CW01426214

LET IT CONSUME YOU...

BLOOD BLACK THORN

THE ETERNAL CURSE BOOK ONE

ROCIO CARRANZA

QUEEN OF WANDS BOOKS
since 2024 | Austin, Texas
contact@queenofwandsbooks.com

Blood of the Blackthorn is a work of fiction. Names, characters, places, and incidents either are the product of the author's imagination or are used fictitiously. Any resemblance to actual persons, living or dead, events or locales is entirely coincidental.

Copyright © 2025 by Rocio Carranza

All rights reserved. Published by Queen of Wands Books.

No part of this publication may be reproduced, distributed, or transmitted in any form or by any means, including photocopying, recording, or other electronic or mechanical methods, without the prior written permission of the publisher, except in the case of brief quotations embodied in critical reviews and certain other noncommercial uses permitted by copyright law.

Library of Congress Control Number: 2024926867
Paperback ISBN 979-8-9921892-1-6
eBook ISBN 979-8-9921892-0-9
Hardcover ISBN 979-8-9921892-2-3
www.rociocarranza.com

Cover Art & Illustration by Irina Koryakina
Cover Design & Map by Rocio Carranza
Editing by Heather Hudec, Simply Spellbound Edits
Interior Formatting by Dream Echo Designs

First edition March 2025
Published in the United States
9 8 7 6 5 4 3 2 1

For the dreamers whose hands are perpetually stained in ink and hearts are swelling with untapped potential.

For the girls who continue speaking up when the world tries to silence them.

And for Giovani and Alonso, my sun and moon.
This may have been completed months ago if not for your love, attention, and occasional hijinks.

SERIT

Occult Isles

Luna

Alvyna

Veneno

Arric

Petris

The Crescents

The Blackthorn

Raven's Holdfast

Coven Capital

Dallise Sea

Givensmir Capital

Catalina's Port

Sandstone Bay

Mistral Island

Give

Costera Mines

Zafira

Golden Ruins

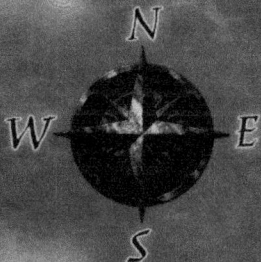

N
W   E
S

Bastards Haven

Sea of Sorrows

Unclaimed Wastes

Gods
Protection

Horned
Cove

Teros

Dragon Sea

The Clutches

Alcanza Peaks

Mytar

Rubianes Keep

n s m i r R e a l m

Larrea

Bay of Chaos

Azurea Sea

CONTENT WARNINGS

Blood of the Blackthorn is a dark fantasy novel and book one of The Eternal Curse series. This story contains content that might be troubling to some readers, including, but not limited to, depictions of and references to abuse, attempted sexual assault, blood, death, genocide, gore, manipulation, PTSD, strong use of language, and violence.

PROLOGUE

"The enchantress is dead."

The room quieted and stilled; the chanting now ceased. Malin took a deep breath before repeating his words, still not believing their conviction, cursing himself for not controlling his impulse to speak aloud. "The enchantress of Givensmir is dead."

The coven, who had only seconds before chanted as they hedged between the land and spirit realms searching for answers, stared in his direction. Grave faces met him, burning holes in his skull, but he kept his head down, grief seizing his heart.

"Of this you are certain, Malin?"

"Yes, My Queen." He nodded, slowly. "Our goddess, Isila, has visited me. She has told me so herself."

A foreboding chill crept up his spine, for that was not all she told him, but he kept silent.

"It is for the best," the witch queen responded after a few moments. "We do not know what she intended to do with those mortals, as you have said so yourself."

Malin turned from her gaze, shamefully.

"Did Isila speak of anything else?"

He held his tongue, not wishing to divulge any more information.

"No," he breathed.

"Look at me, Malin, and speak the truth."

He forced his eyes once more upon his queen, her long, black hair spindled down to her waist, her bright blue eyes, like the ice of her heart, bore into his. Malin opened his mouth, unsure of what he would say.

Then, all at once, the rest of the coven began to speak, as the truth came to them.

"Isila has warned of a half-witch headed our way," one witch announced, the white of her eyes filling the dark room. "A half-witch of our *dear* enchantress. Her flesh and blood."

"Impossible," said another.

"Flesh of a mortal, blood of the sea, heart of a divine," the witch with the white eyes replied.

"Is she the one who was promised?" the witch queen asked.

"She crosses the Dallise Sea, shall I kill her?"

Malin felt a cold chill. "No, let us meet the child, My Queen. Perhaps, she can be of some use to us." Malin bore his eyes into hers, pleading silently.

She only raised her brow as another witch spoke.

"Let us be rid of her, she doesn't belong in this world."

"My dear"—the witch queen grinned—"neither do we."

EVE

ONE

Fifteen Years Later

E ve opened her eyes, no longer in the hazy nightmare that had gripped her forcefully only moments before. Her dream slowly escaped her as the seconds passed and her mind focused on her private bedchambers, a luxury afforded to members of the royal court within the fortified castle of Givensmir. Her silk sheets warmed her prickling skin, slight embers crackled weakly in the fireplace, and the books on her shelves collected dust as they had every morning of her life.

She could hear the guards making their rounds out in the halls, their footsteps echoing along the dimly lit corridors and stone floors of the maiden's keep—the northern section of the castle where the ladies rested their noble heads. There was no place safer, she reminded herself, than where she lay.

Eve thought of the men at war, hundreds of miles away, and how they must be yearning for a warm bed and the comfort of security. Men at war and the women who waited here upon bated breath for them to return. She was no different, she thought, as her mind tried and failed to suppress memories of Prince Theo. He was not her betrothed, but . . .

Yesterday was the first name day celebration of hers that he was not present at. Where she did not see his face nor hear his voice singing with the court as she bit into her sweet lemon cake. Over several months, a truth began to unfurl within her, the sickening possibility that she would not speak to him again. Not finish what they had started. Word of possible victory passed as rumor, but nothing further had been heard in over a fortnight. It unsettled her, no matter how she tried to calm herself, assure herself that amongst the vanguard, the prince was well-suited for battle.

Yet, it did not seem to steady her quickening pulse or the shallow breathing she tried to control. The darkness of the early morning lingered with her as she sat alone, contemplating a return to sleep or a commitment to begin her day. It was too early to seek out her friends at court, and through her balcony she could see the sun fighting for purchase with the night. They clashed together in an array of speckled pinks and dark-gray skies reflecting off the surface of the Dallise Sea toward the edge of nowhere.

Nowhere, yes.

That is what she had been dreaming of. A ship headed for nowhere, taking with it all who had gained passage. It came back to her slowly, as she sat hugging her knees close.

Her older sister, Clarisa, gripping her hand as they ran through the forest, cutting their skin on the sharp bushes they barreled through. Her father's voice as he called out to them, desperate and terrified. The clearing, leading out toward the rocky beach. A boat in shallow, but tempestuous waters, waiting to transport them to the ship just beyond the shore. And then Clarisa was gone to nowhere, and Eve was caught in her father's grasp. She returned to the castle forever changed, the only child of a widower and the daughter of an executed traitor to the realm.

It was all a memory she did not care to revisit, but one that in fifteen years never left her. How young they were when they were separated,

4

constantly wondering if her sister was still alive. Eve hated to admit it, but she could scarcely remember what Clarisa looked like anymore. It was as if her face was obscured by the distance time kept between them, slipping from her consciousness in her waking hours.

The king had sent many men in search of her, but none succeeded, and Eve could clearly remember her father telling her that Clarisa was presumed dead, just like her mother. Eve was no older than nine, sitting across from her father in his study, her small feet barely touching the floor. Even to this day the hate she had for the woman who gave her life, *the enchantress*, for everything she took from her, still made her face burn and hands shake in solitude.

Eve took a deep breath, trying to control herself. She wished to be the child she once was, before everything, to have the simplicity of life thrust upon her once more. Before these memories plagued her mind and weighed on her soul.

She was not sure how long she had been sitting on her bed going over such thoughts, but when she looked toward her balcony once more, the sun was high in the sky, having won its daily battle, and the water sparkled happily in response.

Boooooong. Boooooong. Boooooong.

The tower bells began to toll in the distance, jolting Eve from her contemplation. An icy chill gripped her heart as she leapt out of her bed and toward the balcony.

The bells in Givensmir only rang for two reasons: life or death.

The market square was packed with people when the carriages dropped Eve and the rest of the royal court just outside the city gates. Their guards walked through the crowd, setting up a barricade for them to go to their designated viewing point, unharmed and unbothered by the city folk.

The last of the summer sun cast long shadows in its morning light, covering Eve as she walked toward her standing area. However, the scorching of its relentless heat enticed beads of sweat that lingered at the base of her neck. She stood alongside her friend, Adriana, princess of Givensmir, as they watched men gather firewood and kindling, piling it all against the stake before them.

"It is a bad omen, I fear," Eve whispered to the princess, "to cast fire on a day the gods have already graced us with warmth."

"When was the last?"

"Nearly a decade ago, in the city, at least."

"I had prayed that I would never have to witness one in my life."

"Yet, here we are."

"Here we are."

They stood in silence, as the men completed their task, and Eve listened to the sound of raucous noise from a distance. It grew louder and louder as she realized the crowd of people began to jeer at and throw stones at a woman walking between the guards' barricades. She was chained in irons to the backend of a horse, barely standing as it dragged her through the street.

A few women of the court gasped, and Adriana brought her hands to her face, hiding the scene unfolding before her. Eve could not move, her eyes focused on the woman before them, now being tied to the stake. From where Eve stood, wounds and bruises lined the woman's body, barely covered by a pale, blood stained, linen dress. Her hair was dirty and untamed, obscuring most of her face as she breathed heavily, gulping air into her lungs.

"I can't look, Eve," the princess whispered. "I can't."

"You must," Eve replied, her eyes still fixed upon the woman. She was helpless, forlorn, *powerless*—not at all resembling the witches described to her.

An elder of the cloth walked slowly up the steps toward the stake, his long, white robes draped over him with touches of gold lining and the symbol of their faith—grape vines carrying five grapes, representing each of their gods—affixed to his chest, and a large book in his hand. His pale face amplified the greens of his eyes, and he trudged as any old man would until he was face-to-face with the woman. He studied her closely, before leaning over and whispering in her ear.

The woman's eyes sprouted open, and she tried to bite the elder, growling and screeching as he stepped back, a smirk on his face. One of the guards hit the woman with the back of his hand, and she moaned in pain. The crowd gasped and a few screamed in terror, but the elder raised his hands, silencing them.

"Many of you may wonder why I have chosen white for this occasion. As you know, when death is the will of the gods, us elders dress in black. It is to mourn, to reflect on loss, no matter if it be a thief or a whore. However, white represents celebration, to begin anew, to cleanse ourselves of malintent." He watched the crowd as he spoke with a confidence that Eve felt inclined to agree with. Everything he said was reasonable. "Today, I wear white to celebrate the victory the gods have given us over evil. To celebrate our right to live freely without fear as the gods always intended."

The witch continued to growl and screech in the background, but he continued his speech, unbothered. A small part of Eve felt he may even have wanted her to act this way, but she quickly dismissed the idea.

"No one in Serit, no one in our kingdom of Givensmir, should behold a power over us mere mortals besides the gods. This woman, this filth, has been found guilty of witchcraft, consorting with the fallen goddess to spread her evil ways into our city, and for that we shall see her burn as the gods have willed."

The elder turned back to the witch, who was filled with tears and rage trying to grapple with the tight chains that held her to the stake.

"Do you have anything to confess? Any repentance that may bide you favor among the gods in their kingdom?"

"Curse you three-fold, Elder!"

"Ah, what a pity." The elder shrugged.

He began to turn, when the witch stilled suddenly, her head hanging awkwardly from her shoulders, and another, deeper voice seemed to speak from within her. "You have not seen the last of me, Borgias."

Eve watched in horror as the elder paled, his mouth slack. "W-what did you say?"

"I watch you while you are sleeping, dreaming of depravity, sinking into your cups and women."

Eve held her hand to her lips, stifling a gasp, as she watched the elder take several steps back, nearly falling from the platform.

"She lies!"

The witch raised her head, a crooked smile on her face. "Am I?"

Borgias stared incredulously at the witch, before running down the steps, yelling at the guards. "Burn her, burn her, I say!"

The crowd became feral, throwing things at the witch, who began to laugh. A few men surrounded the stake with their lit torches, throwing it into the kindling and backing away in fear. Fire engulfed her, but she continued her laughter.

"By the will of the gods!" Borgias bellowed into the crowd, raising his fist in the air.

"By the will of the gods!" they repeated.

Adriana grabbed Eve's arm burying her face into it, but Eve could not look away. Screams and genuine terror rattled her ears, filled her mind, and sent her heart into hiding. And for just a moment—only a moment—she thanked the gods that her mother had died quick by a knife and not as a slow spectacle.

The fire took its time feasting on the body before it became clumps of ash in the earth and smoke in the wind. And then the witch was no more.

EVE

TWO

Weeks Later

"My lords and ladies"—King Eryck raised his cup, standing behind the royal table of the great hall—"we welcome back our men from war. Amongst them sit the greatest of our kingdoms—champions, warriors, knights—who all brought Givensmir our long-awaited victory. Larrea was no match for our forces, their civil war done in haste and foolishness, and now we cheer for the reunification of our kingdoms, our gods-given right to prosperity!"

"Here, here," the room chanted.

Eve looked about the hall, watching as each of the nobles, herself included, stood cup in hand from behind their large tables hanging on to every word the king spoke. All wondering if the time of war was truly over, no more enemies left to fight, no more inhabitable lands left to conquer here.

"We could not have done it without our men in the east, the Mytar lords who will be joining us in a few days, and to whom we extend our gratitude. It is for their courage and unwavering support that I look forward to the alliance of our houses soon. As many of you know, my son, Theo, and Lady Felicity are soon to be wed. A golden prince and his lady of the mountain, fierce and strong will the two of them be."

Eve's eyes lingered toward Theo, sitting a few seats from the king and watched as he shifted uncomfortably. He avoided returning Eve's gaze, much to her disappointment.

"Now eat and rejoice in our success!"

The room cheered and began to feast. Eve picked at her food, pretending to listen intently to the lords and ladies seated at her table, smiling on cue, laughing at their horrid jokes. She wished she could be seated among her confidants at the royal table, Adriana and Theo, or even her good friend, Lord Callum, three tables to her right.

She glanced their way occasionally and felt solidarity in seeing them pained or bored by their respective company. Her uncle and royal accountant, Lord Agustin, sat across from her, deep in his wine cup between rather innocuous remarks about the state of political affairs to anyone who would listen.

"Givensmir may now rest easy that this war has settled. The hard times are over, that is to be sure."

"There will always be hard times, Lord Agustin. We are but men, after all." Lord Wesley, the king's informant, chuckled as he tapped his cup for a refill. A servant girl rushed to him, filling it carefully and nervously. Eve watched as Lord Wesley leered at the girl, arrogantly. His light blond, straight hair nearly touched his shoulders, and his face was full of crevices; he held secrets in his eyes and smile. He was nearing fifty, Eve knew, and after decades of service to the crown showed no sign of relenting his position to anyone. She was certain he was grabbing onto any bit of power by the reins until it took him to certain death. Even if that meant intimidating poor servants. The girl squirmed and made herself scarce once the cup was filled.

"Ah, that is true, but I only hope that we do not see one again in my lifetime." Her uncle chugged the last of his wine, bits of it dribbling down

10

his bearded chin. Eve wished he would have some modicum of table manners or at least be presentable in company.

"It is in the nature of men to quarrel, is it not, Uncle?" Eve chimed in, smiling politely. "We may see such tidings of battle again sooner than we may hope. I wonder what that will look like to the royal purse."

Her uncle rolled his eyes. "My dear, I feel that this conversation may be far beyond your comprehension. A woman cannot discuss the nature of money and men, because she is not"—he hiccupped—"a man!"

The people at the table laughed, all except for Lord Wesley, who narrowed his eyes at her. "It is true that us men can be quarrelsome as you say. Yet, I wonder why women would bother to deal with us at all if we were so awful. It would seem counterintuitive."

Eve smirked, feeling a bit venomous, partially due to the wine, but mostly due to Prince Theo's lack of attention toward her—he still had yet to so much as glance at her since he arrived. "I wonder more how men would deal *without* us women, Lord Wesley. That is the true riddle."

The table fell silent, and Eve felt herself slipping away, wishing that she could light it on fire and go back to the comfort of her chambers. It dragged on, save for the noise of the rest of the hall filling in the tension.

She stared him down for a moment longer than necessary, before giggling with mock timidity. "Oh, Lord Wesley, forgive me. I did not mean to make the conversation so dull. Of course, I know not of men and their natures."

That seemed to please her group, as they began starting up conversations amongst themselves once more.

"Very good, very good, Eve," her uncle said drunkenly. "It is a sign of good manners to know one's place in the order of things."

Eve nodded rather sharply but kept her pleasantries about her.

"Your father should be here before the next moon. Are you excited to see my brother? How long has it been? Two, three years?"

"Five years, Uncle."

"Ah, yes. Where has the time gone?" He raised his cup, waited as the servant girl filled it, took a sip, and continued, "You know, Lord Wesley, it has been my life's privilege in raising my niece while she's been a ward of

11

the court. Great honor, indeed. The fine woman she has grown into. These three years—"

"Five," Eve interjected.

"—five years have had their struggles, but I have always considered her the daughter I never had."

Eve took a deep sigh, knowing this to be a glorious stretch of the truth. She had been a member of the court since she was born, only a ward when her father left back to Rubianes Keep to prepare and accompany his men for war. Her uncle, broken by a jousting injury, was kept at court to sit in at the royal council in her father's stead. They barely spoke more than a few words every other day, her opting instead to converse with the fourth of his five sons, her cousin, Pedro. She idly wondered how he was doing in the healer's chambers since his return earlier that day and made a mental note to visit him later.

"You have done well, Lord Agustin," Wesley replied, a sly smile creeping on his face. "Now is the precarious time to find her a match, is it not? The final duty owed to her as her caretaker."

Eve choked on the wine she was sipping, coughing violently into a handkerchief passed to her by someone at the table. A match made by her uncle would be absolutely unthinkable; she could only imagine the choices presented to her and the daft decisions he would make. The gods would have to drag her down the altar to make any such notion a possibility.

"Are you all right, Lady Eve?" Lord Wesley asked, amused.

"Y-yes"—she cleared her throat—"yes. I seem to have drunk too quickly."

"We were just discussing your future, your duty to your house and father."

"My father has a son now, thank you. There is no rush on any decision as my father will have the final say on any future prospects, I'm sure."

"Your brother is only a boy. It would be good of you to remember that your father may seek your uncle's advice. After all, he has been your father-figure these past *five* years."

The thought made Eve's skin crawl. "I'm sure he shall."

"My niece will make for a fine companion to any lucky suitor. She is accomplished in song, dance, and horseback riding. What more could any lord wish for?"

"Being a lady to one of the five great houses has its benefits, as well." Wesley smirked.

Eve, wishing this conversation would end, drank a large swig of her wine.

"I'm sure it does."

"Are there any other *gifts* you may have that a suitor would be intrigued to know about?"

Eve nearly dropped her cup, fingers fumbling with the stem before placing it carefully on the table. She knew exactly what he meant, and how much insidious questions like this irked her. She glared at Wesley. "No, I do not."

"Well, of course you do—of course she does." Her uncle chuckled between hiccups. "She can paint and sew. I'm sure you made that dress herself, didn't you? It is quite lovely with the golds and blacks; colors of our strong kingdom."

Eve now wished that her uncle would have been the one to choke on his wine.

"I did, Uncle, thank you," she said, trying and failing to maintain an agreeable tone.

The sound of gentle, but loud chimes filled the hall, signaling the end of the feast.

"Well, I must retire for the night," her uncle stammered, hiccupping once more. "Until next time, Lord Wesley. Niece."

Eve watched as he stumbled his way into the crowd that had begun to leave through the main double doors. *The fool,* she thought, *what a fool my uncle is.*

"What luck," she heard Wesley say, and Eve turned back to him, noticing the rest of their table was empty save for the two of them. "What luck for you to not have acquired your mother's gifts. It would make it far easier to distrust you."

Eve stared at him, stunned and unable to think of a reply. It had been years since anyone had the audacity to speak so boldly about what he was implying.

He moved toward her, bending to her ear as she sat frozen in place. "I would hate to ever have to see your lovely dress burn like the witch did yesterday. Not after all your hard work."

He traced a finger down the black silk on her sleeve, before leaving into the last of the crowd.

Eve shuddered, wishing she had kept her mouth shut during dinner. Now, she knew, for whatever reason he may yet reveal, she had his attention. She took a calming breath before standing and forcing a pleasant expression on her face as her friends, Callum and Adriana, approached her.

Eve closed the door to her chambers behind her, resting her back along the wooden door. It was unlike her to lose her senses, but more unlike her to let Wesley of all people get under her skin. As the king's informant, any notice by him, good or bad, would invite unwanted scrutiny. Eve did not seek any more attention than she already had; she was beloved by the court for her beauty, passion, and vivaciousness. That was all she needed.

She made her way to the vanity, removing the pins from her hair and letting her long, brown strands flow down her face. The only silver lining of her conversation with Wesley was the distraction he provided her from Theo's betrothal. Eve stared at her reflection in the mirror, wondering what Felicity looked like, and what Theo thought of the arrangement.

In truth, it was foolish of her to think that she would have a chance at marriage with him. She was the daughter of a traitor, a ward only by the graciousness of the king, retaining all her titles as a show of his mercy to her father. A mercy bestowed upon him after he informed Wesley of the enchantress's treason, enough for the king to kill her before she did any more damage to the royal line.

Another reason, of many, that Eve despised her. All her mother had taken from her then, and still years later, the rippling effects of her perniciousness was felt by Eve.

She ripped the last pin from her hair, slamming it down on the vanity, and squeezing her eyes shut, trying to think of anything else. She breathed deeply, once, twice, and once more.

Get a hold of yourself, Eve. You cannot change the past.

She repeated this to herself a few more times. Then, she looked up into her reflection once more; except now, there was something in it she did not notice before. Red eyes where her brown ones had been.

Eve gasped, standing quickly. But when she blinked, they were brown once more.

It was only the wine, she told herself, *the stress, and the damn wine.*

She turned away from the mirror, and toward her bed, startled to see something there, something she had never seen before.

A book, large and old, with dust coating the binding and cover.

She approached it curiously. It bore no name, but on its cover was an owl beneath three stars and unlike anything she had seen before. She looked around the room, but there was no sign of how it ended up there, nor who had left it.

How did I miss this?

She considered asking one of the guards if someone entered her chambers while she was at the feast but thought the better of it as she opened the book and read the first page.

BLOOD OF THE BLACKTHORN

SOUL OF ISILA

A COMPENDIUM OF WITCHCRAFT & MAGIC

Eve closed it immediately, her heart racing, her blood pumping, thrumming loudly in her ears.

This cannot be, she thought, *it cannot be real.*

She grabbed the book with both hands and ran to the balcony, checking quickly to make sure no one was watching, and threw it off. She watched as it fell into the dark depths of the sea below, splashing loudly before it disappeared. She closed her eyes, praying to the gods for their protection. Then she turned back into her room, and her blood turned to ice.

The book was back on her bed, dry as if it had never touched the water.

Fear gripped her heart, but her damned curiosity gained the better of her. As if in a trance, she reached out and touched the book, opening the cover to the first page, her fingers shaking as she touched the parchment.

Eve read the first page once more, her heart thundering in her chest as she realized what she was beholding. This was a grimoire, a magic book, one of witchcraft that would damn her to death if she was caught with it.

In her rising panic, the book slipped from her hands, and she cut her finger on the edge of the page. She flinched as a few drops fell onto the parchment. The red intermingled with the orange-brown colored ink of the page, making a swirl of dark reds and browns before it disappeared. She raised her finger in horror, the cut was deeper than it should have been.

She stood, backing away from the book, a scream rising in her throat but unable to be released. The room was too cold and too warm all at once, the darkness rising and the candles lit around her burned to the wick. Branches, long, dark, and spindled, sprouted from the open pages toward her. They consumed her vision and wrapped itself around her body, pricking her skin and drawing blood. She could hear voices, chanting louder and louder in a language that was foreign to her, until she could not even hear herself think.

Then it all went black.

THEO
THREE

Theo was the last to leave the great hall, watching as Eve left with his sister and Lord Callum. There was an ache in his chest as he watched her smile at them, a smile he wished he could be on the receiving end of. Then, the hall was empty save for his personal guards standing at the other end of the large room. He sighed, standing from his table as the servants now entered, cleaning the mess of the feast. Some, he noticed, picked at the food as they worked, but he pretended not to see them as he walked briskly out.

He could hear the footsteps of the guards behind him as he headed toward his tower on the eastern side of the castle. His chambers faced the massive expanse of the city below that had grown too fast over the last few years; it now resembled a maze full of people, young and old, rich and poor—a constant reminder of his duty as the second heir to maintain order and support his older brother, Eryce, in his future rule. Tonight, however, he did not want to think of his duty to the kingdom, his brother, his father, or anyone.

He continued down the large, dark hall, lit dimly by torches that hung stoically along the walls, and ventured past his tower door.

"Your Highness, are you not going to your chambers?" one of his guards asked.

"No," he responded, "I think I will take a short walk through the gardens; you are dismissed for the night."

The two guards looked at each other, but bowed nonetheless.

"I will see to it that David takes the evening shift at the base of your chambers, Your Highness. Have a good evening."

Theo nodded, and continued his trek, there was somewhere he felt he needed to be.

***

Fifteen Years Ago

Theo ran into the new, small maze of the castle gardens, his heart beating thunderously within his chest as he chased after Eve. He turned left, then right, then left again—or so he believed; it all became a blur as his feet quickened the pace and his breathing became labored with the effort. The wind whipped wildly at his face, and he felt as wild and free as nature itself.

Soon he found himself in the middle, watching as Eve approached the large fountain in the center. It spouted water from the top and into the pool at the bottom. Theo slowed to a walk as he beheld it; this was not something that either of them had seen before, and its architecture was stunning as the sun reached its peak, brightening the light gray stone.

The fountain was ornately carved, displaying the top halves of horses protruding from all sides, almost as if they were emerging from the water. Further up, there was a half-dressed woman carved into the stone, lifting a basin from which the water spouted out of.

Theo approached the fountain with wonder, all eleven years of him delighted at the sight of something new and beautiful. His heart was pounding now for a different reason, their running away now forgotten. As they walked along the pebbled stones, the ground crunching beneath their small feet, Theo could have sworn that the woman turned to face them, ever so slightly. But when he looked once more, she was still and stoic in the daylight.

Eve placed her hand on the cool stone, feeling its smooth texture, and seemed to admire the water that appeared ever so inviting. Before Theo could think to speak, she lifted herself onto the edge of the fountain and jumped in excitedly, splashing about until she turned to meet his eyes.

"What are you staring at, Theo?"

"I–I have never seen a fountain like this one," he replied, trying and failing to appear disinterested in her.

"Yes"—she splashed water over the edge—"join me!"

"Oh"—his eyes trailed the ground, stepping back to avoid the splash—"I don't know, Eve. Father says I can't make any more messes."

"Messes? This is *water*, no harm ever came from *water*."

Before the prince could respond, another far harsher voice called out, "Prince Theo, Lady Eve! Come out and reveal yourselves, this instant!"

It was their governess, a fierce woman from whom they had both been running away. Their studies were a bore, and the outdoors far too inviting to pass in stuffy rooms, so the prince and Eve scrambled away at first chance, running into the maze as they—well, Eve—had planned earlier that day.

Theo's eyes widened and in a split second decided to run toward Eve, jumping into the fountain beside her. He barely peeked his head from over the edge to confirm it was the governess. She was a rigid woman with a scowl on her face that scared him; there was no way he could see himself facing her now. Part of him wished he was the heir and not the second born, then he would have the power to talk back without much retort, not that Eryce did anyway.

They both watched as the governess completely disregarded the new addition to the maze and stalked past angrily, waiting silently under bated breath to make sure she didn't make a reappearance.

"We should run somewhere else before she thinks to look in here," Eve

19

whispered, her eyes scanning the space of the maze around them.

"Good idea," Theo whispered back. They both lifted themselves out of the fountain and stayed still, their ears perked for any sudden sounds. They were drenched and puddles began to pool at their feet.

"Let's go," Eve mouthed, and before Theo could respond, she took off in a sprint. Her shoes made squishing, crunching noises over the pebbled ground. It surely had to have caught the attention of the governess, if she was still in the maze looking for them.

Theo gave chase, not thinking to ask questions, but to run without rhyme or reason, placing his full trust in his dear friend.

"Your Highness! Lady Eve! Your fathers will be hearing of this!"

Theo could hear the governess's voice becoming a distant yell and knew that she would not dare to disgrace herself by running after children in her skirts. This was the only thing that eased his mind, for he knew that when he returned to the castle, it would not be a pleasant welcome.

Eve led them down the weathered steps and toward the second gardens further from the castle itself, more unkempt than the ones they came from. She pushed through the thicket, moving so fast that some of the branches whipped back and hit Theo in the face.

"Ow, Eve," he snapped after the fifth time.

"Sorry." She turned and smiled, grabbing his hand and pulling him through more carefully.

They finally reached a small clearing where a pond rested, with moss and lily pads floating on top. The sun barely broke through the trees, casting a soft light onto the thick grass around them. Weeds and various flowers surrounded them, providing some color to the overall green scene. It was their hiding spot, where the greenery grew like a wild forest, but unbeknownst to them, their mothers could see them clearly from one of the northern towers.

The two sat in the grass in relative silence, occasionally casting stones into the water.

"I hate our governess," Eve announced suddenly. "I wish I could do other things besides sit down and listen to her lectures."

Theo nodded in agreement. "I wish I could tell her to listen to herself, but she would fall asleep, she's so *boring.*"

"Then we would be able to escape, but even easier, because she'd be sleeping." Eve giggled.

"Yes, and then we could spend all day just doing whatever we wanted; like run or play swords." His excitement faltered suddenly. "I need to learn how to fight soon, Father says."

"For what?" Eve asked, her eyes downcast as she scoured for another rock.

"So that I could lead men and do well in combat," Theo said, bravado thick in his voice. In truth, he was not sure what any of what he said meant, only that it was repeated to him by his father often.

"Why would Givensmir be fighting?" Eve looked at him curiously, her brown eyes bore into his hazel ones.

He noted her tan skin and dark long hair, fashioned halfway up as most young girls of the court were. He had known Eve for nearly his entire life since his grandfather, the king, had married her mother off to his close friend and political aide, Marcelo, Lord of Rubianes Keep. They had remained at the court ever since. To him, and most everyone else, Eve looked very much like her mother.

"I don't know." He shrugged and tossed a small pebble into the pond.

"My mother says I'll have to learn how to be a lady soon." Eve tried and failed to juggle a couple of pebbles as she said this.

"Are you not going to be an enchantress like her?"

"No." She took a deep breath. "Clarisa has her magic, it would most likely be her."

Theo considered this, tossing grass in front of him when pebbles could not be found. They didn't go far, the wind now a feeble breeze in the hot, summer day, and he huffed. At eleven, Theo was not particularly knowledgeable about the inner workings of magic, only that he had ever been raised around two half-witches who seemed completely normal to him—Clarisa's magic was coveted by the enchantress and the king, something about fostering a new enchantress to take after mother, or at least that is what he had heard his father say once. Stories of the Blackthorn began to fill his head, of the witch kingdom that lay beyond the Dallise Sea, hundreds of miles away full of black magic and evil, harming any mortal who dared to pass through. He could still hear his former governess's voice, grave and deep, *if you don't behave yourself, Your Highness, they will come and snatch you away as you sleep. They prey on naughty children.* It took Theo nearly a week to be calmed down enough to sleep through the night without nightmares, and after she admitted to telling him the story to his mother, she was never seen by him again.

He wondered if all talk of magic—the enchantress, Clarisa—was a big trick and if magic even existed at all, if no one had actually shown him. He considered voicing this to Eve but thought better of it.

"That's okay. It means you get to spend more time outside of that stuffy castle. Can you imagine if you had magic, having to be holed up practicing all day, with my grandfather present, no less?"

"That is true, I suppose."

"Does it make you sad?"

"Sometimes."

"What does your father say about it?"

"Not much."

They sat quietly once more, appreciating their borrowed time; one of their servants was sure to come and fetch them from their not-so-hidden hiding spot. The wind blew the grass softly and it tickled Theo's hands as he ran his fingers through it.

He was not sure what Eve's place was at this castle; not sure what being a lady really meant outside of staying up late, drinking wine, and dressing in better fitting gowns. While none of that seemed particularly boring—admittedly, Eve talked of her excitement to one day enjoy those splendors—he never saw any of the ladies look completely happy. They talked all day long about things that went over his head, except when they were about people he knew.

He thought of Clarisa, older than Eve by three years, and how her life already seemed to be mapped out for her, a course, a purpose, all of which Eve herself seemed to lack.

Eve was simply a mortal, and despite the disappointment of everyone else, he did not wish for her to be anything more. He watched as Eve successfully skipped a rock twice in the water—how she laughed and hugged him. Her bright smile and brown eyes the color of flying sparrows in the summer sun and warm hearths in the winter.

Present Day

Theo was back in that spot alone under the moonlit sky, listening as the last of the summer mayflies buzzed around him. He reached down and picked up a pebble, looking out toward the pond, trying to remember the last time he had come out here. Before *that* night, it had been years—before he was sent to war, and before the harsh expectations of his position had taken control of his life. Now he was a seasoned warrior, fighting in battles of his father's making, and set to marry a woman he neither knew, nor cared to.

Theo idly wondered if Eve ever brought anyone else here and was ashamed to admit the thought made him jealous. It was ludicrous to think that he could maintain some sort of connection to her now; it would only cause scandal and heartache for them both.

Frustrated, he tried to skip the pebble into the water, putting more force than necessary on the spin and watched as it plopped straight down instead.

Eve would have made it skip. She could do anything.

No sooner had the thought entered his head, than Theo realized what he hadn't all those years ago. That to him, simply being next to Eve was all that magic he could ever wish for.

EVE

FOUR

E ve gasped, lurching into a sitting position on her bed, cool sweat clinging to her skin. She scanned her chambers frantically as her breath shuddered. The morning light peered invitingly from her balcony, and all appeared normal—the dust on her shelves, the weak embers in the fireplace, and the book.

The grimoire.

She leapt from her bed, tossing the covers without restraint, but there was no book to be seen. Eve tried to remember the events from the night before, the *Blood of the Blackthorn*, tossing it over the edge, cutting her finger. She closed her eyes tight, too scared to check, but after counting to three, turned her hand over to face her.

There was no cut on her index finger.

She breathed a shaky sigh of relief, it was just a dream, a nightmare.

"It has been fifteen years, Eve," she whispered to herself. "You cannot go back there. You will not go back there."

She repeated this to herself as her handmaids arrived to dress her and braid her hair. Eve kept her focus in the mirror to confirm her brown eyes were all that stared back.

It was.

She tried to distract herself, between the idle talk provided by the handmaids, but the only thing besides her dream that entered her mind was a certain prince that owed her an explanation for his avoidance.

"Tell me, honestly, do you think you'll love her?" Eve asked, staring at the bright blue sky above her. Her head rested on a bed of grass beneath her, her corset tight against her ribs as she tried to keep track of her breathing. She hoped she sounded far more casual than she felt.

"Why? Are you jealous?" Theo replied, sitting next to her, throwing small stones into the pond before them. He looked far older than she remembered after all this time—his face held a faint stubble, his soft curls long and resting against his face. Eve nearly forgot what she asked as she appreciated the man Theo had grown into.

They had been relaxing in their hiding spot for the first time since he left for Larrea. The one night he had yet to even mention. She breathed a bit shaky. The fresh autumn flowers peeking through the summer trees cast pastel-like colors in Eve's vision. The birds chirped happily, antithetical to her feelings. But even so, she sat up, shoving him playfully.

"No, I'm simply . . . curious, is all."

"Did you kidnap me from the castle to ask childish questions?"

She knew he was right, but her pride wouldn't allow her to admit it. He always left whatever occupied him at the sound of her voice, her beckoning call a lure that ensnared him. Today was the first day since his return where he could simply exist outside of the tedious meetings of the Gold Council, and she took full advantage.

"I don't think it is childish."

Theo smiled slightly, his jaw tight. "I don't think my father had love in mind when he arranged it."

Eve said nothing, unsure of what her intentions were with beginning a conversation like this. It was a foolhardy move, one that only she would suffer the consequences of in the depths of her emotional turmoil.

"And what about you? Lord Callum seems to have taken an interest in you since I left."

Lord Callum, firstborn son to the Lord of Teros, was a kind soul even when Eve was far more preoccupied with other matters during Theo's absence, such as wishing he would make it back in one piece, *alive*. Even so, she knew better than to believe that Lord Callum would ever be interested in her or any other woman for that matter. Was it so wrong to have a confidant of the opposite sex?

"He is *nice*, I suppose."

"I heard rumors."

"Pray, tell me." She scoffed, but avoided his gaze, her cheeks burning; she knew exactly what these rumors were.

"That you may be Lady of Teros soon."

"That's ridiculous."

"I hear he fancies his mares more than women."

"I suspect *you're* jealous."

"Jealous of his mares, perhaps, they cost quite a bit."

"I meant the rumors of his proposal."

"Depends, is it true?"

"I don't know, why don't I ask him?" She felt a tinge of anger that flared unexpectedly, surprising her.

Theo narrowed his eyes. "Maybe you should."

They stared at each other a while, Eve unsure of how to proceed. They had been in this same position before, the memory heating her skin as his hazel eyes burned into her brown ones. She felt a longing to close the distance, to ease the tension with what she wanted more than anything. He seemed to feel it, too, slowly moving closer.

"I do not care for him that way," she whispered as they breathed in the same air.

Eve's heart skipped beats as she could feel the touch of his lips on hers;

he smelled of the seasons they had lost to war—fresh grass and summer rain that quenched the grounds they laid on once. Perhaps, that was just her wistfulness or maybe it could just be . . .

She no sooner closed her eyes then images of the grimoire flashed in her mind. The cut on her hand, blood dripping onto the weathered parchment, the sharp branches, fading to black. It removed her from the present and brought back that feeling of dread and terror.

She moved back suddenly, gasping and blinking a few times as she beheld Theo's confused face.

He shook his head but moved back slowly. "I thought so, too."

She blinked a few threatening tears away, angry at herself for letting a childish nightmare ruin this moment. "It's not like that. I was more worried about whether you would return, than caring for the men at court."

It was partially true. She had made herself scarce during the past year, depression seizing her soul. The first time she emerged willingly from her chambers was when Callum invited her for a walk along the castle grounds, the start of a friendship that she began to look forward to—she kept the last part to herself.

Theo adjusted his posture, his shoulders now facing the pond. "I thought about you while I was gone. War is unlike anything I was told as a child. There were no heroes, no sense of victory when all had fallen around us."

"I'm sorry," was all Eve could manage.

"The only one who should be sorry is my father. King Fidel was only a boy."

She did not want to hear anymore, did not want to be reminded of what happened. Givensmir's years-long war with Larrea ended with two dead kings, the latter being a child of only thirteen. King Eryck now had his lands, but everyone wondered if that would be enough to satiate him.

"Do you believe your marriage will put an end to it all?"

Theo considered this, biting his lip and shaking his head. "We can only hope. But with my father, you never truly know. How many lands must we conquer before he will be satisfied?"

Eve wasn't sure.

"I never want to see you leave these gates again, not like that. Not to go somewhere you may not return from." The words were out of her mouth before she could stop herself, and she realized that she was treading uncharted territory, so quickly added, "You are my greatest friend, Theo."

Theo lifted his eyes to hers, softening, taking in everything she said. "I will try."

They sat in familiar silence, the bright blue sky turning into a soft pink as the sun began to sink behind a few of the clouds and into the earth.

"How much time do you have?" Eve asked.

"Not enough."

"It will never be enough, will it?"

"No," Theo sighed, then chuckled to himself.

"What is it?"

"I only thought, 'what if you had magic—'"

"Then your father would have sent me to burn."

"I didn't mean it like that."

"Magic is dangerous."

"Your mother—" Theo began.

"My mother became so consumed with her power that she killed your grandfather. No good can come from it."

"Eve," Theo began, "you would tell me—if you—if there was a chance that you had—"

Eve interrupted him, "Magic is murder, I'm glad that I never inherited it. My mortality is the only reason I am here, *alive*."

Her hands felt hot, her breathing quickened, and she stood trying to calm herself.

"Wait, I'm sorry, Eve, don't go," Theo stood, gently holding her arm. His eyes bore into hers, pleading.

His touch, his eyes, it was too much.

"I–I believe I have kept you away for too long."

"Since when have you cared about rules, Eve?"

"Since you became betrothed," she couldn't look at him as she said it, but he dropped his grip.

Before she could see the anguish that was sure to be on his face, she ran out through their weathered footpath, heading to the castle, the only home she had ever known, her only sanctuary. Yet, now she was returning, having surely lost another person she loved.

CLARISA
FIVE

It was a bleak, misty morning in the Blackthorn and Clarisa felt the chill within her bones even as she stood in the crowded throne room of the castle. All of them, witches, representing the six covens of the Blackthorn, all present to witness the trial of two accused of treason.

The entire thing was a spectacle, she noted, as the consensus of the whispering crowd leaned toward guilt even though none of them had been told what the specific charges were. If what they were saying was true, it would be the first time in years that one of their own would be found guilty of betraying the coven, a certain death sentence.

Clarisa breathed deeply to calm her nerves and steadied herself next to Ana. Even as a grown woman, she felt so much like a child as she looked to her companion for comfort. Ana stood tall and poised, her skin a warm sienna like amber kisses in summer bloom, though her face was grim and ashen. Her usual cheerful disposition was traded for a grave one, and Clarisa dared not question it.

BLOOD OF THE BLACKTHORN

Ana was one of the witnesses selected to attend on behalf of the Alvyna coven from the west. And much unlike Ana's trek through the crowded city, escorted by her mother's staff in the unrelenting rain and mud outside the castle gates, Clarisa walked on her own from within the castle. The place she had been raised these last fifteen years.

Ana's braided hair was damp, and droplets fell from the ends of her tight, twisted tendrils, making small pools on the marble tile beneath her. It had been nearly six months since the rain started, and it showed no signs of letting up.

Clarisa softly placed her hand in Ana's, it had been so long since they last saw one another. Ana gave her hand a small squeeze in response but released it as she remained facing the throne.

Behind them stood Clarisa's familiars, Tabor and Brisa, their chins held high and eyes wandering purposefully. Tabor met her gaze as he adjusted the quiver of arrows on his back. He gave her one of those smiles, very faintly, and she righted her shoulders to steady herself. She then made eye contact with Brisa, whose hair today was blonde and cropped short. Clarisa stared for longer than necessary at the change; sometimes she felt that she could barely keep up with her familiar's shapeshifting ways. Brisa merely thinned her lips and nodded slightly to her.

It made them nervous to have her in large crowds, as if she might run away or disappear within one under their noses. Clarisa would be lying if she said the thought never crossed her mind.

Where would she even go when the Blackthorn was her home?

The last of the witnesses ambled into the throne room, muttering and whispering to each other, and it sounded to Clarisa like birds chirping in the forest. She faced the two identical thrones, one for both of their rulers. The chairs were made of numerous blackthorn branches, spindling off into different directions from the backrest which held the seal of the kingdom—a large owl beneath three stars. The owl represented their fallen goddess, Isila, and each star symbolized the three original witches created by her. The armrests and seats were fitted with thick, black-and-silver cushions; each chair looked mighty and intimidating, and Clarisa could practically feel the magic coursing from them.

The Blackthorn—kingdom of witchcraft and magic—was the only kingdom of its kind and was strategically located hundreds of miles from the shores of the warring kingdoms on the mainland. The Blackthorn had achieved a sort of peace within the isles, protecting themselves with the treacherous Dallise Sea between them and the mortals that threatened their livelihood. It was the only kingdom to withstand all wars and battles, remaining united under the same lineage of rulers since its creation over seven centuries ago.

Clarisa could hear the heavy wooden doors being closed behind them, and the high priestess of the Blackthorn, Giselle, called order to the room. The entire crowd fell silent, except for the shaky breathing of a few, Clarisa included. In a matter of seconds, the room darkened despite the afternoon light outside, and before her very eyes, the coven leaders appeared seated on the throne.

Saryn and Gareth, the queen and her king consort, rulers of the Blackthorn, the Occult Isles, and the six covens. Legend had it their ancestors were from the original three, blessed with magic and power from the gods themselves, but cursed to have it only so long as they remained within their kingdom. Clarisa could not recall a tale or time when any of them had ventured outside of their borders.

Magic is not immortality, Ana would often tell her.

The only heir, Navir, son of Saryn, typically upheld the duties of the kingdom in other lands. He was not present that Clarisa could see. Apparently, his diplomatic mission for the queen was taking him longer than expected.

She did not realize how deep in her thoughts she was until Ana held her hand once more, bowing her head as the rest of the witches did, and Giselle's voice filled the large throne room, reciting the introductory prayers aloud:

Ever merciful Isila, our goddess and divine creator,
Grant us the wisdom of your divinity,
The strength of the seas you rule,
And the passion of your fire
To align our spirits with yours,

BLOOD OF THE BLACKTHORN

We shall forever pray for your just return,

Clarisa raised her gaze toward Gareth as the prayer concluded; he was an old, but strong man and sat on the right, his emerald-green eyes seemed bored of this affair before anything had even started. He stared lazily throughout the crowd, seeming to find nothing of particular interest, his crown tilted slightly off his head. Saryn, the queen, stood before her seat, her raven hair adorned in a braid and her blue eyes scanned the room, her crown was black as night and affixed with dark purple jewels that somehow still glinted in the small amount of light present.

"Bring in the traitors," Saryn ordered.

Clarisa felt as if Saryn's eyes were fixed on her, despite being one in a sea of nearly fifty people. Clarisa averted her eyes toward a hall off to the right, where a number of guards forced two people in shackles to the bottom steps of the throne. They were pushed onto their knees, forcefully, and each stared at the ground. The guards behind them removed their hoods and revealed the faces of a man and a woman.

Clarisa held her breath, and recognized the man as Malin Flynne, a trusted member of the covens and a close confidant of the rulers. Except, he looked nothing like the proud, confident man she was used to seeing in the halls of the castle, he was now thin and scrawny with a bruised face and dirty, blond hair. The woman next to him was unfamiliar, with amber hair and a pretty, but heavily bruised face.

"Proceed, Deyes," Saryn ordered one of the guards.

The guard nodded, and then procured a thick scroll from his belt and read:

"By Order of the Queen, Malin Flynne, of the Blackthorn Kingdom and River Strant of Givensmir, will face a trial witnessed by those present for the accusation of treason against the crowns. The accusations are listed as such: providing secrets regarding the Blackthorn realm to Givensmir, providing false intelligence to the Blackthorn guard, resulting in the death of thirty-nine witches in a massacre against the Petris coven, and orchestrating recruitment efforts on behalf of Givensmir. If found guilty, the accused will be subject to the penalty of death."

Deyes finished the last sentence and furled the scroll once more, placing it back in his belt.

The room stood silent in shock, before Saryn broke it, a deadly look on her face, and addressed the witnesses. "This witch and this mortal have dishonored our kingdom and allowed our brothers and sisters to be killed by our mortal enemies. Blood was spilled in our waters, lives were needlessly lost, and families torn apart. All for the sake of a *few gold coins.*"

Those last words she said very slowly, emphasizing them with a venomous quality, and Clarisa felt a shiver run down her spine. She could not imagine any price that would be worth being in the position of Malin and the mortal.

Saryn twirled her hand, and a small sack appeared on her palm, she stared into the eyes of Malin as she turned the sack over and gold coins spilled around them. Each seemed to make the loudest *tink, tink, tink* sound on the stone floor like a thousand ringing bells. There were audible gasps by some witches in the witnessing crowd, and Clarisa put a hand to her mouth to silence hers.

Saryn began to return to her seat, but not before Malin lunged at her. Before any of the guards closest to him could react, he was suspended, frozen in his shackles and chains in the air. Clarisa looked to see Giselle's hand raised, controlling Malin's body and keeping him paralyzed in that state. Saryn, unfazed by anything that had occurred, calmly continued her trek up the throne steps and sat in her seat. Once she was comfortable, she nodded at Giselle, who lowered her hand, and Malin fell on the steps, hitting his chin hard on the stone. Guards were quickly upon him, clubbing the back of his head and sending him back on his knees next to his co-conspirator.

"Malin," Saryn said, "I see the fire in you has still not died out."

Malin's nostrils flared, and through gritted teeth, he replied, "If you took off these iron shackles, you would see how bright my fire burns."

Iron, the only thing capable of disarming a witch's magic, making them no more than mere mortals. The dungeons of the Blackthorn castle were made of iron, to simmer any criminal intending on using their gifts to escape. None had been successful.

River shook violently in her shackles, appearing to lose all control of her senses, "Malin, please! Stop!"

"Deyes," Saryn said mildly, ignoring River's cries.

With a bitter, angry look toward the accused, Deyes spoke, "How do you plea to the charges Malin Flynne?"

"Damn you." Malin spat and said nothing else.

Deyes took out a handkerchief and wiped up the remnants of spit on his boots, before continuing, "River Strant, how do you plea?"

River was nearly convulsing for the fear that emanated within her. "I-I'm sorry. I'm sorry. But it was either obey my king or face death, I had no choice!"

Deyes ignored River and continued, "Do you both have anything to say on your behalf?"

River continued to shake and stuttered too violently for Clarisa to make out anything she had to say. Malin on the other hand simply announced, "I did what any other witch would do to survive. Mark my words, the mortal kingdoms will overpower every witch on this island. We either join forces or cease to exist." He spat a tooth on the ground, no doubt a result of his blow on the stone steps.

Clarisa nearly forgot to breathe, and her blood ran cold in her veins. She knew that the mortal kingdoms were wary of witches, but she did not realize that there were kingdoms set to eradicate them completely from existence. Brisa's warnings about never leaving the Blackthorn rang in Clarisa's head: *they do not understand our kind out there.*

Deyes turned toward the crowns. "My rulers, how do you find the accused?"

"Guilty," Saryn announced, chin held high.

"Guilty, as well." Gareth sighed, and Clarisa could not imagine how he could still appear bored and unbothered by the events that had thus unfolded before him.

River cried out, terror etched on every crevice of her face. Malin remained silent, but fuming.

"And the punishment?" Deyes continued.

Gareth looked toward Saryn, who had a faint smile on her face. *She had been planning this*, Clarisa thought.

"Cut the head of the mortal, post it on our border in the eastern province, may it serve as a warning to every ill-intended who dares pass through."

"And the witch?"

"Have we received all the intelligence on his affairs with Givensmir?"

"Yes, My Queen."

"Good. He will not receive an honorable death, nor will his ashes be presented to our goddess at the sacred Blackthorn. Anyone who betrays their coven, is not worthy of a peace in the afterlife." She turned to Malin as she finished. "You will suffer the rest of your existence in a purgatory so dark and quiet, that the silence will drive you to an endless madness."

Malin stared back, hate in his eyes, and Clarisa could see smoke emanating off him, but the iron kept the full force of his fire smothered. "Then it would be no different than lying in your bed."

The crowd gasped at his insolence, but Saryn only laughed and waved her hand to Deyes. "Feed his tongue to the pigs as well."

Deyes turned toward the crowd. "Clarisa, step forward, see to it that the will of our crowns be done. Guards, take care of the woman."

"Malin, help me! Please, save me!" River cried out to Malin as a large and terrifying guard pulled her to a chopping block.

"Use your magic, please!"

Malin said nothing and kept his head down as she continued screaming out for him.

Clarisa squeezed Ana's hand before stepping forward, understanding her role, and trying her best to manage indifference as she moved past the screaming woman.

River begged for her life as two guards set her into the chopping block. She tried to push and thrash away, but Giselle held out her hand, her power forcing the woman down into the block and held her still. It was over before Clarisa could process anything else, and River's severed head rolled on the ground, stopping at the foot of the throne steps. A few from the crowd screamed with shock, and Clarisa could not stop looking, as much as she wished she could, her eyes fixed on the gore before her. She could see Ana from her peripheral vision, shutting her eyes tightly. The blood spilled all over the floor and sprayed onto Malin's face, whose eyes were still fixed on Saryn's.

"I didn't love her," Malin seethed, his nostrils flaring as River's blood pooled down his temple.

Saryn stared back at him as he was lifted by the guards and tied to one of the pillars. The moments before his death were tense; he refused to drop his gaze from Saryn, nor she his.

"Goodbye, Malin." Saryn smirked, finally shifting her gaze, and nodded to Clarisa.

Clarisa took several painful steps toward Malin, staring into his eyes as she lifted her hand to him, the least she could do to the man who mentored her all these years.

Find her, please, he mouthed to her, and for the first time she noticed a fear in his eyes that she had never seen before.

She wasn't sure who he was referring to but had no time to ask.

I will, she mouthed back, because it was all she could think of to say.

Malin did not reply but closed his eyes before letting out a bloodcurdling scream. Soon he began to choke, water now coming through his mouth and nose as if he were drowning in it. It was excruciating to watch, but Clarisa had done this many times before. It should have been no different, she told herself, but it was.

In seconds, he turned into a withered mess of dry skin and bone before his carcass fell to the floor. A guard came by with a knife and cut the remnants of his tongue, eyes, and heart and walked away. It only took a few seconds, but it felt like a lifetime as Clarisa stood before the death in front of her. This was who she was, who she had become in this place: a murderer, their personal assassin, a weapon.

She stared down at what was left of Malin's body. It was a shameful, cursed death, Clarisa and everyone present knew. It was custom to burn the body of a dead witch at a pyre and spread the ashes at a blackthorn tree. To leave a body without its tongue, eyes, or heart after death meant only a cursed afterlife in purgatory, a place of infinite nothingness. The bodies of the dead were quickly gathered by the guards, but the bloodstains remained on the ground, Clarisa stared at it—and for the first time realized that the color of blood could be nearly black. She tried to control her shaky breathing, but her lips quivered. She felt a hand squeeze hers and looked down. Ana was holding onto her with a firm grip, bringing her back into the crowd. She tried to calm her by stroking her thumb over the top of Clarisa's fingertips. This was certainly not how she expected this day to go and was nothing like how she thought it would turn out.

Saryn stood once more when the bodies were no longer in sight and looked upon the crowd, a triumphant gleam in her eyes. "We will mourn the deaths of our beloved fallen at the hands of these traitors. We dedicate our lives in service to you and will continue to maintain a safe haven for magic in our kingdom as we have done for hundreds of years.

"Malin, as many of you know, was once a faithful servant to our realm, a loyal servant to the crown, but allowed his greed to be his downfall, and chose to conspire with our enemy. Let this be a warning to all our constituents, any witch that endangers the life of another will meet the same fate as him. No witch is above the law of our kingdom. The coven must come first, always."

"The coven first," the witches chanted in response.

Saryn paused, assessing the faces of each in the crowd, Clarisa held her breath when Saryn's gaze landed upon her, but it was only for a fleeting second, before she continued, "Now, go back to your covens and spread the word of what you have witnessed today. May Isila protect and guide you on your journey home."

Without another word, the queen and king disappeared, and the throne room brightened, but only slightly, as dusk began to overpower the daylight. Clarisa wondered how long the entire event had taken—an hour, four hours?

The doors behind the crowd were opened by a few of the guards, and the witches began to file out silently. The crisp air, a reminder that fall was near, lingered around Clarisa as she followed Ana out of the castle, intending to escort her to her carriage. Brisa and Tabor followed closely behind. A foggy drizzle and a gloom permeated the castle grounds; Clarisa hoped that Ana would reach the dense forest a few miles outside the castle before a downpour arrived and soaked her carriage.

"I'm sorry we had to meet again under such circumstances," Ana whispered.

Clarisa looked at Ana, her dark brown eyes nearly mirroring her own, but within them held strength and secrets she yearned to uncover. "I was not prepared for it, admittedly."

Ana hesitated but nodded before grabbing Clarisa's hands. "Are you ever?"

Clarisa shook her head slowly.

"Before I go, I want you to know that I will be back upon Navir's return."

For the first time since Ana left to accompany her widowed mother, Clarisa felt relieved. The castle was lonely without her. Ana's work as a healer, recently assigned to Navir, meant she would be around more often.

Clarisa smiled. "This is the best news I've heard in ages."

"We will be together soon, I promise."

A footman checked the ties between the horse and the carriage before calling out, "Ana, we should leave before the rain worsens."

Ana nodded to him before returning her gaze to Clarisa. "Take care of yourself. I don't want to return to a gloomy castle and an even gloomier you." She lifted Clarisa's chin and smiled faintly.

"I will."

"Good." Ana released Clarisa's hands and walked away, lifting her gray linen skirt from the worst of the mud as the footman helped her into the carriage.

It wasn't until she watched Ana ride outside the castle gates minutes later that Clarisa finally felt a heavy burden on her shoulders once more. Her mind was running with all that she had seen, and all that she could not unsee. She could not understand, no matter how she tried to go over the events in her head, how anyone would ever dare challenge the wrath of the most powerful witches. Especially someone like Malin, who worked alongside them and surely knew how they punished their enemies.

Did some gold really convince Malin to risk his life, his legacy, to betray her? To betray the Blackthorn for Givensmir? The kingdom that sought to kill them all, who was now recruiting spies for their cause, and who had killed her entire family for sport.

Eve.

Clarisa hadn't thought about her fully in so many years and had tried to keep her a distant memory. The thought of how she must have suffered before inevitable death rendered Clarisa helpless. She had watched her get captured. The salt of the sea hit her like a slap to the face as she watched her disappear in the distance. *Did she suffer?*

No, she thought. It was dangerous to think like that, too dangerous to consider that a child like her could have been subject to such torment.

Clarisa remembered the cold throne room as she kneeled before the crown with Malin by her side. He was there when they had made a promise to a twelve-year-old, scared little Clarisa, recently orphaned and left to an unknown land among strangers. Malin held her hand and walked her back to her new chambers in the castle, where she would live for the next fifteen years.

Clarisa thought once more of Malin, the version of the man before he was executed. While it had been months since she last saw him, she remembered his kind smile and protective nature. She had felt a comfort in him and considered him a rare warm presence in her life as a child. He was always a strong, fervent supporter of the Blackthorn, of magic, of all those he served. Never once in her recent memory did he display any actions that would have made her suspect his traitorous nature.

The more she thought about it, the more an unsettling notion began creeping into her head that surely something more influential than some gold had persuaded Malin to betray the coven.

THEO

SIX

Theo did not care much for the follies of the noblemen. Did not care to entangle himself in the quarrels or minute power struggles between them. It irked him beyond reason how they clamored and groveled for his father's favor, and recently, that of him and his brothers.

As he rode on horseback alongside the men at court, he wished he was far away from them. It was the first hunt to celebrate their return from Larrea, and the entourage was full of men and their sons hoping to get a taste of game and gossip. His father traveled in his carriage, not willing to admit he struggled on horseback.

"I can't wait to kill my first man." Marc, his younger brother, smirked from upon his horse to no one in particular. Those around him nodded and made approvals as they rode, Ser Kyron James, commander of the armies, more than anyone. "I wonder if he will cower under my strength and beg for mercy or if he will actually fight me like a man . . ."

Theo rolled his eyes and rode faster to catch up with his older brother,

Eryce, and Lord Callum. The two were deep in conversation regarding Callum's struggle to maintain peace between the castellans left in his charge during the war.

"The man pulled his axe and swore to tear apart the steward, right there on the spot. It took five of the guards to hold him back." He shook his head and laughed. "All for a couple of meat pies that were the steward's to begin with, can you believe it?"

Eryce laughed with him. "At least that sounds a bit entertaining"—he turned noticing Theo approach—"my brother could barely smile the entire time we were camped out in Larrea. And I know I was laying my humor on thick."

"A shame." Callum feigned a grimace. "I wish we could have switched places, Prince Theo."

Theo nodded, coolly assessing him. "I'm sure you wouldn't."

Eryce's cackle thundered through the wood. "Relax, Theo. Callum is not serious. We are home now. We can enjoy a bit of life as the gods intended."

Theo shrugged. "Forgive me, Lord Callum, I did not sleep well last night."

"It is quite all right, Your Highness." He smiled genuinely, revealing a small birthmark upon his left cheek, and Theo wondered if he gave Eve that same smile. It was no wonder the two were close, the man was practically without fault, confident and friendly as he rode alongside him. Perhaps, that irked him more than Marc at the moment.

"After the feast, most of us went to drink in the city. I am surprised you did not join us," Eryce said.

"I was preoccupied," was all he could manage, and while Eryce raised his brow, he did not question him. Theo did not want to divulge his walk along the pond, how he pined for Eve, despite his betrothal. That was not a conversation for Callum's ears.

"A shame," Callum mused, "you were missed. However, considering how lethargic and drunk most of the men were the next morning, I imagine you made the right choice."

"Maybe next time."

"It was rather crowded," Eryce said, "Ser Elliot, the new commander of peace, mentioned we've had an influx of people from the east move into the capital, but I did not realize how many that was until I saw them crowding the city center."

"Lord Agustin said that the crown has had to pay nearly double to transport food from Rubianes," Callum replied. "It only makes sense considering the demand has increased."

"War will do that to people." Theo sighed. "No one wants to live where they may die."

"Then I wonder why they came here." Callum shook his head.

Neither of the princes replied, thinking more about the truth of his words, than the offense they should have taken to them.

The scouts and hounds tracked down a considerable number of game to keep the men occupied for most of the day. Deer and hares, pigeons—from the falconers and archers—two boars, and a stag were dragged by the king's servants through the royal forests and toward their encampment.

Large pavilion tents were erected and lined throughout a clearing to accommodate the court. The king preferred the company of the Gold Council in the tent, whereas Theo and Eryce wandered the grounds. Smoke from the spits and the scent of various meats filled the area late into the afternoon as the rest of the court began to congregate around a large fire in the center of the camp, sharing stories of war and their personal victories on the battlefields.

"I was this close to killing the false king myself," Ser Seymour, a member of the vanguard, exclaimed, squeezing his pointer finger and thumb in front of him, "but I wanted to give Prince Eryce the honor. It is only right our future king take the life of a usurper. Sends a warning no mere knight could."

Theo noticed from the corner of his eye how Eryce clenched his jaw. Callum shook his shoulder gently, trying to lighten the mood.

"Gentlemen, the war is over. Must we continue beating a dead horse?"

43

"You weren't there, I reckon you've never seen a dead horse," Ser Seymour replied, much to the amusement of the group. Laughter filled the air, and Callum laughed along with them, standing and raising his cup high.

"If I was in Larrea, who would have watched over the safety of our women and children? A mighty task I take charitably." He took a swig of his drink and bowed theatrically before the crowd who jeered and booed him playfully.

Theo watched as Eryce pulled Callum back down next to him.

"I say we change the subject, something that will scare the youngest among us." Callum gestured to the sons of the nobles; they peered up at him nervously with their boyish features next to their fathers.

"What do you propose?" Theo asked, interest piqued.

"A tale. Come now, am I to believe I sit with the fiercest among us and not one of you has experienced a near-kiss of death? Not related to war."

The men were a mixture of grunting in boredom, while others joked they tackled bears on other hunts. As the conversations grew in enormity, the tales began to thrive in absurdity, the drinks surely making the tongues of men spew exaggerated tales of their encounters. Deadly sirens, wraiths, and shapeshifters. Theo thoroughly enjoyed himself, listening as the men felt conviction in their drunken slurs, laughing as he truly hadn't in quite a while.

Finally, a man rose on Theo's left, he was burly with a dark, long beard and a head that glistened with sweat from the heat of the flame. Lord Enneco from a minor house in northern Teros.

"I saw a gytrash, when I was a boy," he grumbled, his deep voice carried through the noise, and the group silenced as he spoke. "Fur black as night, and eyes red as blood. Its teeth were like daggers that glistened in the moonlight and could tear a bear apart with ease."

Theo noticed how animated he was when he spoke, focusing most of his attention on the youngest of their group. They stared slack-jawed at Lord Enneco, their eyes wide and nervous. Theo smirked, knowing this to be a bit of folklore from centuries passed.

"I was traveling with my father and brothers through the woods near Gods' Protection, the wide river separating our kingdom and the frozen wastes. The trees, they grow like giants, I swear to you they can reach the heavens. I was the youngest of my brothers, and it was my first time traveling outside our lands. When we set up camp, they abandoned me in the woods, telling me I needed to prove my worth and manhood to them. I was but ten." He held up both his hands in exaggeration, and the boys were silent, captivated by his storytelling.

"I wandered for hours—every noise was a beast come to feast upon me, every twig I snapped another reminder of my inept ability to hide even in the dark. I could not so much see the light through the branches above me, nor could I make out what direction I was headed. It was the dead of night, and while I had become familiar with the sounds of the insects and the scampering of the opossums, I was not prepared for the growl of the gytrash I encountered. It was unlike anything I had seen before or since, I damn well pissed myself as it neared me. I forgot my sword at the camp and only had my cutting knife—courtesy of my dear brothers." He snorted, as if the thought brought back fond memories.

"What happened next?" Theo asked, hating to admit his curiosity got the better of him.

"Oh, it led me back to my camp. I was not that far from it, after all."

"You mean to tell me a ferocious beast came upon you as a boy, and you followed it to camp? Did it give you a kiss on the forehead before it left?" Ser Seymour spat, incredulous.

"And tucked me in to sleep, of course," Enneco quipped.

Theo and the men of the group laughed. The boys, however, seemed far less enthused.

"W-what is a gytrash, my lord?" one of them asked.

Enneco smiled, a wicked gleam in his eyes. "They were created by the witches as were the other creatures of the night, little lordling. They are spirits that roam the dark forests leading travelers astray. If you are particularly favored by the gods, they may even lead you right when you are lost."

"Do they eat us? Mortals, I mean," the boy continued.

"Anything created by magic can kill us, it would be good of you to remember this."

Somehow, Eve ran through Theo's mind. He scoffed. "A man gets lost, no doubt drunk, and sees a wild dog and the stories abound over the centuries. I wager we'll hear a story about hares turned into seductresses, or the boar on the spit becoming a dragon."

Enneco smiled, shaking his head. "Oh, My Prince, unfortunately for us, the truth is always far more terrifying than folklore."

DAKON

SEVEN

D akon had made great efforts over the years to avoid the king
in person. It was not that he despised him, necessarily, it was
simply a matter of avoiding the brutality he had been rumored
for toward servants. Unfortunately, when a regular serving boy twisted
his ankle, the castle steward chose Dakon to take his place. As one of the
only other servants with a modicum of gentlemanly manners, a regular
sparring partner of the royal sons, and his work in the stables where the
princess was a regular, he was not given a choice in the matter.

"It is for the temperament of the king that all servants be practically
invisible," the castle steward repeated to him, his feeble hands picking a
piece of lint from Dakon's shoulder. "I cannot defend you once you are
in his sights. Do your duty and be quick about it. Take your cues from
the other servants."

The livery uniform, bearing the merlion sigil of House Ebron, that
of the royal family, was stuffy and uncomfortable on Dakon's skin, and

it took considerable effort to avoid scratching. The dinner was an intimate one, meant for members of the king's Gold Council and his family to prepare final arrangements for the arrival of the Mytar nobles in the coming days, or so Dakon was led to believe. He stood along the back wall with the other servants, only moving when a member of the party lifted a glass to be refilled. Guards flanked the entrances, standing stoically in their golden suits, weapons affixed to their belts.

Dakon recognized most at the table, having served them at one time or another. Queen Alondra spoke lively amongst the party, her jewels glistening against her skin. The princes spoke casually amongst the table, the eldest two with each other and the younger with Ser James. He had a war-torn face, and thick wrinkles, and spoke often and loudly next to the king. Lord Velant, master of law, a man of nearly sixty, kept mostly to himself, picking at his food and barely touching his wine. Lord Agustin, a portly royal accountant, kept cordial amongst the men, but mainly spoke to tap his cup for more wine. Lord Matias a newly appointed commander of ships, laughed heartily at every one of the king's jokes, his face alight with feverish excitement. Dakon's eyes trailed to Princess Adriana, who seemed rather bored of the affair as soon as it began, mustering a semblance of a smile only when her mother would whisper sternly in her ear. Her long, light brown hair was braided neatly, her jewelry less ostentatious than her mother, dubbing a simple emerald necklace that complimented her hazel eyes. Occasionally, she peeked at Dakon from beneath her lashes and raised her lips in a soft, dimpled grin. He couldn't help but return it, nodding slightly toward her before she was forced to socialize with her table once more.

Over the past few months, she and Dakon had become well-acquainted as she frequently visited the stables to get distance from her mother and the court. Their conversations, which started as small remarks on the weather and her horses, had recently become impassioned discussions on the state of their futures, pretending for an hour or two that they were not separated by class and wealth.

"Quit staring, Dakon," his good friend and one of the servants, Pazel, whispered to him, "you'll get their attention, and I like my hide where it is, thank you very much."

Dakon flitted his eyes to the floor, nodding.

The dinner appeared simple enough and the conversation dull and uninteresting, until the king rose and addressed his party. "My friends, we are on the cusp of greatness. Our names will be written in the texts and carried through the songs of the century. We must celebrate our victories and our coming glories!"

The people at the table cheered and drank heartily from their cups.

"Now, let us be done with this business and enjoy ourselves," the king continued. "Where is my fool?!"

A lanky, tall old man was quickly let into the room with an astounding stride for one of such advanced age. His eyes were a faint blue, nearly purged of color, and his arms shook awkwardly as he moved. He wore the colors of Givensmir—gold-and-black striped pants and an ill-fitting top—as he pranced about the room, much to the delight of the mostly drunken party.

"Tell me a joke, fool." Lord Matias laughed. "Make it good!"

"The only joke in this room is you, Little Lordling" he replied, and the table roared with laughter.

Lord Matias drank his wine and feigned a chuckle.

"Your Majesty," the fool continued, "where is his wet nurse? Shall I inform the navy they must bring a crib aboard their ships?"

"Perhaps, I should," the king replied through winded laughter.

"I order you to leave at once, Lord Matias. tell your mother you missed her and beg forgiveness." The fool placed his hands on his hips theatrically.

"She knows I am here and have been a man grown for nearly a decade, *fool*," Matias spat.

"Oh, a temper this one," the fool said. "Is it past your bedtime, child?"

Dakon watched as Matias looked about the laughing faces, particularly that of the king, and reddened with embarrassment.

"Do leave us, Lord Matias, bed your wife and bid her good night from the men at this council." The king snorted.

Matias stood, words seeming to appear on his lips, but his voice found no strength to carry them. He instead forced a smile, bowed, and exited quickly from the room.

Throughout the next hour, the fool continued his jokes and sang various medleys to the party, all much to the delight of the drunken king.

"Now, sing me another," the king shouted above the thunderous laughter. "Make it a good one."

The fool smirked and nodded. "Oh, for you, Your Majesty, I have prepared a special song." He cleared his throat theatrically, grabbing Ser James's cup and downing it in one sitting. Then he began to sing in a silly, deep voice:

The boy king stood no chance,
To our great king with a lance,
A babe upon his bed,
And a lion on the prowl,
Our fierce king knows no fear,
Except for the witches that grow near,
He shrieks like a child,
And gets mad and wild,
Ah, but burn them down, all around
Claim their lands!
Let it stand!
Our king of ash is so renowned!

Dakon watched each of the noble faces, focused on the fool's song with glee, but felt an ache in his chest as he came upon the king. His face was twisted in an amused grin that chilled his blood. Dakon felt a tightness in his chest for what might come—a rising anxiety—when he felt something soft like fur beneath his fingertips. He stared down curiously and leapt from where he stood as a large, black dog panted next to him.

"What are you doing?" Pazel hissed, keeping his position rigid against the wall.

"Y-you don't see it?" Dakon breathed, "The dog?"

"See what? Get back in line unless you have a death wish."

Dakon looked at the dog once more, it was massive with its matted black fur and red eyes. Perhaps, Pazel and the rest of the servants were used to seeing the different animals the royals owned, and Dakon cursed himself for his foolishness. It was only a dog, not a ghost—and he ignored it as it licked his hand.

The fool continued to play the lute to finish out the melody as the men of the table continued to clap and cheer. The king was not laughing, but simply nodded and clapped when the song was finished. He stood, gesturing to his guards to accompany him.

The fool, none the wiser, swayed slightly before the king, a wide, crooked grin upon his face. The guards now lingered on either side of the fool, and the rest of the party was silenced, the tension thickening the room.

The dog barked twice and Dakon squeezed his eyes shut, praying that the royals would ignore his presence. But when he opened them, it seemed no one heard the animal. Even stranger, no one seemed to notice as it left his side and padded across the room, lapping its tongue and whining as it went. It ran through the wall and disappeared as if it never existed.

Dakon could not believe what he saw, but had no time to think about it before the king spoke.

"Wonderful, did you make that song yourself?"

The fool, drunk himself now, responded, "Yes, Your Majesty. All to entertain from the words of your people."

"I am entertained." He nodded, standing before the fool. "It seems that I was unaware that my people believed me to be a boy killer, nor that they believed I feared the witches."

"Ah, but what king doesn't have trouble with wrongdoers?"

"True. And what should I do to these wrongdoers?"

"Why, kill em as you would any other, Your Majesty."

"Excellent response," the king replied, nodding to his guards.

The men held down the fool, while one held a knife to his throat.

Dakon's heart hammered in his chest, and from the corners of his eyes, he noticed the rigid stillness of the rest of the servants as they faced the floor. He did the same, trying to avoid incurring any of the king's wrath.

"Wait, Your Majesty, it was only a joke. I meant you no disrespect!"

"Good to hear," the king replied, as he walked back to his seat, "so you shall have a clean death as a token of our mutual respect."

Before the fool could utter another word, the guards slit his throat and quickly removed the body from the room. Adriana let out a shriek, and the elder of the two princes stood from their tables, arguing with their father. But Dakon could not listen, his mind was occupied by the trail of blood leading out the door.

"Am I to look at this mess for the rest of the dinner?" the king complained, ignoring his sons, and he sat once more as the servants rushed to clean it.

Dakon retrieved a rag from his pocket and joined them.

"Come, Adriana, we will take you to your chambers," Eryce announced, as he helped Adriana from her seat with Theo. They began walking from the room, as Adriana cried about the loss of her favorite fool.

Bits of flesh converged with the blood and the putrid, iron scent invaded Dakon's nostrils. He stood to grab more rags from the kitchens, when the king called out to him.

"And who are you?"

Dakon froze for a moment and turned slowly to face the king and all his party. He could hear Adriana gasp behind him, her brothers trying to force her to go. He tried to avoid the princess's stare. Embarrassment filled him and all pleasantries were lost upon him as he spoke. "Dakon, from the stables."

"The stables! Why is a stableboy serving a king?" Ser James inquired, shoving a piece of pork into his mouth.

"A servant was injured, I merely replaced him—"

"Your Majesty," Ser James sneered. "When you address the king, you must use the proper courtesies, you fool."

"O-of course," Dakon's eyes were wide, and he looked at the king once more, "Your Majesty." He bowed, and stood awkwardly before him, waiting to be released. Wishing that the princess was not bearing witness to his humiliation.

"What did you think of the fool's song?" the king asked, taking a sip of his wine.

"Father, must we kill all our servants?" Eryce began, "This is a good man—"

"Take leave or I shall see to it that all of them are killed at once," the king growled.

Dakon could hear Adriana's whimpers as the three of them left the room.

"So," the king said, focusing on his wine before him, "what did you think?"

Dakon weighed his words carefully. "It was in ill-taste, Your Majesty."

"Do you sing?"

"Not very well, Your Majesty."

"A handsome, young man like you? I do not believe it," the king mocked. "Come, sing me a song to make me forget the last. Entertain me, *Dakon from the stables.*"

Dakon felt the eyes of the room upon him, some in fear, others in curiosity, but most in pity. His next words may very well be his last, he knew this. Yet, to not obey the king would be to put all hope in the hands of death itself. He buried his rising anger and began to sing a song known among the common folk.

"The halls of the great—"

Fortunately, the king raised his hand to silence him before he finished the first line.

"You have a good voice. But I am in need of a fool, not a troubadour."

"Of course, Y-Your Majesty."

The king studied him, his brows creasing as his table watched him precariously. "I am feeling rather merciful tonight, tell me, how would you like to die?"

Dakon felt his breath hitch as the guards brought him roughly to his knees, holding him tight. The reality of his situation bore down on him with full force, and before he could censor himself, he spoke true. "When I am older than the fool, Your Majesty!"

The silence stood and Dakon closed his eyes tightly, waiting for the pain to come, but instead he heard laughter. The king's laughter.

"Clever," he grinned, wiping tears from the corner of his eyes. "Older than the last, hmm?"

A few of the men around the table laughed nervously along with him. The king took a deep breath, trying to calm himself before he spoke once more.

"Gentlemen, I believe we have met our new fool."

Dakon stalked toward the servants' quarters, his tunic filled with wine and blood, the stench of it filling his nostrils unpleasantly.

From cleaning the stables as a boy, he worked his way through the servant ranks to be considered a sparring partner for a few of the nobles, practicing until late into the night at a craft he surely would be unable to put into practice as the war effort never spared castle servants. All this work, only to be made a fool. He groaned, the humiliation bearing the heaviest weight on his pride.

Then there was the matter of the dog, Adriana never told him she owned a dog like that. He began to wonder if maybe he was going slightly crazy, insane even. *Dogs do not go through walls, you idiot.*

The quarters were dark and dimly lit with candles whose wicks were nearly gone. The bright evening sky led him through the relatively quiet halls save for a corner room filled with servants listening attentively.

A woman's voice raised and lowered in dramatic fashion and as it fell upon his ears he began to calm.

"And the blood of witches ran black in the rivers, poisoning all who drank from it . . ."

He approached the crowded room, filled with servant children and others who wished to find some means of escape from their daily lives, if only for a few moments. They all encircled an elderly woman, sitting at a wooden chair telling another tale of intrigue and mystery. Sitting there, she was not just an old servant, but a vivacious, lively woman with her raised hands and theatrics.

The woman paused for effect, and her eyes reached Dakon, and she smiled. This woman, Cerene, the only mother-figure he had ever known, was the only person he knew who could truly captivate a crowd with her voice alone.

"Sons turned against their fathers, daughters against their mothers. Death encroached the lands like a dark cloud, and all seemed lost."

The children gasped, and Dakon felt a slight smile creep across his face. He remembered this tale well; she told it to him many times before.

"That is, until the mighty king thrust his knife into the heart of the witch, killing the dark magic throughout the lands, and saving our kingdom from ruin. Blessed by the will of the gods themselves."

"By the will of the gods," the crowd repeated, bowing their heads for a moment.

When they all raised their heads, Cerene finished as she always did: "Now, it is time for bed children. Go off, it is an early morning tomorrow."

The crowd began to disperse, the children talking excitedly as they did. Dakon walked into the room, helping to lift Cerene up from her chair. It was the first time he really noticed how frail she was becoming; it unsettled him.

"I told your favorite." Her eyes flicked to him, her hand patting his as she released herself from his gentle grip. "I had a feeling you would visit this old woman today."

"I almost didn't," he admitted, walking alongside her. "Cup bearing duties today."

"Ah, that upsets you."

"How did you—"

"I have known you long enough to know when you are unhappy."

"I can be of far better use outside of this castle. I have been training . . ." his voice trailed off, unsure of what he truly meant to say.

Cerene stopped, turning to him, her eyes assessing. "Swords in play are not the swords of battle, my child. You would do well to humble yourself."

"What glory can be found in these castle walls? What pride can there be with serving unworthy men who look down on people like me—like us?"

"And what do you know of the consequences of glory, of pride? None of these come to people without a high cost. Do not confuse the chanting of an imaginary crowd with the affection of family."

"I would never—I just, I only meant—"

"You seek a life that is not meant for us. Carrying after dreams and wishes as if they will win over the woman you desire."

This silenced Dakon, and he chewed on his tongue, turning from her. Cerene lifted her feeble hand to his chin, turning him slowly toward her, eyeing him warily.

"Gaining her affections through lies, does not make them truer."

Dakon cast his eyes down, wishing she understood how the princess felt for him, or at least how he felt about her. Memories of the last precious months came to his mind, riding horses into the thicket, talking gently under the silver birches of the Givensmir forests. Her bright eyes reflected a mixture of the summer greens and earthy browns, a nature he did not ever wish to part from. It was all a secret only they could share, and it felt heavy in his soul as he kept silent while Cerene continued her lecture.

"Do not covet her heart, my child, it will only bring you misery and death."

EVE
EIGHT

There it was again.

The grimoire lying open on her bedsheets, waiting for her, beckoning her. Whispers flitted from ear to ear, a voice she was unfamiliar with, but felt a peculiar connection to.

Touch me, Eve.

A cool chill filled her bedchamber, prickling her skin with its bite. Feasting upon the warmth of comfort and familiarity and replacing it with the fear of the unknown, the uneasiness of what it all meant. The moon evaded most of the dark clouds of midnight and shined its ethereal glow through the balcony. Lighting her way to the book in the night.

Eve, wrapped in her nightgown, hair cascading down her back in an unruly fashion, took a step toward it. She could not remember from whence she came or how she came to stand before it, but there she was, listening and watching the book from a short distance.

It felt surreal and dreamlike, the whispers in her ear and the book growing ever closer in front of her. Its dark leather-bound cover frayed and cut at the edges, depicting the same owl beneath three stars. She did not remember taking those steps, but somehow, she must have, for now she could reach out and touch it.

Sweat pricked from her temples, the hair on the back of her neck rose, and part of her tried to look away, to resist the temptation of discovering more than she would ever dare to in the light of day. But she felt weak before it. Its power was too strong for her, she could feel it now coursing through her veins as the voices rose.

Blood of the Blackthorn.

It is you.

The floor beneath her was ice now, her feet red and aching with the numbing pain, and she let out a whimper as she stood in place, unable to move. From her peripheral vision she could see ice and snow claim her space, freezing over her chambers as if it were left to the elements in the dead of winter. Eve tried to breathe calmly, but the cold bit at her throat, seizing it with every inhale.

I can bring you everlasting fire.

It glowed invitingly, a golden-orange hearth in a blue storm. She precariously rested an icy, trembling hand on the book, relishing in the warmth it provided her. The small reprieve from the cold that now overtook her room.

Anything you desire.

The truth.

The truth is what you seek.

She could not bring herself to think of anything but the cold, nipping at her extremities, slowing her blood flow, her throat ached for relief from the burning sensation. Eve felt a lone tear escape from the corner of her eye, and in desperation opened the book, shivering uncontrollably and squeezing her eyes shut as the wind picked up in her room.

Except, when she opened them, Eve was no longer in her chambers, no longer in the castle, but somewhere dark and foreboding with the most peculiar, thorned trees. The book cast a faint light as it laid open on the ground before her, revealing a story she had never read before.

It began seven centuries ago, a time when the gods and mortals warred to ruin and destruction. Misery and death plagued the lands of Givensmir and the five realms that ruled within—Teros, Rubianes, Mytar, Larrea, and Zafira—all inhabiting mortals who no longer wished to follow the will of the gods, instead seeking solace and faith amongst new leaders, men of their own who promised salvation.

Angered, the gods sought to create something that would change their minds. Something for the people to fear and return to them. Each creation failed to come to fruition and only further enraged the mortals who tore down statues and tributes in retaliation. Desperate, the gods sought counsel from the most chaotic among their kind.

Isila, a goddess known for her trickery and magic, promised the gods eternal admiration from the mortals in exchange for something simple—a seed to plant in her gardens, forged by pieces of their souls. The gods, weakened now by the near desertion of their most ardent followers, gifted her as she asked—a seed containing bits of their souls molded together.

Isila took the seed, secretly planting it on a lone island three days from Givensmir across the Dallise Sea. The goddess watered it with drops of the ocean and the blood of men who denounced the gods. She gathered three mortals who swore fealty to her above any other. And when the seed took to the soil, Isila and her mortals watched patiently as the tree grew from the earth—its branches spindled crookedly in the spring and bloomed white, five-petaled flowers—one for each kingdom that went against the gods.

The goddess gave the flower to one of the mortals to eat, but, unable to handle the magic within, he succumbed to death. In the summer, the leaves changed to green, symbolic of the greed of men. Isila gave it to the second mortal to boil and drink; she, too, met the same fate as the first. In the late fall, dark black-blue berries clung to the branches, their taste representing the bitterness between the gods and the mortals. She gave it to the third to eat, and she, too, fell. And when the winter's harsh breeze began to strip the tree of its life, Isila pricked herself on its thorns, letting her blood flow freely along the branches. The goddess burned the tree and the bodies of the mortals with it. And when the fire died, the mortals and the Blackthorn were left unscathed, rising with magic, and Isila rejoiced for it symbolized the end of sole mortality and the beginning of the Age of Witchcraft.

<hr/>

Eve found herself standing at the edge of her balcony in the darkness, looking once more into the sea, the book raised above her head as if ready to throw it in. A sense of deja vu filled her; she could taste the salt in the air, feel the blood that dripped from her finger and down her arm, the thick night drenched the evening in shadow. She slowly brought the grimoire back down and cradled it against her chest. It was hers now, only hers. Eve took one last look out toward the water, feeling a pang in her chest for something felt lost once more, and walked back inside.

<hr/>

"My lady," the handmaid said breathlessly, "wake up, it is late. You are to accompany the princess within the hour."

"M-my book," Eve mumbled, her vision foggy from her deep slumber as the light of dawn intensified the ache in her head.

"Why, there is no book here, my lady," she replied, lifting Eve into a sitting position. Her words were coming too quickly as she chatted excitedly. "All your books are on your shelf. I say again—encourage you, rather—to read them every once in a while instead of visiting that dusty library. Oh, and before I forget, the handsome Lord Callum has called upon you. I know it is not my place, but you should try and be reasonable. You would not wish your uncle to choose for you . . ."

THEO
NINE

"**N**ow, brother, you will never be able to lead any soldier into battle with such weak posture," Prince Eryce lectured Theo as they sparred with wooden swords.

"*You* woke me early this morning; *I* was not ready for exercise before dawn," Theo moaned. His brother was his closest confidant, his best friend, and a worthy sparring opponent, but damn him for rising before the sun. He aimed for Eryce's exposed ribs, but his sword was quickly deterred by a strong blow—the wood made a loud clack against each other and Theo came back into the defensive.

"Ah, you have been away from battle for too long," Eryce replied, striking Theo's sword as he attempted to jab his midsection.

"Have I?" Theo ducked to miss Eryce's attack, barely making it under. He responded with another jab to his brother's torso, but Eryce was far too quick.

"Yes, the battlefield was far too lonely without my brother beside me."

Eryce mocked a sad face, while taking the lead in the dance, his stamina picking up while Theo's began to falter.

"I was injured in battle, you fool." Theo laughed and barely dodged another presumably fatal blow toward his chest. "My arm has only just begun to feel normal."

He shuddered for a heartbeat recalling the events of six months ago; the final stretch in the war for Larrea, his father, King Eryck's, continued battle for expansion of his realm into neighboring territories. This war was barely won, with thousands of their men killed and barely two hundred left as they carried Theo's beaten body to the healer's tent. His right arm, sliced by an enemy soldier, and more superficial than fatal, leaving him with a large scar, began to fatigue with the strenuous duel.

Eryce expertly deflected another blow by Theo and disarmed him before Theo could figure out what had happened. In seconds, Theo had found himself on his back, with a wooden sword at his throat.

"That is why you have me to practice with, so we can try to avoid such annoyances in the future." Eryce smiled, and reached out his opposite hand toward Theo. He took it and stumbled back onto his feet.

A servant approached with water and filled their cups. "Excellent fight, Your Highnesses," he remarked. "Do you wish to continue? Need a sparring partner, perhaps?"

"Thank you," Eryce replied courteously, "but we are needed elsewhere. Feel free to work on your technique while we're gone. I'll need someone to spar with that has *two* useful arms since Dakon is no longer in our service."

"Will do, Your Highness." the servant bowed graciously and moved aside.

"A shame about Dakon," Theo muttered.

Eryce sighed heavily, "a wasteful man our father is."

The brothers finished their water and deposited their wooden swords in the equipment boxes as they began to leave the sparring room, headed toward their chambers to freshen up.

As Theo and Eryce walked down the long corridor Theo took note of the serene landscape outside, the Dallise Sea rocked gently, inviting, from a distance.

Eryce interrupted his thoughts. "It's a shame Marc does not join us in our sessions."

Marc, their youngest brother, was known to be rather aloof and opinionated, opting to spar with his personal trainer rather than his brothers. Marc often declared that he was the finest swordsman in the kingdom, but refused to take up offers to test his boisterous claims.

"He is probably holed up in some woman's room discussing how grand he is." Theo circled his hands animatedly around his curly hair as he rolled his eyes. It was no secret that Marc and Theo were often at odds, with Theo calling out Marc's atrocious behavior, while Eryce tried to simmer the tension.

"True," Eryce replied, "we can only expect so much out of a man who has been spoiled by everyone around him with all the privileges of royalty, and without any of the inherit responsibilities."

Marc, it was known, would not see himself as king to the Givensmir throne in his lifetime. With their father's illness and two brothers—twenty-eight and twenty-six, respectively—there were too many heirs with good health and youth in his way. It was a known sensitive topic for Marc who often declared that birthright should go to a chosen prince, instead of the eldest. It had been a while since their last discussion on the matter, however. Marc often kept to himself, while Eryce and Theo kept busy on the battlefields.

"If that is wholly true, then why is Adriana so much unlike him?"

Princess Adriana, their only sister and the youngest of the four siblings, was beloved throughout the kingdom and known for her kindness and charity. Her wit and taste for knowledge were practically unmatched, compared to her brood of brothers.

Eryce sighed. "Adriana certainly understands the importance of compassion and humbleness, but she was never raised believing she could have had a chance at the throne. Marc, for some reason or another, believes that he will one day rule us all by charming Father, as if it were truly in his hands. Give him another year, certainly he will mature."

Theo and Eryce, freshly changed in their royal garb, walked to the council room; their father had demanded their presence at noon. It was where the men of the royal family congregated with the Gold Council to discuss important matters of state and politics. A place that Theo would rather avoid if given the choice; it had become a haven for the sycophants of his father at court, rather than a forum of healthy debate. Too many ill-advised decisions carried tremendous weight, and he stood witness to all regardless of his or Eryce's opposition.

The men strode in side-by-side, having finished laughing about a joke. Their father, standing behind one of the war tables looked less than amused, his face in a grimace as he eyed them with irritation. Marc was standing next to their father, as well as three different men of the council. Ser James, and Lord Wesley of Asturi, a minor house of Givensmir, and the king's most trusted informant. Both men enriched themselves by association with his father, and Theo maintained a steadfast wariness around them. The last was Lord Agustin, the royal accountant, who seemed sickly this morning, no doubt from his excessive drinking the night before. A few other members seemed to be missing.

Each man stood around the war table—a table fixed with a large map of Serit and the non-contiguous outlying lands, various borders, topographical features, seas, and kingdoms stenciled within, wooden pieces were placed on areas of the board, depicting the allies and enemies and their last known locations to the spies in Givensmir's hold. It appeared that the group was discussing strategy as the princes walked in.

"Nice of you to join us, glad we could make it into your schedule." His father sneered as he lowered his eyes back to the table.

"Father, you said noon, and we are here as instructed," Theo replied.

"Does your brother speak for you now?" The King glared at Eryce.

"No, Father," Eryce replied, "we apologize for our delay."

Their father stared at both of them for a few moments, before finally lowering his gaze once more onto the table.

"Marc, feel free to brief your brothers on what we have discussed."

"Certainly, Father," Marc replied. Theo glared as Marc smirked at him and they joined the council around the table. "We will subvert the remainder of our forces from Larrea now that we have achieved victory there. As we know, the last of the treasonous family—mother and sisters to the false king—have committed their rituals of submission and denounced their titles. Father has spared their lives and sentenced them to a life of exile in the Bastard's Haven." Marc let out a slight chuckle, moving the wooden goat piece, representing the Ivari family sigil, from Larrea to the island before continuing. "We will move our armies into a renewed campaign that we have left neglected for the past decade, focusing our efforts across the Dallise Sea. It's about time we rid this world of witchcraft and finally claim the land as part of Father's impressive expansion of Givensmir."

Ser James nodded. "Excellent, Your Highness." He turned to Theo and Eryce. "It is necessary to go forth when they least expect it and when they will be less likely to commit any form of suitable retaliation."

"Witches are a rarity among our lands, Father—" Theo began.

"We only burned one weeks ago," Marc spat.

Theo flared his nostrils but ignored his brother and pressed his father. "What do we hope to gain from attacking their lands? They have nothing that we could benefit from, and that witch was the first in years that we have executed. You have said so yourself, they have no power over us."

Their father coughed into his handkerchief, his eyes bloodshot and vile as he returned Theo's gaze. "Everyone who is not us is our enemy. They have no power *now*, but that witch was a sign. How many more are among us? How many more may fall into the hands of our enemies to use as weapons of their own?"

"The only true enemies we have are nobles like the Ivaris who wish to usurp our rule. This is sure to be the case if we do not tend to the needs of our people."

"*Our* rule? Do you hear that Eryce? Your brother thinks he is the heir now."

Theo did not rise to the bait. For his father to think this way was madness. His sentiments seemed to be mirrored by Eryce who chewed on the inside of his cheek, a tick indicating his discomfort. Theo knew an argument was brewing, and he decided to take a step back to listen.

"Father"—Eryce straightened—"is there no plan to rest our forces? We have been in constant war for nearly a decade and have only recently completed our last attack a couple of weeks ago. Our men need rest."

"What our men need is discipline," their father spat, moving one of the wooden Givensmir pawns on his wargaming set to a forested area of the table. "We took eight years to do what should have been done in three."

"Without proper rest, we assume a larger risk of injury or illness of our men. We are entering autumn, temperatures will plummet soon and the mountainous, dense forest terrain of the Blackthorn isles, not to mention the rough waters between our lands, will significantly impede our forces. Let us delay—"

"Prince Eryce, perhaps you have forgotten, but our forces have only known consistent warfare for years. The least we'd want to do is weaken our army by encouraging too much lethargy amongst our soldiers," Ser James interjected.

"We won't have any men to fight if they cannot heal properly," Eryce retorted.

"Perhaps the prince has a point," said Lord Agustin. "If we delay until the spring, then perhaps we can replenish our supplies and ensure we have enough coin to fund this venture."

"We can take the money from Blackthorn once we've conquered them, and the acquired funds from the Larrea kingdom should be good to start a small skirmish shouldn't it, Ser James?" Marc raised a brow at the commander.

"No, that is not how war funds work," Eryce chastised, then turned to his father. "Father, I was out there on the battlefield as you commanded. For the last eight years, I have watched as our men have died and fought to survive. Believe me, the best thing for our kingdom is to replenish our armies and let our men—our soldiers—go back home to their wives and children."

"You speak like you are a king already; how disgraceful, brother," Marc said, nostrils flared. Theo noticed a hint of envy in his eyes.

"A true king is present for his battles. Eryce is more than fit to speak on such matters," Theo interrupted before he could stop himself, holding firm as Marc looked as if he had been slapped. Their father always kept one of the spares at the kingdom during the war, in case he or Eryce should die. Marc never got the chance for battle, much to his chagrin.

"Enough now, all of you!" King Eryck roared and turned to face Eryce. "You are not king yet, boy. You would be wise to keep that in mind when you start speaking of rest and delays. No one will follow a king who cannot keep a *powerful* and *loyal* realm."

Theo watched as Eryce clenched his jaw, but kept his gaze firm on their father, never lingering, never faltering. He turned his eyes toward Marc who smiled as his head was lowered, enjoying every second of Eryce's beratement.

The king turned his gaze to Lord Wesley. "Update them of our reports on the Blackthorn."

"Certainly, Your Majesty." Lord Wesley stood upright. "Your Highnesses, I have received reports that one of our spies in the Blackthorn has been murdered, sentenced to death after being caught during a skirmish that was simply testing the strength of the outskirt villages of the Blackthorn's southeastern provinces. Our forces were defeated as expected, but I was able to receive intelligence from a few who escaped. The witches are indeed mortal-like in physical combat, most are not able to sustain their magic against a formidable force. If we attack with large numbers—a minimum two-to-one—against them, they will be defeated quite easily as they do not have a sophisticated army. The spy I employed, River Strant, now has her head on a spike on their border, a sure indication of warning and a threat to us. However, she is one of many I have currently serving you." Wesley paused, moving a few pieces across the board toward the Blackthorn portion of the map. "She was executed alongside a witch, Malin Flynne, who must have been an informant as he had not been previously added to our list of insiders."

The men were silent, taking in this information.

"We cannot allow them to kill our people and get away with it," their father announced.

Theo did not care much for his father, nor did he respect him, and he knew that this death was merely an excuse for his father to do what he had already been planning. It was common knowledge that his father had succumbed to a love of war and terror, focused solely on expanding his realm versus caring for the people within it. The second their father received his crown, the worse things had become for the kingdom. Practically overnight, they were sent into mayhem with unnecessary battles that had not ceased since his coronation. He had orchestrated the near extinction of witches throughout the kingdom, the last execution a few days ago was among the first in years.

His mother, Queen Alondra, was not much better, succumbing to silence to avoid any brutality at the hands of his father. She feigned a carefree existence in the comfort of her court, more focused on keeping the peace than challenging her tyrant of a husband. A match made from the necessity of alliance rather than any affection. Theo tried to block out the glaring similarities between their marriage and his betrothal, or his brother's marriage.

Eryce had been wed to his wife, Gabrielle, for years, but had yet to produce an heir, nor did he seem interested in doing so, much to the detriment of his mother. Now, with Eryce growing to be more compassionate and less like his father daily, Theo could see a rage building within the king. A bitter resentment that his legacy would be left to someone intent on pacifying the kingdom within rather than enforcing control by fear throughout.

Theo studied his father, the king's hands shook involuntarily, his face was contorted into a fierce rage, his nostrils flared, and he coughed into a handkerchief after nearly every other sentence. Theo often overheard his father repeating commands, forgetting things, or—even as the night before— ordering severe punishments on innocent staff members for no other reason than for his entertainment. He wondered how much time his father had left, wondered how deep his illness would plague him and his decision-making before finally taking him out of this world.

Theo snapped back into focus when his father clapped a hand on Marc's back proudly and announced, ". . . and Marc will accompany your men on this journey, Ser James. See to it that he has a first good taste of battle."

"Of course, Your Majesty." Ser James bowed.

"All of us at once, Father?" Theo questioned.

"Yes, pay attention, Brother," Marc sneered.

"Who will remain behind in case—"

"Do not be insolent, boy. I have made my rule, and it is final," his father gritted through his teeth.

The room held a silent tension before he continued, eyeing Theo warily. "One last order of business. As we all know the nobles of Mytar, Lord Joseph and his family—wife, son, and daughter—will be staying with us for a few weeks. Our success with our new campaign relies on their happiness and comfort in our castle and with our kingdom. Theo, I'm warning you, you have one chance to prove to me of your worth, see to it that you are attentive to Lady Felicity. We need your marriage to the girl to secure this alliance, and their coin."

"Yes, Father." Theo's eyes locked back on his father's.

The king leered at Theo for a few seconds before finally turning his gaze to Marc. "Soon it'll be both you and your sister's turn to secure an alliance of some sort; wars are expensive. Betrothals can be changed, perhaps as a last resort I might throw the half-breed your way to appease the witch kingdom if all else fails."

Theo clenched his jaw, narrowing his gaze at his father. He knew exactly who he was talking about, and he would be damned before watching her walk down the aisle with his snake of a brother.

"Say the word, Father, and your will shall be done." Marc grinned at Theo.

"That's the attitude of a true man. I hope you two"—King Eryck eyed Theo and Eryce—"learn from this. Now take care of any final arrangements on your part, they will arrive tomorrow."

The group began to file out of the room.

"I wonder what meals the cooks will prepare for this welcoming celebration," Lord Agustin said aloud to no one in particular. "I am quite fond of the honey wine, though, I know that our stock was running low last I had the steward count . . ."

Theo ignored him, following alongside Eryce out of the council room. "This was a waste of a meeting," Eryce breathed in frustration for only Theo to hear. "He is set on ruining our kingdom and our names with it."

"Agreed, Brother. We just need more time for him to see reason."

"He would sooner give Marc the crown than to stop this madness."

Theo could only nod, unsure of how to respond.

As they moved out the door, Theo turned once more, noticing that Marc opted to stay behind and talk to their father. The king spoke to Marc with a rare smile on his face, clasping his hand on his shoulder in pride. Marc turned his eyes to Theo and smirked, before setting his attention back on their father, clasping a hand on his shoulder in return.

DAKON
TEN

"I am so sorry, Dakon, truly."

Dakon and Adriana stood alone in the stables, brushing and feeding their horses as they spoke. They were positioned along the right corner, obstructed from view, and Dakon relished the cool breeze of the early autumn morning making its way through the structure. Their horses waited patiently and ate vegetables off the ground as a treat. Today they would only have half an hour before the princess was expected to prepare for the welcoming ceremony.

"It is not your fault, Princess."

"I should have done something." She placed her hands on his, and he looked down at them, clean and polished against his callused ones. He removed his hands slowly.

"There was nothing anyone could do."

"But I wish there was."

"Your father is a king—"

"That does not give him the right to act so atrociously," she remarked, and after a moment, added, "poor Trent."

"Trent?"

"The fool—or former one, I should say." She sighed.

"I only hope that I do not succumb to his fate."

"No, I won't allow it. There must be some way—"

"Apart from running away, at which point your father would quickly seize and execute me, I have no choice in the matter."

"There is always a choice."

"Maybe for you, but not for people like me."

"You think I have a choice in my life?"

"You're right, between gold and silver necklaces, it must be difficult for you."

She paused, hurt etched across her face, and he regretted the words as soon as he said them. "Forgive me, Adriana. I have not slept much; that is no excuse to take out my frustrations on you."

She bit her lip and narrowed her eyes, but Dakon breathed a sigh of relief when she did not leave. He continued, "let us talk of something else."

"I may not be able to see you for a few weeks . . . so informally, I mean."

"I understand."

"I'm not making this conversation any better, am I?"

"Adriana, I am happy when you can spare me any of your time. Now and in a few weeks is perfect."

She smiled, giving her horse another carrot. "If I give you a gold necklace, will you then tell me the name of my admirer?" Princess Adriana smirked playfully.

"My word is worth more than gold, Princess," he replied, a wicked gleam in his eyes and mock hurt in his voice.

"Of course, I meant the silver. Silly me."

"How you wound me, Princess." He placed a hand dramatically on his chest and watched as she laughed.

"It is merely a test, you see."

"A test?"

"Yes, I wish to test your word." She raised her chin toward him.

"However, I would like to know if I can ask a few questions about him."

"The point of a secret admirer is that it is a secret. How can this poor man admire you from afar without reservation if you were to know his identity?"

"Please, Dakon. It isn't fair!" she complained playfully.

He stared at her for a moment longer than he should have before casting his gaze elsewhere. "One question."

"Four."

"None."

"Three."

They narrowed their eyes at one another, before he relented. "Three."

"Oh, this is so exciting, um, I was not prepared for this." She appeared to rack her brain for questions.

Dakon simply appreciated the view.

"Is he someone I know?"

"Yes."

"Is he handsome?"

"How should I know?"

"You cannot answer a question with a question, Sir. Think like I would. Would I find him attractive?"

"I think so."

"Is he you?"

Dakon felt his breath catch and his heart skipped a beat. Her eyes were wide and curious, and he allowed himself to believe, just for a moment, that she would have wanted it to be him. He swallowed, clearing his throat. "No."

"Oh."

They stared at the ground silently for a few moments.

"But, of course"—Adriana laughed anxiously—"that would be silly, wouldn't it? I mean, you would have to know how to write and read first and foremost."

"I can—"

"Dakon!" Pazel called out to him from beyond the stables, his black hair and ochre skin contrasting against the pale stone of the castle, "Dakon, the steward calls for you. Come inside, quickly!"

Dakon looked toward Adriana. "My apologies, I trust you can make your way back to the castle?"

"As always, I am a very capable woman."

He smiled, and kissed her hand, discreetly leaving a note in it. "Until next time, Princess."

<hr>

"So, shall I ask the king to hang us now or later when we are caught?" Pazel asked a short while later, as he walked Dakon back to the servant's quarters.

"We are breaking no laws, Pazel. Me and the princess only talk, and you are only my eyes to make sure no one bothers us."

"Ah, see, but here is where you are wrong. You would not need me to keep watch if you believed the king would be fine with your dalliances. You and me"—he placed a hand, palm up, below his chest—"are little men, *servants*. The princess,"—he raised the opposite hand above his head—"is *royalty*."

"I know, I know."

"Actually, you are a fool now, so I guess that is befitting your new position."

"Don't remind me."

"Remind you, I must. For if I don't, who will?"

"There is nothing to worry about, she will soon be married off to some noble or other, and I will still be here, beating you like any other day."

Dakon grabbed Pazel in a playful chokehold, when, from the corner of his eye he saw the black dog sitting at the edge of the castle gardens. He released Pazel, and turned toward it, but he only caught a glimpse of its tail as it disappeared into the bushes.

"One day, Dakon," Pazel said, breaking Dakon's concentration, and brushing bits of dirt off his tunic, "one day, I will learn to fight and then you will be the one watching for royal guards as I whisper sweet nothings into the ears of ladies."

"Uh huh."

They no sooner opened the door of the servant's keep, then a little girl ran headfirst into Dakon. Her face was flushed and her eyes wide as she looked up at him.

"Are you alright?" he coughed, grabbing his throbbing stomach.

"Dakon—" the child said, breathing heavily, "Cerene needs you, now! She is hurt!"

EVE

ELEVEN

Eve watched as the guard knocked on the large, steel door before her, not paying any mind to the other intimidating ones flanking close behind her. Times of celebration and large crowds tended to make the king nervous, ensuring that most of the royal court was escorted during such occasions. Eve had grown accustomed to them long ago, as if they were temporary extensions of her. A shadow, or non-contiguous limb. Their large, golden armor gleamed in the sunlight that filtered through the open windows of the hall. The weather outside was fair and bright, as most days were at the castle—the primary residence of the Givensmir royals and their royal court, and the only home Eve had ever known.

A light breeze cooled her face in the warm hall, and she welcomed it as she smoothed the near invisible wrinkles of her silk gown. Her burgundy dress was multi-layered and fitted over a tight corset that was like a second skin she longed to shed. She knew better than to change, though, especially today, when the whole royal court was expected to be in their best attire. Her handmaids had fastened her braids tighter than usual, fixing them with small pearls. Her favorite necklace, a sun adorned with a diamond in the center, given to her by her father rested against her chest. He claimed she was the sun and vitality of his life. While Clarisa was his moon and guiding light and used to wear a moon pendant on a thin, silver chain.

Blood of the Blackthorn.

She quickly shook her head to dispel thoughts of her dreams, needing focus above emotion today.

In a few hours the castle would host a special feast welcoming the nobles of Mytar—Lord Joseph, Lady Marie and their children, Lord Joseph II, and Lady Felicity after a long journey from their kingdom. To Eve's knowledge, they were visiting for the first time in years to make a show of their allegiance to Givensmir. It was a day she had dreaded for months, however, for other reasons. Eve tried to think of something else, anything else, while she waited to be let inside the chamber.

"Come in!" an exasperated, but sweet voice finally called from beyond the door, and the guard to her left opened it.

Eve strolled in casually, taking in, for what was perhaps the millionth time, the room of Princess Adriana. The guard closed the door behind her.

It was a large chamber, with a four-poster bed, a large vanity, numerous wardrobes, and a seating area, among other lavish furnishings. The door to her balcony was slightly ajar, overlooking the Dallise Sea. The waves gently rocked in the distance, and the brilliance of the water was enhanced by the cloudless sky. Eve would have appreciated the view more, if it was not for the twenty-one-year-old princess before her tossing and throwing various articles of clothing from a trunk and sighing heavily every few seconds.

"You seem out of sorts this morning, Princess," Eve said, eyeing her young friend. "Anything I can help you with?"

Princess Adriana began rummaging within her desk drawer, tossing out quills and paper. "I can't find it, Eve! My note, oh, I am such a fool." She stood, pushing her hands through her long, wavy hair. Her face was flushed from her stress, but otherwise, was as youthful and pretty as ever. Adriana's hazel eyes searched Eve's brown ones, as if the answer to her problem lied there.

"You are not a fool, although, you are a lousy searcher. Your handmaids will certainly be shocked upon seeing the state of your chambers." Eve offered a slight smile as she descended the steps into Adriana's room, now riddled with articles of clothing, papers, and bedsheets. Her stone floor was barely visible underneath the mess.

"I was supposed to burn the note," Adriana whispered, glancing at the door, "but I left it when I went riding this morning, and when I returned it was gone. Disappeared into thin air." She threw her hands up dramatically.

"What was in the note?"

Adriana cast her eyes downward. "I would rather not say."

"Who was it from?"

Adriana glanced at Eve, fiddling with her hands. "From Dakon, the stable servant, well, not from Dakon, really."

"Then who?"

"I am not sure, a secret admirer who uses Dakon to pass me notes."

Eve let out a laugh. "And you are sure it is not Dakon himself?"

"Dakon does not know how to write, Eve, of course it is not him."

Eve nodded, sighing. "Well, did anyone come into your room?"

"I'm not sure." Adriana began to pace back and forth, mumbling to herself all the places she had looked.

Eve turned her attention to the fireplace close by, it had a dying flame with nothing but a bit of ash underneath, not very promising.

"Perhaps you burned it without realizing."

Adriana blew a raspberry into the air, rolling her eyes to the ceiling. "I hope so, I have never been this careless before."

Eve placed her hands gently on Adriana's shoulders. "I will help you for a few minutes, but you know we have to leave soon, or we will be late."

"I hate these welcoming parties, they're so dull!" Adriana turned on her heel and began searching fervently through the same trunk.

Eve picked up a few articles of clothing, trying the pockets of some but turning up empty. "I know—it's the last place I want to be too."

Her words were barely audible, but Adriana turned from the trunk, registering Eve's tone.

"Of course, I am sorry," she replied gently, approaching Eve. "I nearly forgot."

Adriana gently stroked Eve's arm, a friendly, comforting gesture, but Eve's heart sank regardless.

"It is fine, truly."

"We can talk about it, if you want."

"No, we have no time for that," Eve murmured, turning away, trying to think of anything to change the subject. "Hmm, if I were a scandalous love letter where would I be?"

Adriana laughed nervously as she returned to searching, this time under her bed where somehow even more clothes lay. Eve focused atop the bed, pulling the rest of the sheets and pillowcases apart.

Dammit, Adriana, you can't be making silly mistakes like this.

What if someone found you out?

She no sooner finished her last thought, her hand in the process of feeling the inside of another pillowcase, when there was another knock at the door.

"Come in," Adriana said rather exasperated from under the bed.

A handmaid, Cerene, walked in and her eyes widened at the scene before her. "Oh, my gods, Princess. What on earth happened here, I thought you had left already!"

The princess crawled from under the bed, and smoothed out her blue gown, "I–I was looking for . . . my broach."

Cerene looked to Eve as if for confirmation, mouth agape. The second Cerene's eyes locked with hers, Eve's senses became alert, and intensely focused. Her mind fluttered through images of Cerene eyeing a note beneath Adriana's pillowcase, the very one in Eve's hands.

"Uh, yes"—Eve tossed the pillowcase to the bed, straightening—"do you know where it is? The *broach*?"

The handmaid looked between the princess and Eve, and something in her eyes—a preoccupied, concerned look—told Eve she knew exactly what they were looking for.

"No, my lady," Cerene began as she righted herself, putting her hands in her apron pockets. For a woman of old age, she appeared to be young and confident of her position.

Eve felt her skin prick, the hair on her arms stood up, and she knew, somehow, she knew that the note was with Cerene. Resting in her left pocket.

"Why don't you help us?" Eve pressed.

Adriana looked at Eve with confusion, but Eve continued making eye contact with the handmaid.

"I would, my lady"—Cerene bowed, slowly removing her hands from her pockets—"but I must hurry back to the servants' quarters, there is much preparation for today, you see. I will be back to clean your chambers, and it will be bright and new when you return, Princess." She bowed to Adriana as she finished her sentence.

Eve could picture the note, folded in fourths on parchment, the ink smeared by a fastidious writer. Her instincts had her concentrating on the note, and she pictured it in fire, burning to ash, while she held the gaze of the handmaid who maintained her steadfast composure despite the surreptitious accusations lurking beneath their gazes.

Adriana approached the handmaid, studying her closely. "Can you turn out your pockets, please? Maybe it is with you from when you were helping me this morning, a simple mistake seeing as how everything is so stressful today." She smiled sweetly, her eyes endearing, but Eve knew this look was no more than a facade of the venom that lurked beneath.

"Your Highness, I—"

"Now, please," Adriana urged. "I would really like my broach; we are running late you see." She gestured to Eve who continued concentrating on the yellowish-white folded note and the dark black ink that was smeared by someone who was surely left-handed.

Burn, fire, ash.

Cerene bowed once more, and leisurely began to turn out her pockets. Her right one first had nothing but a cleaning utensil and a rag. She began to protest lightly, but Adriana would hear none of it, tilting her chin to the other pocket. Cerene slowly lowered her hand into it, before her eyes

80

widened and her mouth opened in a silent scream. Eve watches as Cerene paused for a fraction of a second as panic rose up her spine, and she quickly pulled her pocket out.

It was empty.

Of a note, at least.

Cerene lifted her hand and a handful of fresh ash fell through her fingertips and onto the floor.

"Ah!" she shrieked, waving her burnt hand around and turning out the rest of the remains of her pocket. Her hand was quickly turning red, and the skin was peeling from the injury.

A sliver of parchment fell out. Eve looked at it, surprised, then to Cerene who looked confused and horrified back to her.

"It is you," Cerene whispered, her hand now blistering a reddish-green color.

Adriana turned to Eve, raising her brow.

Eve stood silent, stunned, watching as Cerene retreated slowly away from her. Facing her so as not to leave her back exposed, as if Eve may hurt her should her eyes dare look away.

"My apologies, I–I will send the other handmaids to clean your room, Your Highness. I must go to the healer."

Adriana only nodded and their eyes followed the handmaid as she rushed out, sweating profusely, and startling the guards on her way out.

After a moment, Adriana walked toward the pile of ash slowly, carefully, before picking up the bit of paper on the ground. She brushed off the now cool bits of ash and inspected it in her fingers. "It seems I have found what I was looking for."

"Let it be a lesson, Adriana," Eve replied, rubbing her tired eyes. The nightmares still had not ceased to keep her from a pleasant sleep. Not since . . .

"Do you think she—" the princess began.

"No," Eve replied firmly, "I'm certain she tried burning it and hid it quickly. There's no magic involved here."

DAKON

TWELVE

Dakon hurried to the kitchens where he beheld a healer's apprentice bandaging Cerene's hand in the far corner. She looked uncharacteristically disheveled and shaken, her lips trembling as he watched from the doorway. The kitchens were alive with cooks, bakers, and other servants preparing the feast for the upcoming welcoming ceremony, and he had to dodge the fastidious movements of the workers within as he rushed toward her.

"Cerene? What happened?"

He inspected the rest of her, she seemed otherwise unharmed. He watched the last of her hand's wound—blackened and blistered—before it was completely covered by the bandage.

"That should hold, Cerene," the apprentice said, placing Cerene's hand gently on her lap. "If it worsens, it would be best to see the healer himself. And mind the kindling, I wouldn't want to see your other hand meet the same fate."

Cerene gave her a gentle smile. "Thank you. It was an old woman's mistake."

She returned Cerene's smile, gathering her herbs and belongings before leaving.

"What happened?" Dakon repeated, searching her eyes for some answer to the urgency with which he was summoned.

He could hear the shouts of cooks barking orders at one another, and he couldn't be sure Cerene even heard him through the noise. She beckoned him close, and he leaned in.

"Let us go for a walk. I need to speak with you," Cerene nearly shouted in his ear, trying to make sure he heard her. He nodded, and held out his arm for her to grip, leading her out of the kitchens and into the kingdom's first autumn day.

They walked a considerable distance toward the stables in silence, servants moved to and fro around them like the wind through the trees completing one task or another. Dakon peeked down at the feeble woman he considered to be like a mother to him, and then at the bandage. A nervous energy began to unfurl within him.

She led him within the stables that seemed to be untouched by the servants for the time being. Horses brayed and others snored almost as if they knew their duty would come upon them soon. No doubt sensing the tension of their masters as of late.

"Make sure we are truly alone, and close the stable doors," she ordered, and he abided, though confused. He lit a small torch hanging from the stable wall and left it there. Lighting just enough for them to see each other and a few feet around them. He pulled out a stool and led her gently to sit. He knelt, trying to meet her at eye level.

"What happened, Cerene? Why are you acting so secretive?"

She took a deep breath and released it, keeping her eyes on his, "I have not been . . . forthcoming with you, Dakon."

"Did you really hurt yourself in the fireplace?" he asked, meeting her steely gaze.

"No," she replied simply, then paused contemplating her next words. "I had found a note from you in the princess's chambers. It was left about carelessly, and I grabbed it before the other handmaids could see it. I was caught by the princess and her friend."

Dakon felt a sweeping sense of shame and guilt come over him, "Cerene, I'm sorry. I–I did not mean for this to happen to you."

Cerene seemed to ignore him, shaking her head. "I had hoped that this day would never come."

"What day? What are you talking about?"

"The stories—the ones I tell the servants, to you—they are not quite true."

"Cerene"—he let out a nervous laugh—"of course they aren't true. They are fables, children's tales. Goblins do not steal babies from their cribs and neither do sea serpents tread the Dallise Sea."

She grabbed his hands, gripping tight and flinching ever slightly at the pain it caused her wound. "I am serious, Dakon. Listen to what I am to tell you. I may not have enough time to speak it."

He paused, furrowing his brows, unsure of how to make sense of her reaction. "I am listening," he whispered.

"There is a witch among us, a powerful one. She does not yet know the magic she wields, is inexperienced with it."

"Who?"

"Lady Eve."

"The enchantress's daughter? No, Cerene, you must be mistaken. She has no magic. The king attested to this himself years ago."

"She does and she has been under a binding spell that has now ended."

"How do you know this?"

"Because I helped cast it. I was the enchantress's familiar."

Dakon stood, ripping his hands from Cerene's grip. This was impossible, this woman before him made earth teas, nursed him from sickness, and told tales of heroes and their adversaries. She must be telling him another story, perhaps she hit her head, or her old age was making her senile. He felt gutted and sick.

"No more stories, Cerene. Tell me the truth."

But her face was still as stone, "this is no story, Dakon."

He stood before her, frustrated. "What you are speaking of can condemn you to the stake. To be associated with witches is to embrace death with open arms. Do you think I want that for you? Did you not see what happened to the last witch that was caught? They will do that to you too!"

"I will soon die, and I do not fear death. And you, Dakon, will fulfill your duty."

He faced Cerene, grappling with shock and confusion. This must be a terrible nightmare, a terrible dream that felt real and horrid. Dread crawled from his chest, consuming every inch of his body. He could not find the words to speak and Cerene continued.

"The original witches, the three that roamed the earth centuries ago, were created by a fallen goddess, Isila. Together, they created spirits, beasts, and creatures that have prevailed throughout time, manifesting an energy within nature itself, tethering their powers with the earth, sea, and sky. Familiars were made to guard and protect their witch—to die for them, if need be—and to aid their witchcraft. The enchantress chose me, protected me, as I disguised myself as a servant within the castle walls. When her youngest daughter was born, I aided in her labor and helped her bind the child in mortality for as long as we could. The time has come"— she lifted her bandaged hand—"and it seems she likes to play with fire."

"Cerene"—Dakon knelt once more—"even if what you are saying is true, I do not possess magic. I am as mortal as they come."

"That is not what your pet seems to think."

He froze. *The dog creature?*

"Gytrashes only appear for those who are lost, and lost you will be for a while," Cerene said calmly. "You may find this castle holds more halls than meets the eye . . ."

Dakon shook his head and pinched the bridge of his nose. "Cerene, you are not making any sense."

"The enchantress found you left outside the castle gates. Witch hunts were far more prevalent throughout the kingdom at that time, and she knew from the moment she saw you that you were destined as her daughter's familiar." She gave him a solemn look, "I do not know of the

85

magic your mother possessed, but your father was a shapeshifter, taking the form of various creatures throughout Serit." She held up a hand gently, silencing Dakon as he was about to ask the obvious questions.

"I do not know where he is, child, and he is not the gytrash that has become tethered to you as of late."

Dakon considered this, silencing the pang of hope he had felt blossoming. He focused on the latter of her remark. "Why is that?"

"I suspect it has something to do with the binding spell ending. Your witch is slowly gaining her powers that have been dormant for years, the same will happen to you—already has begun."

"How will I know?"

"Trust me, you will." She grasped his hands once more. "Eve is the witch that will recover the grimoire hidden for centuries and bring back the goddess. She will need you when the time comes."

"But what about you?"

She paused, and then sighed heavily as if the weight of her words held new meaning. "I am nearing the end of my journey." "Ridiculous, if you have the magic to aid a witch, can't you prolong your life with it?"

"We familiars can die a mortal death and burn as they do." She caressed his cheek, as she did when he was a boy. "But as your first lesson, I want you to remember that magic is not immortal."

EVÆ
THIRTEEN

E ve and Adriana walked arm in arm toward the expansive dining table in the great hall. It was decorated extravagantly for the evening's event, banners bearing the royal sigil—a large merlion, aggressively postured with its claws out as if in mid-fight—were strewn from the ceiling, the stone pillars were decorated with black and gold streamers, and long tables decorated with candles, cutlery, and dining-ware were positioned in the center. Most everyone required to be in attendance was seated, talking animatedly amongst themselves and barely registering their arrival.

Eve tried to keep her chin up as she walked toward the large table, positioned at the far end of all the others, trying to maintain some sense of confidence.

This is really happening, isn't it? She thought to herself as disappointment and heartbreak filled her.

Eve tightened her grip slightly on Adriana, as they were now only thirty feet from the royal table, then twenty-five, then twenty.

Adriana whispered to Eve under her breath as they closed in to the royals seated at the front. "Just smile, Eve. Do what you do best—at least for now."

Joined in the center of the table were King Eryck of Givensmir and Lord Joseph of Mytar in a discussion that was much muted by the sounds of the hall around them. To the left of King Eryck was Queen Alondra and their sons. Eve drew a quick breath into her chest as she spotted Prince Theo seated next to Lady Felicity of Mytar. She was now in a delightful looking discussion with Princess Gabrielle of the Mistral Islands and Prince Theo.

Eve fluttered her lashes, trying to avoid looking in that direction, but it only made her heart pound more to wonder, *what does he think of her?*

Adriana tugged her arm lightly, chastising under her breath, "I will feign an illness once the main celebrations are complete, then you can accompany me back to my chambers. You must hold it together until then, promise?"

Eve nodded, keeping her eyes forward, trying and failing to not stare at Prince Theo and Lady Felicity, who were now engaged in conversation. Felicity laughed sweetly, her hand covering her mouth as the beautiful sound was heard. Eve swallowed, and blinked threatening tears away, forcing a smile on her face. Deceiving her real emotions was something she had become an expert at over the years as a means of protecting herself in this cutthroat and subtly poisonous environment. But today was different, today seemed harder, somehow, to play pretend, but she would. She would make it through, clap when needed, speak when required, and smile always.

She released Adriana's arm as they approached the royal table, and the girls both bowed deeply to the king. He nodded absentmindedly, paying more attention to a conversation he was having with Lord Joseph. The queen inspected Adriana and Eve, her eyes narrowing on Adriana.

"You are late, my daughter," she said, disapprovingly.

Adriana smiled as she walked toward her mother, placing her hands on either side of her mother's place setting. "Oh, Mother. It is only a few minutes, and it seems that our presence was not missed." She gestured to the lively nature of those within the great hall, everyone present seemed to be enjoying the company of the Mytar nobles—laughing, smiling, talking.

"You are a princess and grown up enough to know better. Let it not happen again."

Adriana nodded, but sighed heavily, walking to her seat at the far end of the table next to a disgruntled looking Prince Marc.

Queen Alondra scanned Eve with a suspicious look. "You look well, Lady Eve. Burgundy suits you. I thank you for escorting my errant daughter."

"A pleasure as always, Your Majesty. You look wonderful."

The queen smiled faintly, and lifted her chin, showing off the sapphire diamonds adorned to a thick chain around her neck. "Enough of that. Go join the court and enjoy your evening."

Eve bowed and glanced sideways at Adriana, who gave her a reassuring nod. She stood and nodded back, taking a deep breath before she walked to her table. It was to the left of the great hall, meaning she would have to walk by Prince Theo, she realized. She held her head high, eyes focused on her seat at the table, hoping that she could get there before he saw her pass. If she could just make it to her seat, then the king would deliver his speech and the feast would begin. Perhaps she could feign an illness before Adriana and leave before the rest of the evening's celebrations would start.

"Lady Eve!" she heard his voice and felt her stomach drop.

No.

Eve closed her eyes momentarily before opening them and turning to face the royal table once more. "Yes, Your Highness?"

Prince Theo stood from where he sat, waving her over to his side of the table. Eve glanced at the king, noticing he was still in heavy discussion about something or other with his counterpart. She turned back and met Lady Felicity's gaze. She sat like a goddess in her chair; her long, red hair fell below her breasts, the emerald-green gown fit her like a glove, and her catlike blue eyes assessed her. Eve felt greatly unmatched in beauty and form compared to her and wished nothing more than to just sit in her chair hidden amongst the crowd of other court members.

"Come, meet my betrothed." He smiled genuinely, kindly.

Oh, I wish you'd spare me.

89

Even then, she couldn't help but smile back, his handsome face like nothing she had ever beheld in her twenty-four years of life. Eve cursed the gods for giving the king the bright idea to marry him off so soon to secure an alliance. All this despite the fact that she had kept her love for him a secret for years, and despite the fact that she had always swore she would tell him the truth before something like this happened. But she had never found the courage, had always made up some excuse in her mind and now the thing she feared the most was happening right before her eyes. Even with all their years of friendship, she could not tell if he was pretending to be happy or if he truly was as the beautiful princess placed her hand on his as Eve approached.

Theo's curls bounced slightly as he cocked his head with his boyish, dimpled grin, his eyes alight with happiness, and Eve wished that they held something stronger as they looked into hers.

Stop it.

Eve breathed deeply, and her heart thundered in her chest as she ascended the steps slowly, thinking of some excuse she could use to escape the situation she was being forced into. Each step felt like she was trudging through thick mud, but even so, she was soon bowing to the soon-to-be spouses.

"I am honored to meet you, Lady Felicity," Eve smiled politely, avoiding her gaze.

Lady Felicity looked her up and down before smiling tightly back. "As am I, Lady Eve. Prince Theo speaks of nothing else but you and hunting."

She lifted a brow and reached out her hand. Eve took it as she bowed her head, lost for words.

The second their hands touched, Eve felt a spark and lifted her head quickly. She was no longer in the great hall of the castle, no longer touching the princess's hand, but outside among the mountains of some unknown land in the blistering cold.

A child, a little girl, lay on the ground, bleeding from beneath her head as a boy screamed and cried to the gods over her. The wind whipped wildly at Eve's hair, the frigid cold chapping her lips and cracking her skin. She reached out to the girl, whose eyes sprung open, landing on Eve's. The girl opened her mouth to scream . . .

"Lady Eve? Lady Eve! You can let go now." An exasperated voice snapped Eve's focus back on Felicity whose hand she still held in a firm grip. Eve dropped it immediately, muttering her apologies as she recognized she was back in the great hall, the candlelight showing throughout the room, people feasting and rejoicing around her. She was no longer cold, but warm to the touch, and she realized that she had been silent too long.

"Are you well, Lady Eve?" Felicity narrowed her eyes warily. "I did not expect such a great friend to my betrothed to be so mute."

Eve smiled tightly. "I–I think I am just a bit tired, nothing a little celebration won't fix."

Prince Theo, oblivious to the tension that was arising so soon between the two women, spoke. "Lady Felicity is a gifted singer, such a beautiful voice." He placed his hand on her shoulder, as their gazes met. "Perhaps she will do us the honor of singing later this evening. You must watch, Eve."

Felicity feigned timidity. "Oh, Your Highness, you greatly exaggerate my abilities."

"Of course not, it is quite enchanting to hear you."

Eve felt out of place and was about to offer her congratulations and turn on her heel when the prince continued, "And Lady Eve here is a remarkable dancer, very graceful."

"I see," Lady Felicity breathed, smiling tightly back.

They were interrupted by a pounding sound on the table, signaling the start of the king's speech. Eve took it as her cue to leave and she bowed quickly before rushing down to her seat with the rest of the court. No one paid her any mind as she settled into her chair and took a long sip of water from one of her glasses, her mouth dry from the awkward encounter. She reached her fingers to touch her lips and realized they were chapped, nearly bleeding. Her thoughts trailed back to the harsh wind that fought her in the mountains.

The girl.

Eve quickly used her handkerchief to dab at the blood, making sure no one saw. She tried to settle her breathing, cursing internally for making a fool of herself.

She took another long sip, this time of wine, before Eve looked about. Most everyone around the table were people she had known all her life—lords, ladies, knights, and other nobles. The seat next to her, however, was empty. Before she could inquire as to its occupant's whereabouts, a familiar voice whispered from behind her.

"So, Cousin, what do you think of our new princess?"

Eve rolled her eyes, as her cousin Pedro, a knight of Givensmir, sat beside her, raising his brows as he lifted his glass to his lips.

"I think you had better mind your business. Cousin or not, I can still beat you in front of all these lovely people," she whispered back, smirking.

Pedro chuckled quietly. "One—that day you caught me off-guard. Two—we were *eleven*. A lot has changed since then."

"You're right, I'm a lot stronger now than I was as a little girl." She gave him a mock glare. "Don't make me prove it."

Pedro raised his hands, laughing a bit harder than intended. "It's always a pleasure to see you, Eve."

"Shhh!" one of the lords, a stout, bald man with a red face and thick mustache glared at them.

"Our apologies, Lord Cameron, but it doesn't look like the king has started speaking yet. Can you be a doll and tell me when he does?" Pedro raised his glass with a smirk. The look in his eyes was quite deadly, and Eve, for all her joking, was glad she was not on the other end of that stare.

Lord Cameron huffed, but turned quietly to face the king, as the rest of the crowd was now doing. Eve and Pedro snickered silently like errant children, as they always did each time they sat next to one another, especially at important events. Eve wished she saw more of her cousin, but with their youth now past them, and the responsibilities of their positions now upon them, it was harder to make time to see one another.

Pedro was the fourth of her uncle's sons and the only one Eve had befriended. With five sons, Lord Agustin granted Pedro's request to become a knight—forfeiting all lands, assets, and inheritance in order to serve the Givensmir realm, and bring honor to Rubianes Keep. Eve had only visited the land once, when the king took the court to celebrate Lord

Agustin's name day when she was a child. It was the first time she stepped foot onto the land her father called home, and it was truly an enchanting experience. The land was filled with soft rolling hills, fertile ground, and some of the best wine that ever passed her lips.

Her uncle, however, was much unlike her father, very much a drunkard, clueless, and aloof to his children, and her by extension even though he claimed the contrary. It was odd that a man of such a peculiar disposition would be a lord of one of the most beautiful lands of Givensmir, as if even that was not enough to entice at least a bit of appreciation from him. She looked at him, sitting on the other side of Pedro, deep in his fourth wine cup of the early evening and rolled her eyes. Yes, very much unlike her father and better than her mother.

The thought of her parents brought about the familiar rage-induced feeling that always morphed into anxious confusion and a downward spiral of conspiracy theories as to what might have happened to Clarisa. The court was unusually tight-lipped when it came to matters of her family around her and their unusual demise or even the reasons that propelled a witch hunt that saw hundreds of witches executed in the immediate aftermath. And most history books were focused on the evil intent of magic and the extinguishing of all witchcraft in the kingdom, but gave little else that would help her understand.

Eve looked at her cousin, taking in the sight of him after a year of practically no contact. Pedro was the closest thing she considered family, the only person who ever paid her a visit when he could. He looked back and smiled, taking a deep breath and another swig of his wine before directing his attention to the king. Eve did the same.

There was the clinking of glass once more, and the king stood before the great hall. Eve took him in from a distance, assessing the most powerful man of the kingdom. In the past couple of years, he had become more rotund in size, his hair now riddled with gray, and the bags under his eyes had become more pronounced. It was no secret in the court that the king was secretly battling an illness of some sort, with many suggesting it was due to the stress of numerous campaigns and war efforts. It was a sensitive topic of conversation among the nobles, and one that Eve made sure to avoid at all costs. It would not be wise for someone like her to be an active participant in even nonsensical discussions regarding the death of their monarch.

Fifteen years ago, the king had granted her mercy when she was brought back to the castle, trembling and crying after her mother and sister. She could still remember the look on his face, the distant stare that told her he was deep in thought about something else. It was not until she inquired after her mother, that the king had asked if she possessed any magic—it was not a request, but a plea that much she remembered. It was the first and only time Eve had ever seen the king so out of sorts, as if Eve held the answer to something she did not understand yet, and that the king badly wanted.

She informed him that she did not, and the matter was settled. Perhaps, that was the answer he was looking for, perhaps it was something that told him she was not a threat, because he treated her far more sympathetically as opposed to other witches who met a grisly end at his command. Even so, she knew that the court closely watched her, monitored her for any signs that she may be more than just a mere mortal. She was kept busy enough to not think about it much, and in time the excruciating pain of her losses became a dull ache in her chest when they came to her mind.

"My constituents," the king began, his voice much more powerful than the body it came from, "tonight there is much to celebrate for our kingdom. Today we welcome our friends, the Lord Joseph of Mytar, his wife, and children. We thank the gods that they have arrived safely and are present to enjoy this wonderful feast with us. Tomorrow is the start of the Harvest Festival, a tradition in our great kingdom to celebrate our bountiful harvest, the sustenance supplied to us from the gods through our hard work. May the gods continue to bless our lands with plentiful food and even better drink as the year progresses!"

"Here, here!" The crowd chanted to the king, glasses raised before clinking them with their neighbors and taking a swig. Eve and Pedro clinked their glasses together, nearly spilling its contents and laughing like fools. They calmed down as the room silenced, waiting for the king to continue.

"It has been a great year, the end of our conflict with Larrea, and an even greater year for Givensmir for *another* reason." The king turned to face Theo, a sly smile on his face. Eve noticed Theo shrink ever so slightly in his chair.

Something was off.

"As most of you know, my son will wed the beautiful Lady Felicity of Mytar, the enchanting woman seated next to him. This alliance will secure the houses of our kingdom in a union based on strength, power, and prosperity to continue our friendship for many generations to come. Such an alliance is imperative to a thriving kingdom, and one that Lord Joseph and I feel is better done sooner rather than later."

The crowd gasped excitedly, and a few began to clap loudly for the announcement that was sure to come. Eve took a sharp, unsettling breath.

Sooner rather than later?

The king raised his hands to settle the crowd, a wide grin on his face. "Thus, we officially announce that Prince Theo and Lady Felicity will be married by the end of the next moon."

The crowd stood and clapped, whooping and whistling with excitement. The roaring cheers seemed to vibrate around the room and the men shook hands happily. Eve knew she was clapping, knew that she had something of a smile on her mouth, but when she turned to Adriana and saw the pitying glance in her direction, it became too much to bear.

Eve felt her heart stop and the entire room stopped with her.

Everyone was frozen in place, unable to move or stare or speak. She thought it was just her imagination, or a trick of the eye, but when she put her hand on Pedro's shoulder, intending to have him escort her back to her chambers, she realized that he, too, was frozen in place. The look on his face was of genuine happiness, mid-clap, unmoving.

How did this happen?

Did I do this?

How did I do this?

The questions came rapid fire to her mind as Eve could feel the prickling sensation of fear creep up on her. She kept closing and opening her eyes, willing everything to turn back to normal, but it was as if she was beholding a painting of incredibly realistic quality. The king was still standing, a wicked look on his face as he beheld the excitement of the crowd. People were frozen with looks of awe and elation, and a few were suspended midair from jumping with excitement. Theo had a nervous look, his brows furrowed, that mismatched the euphoric expression on Lady Felicity's face.

The grimoire flashed in her mind, over and over and over again. Opening, her blood on its pages, the words of that voice echoing through the walls of her mind.

"How did you do that?" a voice echoed to her from within the room.

Eve turned quickly, her chair falling behind her. "Who is speaking?!" she demanded.

She turned right and saw the fool, eyes wide as he peeked out from behind the tablecloth of the royal table. He had copper hair and green eyes, and seemed nervous as he moved out where she could see.

"My name is Dakon, my lady," he said, his voice shaking. "I am your familiar."

"My what?" She couldn't make sense of how he was the only one among the crowd unfrozen.

"I am bound to you, to help you. The handmaid told me so."

Eve couldn't speak, her heart thundering in fear. She had heard the tales long ago of witches and their familiars, but they were supposed to be creatures and beasts. The man before her was nothing like that.

"I don't understand," she said, and her voice cracked as she began to realize that someone may soon come back and see what she had done. She began breathing short, quick, frightful breaths.

"Be calm, just breathe. It will go back, I promise," Dakon said.

This stranger, his voice was comforting, soothing. And she closed her eyes, trying to will everything back to normal. Trying to find something within her that would make time move again.

The sounds of roaring laughter and cheering sent her into a panic, and she accidentally tripped backward over her chair. Everything was sent back into motion—the noise of the crowd, the movement of the people. It was as if nothing had happened, as if the whole experience was in her head. Even so, Eve's eyes darted around the room, searching for anyone who may have had a clue or suspected a thing. Even the fool, Dakon, appeared to be acting normal as he sat on the steps in front of the royal table. Not a single soul in the crowd looked suspicious.

She dared to look toward the king, who was staring at her on the ground over a fallen chair. Eve prayed to the gods that he was more concerned for her well-being than suspicious about the stop in time she caused.

Her cousin was at her side in a second, picking her up from the floor before too many people noticed.

"I know you aren't happy about this, but you don't have to hurt yourself," Pedro whispered gently, as he brought her chair back upright. He looked into Eve's eyes, with a hint of concern. "Are you going to be okay?"

Eve collected herself and smoothed out her dress once more, trying to find a modicum of confidence. "Yes, I think so. Thank you."

"You just have to pretend a little while longer."

"I'll try."

Pedro gave her a sidelong glance but nodded.

She knew she had to do more than just try, but even as she put on her brightest smile and kindest eyes, she could feel the king burning holes into her skull.

ADRIANA
FOURTEEN

Adriana walked the dark corridor to her chambers, escorted by Timothy, a knight with light blond hair and gray eyes, strong and robust as any young maiden would wish for. He had been her personal guard for nearly six months, and since his appointment, she had noticed his eyes linger on her longer than most. Even the start of the notes being passed to her, complimenting her, speaking of her beauty and kind soul.

This is someone more appropriate for me, she thought. And she tried to quell thoughts of Dakon from her mind and heart. If there was someone else that could give her what Dakon did, and of better station, then perhaps she could find true bliss and not bring shame upon her family.

The wine and the overall merriment of the welcoming party, set her in a fixed determination as she contemplated this next to her guard.

"Ser Timothy"—she slowed her walk as they were now alone in the corridor—"is there anything you wish to tell me?"

Timothy looked confused, staring down at the princess as he walked beside her. "No, Your Highness."

"We are quite alone, I assure you." She smiled "You can speak freely to me."

He continued walking and his brow furrowed as if he was not sure how to respond.

This is maddening, she thought, *surely this cannot go on forever.*

Adriana tried a different strategy. "What is it you wish to know about me?"

"Only what you wish to share, Your Highness."

"Hmm," she sighed. "This is not a trick, I promise. I only wish to know your intentions."

"My intentions?" He stopped and turned to her. The halls were eerily silent, and Timothy lowered his voice. "What is it you want, Princess?" His face a mixture of curiosity and concern.

"I only wish to know how long you have felt for me as you do."

Timothy looked bewildered and stepped back slightly.

"Your Highness, I—how did you—"

"It was plain to see, Timothy," she said as she moved closer to him. "I only wish you would have told me sooner."

Timothy looked both ways down the hall, and assured by its vacancy, seemed to relax.

"Princess, I fear that I have always had affection for you, as do most in this castle."

Adriana looked up at him and moved closer. "But no one looks to me the way you do."

It felt wrong to lie to him, but she needed to see, needed to at least try and forget Dakon.

Before Timothy could respond, she placed her lips on his, savoring her first kiss. He brought his hands into her hair, gently, as if practiced hands had done this before, and kissed her fervently, desperately back.

She no sooner closed her eyes, trying and failing to enjoy the kiss, than a loud voice boomed in the hall. "Ser Timothy, I fear you have taken your duties far too seriously."

Timothy quickly pushed himself away from the princess, collecting himself. Adriana, in her confusion turned to the voice; it was her brother Marc.

"Marc, I—" she began.

He held up his hand. "I am not speaking to you."

She held her breath, fearful of the danger she now put Timothy in. "This was all my fault. I threw myself on him!"

"So, my sister is a liar *and* a whore." He moved closer to them.

She did not respond, shaking and wishing that she would have invited Ser Timothy into her chambers instead of foolishly lingering in the hall.

Marc stood a few inches shorter than Timothy as he leaned in close to the guard. "Get out. Say a word of this encounter, and I will see to it that you lose your tongue."

Timothy bowed and immediately left them, turning a corner. He was gone.

Marc turned his sights to Adriana as her heart pounded in her chest, words unable to escape her. The dire consequences of her situation very real to her now.

He looked at her, as if from a new light, and smirked. "Who knew the darling of the court could be so secretive with her affairs."

"This was the first time."

"Is it? It seemed to me as if you had a practiced form."

Adriana turned, humiliated. "What do you want?"

"I only want to know that my sister is not spoiled before we wed her to secure another alliance. We can't share spoils on the tables of our guests, can we?"

"Theo is marrying Lady Felicity, Father has conquered Larrea. There is no one left to secure an alliance with. War is over."

"War is never over."

She narrowed her eyes, assessing him. "What are you talking about?"

"Father wishes to secure the Blackthorn, subdue the witches, and claim their lands. It might be easier if we had a chaste princess to marry off. You know, to bolster our pocketbooks."

As his words settled, a chill went down her spine. Thoughts of Dakon filled her. "No."

"Yes."

"W-who do they have in mind?"

Marc's lips raised into an unsettling smile. "That is for me to know, Sweet Sister. I could have put in a good word, but it seems to me that you are in a far more precarious situation. Your virtue could stand to be questioned."

"What is it you want?" she asked again, anger flaring.

"I need information, something that only you would be able to get for me."

"Go ask Lord Wesley, I am not a common spy." She turned to walk away.

"If I do, I will stop by Father's chambers first. You know how much he likes to receive bad news in the dark."

Adriana stopped, biting her lip. Desperation shook her rage, crushing it with a rising panic. She could hear Marc's footsteps as he approached her. His cold fingers lifted her chin until their eyes were level with one another. She could nearly see her startled reflection within them, and her skin began to crawl.

"You will find out if Eve inherited any of her mother's magic."

CLARISA

FIFTEEN

The skies were black, and the waves of the sea grew into seismic portions, nearly reaching the highest peaks of the castle towers along the cliffs. The winds blew with a rage and fury unlike anything Clarisa had ever witnessed. Rods of lightning pierced through the clouds and struck the water in a continuous deadly pattern, charging it with its force. She could feel the spray of the sea on her face turning to blood in her hands as she wiped it off. Many witches died trying to stop the incoming storm, using their full force until the magic drained them of their lives. Their bodies littered the shore, and she watched as the last of them began to fall, joining their coven in death. Something was calling out to her, a message carried in the wind, and she began to walk to the edge of the sea to hear it, down the steps of the castle toward the beach that was becoming quickly flooded; she could not stop as she blinked through the heavy rain clouding her vision.

A large fleet of ships were cresting over the tumultuous waves in the distance, larger and larger they grew as the storm carried them over even the fiercest of waves. And she could feel it within her bones, within her soul, these were no ordinary ships. They intended to kill them all, to seal their fates upon landing. As if the gods themselves wanted them to all die – Isila abandoning them in their time of need. To carry themselves to the land of witchcraft and magic and destroy them all as they did to all others they conquered.

Clarisa felt the edge of the water at her feet now, and did the only thing she could think of, the only thing that felt right in the moment. She cut the palm of her hand with a knife and watched as the drops fell. The blood and water met, and instantly the ships began to meet their deadly end, swallowed by the sea. The screams pierced the night from a distance, carrying over the ocean, desperate to make sure it was heard by all present.

Then, she heard a familiar voice calling out. A voice that brought her back to her childhood. It was so close it was nearly tangible. If only she could reach out and touch it.

"Eve! Eve!"

<hr/>

"Clarisa! Clarisa, you're okay. You're safe."

Clarisa sprang awake, thrashing and screaming as she got a hold of her surroundings. Sweat dripped from her temples and her mind was a blur as she realized she was in the arms of Ana.

Clarisa looked into her dark, concerned eyes, only inches away from her face, barely visible by a soft candlelight. Ana's face was etched with worry, and Clarisa realized that although they had been here before, in this same position, that the pain of watching her suffer was still enough to wound her.

"Ana?"

"Shh, shh. Yes, I'm here, I'm always here."

"I-I'm sorry." Clarisa began to cry, her voice cracking as she tried to steady herself.

She raised her hand to wipe her eyes, and drops of blood fell from her palm. Ana grabbed her hand quickly, reciting a healing enchantment. The wound began to heal itself as she spoke. "It's not your fault."

"But it is," Clarisa whimpered. "This is who I am."

Ana stiffened, holding her breath before she finally spoke. "You have a power that no one yet knows how to behold. It is *not* your fault."

"I can't control these dreams. I can't control what they do to me in real life." She raised her now healed hand in front of her. "I'm scared, Ana, they are getting more real, they come now more often than ever."

"I promised you I would find a solution and I will." Ana's eyes bore into hers as Clarisa settled her breathing. She could barely make out more than her features in the near-total darkness of night, obscuring the rest of her chambers. She listened as only the sounds of their breathing and the midnight rain, that made its way inside from a cracked window, filled the room.

"What if there is no way?"

"There is, there has to be," Ana whispered. "Have you considered going to Raven's Holdfast?"

Clarisa shook her head, "I do not know if scholars of our craft can teach me anything that can subdue my dreams."

Ana's jaw tightened slightly, and Clarisa sighed. "I will go there, if that makes you feel better."

"Thank you."

They sat, still and silent for a time, until Ana rose suddenly retrieving a black candle from a nearby drawer.

"What are you—"

"Clarisa, have you released yet?"

"No."

In truth, Clarisa was losing faith in their goddess and had chosen not to this dark moon. She had seen far too many bodies and not enough life recently to encourage her. Thoughts of Malin seeped into her mind, he was the most devout to their coven, and even he grew corrupt. Now he rotted in the ground, instead of burning above it.

"Maybe that is why your dreams plague you." Ana opened the window completely, more rain gently made its way inside, making a small pool on the stone floor.

"I doubt it." Clarisa sighed but gathered an empty bowl, using her magic to fill it with water. She sprinkled some salt from a small vial and set the bowl on the floor. Ana lit the black candle setting it between them just out of reach of the rain.

Ana's features became more pronounced in the added candlelight: the knit between her brows as she concentrated on her task, the way she bit the inside of her cheek, and the healed scars she bore from removing Clarisa's etched into her skin like tattoos. One can only heal by giving up a piece of themselves, and she did it for Clarisa every time, despite protest. She reached out to touch her palm, the fresh wound scarring over already, but Ana shook her head.

"Focus, or at least try to." Ana burned incense, allowing it to fill their space, and filter out bit by bit into the cold, wet air.

Clarisa had done this ritual many times before, but for some reason she felt unable to connect as she usually did. The incense clouded her mind, instead of freeing it, the *drip, drip, drip* of the rain against the stone sounded like a blacksmith's hammer against her skull.

"Sit," Ana said, sitting cross-legged in front of Clarisa. "Listen and sit."

Clarisa's movements felt slow and agitated, her mind filled with chaos as she had yet to fully process her nightmare, but she sat across from Ana as instructed.

"Isila, this dark moon we honor and cherish you. We call upon thy energy. Release Clarisa of this torment, bring to her your will."

Clarisa took a deep breath, repeating Ana's words aloud.

They sat in meditative silence for a few moments, Clarisa feeling the burden upon her heavier than ever.

"Scry, Clarisa."

Clarisa cleared her throat; Ana's eyes were still closed, focused on the ritual, much unlike herself.

"Please," Ana breathed.

Clarisa felt a tingling sensation within her, a prickling of fear coming forth, but looked into the bowl. At first, as always, she could see her reflection—her dark hair and eyes, her lips and nose reflected clearly back at her as if she were staring into a mirror. Sometimes, she felt as if she were looking at her mother instead. It unsettled her.

Clarisa hated to scry and hated seeing the visions that came with it. Often, they showed the death she would soon bring upon another, the fear in their eyes as she completed the will of her crowns. It would linger with her, haunt her very essence for days and weeks and no amount of cleansing would keep it at bay.

She thought about the men who warred to glory in Serit, bringing pride to their kingdoms and their houses. Showered in gold and silver, paraded for their valor and bravery. It was quite unfathomable to her.

To take life, was to give up a piece of yourself. For the very foundation of nature was balance, and death was not glorious, but final.

Clarisa stared into the bowl and could see the makings of a vision painting itself in the water.

"There is a storm coming," she said as the dream came back to her. "One that will rival anything our kingdom has seen before. Many witches will die, and dozens of ships will attempt to reach our shores from the mainland."

Ana opened her eyes. "Are you certain?"

"Yes. My blood was the only thing to stop them."

She tightened her jaw. "What does that mean?"

"I don't know."

Clarisa watched as Ana took a deep sigh, blowing out the candle. They both repeated their thanks to Isila, closing out the ritual.

Ana knelt, placing the incense in the water. "The crown wouldn't dare sacrifice you."

Clarisa nodded, closing the window. A half-witch was a rare occurrence, one that lived through infancy even more unheard of. She was either blessed or cursed, but knew the queen kept her alive in hopes of the former.

"I may not have a choice. Between me and the kingdom, we know what they will choose. Perhaps, this is why they wanted me all along."

"They saved you—"

"Saved? Is that what they call it?"

"You could have been killed in Givensmir, do not deny it. Your sister *might* be alive only because she did not inherit your mother's gifts."

It was true, and Clarisa considered this, biting her lip in frustration. As children, only Clarisa was able to use any of her magic, which was now tantamount to a death sentence in Givensmir. Eve was more than happy to simply live as a normal, mortal child—her only hope of survival. Her heart ached hoping that Eve was somewhere safe and not buried deep beneath the earth.

"Out of all those witches killed in Serit, why did she choose me? Why not save anyone else? There were hundreds far more experienced."

"Because you are the one that is prophesied." Ana spoke the words fervently, grasping Clarisa's hands tight in her own. "The one who will find the book and bring Isila back to us. She will end all wars, all suffering, everything."

Clarisa pulled her hands back, frustration building within her. "Magic can barely keep us from war, to think a book can is absurd."

Ana tensed. "I have told you before, *magic is not immortality*. The book is more than that."

"A book is a book. Everything is fallible."

"One of mortal heart and wicked nature shall reveal and become the Blood of the Blackthorn. Kingdoms will rise, kingdoms will fall, and the eternal curse shall break—"

"Stop, Ana!" Goosebumps rose on Clarisa's skin at the words, the reminder of why she was allowed to live. It was too much. "Is this why I am guarded like a caged animal, because they equally believe that I will either cause their demise or be the key to their power?"

Ana did not answer, walking toward the window as the rain pattered against the glass.

"I am not nearly the most powerful witch here."

"You are more powerful than you believe."

"No, I am not!" Clarisa tried to control her voice, but her emotions got the best of her. The room shook along with the flickering of the remaining candlelight. It was only a moment, a minor slip, but when she looked at Ana there was the slightest tinge of apprehension in her eyes.

Her chambers stilled once more, the candles resuming their tranquil burning.

"I-I'm sorry, I'm just overwhelmed and tired." Clarisa rubbed her temples, there was a pain throbbing there.

Ana did not reply but let out a long breath.

"Do you fear me, Ana?" Clarisa asked as she walked toward her.

Ana stiffened as she grew closer, but only slightly. Then, slowly, her lips curved upward. "No," she replied, placing her hand on Clarisa's cheek, "I don't."

"Good," Clarisa whispered, "I don't know what I would do if you did."

They stared into each other and drew close, their hands gently caressing the other.

"You can trust me," Ana breathed as she placed her lips on Clarisa's.

Her sweet scent invaded Clarisa in a welcoming torrent of lavender and rain as she kissed her gently back. She closed her eyes and imagined that the two of them were far from this place, out of the shades of the Blackthorn, and under a golden sun that would tan their skin unevenly and blissfully. No prophecies, no war, no more death. Only the two of them safe and together. This dream was where she wished she could spend eternity.

EVÆ
SIXTEEN

"They say he was traveling along the Winding Roads when it happened. At night, no less. The poor man couldn't have seen it coming," Jayne, daughter of Ser Elliot, said as the court ladies needled. "At least that is what my father says."

Her auburn hair was braided tightly in the court fashion, and she continuously stopped her needling to stretch her neck. Eve watched as the rest of the ladies commented on *how terrible it was, the horror, the poor wife and son, and look how unsafe our roads are getting.*

Eve concentrated on her needling as they spoke over one another, less about the death of Lord Felix, who was killed by bandits as he traveled for the royal wedding, and more about what might have caused it. Considering his possessions and horse were stolen, the answer seemed obvious to Eve, but as the conversation continued, wild theories abounded: from a pack of wolves to thieves of the Six Sands, to a jilted lover hiring an assassin.

The court ladies were assisting the children with their needlework this morning, but most of the young girls were inattentive and bored. Their mothers spent more time scolding them than helping.

Eve tried to ignore them as she continued her task, far more concerned with the welcoming ceremony, the magic that was making a reappearance, and the peculiar fool—her familiar, he claimed. She avoided him like the plague, unsure of what to do with the information. She even tried to ignore thoughts of the book, but it continued to haunt her dreams, willing her to open its pages and read. She shuddered.

"I wonder what the children think," Adriana whispered to Eve.

Eve was just about to reply, when another woman, Grigoria, spoke, as she helped her daughter Sera fix her stitches. "I believe the witches are at it again. I heard they have been growing a small army in the south, causing mischief in the Ruins."

The room grew quiet, as Grigoria's words settled on the group, but only for a moment.

"That's what Father says too," Jayne replied. "It seems to be a new cohort wreaking havoc upon the innocent."

"Vultures," Grigoria continued. "Thankfully our king has been hard at work to exterminate these vermin."

Eve settled for silence, understanding her place. She focused sharply on her stitches, working faster and faster to drown out the new way the conversation was going.

"How are there so many of them? I do not understand how we have burned thousands and yet there are still a thousand more!"

"They worship a dark goddess, who knows what twisted, evil magic they are capable of?"

"I can't believe King Eryck ever allowed one of them to walk these halls."

Eve knew where this was leading, and in her frustration accidentally pricked her finger on her needle. It began to bleed, and she covered it quickly with a handkerchief.

"How do we know this?" Adriana interjected. "Or is this from pure imagination? A story to scare the children, perhaps?"

The few daughters of the court looked up from their needling, but quickly returned before their mothers scolded them once more.

Eve wanted nothing more than to remove herself from this room, this conversation.

"Princess, these are simple truths. The moment your grandsire, may he rest among the gods, allowed one of them into the castle walls, it spelled trouble for our kingdom. They want for power and use any kind of blood magic to get it." Grigoria's eyes settled on Eve. "It is lucky you took after your father, isn't it?"

Eve stood quickly, still applying pressure to her finger. Her nostrils flared, but she bit her tongue. "Princess, I must take my leave to mend my finger."

Adriana's hazel eyes met hers, an understanding in them. "Of course, would you like me to accompany you?"

"No, Your Highness, I shall see you later this evening."

Eve left quickly, and no sooner had the doors shut behind her, than the conversations continued.

Eve left the healer's tower, a guard escorting her followed close behind, as her mind ruminated over the interaction at court—Jayne and Grigoria's words surely meant to vex her. She felt helpless and irritated, fiddling her fingers along the small bandage that kept the blood subdued.

I am normal. I am mortal. I am not a witch.

She repeated those words to herself as she crossed the courtyard a short distance from the fighting yard where most of the noblemen were sparring. Lord Callum, clad in his sparring attire, called out to her.

"Lady Eve!" he ran toward her, "are you headed somewhere of importance?"

"No, Lord Callum," she replied, startled from her train of thought. "I–I simply wished to turn about the gardens, get some fresh air."

"Might I join you?"

She eyed the bit of sweat that gleaned from his bronze skin, and the long tendrils that fell upon his handsome face. His golden eyes shined in the autumn sun, and he smiled gently, inviting.

"Of course"—she returned his smile—"one could always use some company." She turned to look at her guard, who only nodded slightly as they began walking.

"What happened to your finger?"

"Needling." She raised the bandaged finger for him to see. "It is our version of swords and tourneys."

Callum laughed, his bright smile making her forget her earlier woes. She always felt a familiar comfort in his presence, an ease of divulging her thoughts in conversation unlike the other men at court.

They walked into a maze of hedges carrying various colored roses, and Eve admired their beauty as they walked in silence. She had grown quite fond of the Lord of Teros over the past year, considering his appointment to command the castle defense while the rest of the army battled in Larrea. They had grown a kinship during the uncertainties, bonded by proximity and mutual interests.

"What have you heard of Lord Felix?" Eve asked, curiously.

"Only that a band of thieves attacked him and his men last night." Callum shook his head. "The poor man did not deserve to die that way."

"No one does."

"No one," he repeated.

"The ladies of the court claim witches have something to do with it." Eve turned to Callum, assessing his reaction. Her heart pounded in her chest, hoping that she could trust his confidence. Her guard remained aloof a few meters back, out of hearing distance.

He nodded slightly, his tone even. "I have heard those rumors."

"What do you believe?"

"I believe this is the work of common thieves, nothing more."

She nodded and they continued in silence for a few moments more, getting further into the maze. Her handmaid's words began to come to her as they walked, *you should try and be reasonable.* Eve peeked at him from beneath her lashes; he was kind, generous, and a lord to one of the major houses in Givensmir. What more could any lady in her position hope for, than a friend? She turned her attention back on the pebbled footpath.

"I know that your mother was a witch—an enchantress, I mean," Callum whispered, alongside her. "That is no secret to this court as you know. And I understand that you did not inherit her powers as your sister."

Eve stared up at him. "I would not be here if I did."

"It is a blessing, surely."

To this, Eve turned, distracting herself with one of the roses, feeling its soft, yellow petals within her fingers.

"I was only a child when she killed him. Only a child when she decided power was more important than her own flesh and blood."

Callum moved next to her. "You are not your mother, Eve. You do not bear her sins."

"My father never speaks of it, and yet the court still gossips about it even after fifteen years."

"People fear what they do not understand. But you are Lord Marcelo's daughter, heir to Rubianes Keep; you have far more power here at court than you take credit for. The king would not have spared you if he believed you to be a threat."

Memories of her before the king as a mere child resurfaced, the question he asked her again and again.

Do you have your mother's magic?

Can you see the future too?

"I am still half of my mother's blood," she breathed, "does that not frighten you?"

"The only thing that frightens me, Eve," he said, with a slight smile, "is that you will prick your other fingers on those rose stems." Callum moved next to her, retrieving a dagger from his belt and cutting one of the yellow roses from the hedge. He held it within his hands.

"What do you want from me, Lord Callum? I suspect it is not to hear of my traitorous mother."

"I wish to speak to you about whatever is on your mind," he answered, slowly, the rose still held in his hands. His golden eyes bore into her amber ones, a ghost of a smile on his lips.

The thought of her magical mishap the other evening entered her mind for some reason, and a sudden thought occurred to her. *What if I freeze him right here, right now, before my guard? Would I be killed or have a trial first?*

Yet, he was not frozen, nor did he appear in any unusual or unfortunate state. She rubbed her eyes, trying to relax herself from such intrusive thoughts.

"There is quite a bit on my mind, unfortunately."

"Then perhaps you can entertain me with your thoughts"—Callum kneeled before her, rose raised—"for the rest of our lives."

DAKON
SEVENTEEN

They were still a short distance away from the tavern, but the noise of its patrons carried through the late afternoon. Laughter, drunken singing, a lute, and voices—so many voices. Dakon joined two other servants to drink away his frustrations, hoping to drown himself in whatever poisons the barkeep provided him. Kilian, an old cook, with a scruffy beard and light eyes, and Pazel with his lean posture and dirty tunic fresh from the stables. *A humble bunch, but they would do for company*, he thought. They jumped from the merchant's cart, Kilian passing the man a bushel of turnips as promised for the ride.

Dakon felt for the twin daggers beneath his tunic, they rested in a belt on his hip, hidden from obvious view. It was not like him to be so cautious, but his conversation with Cerene lingered in his mind. In truth, he was a little spooked and shamefully hoped her knack for storytelling was catching up with her age, but her eyes—the sincerity and fear within them—and the burn on her hand, then Eve freezing time in the great hall.

He could not unsee it, just as he could not make up his mind about Eve, either, who he had tried and failed to approach on numerous occasions. He cursed himself for scaring her that night.

"This way, lads." Kilian gestured toward the crowd ahead of them. "You'll find paradise this way. Keep alive, the pickpockets are better here than the rest of the city."

Catalina Port, an ill-favored, less-governed municipal, miles across the bridge from the city center was home to many nefarious dwellers and cheap liquor. The stench in the air was musty and filled with unfamiliar spices that intoxicated Dakon's senses, making him feel drunk with the experience before he even had a drink in his hand. People lingered along dirty, unpaved paths or clung to alleyways like spiders between tattered buildings in various states of disrepair. Unlike the parts of the city closest to the castle, there were no city guards walking through the streets, as if the notion of protection abandoned itself across the bridge that led them here.

The thoughts of the princess lingered in Dakon's head; he could never see her entering a place of such destitution. Then, naturally and unfortunately, the embarrassment of the previous night hung heavy on his heart. Another night as a fool singing songs and making jokes to entertain the king and his drunken hoard of rich men, all while the princess cast her eyes on her untouched plate. He shuddered at the thought.

As they arrived in the tavern, Dakon noted the loud and lively crowd commiserating from all walks of the slums of Givensmir. Men played cards and cajoled amongst each other over drinks and a few of the prostitutes from a brothel around the corner—or so Kilian claimed—and barmaids served quickly and quietly to avoid getting their attention.

"This'll do nicely." Kilian smirked as he took one of the corner tables. He eyed the scene around him. "When's the last time either of you had a proper drink?"

Dakon and Pazel sat with him and glanced at each other. Pazel chuckled, his dark curls covering most of his face; he kept moving his hand to brush the tendrils out of the way.

"I've only had the kitchen wines, on a dare," Pazel stammered. "It wasn't very good."

"That piss is for the royals—tasting like fruits and shit. No, this is where the good stuff is." The corner of his lip curled.

"I haven't the time to venture out of the castle much," Dakon explained.

"Whatever happened to men being men." Kilian snorted. "I was drunk and had bedded at least two women by my thirteenth name day. Now, I am expected to believe you both have only had sips of the royal piss?" He howled with laughter.

"I am not thirteen!" Pazel countered, "I'll be twenty-two by—"

"I don't think that's his point," Dakon interrupted, patting Pazel's shoulder.

A barmaid approached, with light blonde hair and blue eyes, she seemed far too gentle to be in this bar, Dakon thought.

"What'll it be?"

"We'll take three, and keep them comin," Kilian answered.

Without another word, the barmaid scurried back to the bar.

"She's a looker, that one," Kilian said, eyeing the barmaid for a moment before focusing his attention on Dakon. "How's being the king's personal bitch?"

"I'm living the dream." Dakon shrugged noncommittally.

"That's not true," Pazel laughed. "You told me just last night that you would rather rip your tongue out than have to sing another song."

"He's not serious, you idiot," Kilian replied. "From riding horses, writing their messages, and sparring with nobles to being the laughingstock of them. That'll rip a man's confidence clean off."

The barmaid brought them their drinks, setting them together in the center. Kilian's eyes lingered for too long, and Dakon spoke to distract her from his unwelcome gaze.

"Thank you. Greatly appreciate it."

She nodded, her eyes alight for a moment, before she turned and rushed quickly away.

Dakon took a long slug of his ale, feeling their eyes on him. It made his head feel heavy, and the cool liquid quenched his thirst.

"The work is terrible."

"I can't imagine," Pazel chimed in, "being at their beck and call. To make them laugh no less. Can you imagine being that rich that you need to pay someone to make you feel something?"

Kilian snorted. "They aren't like us. I reckon they aren't even people."

"What do you mean?" Pazel asked.

"The country is in shambles, and our king is more focused on choosing fools than providing for his people. We've won every war, conquered nearly every kingdom in Serit up toward Gods' Protection. Normal people are happy with what little they got, but them royals, they're always looking for more. It's *unnatural*."

"I don't even know what we are fighting for," Pazel replied, taking a sip of his drink and making a bitter face.

"No one knows what we're fighting for anymore," Dakon said. "Just that it is what is expected of us."

"You won't see me with a lance and armor. I'm not giving my life for some pompous prick who hasn't fought in a single battle in years," Kilian spat. He raised his empty mug for the barmaid to see.

The barmaid came back with a few more drinks and set them on the table with a thud. The bubbles carried over, wetting the table. His friends didn't seem to notice as she left quickly once more.

"And what about the witches?" Pazel asked. Dakon perked his ears, assessing Kilian's reaction. Cerene and Eve began to enter his mind once more, but he brushed it quickly aside.

"What about them?" Kilian shrugged.

"I hear they're coming back. A noble was killed by some along the Winding Roads."

"One witch gets burned and all of a sudden, we have a witch problem. They're distracting us, you fool, don't want us to see what's really going on."

"And what's that?"

"I hear they're thinking about starting a new war."

"No."

"Yes. They want to take the navy to the Blackthorn, or so some of the servants say."

"Isn't the Blackthorn just a bunch of crazy forest folk?"

"Well, the king thinks there's something there, or else he wouldn't want it."

"He can't want magic." Pazel sighed, taking small, trepidatious sips of his drink. "The gods wouldn't like that too much."

Dakon swallowed the last of his drink, the conversation making him feel sick.

"Magic, power, it's all the same. They want *more*. What do you not understand about that?"

"We had the enchantress and look how that went. A dead king who is now the laughingstock for giving too much power to a witch."

"I think that drink is making you smarter, Pazel. Why don't you keep it up." Kilian snickered, lifting Pazel's drink so he was forced to take long swigs.

"I think we should leave ourselves out of it." Dakon spoke finally. "It's a death sentence to cross the Dallise Sea into their territory. Everyone knows that."

"Well, why don't you tell His Majesty next time you're singing melodies and telling jokes?" Kilian responded, placing the cup down.

"I would but I wouldn't want to end up like the last."

"I think he likes you," Pazel said, his eyes glazing over. "Otherwise, he wouldn't have chosen you from the lot."

"I think you're drunk."

"No, I'm Pazel."

"All right, you two. One last drink and we can leave. We might be able to make it to the castle in an hour if we walk before the leeches begin to lurk."

Kilian signaled the barmaid, and she brought the final drinks, taking their coppers in return. Dakon watched as she eyed him, a ghost of a smile on her lips. She was beautiful, but the only thought that came to his mind was how she did not have dimples, not like Adriana did. The barmaid retreated behind a crowd of people.

"If you don't talk to her," Kilian began, wiping bits of his drink off his face, "then I will."

"I don't think she wants that," Dakon replied.

"You don't know unless you try, it's not like you have anyone else waiting for you." Pazel stood clumsily and tripped over his feet before falling onto a brusque-looking man. The collision caused the man to drop his drink on his tunic, and Dakon stood quickly to lift Pazel as he vomited at the man's feet. The man kicked him off, and Kilian rose to help.

"I ought to have your head for this you little shit," the man yelled, unsheathing a sword clumsily from his belt. He held it up high, and the tavern seemed to quiet, the only sounds heard were Pazel's coughs and vomits.

"Wait, wait," Dakon yelled, putting himself in front of Pazel, hand raised. "He is clearly drunk, sir. Let us pay for your drink, as an apology."

The man's face was full of ale that now dribbled down his chin and into his long, red beard. He lowered his sword and narrowed his eyes. "Get out of my way, *boy*, or I will take on the both of you."

Dakon's breathing hitched, his eyes wide as he beheld the man before him. He was not tall, but stout and muscular, his face was weathered and tanned, scars lined most of his visible skin.

"No, I–I can't."

"Then say hi to the gods for me." The man sneered as he raised his sword once more and thrust it down with fury.

Dakon quickly retrieved his daggers and stopped the sword just before it was set to land on his face. He struggled to keep the sword above him, as all the man's might set upon forcing him down. In a fit of strength, Dakon pushed the sword away from him and the man fell to the side, sword still in hand.

Dakon got to his feet just as he saw Kilian carrying Pazel out of the tavern, most people moved out of the way, avoiding the inevitable bloodshed, but eager to witness the action.

"You little shit," the man spat, righting himself. It was clear that he, too, was drunk as he sliced the air in lazy motions.

Dakon stood his ground, his eyes wide and his palms sweaty. He tightened his grip on his daggers, praying to the gods that his strength and practice would not fail him in real life. The man rushed him, and Dakon deflected the blow, slicing the man's side as he moved past him. The man howled with anger and pain, and turned, fire in his eyes as he came to

Dakon once more.

The two were embroiled in deflection after deflection. Dakon focused on a defensive stance as the man was beginning to grow weary. The man sliced the air with a quick deftness, but with an inebriated sense of purpose. *He must be a great swordsman when he's sober*, Dakon thought, as he pushed the man off him once more.

He turned quickly and cut Dakon's cheek, blood flowing down his face and into his mouth as he spat. The tavern was roaring with bets and jeering, pushing Dakon or the man back into the fight whenever they ventured too far away from each other.

Sweat trickled down their faces, bloodshot brown eyes bore into green ones. Then, time slowed and Dakon felt as if he were rushing through his movements as everyone else became sluggish. He turned around, trying to make sense of the situation. The noise of the tavern was nearly muted, but the crowd seemed to slowly open and close their mouths as if they were shouting.

My magic, he thought, *it's beginning to mirror Eve's.*

The man he fought slowly raised his sword, but nowhere near as fast as he should to defend himself. Dakon rushed him, wanting to end the fight and make time move back to normal. With a final hit, Dakon sliced the man's ear. The tip of it fell clean off, and everything sped up back to normal.

The man now stared at the bit of himself on the wooden floorboards. Dakon maintained his posture, daggers like an extension of his hands, his adrenaline pouring through him.

"It's been a good, long while since I've had a decent fight," the man said, slowly, his fingers feeling what was left of his ear.

Dakon only nodded, daggers in hand.

"What's your name?" he asked, weapon now lowered to his side.

"Dakon."

"Dakon," the man repeated, "how do you like the water?"

The question took Dakon by surprise. "What do you mean?"

The man sheathed his sword and stared at him with a sinful grin. "Aye, someone get my friend Dakon a drink!"

Dakon looked around, confused. People rushed in all directions, and the tavern seemed to resume its normal operations. The same barmaid brought two ales for them and the man gestured to Dakon to sit with his group of men. He did so, moving warily in the seat, the daggers in a white-knuckled grip in his hands.

"Is the fight over?"

"It's never over," the man said, chuckling, pocketing the bit of his ear from the floor, "but I think I like you better alive."

The barmaid blushed slightly as she placed the mug in front of Dakon and grinned before retreating.

"I think you'd do well on a ship, boy. My ship."

"A-a ship? I don't know the first thing about them."

"But you know how to fight, very well I may add. Doesn't he men?" The group at the table nodded and uttered various agreements. Dakon was confused by the sudden turn of events. One minute he was fighting to what appeared to be the bitter end, and the next he's being invited to join a crew of some sort. It made no sense.

"What's your name?" Dakon asked, placing his daggers slowly back in his belt.

"Amarin," the man answered, with a gruff tone, "Captain Amarin."

CLARISA

EIGHTEEN

"I did not believe the prophecy would come to fruition in my lifetime," the high priest of Raven's Holdfast mused, setting up the altar. It was only the two of them, her and high priest, Aris, a humble, short man, with thick blond hair that tousled as he moved.

"I don't understand," Clarisa replied, lighting the candles of the covenstead. Her movements were slow and weak, her body feeling burdened by even the simplest of tasks.

It had been days since she arrived at the holdfast. A small fortress north of the castle where the most devout of their coven dedicated their service and lives to Isila and the craft. She wished to visit and learn more about her nightmares, but even with the help of her familiars, they had not discovered anything from the scrolls and texts that rested in the holdfast's extraordinary library.

She had sought out Aris, a powerful high priest of the coven, in hopes that he could give her answers. Instead, he seemed only interested in lecturing her on the coven's histories as he tasked her and her familiars with mundane tasks throughout the holdfast. Earlier that day, he had them filling water barrels with their magic and loading them onto ships bound for the west—that part without their magic, unfortunately. Now her arms ached, and her legs strained to keep moving as they set the altar in one of the worship spaces. Her familiars were giving them privacy as Aris requested.

Aris collected five gray candles from a box and moved back to the altar. "Perhaps, let us start from the beginning, shall we?" He placed a candle on each corner of the altar cloth and one in the center. "Why do we have five candles, Clarisa?"

She tilted her head. "One for Isila, three for the original witches, and one for all witches who come after."

The priest gestured to her to light them. "We cannot know our future without understanding our past." He placed a small figurine of Isila in the center. "Do you know why you were brought here?"

"I chose to come to Raven's Holdfast."

"No," he replied calmly, "when you were a child."

She shrugged, lighting the final candle. "Because the queen believes I am prophesied to bring Isila back."

He nodded. "Yes, that is what we have been told."

"Forgive me," she said as she placed a few dried flowers from a nearby table atop the altar, "but I do not understand how this is supposed to help me make sense of my dreams."

Aris smiled gently. "We are not here to discuss them, Clarisa. We are here to find out who you really are. In order to do that, you must reckon with your past."

"How can I do that when you have occupied me with tasks fit for the tradesmen?"

Aris chuckled, walking back to the box. "I admit it was mostly for my amusement. But it must have been nice to not think about what plagues you, even for a day."

Clarisa opened her mouth to protest but thought the better of it. It was true, as she worked and busied herself, she did not think much about her dream, but more so about the labor of work. In her free time was when the thoughts resurfaced, and she would spend late nights pouring her soul into every readable surface of books she could find.

"Your familiars are very good, very powerful," Aris mused as he retrieved a vial of salt. He handed it to Clarisa, and she began to gently pour it onto the altar.

"I hope so," she said under her breath. "I would be worried if they weren't."

"I only meant that you have those who truly care about you, who wish to make your life easier in the coming trials and tribulations you will face."

"I am beginning to think none will come, all of this anticipation and never once have I received any hint of the book or Isila's presence."

"Maybe you are needed for something else."

She shook her head, placing the top of the vial on and handing it back to Aris. Her whole life was set up to be the one to bring the kingdoms to heel, to bring Isila back and with it the power of witches to thrive once more outside of the Blackthorn. To think otherwise—she couldn't allow herself to consider what her life would be otherwise . . .

"Prophecies are quite an interesting subject," Aris continued, "very fickle, and mostly left up to interpretation by those who receive its message."

He gestured to Clarisa to stand in front of the altar, and she did, her eyes focusing on the candles before her.

"In my youth, when I was but a simple witch studying here in Raven's Holdfast, I encountered a witch who claimed to see visions sent to her by oracles of the night. 'They terrorize me, dark and vicious, and I cannot make them go away,' she claimed. She was as pale as a ghost, her lips nearly blue, her eyes red from lack of sleep. I believed her to be a poltergeist, nearly spooked me senseless. My mentor, Osyn, had me prepare her a sleeping potion, hoping it would help her get a good night's rest and to determine what we should do about her so-called visions."

"Did you think she made them up?"

"Oh, no," Aris claimed, standing next to her in front of the altar. The candles cast long shadows that began to creep toward Isila in the center. "We knew she spoke true, or what she believed was the truth, but had no idea how to go about a solution."

"Did you cure her?"

"Of the visions, yes. Her memories of their afflictions, no. We are limited on such discourse unfortunately."

"So, what did you do?"

"Well, it's a curious thing, these oracles of night. I do not know if you have heard of them, but as we are visiting the past, we might as well add some history to it." He fished in his robe pocket and retrieved an object from it. He held it before Clarisa, and she tilted her head to get a closer look.

It was a necklace, and dangling from the thick silver chain was a small, circular crystal. It was nearly translucent, save for the bits of dark-gray smoke that swirled within it. Some of the smoke began to tap lightly against the crystal, startling her.

"What is that?" she breathed.

"This *luring crystal* is one of only three in the world. And where the witch's oracles—Diani, Sybila, and Amia— are now. The ones that nearly drove her to madness. It took quite a number of days for me and my mentor to seal them inside, depleting our energy for quite a while thereafter. They are not fond of staying locked inside where they are not free to roam."

He placed it gently beside Isila's figurine.

"Oracles are quite dangerous when used by less experienced witches. They can consume your mind, torture your sanity, and even make you believe in things that are not quite real. One begins to believe that they will not survive without the oracles and their visions. Visions that are not always accurate, in the literal sense of the word. They will host and feed upon you until you become a shell of a witch, hollow and in an unthinkable state between life and death, that is until they find their next host. Only witches that can withstand them can procure from them the answers they seek."

"How does one use the oracles without succumbing to them?"

"I cannot say for certain." He sighed. "If they successfully penetrate your defenses, you will need your familiars to put them back inside the crystal, or to destroy the crystal itself."

"*My* familiars?"

"Yes, Clarisa," Aris said, staring at the crystal. "It is time for you to find out who you really are."

She stared at him speechless and then allowed her eyes to drift toward the crystal. It turned a mixture of orange and yellow, mirroring the flames from the candles. The smoke from within began to tap even harder against the glass, moving ever slightly on the altar, beckoning her to release them from their prison.

EVE

NINETEEN

E ve eyed the ring on her finger, noticing it caught the glint of
the dying sun outside her balcony. A red jewel met her gaze.
These jewels, she knew, were found in the mines of Zafira, a
major house within their kingdom in the south. She wondered, idly, how
it felt for the nobles there to sit upon such gifts of the earth—nearly all
the jewels found throughout Serit were recovered from there, making it
a place of vast wealth and a haven for merchants that traded with the
nobility.

Callum certainly would have requested such a ring a while ago as the
war seemed to be reaching its conclusion. She wondered how long he
had known that he would court her, and how confident he was that she
would accept. According to Callum, her father had sent his approval
weeks ago, and the king accepted his request earlier today. It all seemed
too perfect . . .

She let the wind blow freely through her hair, all her braids were

BLOOD OF THE BLACKTHORN

undone and the tendrils waved about gently. It was expected of her to marry, she told herself and better a friend than someone she did not know. Even worse, she shuddered, a stranger her uncle would have certainly recommended.

Thoughts of Theo plagued her then, how she would have to tell him, and when she would. He had no choice but to marry Felicity, the weight of the expectations upon him as a prince were far more burdensome than hers as lady of Rubianes Keep.

Rubianes. Land of grapes, olives, and wine.

Teros. Land of highly sought after darkwood, Teros war horses, pelts, and silver mines.

She laughed to herself. *I will be one of the wealthiest and drunkest wives in all five kingdoms.*

Eve turned from her balcony, set upon retiring early. The day's events were beginning to weigh on her, and she wished for nothing more than to escape her reality, even if it meant a few more unsettling dreams.

She entered her chambers and saw it. Stopping her mid-laugh.

BLOOD OF THE BLACKTHORN
SOUL OF ISILA
A COMPENDIUM OF WITCHCRAFT & MAGIC

The book was laid open to the title page at the end of her bed. She was certain, fairly certain, that it was not there when she had returned from speaking with Callum.

Eve approached it, cautiously, and read the page again. Her heart thudded loudly in her ears, and she looked around to ensure she was alone, then let out a nervous laugh. Of course she was alone, it was her private chambers, after all, no one ever bothered her here. And there were no engagements for the rest of the evening . . .

She lifted the book, feeling and inspecting it.

It was not particularly large, and the quires seemed to be held together by a taut thread. The thick binding felt heavy in her hands. She sat on the floor, back facing the door and positioned a candle carefully beside her.

The afternoon was bleeding into the darkening sea, and light from her balcony was waning gradually.

Curiosity seemed to outweigh the trepidation that gripped her heart. And after a few moments the fear waned completely. In her hands, this grimoire made her feel serene, peaceful. Eve took a deep breath, allowing herself to forget all the reasons that demanded she reject this book. Perhaps, she considered, it is not a grimoire, but a book of histories.

She opened it to the next page.

It was blank.

She flipped once more.

That page, too, was blank.

She continued this, until she had exhausted all of the pages.

"Why is it empty?" she said aloud to herself.

She flipped back to the first blank page and studied it. Willing something, anything to happen.

Touch it.

A voice within her spoke.

She lifted a hand, her fingers barely brushing the page. Her hesitation was enough to question her actions. Eve turned to look at the door, but there was no sound on the other end. No one was expected to visit.

She looked back at the page and closed her eyes as she touched it.

When she opened them, she was no longer in her chambers, but in the corridor that led to the tower of the king. It was not night, but a bright, sunny day greeted the stone-lined halls. A cool, inviting breeze carried through the open windows. Guards lined the hall, shrouded in their gold armor, standing tall as someone approached from behind Eve.

She turned slowly, hearing the footsteps, and nearly fainted from the sight.

It was Lucia Rubianes, First Royal Enchantress of Givensmir.

Her mother.

DAKON
TWENTY

The hours blurred and the night grew darker for Dakon, as he drank to excess with Amarin and his crew. The world blended together in a flash of colors, the dim candlelight of the tavern lighting only the few patrons who remained. He recalled memories of kissing the pretty barmaid to the cheers of men around him and her red cheeks as she blushed and smiled at him, retreating once more into the crowd. He remembered beating one of the sailors at dice, winning nothing but another drink. Then he remembered the captain bidding him farewell.

He stumbled, drunk, out of the tavern into the dark night. Catalina Port smelled of rotten fish and salt, invading his nostrils and making him vomit on the side of the tavern. He was lost, he knew. His friends long gone back to the castle, and he, without memory of how they arrived at the tavern in the first place, unaware of how to get back. He stumbled, nearly falling on his vomit and closed his eyes.

When he awoke, it was pitch black, and the streets were nearly empty. His pockets had been outturned and he was missing the small coppers he carried, nearly four moons worth of work. He cursed, and still felt the world spin as he tried to stand. His daggers were still on his hips, the thieves most likely focused on his pockets rather than what lay hidden beneath. As he tried to gain his bearings, Dakon heard a gruff noise. He spun around too quickly, falling back hard in the dirt. He noticed something peering at him from a nearby alleyway. Dakon squinted his eyes, trying to make out the figure as it moved cautiously amongst the debris of the street toward him.

The black dog, the gytrash.

It approached him until it was nearly face-to-face and the scent of earth filled his nostrils. Its eyes were soft and held a reddish-orange hue like the blood moon. It seemed to be studying him, contemplating its next move. Dakon could barely feel himself breathe, barely hear himself think. Fear took hold, fixing him to the spot.

Finally, the gytrash nudged his side, and Dakon cautiously reached a filthy hand to pet it, it's fur thick and soft under his fingertips.

"I'm a bit drunk," he slurred.

The dog only stared in return, as if waiting for Dakon to do something, anything.

Dakon stood once more, feeling a bit queasy, but better after his awkward nap.

"Friend or foe?" he asked the beast. It was larger than he remembered, and on all four legs nearly reached his chest.

It didn't answer, not that he expected it to.

"I will call you Beast. I do not mean that offensively."

It tilted its head and seemed to smile at him. Dakon felt a bit of deja vu, but it quickly left him as he focused on the eerie street around him and the realization dawned on him that he was unsure how to get home.

"Can you take me back to the castle? I'm a bit lost."

Beast cocked his head, then tugged on the sleeve of his tunic. He began to walk forward, taking a few steps before looking back at him.

"Sounds like a yes to me."

He followed Beast down various alleyways, leading him further and further into the depths of the slums to places he was not familiar with. Shacks made of thin materials seemed to jut at peculiar angles as if stacked haphazardly atop each other. Rats littered the streets and dark alleys eating anything. Dakon trembled slightly, and for once, he wished he were back in the crowded rooms of the servants' quarters. He made a silent prayer to the gods that they bring him back safely. Then he wondered if he should believe in the gods anymore, on account of who—or what, rather—he was.

Through the dark, he began to make out a small gathering of people, waiting outside of a building of dark, rotted wood. He rubbed his eyes trying to get a better look at the crowd, they were quiet, still, and filled this part of the street. He had to go through them to get to the other side where the bridge merged between the slums and the city center. It unnerved him.

"Can you take me a different way?" Dakon whispered, but when he looked down, Beast was gone. He turned around, trying to see where he went, but the gytrash was nowhere to be seen. His head swam and he blinked a few times to focus out from the last of his drunken haze. As he walked forward, trying to maintain a modicum of bravado, he idly wondered if he was meant to be here. Why else would his companion abandon him here?

The doors opened suddenly as Dakon tried to pass through the crowd. And in their eagerness, the group pushed Dakon inside as they all clamored to get in quickly.

Before he could turn back, the doors were shut, and he heard the sound of a lock. He was sober now, he was sure of it, his adrenaline spiking and his mind racing. The crowd faced the front of the room, where on a barrel stood a short man in an unassuming dark, tattered robe.

"Welcome, my people."

The crowd remained silent, transfixed on the words of this unseemly man.

"You are here, because our sources have found that you each possess a gift. Gifts that have been passed down through the generations leading back to our great goddess, Isila."

The crowd seemed to nod in agreement, looking back and forth assessing each other. A few eyes landed on Dakon, but he fixed his eyes on the man, trying to maintain a low profile.

"Our kind is no stranger to hardship, our hands familiar to hard work. Centuries ago, we used to lead the people of this land and used our power to give them life. Everything we see around us, is a product of the work of our ancestors. All fostered to us by the original three in all their graciousness. We were sent here to temper the hearts of greedy men, and instead were overthrown by them. Cast aside, having to hide ourselves behind shadows and cower in fear to live as we please. I say, no more! We are what they need, we are what brings life to the mortals, and we can take it away."

The crowd began to murmur their agreements and a few clapped. Dakon, clapped along with them, realizing with a sickening feeling that he was somewhere he shouldn't be.

Be calm, he thought, *be calm.*

He quickly searched right and left for any escape, but the windows were boarded and the only visible entrance behind him was guarded by two large men.

This would be a great moment to slow time, he thought, and cursed himself for magic he could not yet control.

"We come here to join our forces as one, to do what the Blackthorn could not. What they *choose* not to do. These mortals have grown greedy, deadly, taking what is rightfully ours and killing any of us that tries to stop them. The original three runs true through us, and together we will conquer these so-called noble men and end their reign of terror!"

The crowd cheered, this time unruly and passionate. In the chaos, Dakon tried to dodge the erratic movements of those around him, but he felt sluggish and lethargic, receiving hit after hit by random people. He raised his arms to protect his face, his sides, any part of himself that felt exposed and trampled on.

"Join the Strix and live as gods on earth!"

Gods on earth!

Dakon no sooner heard this, then he felt a stinging, painful sensation on his head. His vision blurred and darkness began to envelope him once more as he fell down, down, down . . .

CLARISA

TWENTY-ONE

C larisa sat at a table with her familiars, the crystal laid out in the center between them. She had divulged what Aris told her, and so they spent this evening drowning in books, texts, and scrolls to better acquaint themselves with the oracles. Something gnawed at Clarisa as she watched the smoke dance within the crystal. A light evening rain pattered against her guest chamber windows, candles flickered in the darkness, and a waxing crescent moon peeked from behind the fog.

Raven's Holdfast sat along a hill, as if the earth pulled the bottom under and grew around it. From where she looked, she could see the valleys and small villages spread for miles and miles. Part of her wished that she could run toward it, where the sky met the lush, verdant grass, sail through the Shimmering Seas and continue west to paradise.

"There is not much regarding summoning and subduing oracles," Tabor murmured as he placed another scroll in the read stack.

"Except that they move from host to host," Brisa added, running her hands through her long, white-blonde hair, "quite a bit of lore, not enough encounters."

"Hmm," was all Clarisa would manage.

Brisa placed a gentle hand on Clarisa's. "We will keep reading, please get some rest."

There was a knock on her door, and Tabor moved to open it. He stood rigid as he greeted their guest. "Prince Navir?"

Clarisa stood quickly, clutching the crystal necklace and placing it in her pocket.

The prince with raven hair looked very much like his mother, with the same eternal attractive qualities. His blue eyes bore into hers as he walked slowly into the room, hands behind his straightened back.

"Your Highness." Clarisa bowed, curiosity at his presence irking her as the questions came like wildfire into her head.

"Clarisa"—he kissed her knuckles, holding her hand between both of his cold ones—"I apologize for intruding. I arrived at the castle only to be told you had left. I came as soon as I could."

"I don't understand?"

"Can we have a moment?" He tilted his head to Tabor and Brisa.

"Yes, I can spare a bit of time."

They gave her confused looks but gathered the documents and headed out of the room, closing the door slowly behind them.

Clarisa couldn't help but feel rather annoyed at Navir's untimely arrival. He was expected at the castle, and they were not particularly close to warrant such a visit. To her recollection, they did not spend much time together save for when occasions called for it—celebrations, death ceremonies . . .

Anxiety filled her, what if something had happened to Ana? Her thoughts began to spiral until Navir spoke, bringing her back to reality.

"Will you take a walk about the castle with me?" the prince asked. "I find it to be a refreshing bit of exercise, even with a bit of drizzle."

Clarisa smiled politely, then looked toward the window. *It would be more than just a bit of drizzle*, she thought.

"Is everything okay?" she asked, a worried look in her eyes.

"Yes, not to worry, but there is something of importance I must speak to you about."

"Of course," she replied as she grabbed a black cloak from her wardrobe. He helped her drape it over her shoulders, clasping the ends together.

Navir smiled as she linked her arm in his and they walked out of her door and into the empty, dank corridor in silence.

***

"So, what is the real reason you wanted to take a stroll?" Clarisa asked as they walked about the stone walkways. It was maze-like, adjusting its course and contents in accordance with Navir's will. The continuous movement of the stone walls and footpaths told Clarisa that he wished to be isolated with her. This must be a subject of great importance if he was going through all the trouble of keeping them hidden from view.

She used her magic to keep the rain from her space, and from afar, she knew it looked as if she walked with invisible shields. The thought made her smile. *It was good to be a witch.*

They came upon a garden sanctuary, filled with plants and herbs found throughout the Blackthorn; statues of Isila and the original witches lined the edges. Navir led her to a wooden bench under a small pergola, gesturing her to sit alongside him.

Clarisa did but felt a faint sense of anxiety blooming once more; it had been a long time since they had been alone. She wished she would have brought her familiars despite his request.

Navir gave her a soft smile that did not touch his eyes.

"I am sorry for your loss. I know Malin was important to you."

The thought of her mentor tugged at her heart, and she blinked away the threatening tears. She did not have time to grieve him and wouldn't let herself embrace that pain.

"Thank you." She cast her eyes to the ground, wishing to change the subject.

"I know we are not particularly close, but anyone could see how much he doted on you. It was clear he loved you like a daughter."

"He betrayed the realm, betrayed me."

"I am certain he never wanted to bring you harm. But it is true, he made his bed and lay in it. And you got your revenge from it."

Clarisa raised her head, cocking a brow at Navir. "I would have rather spoken to him first before being forced to kill him on the spot."

"Why is that?"

"I wanted him to tell me why coins were more important than me."

Navir let out a laugh. "Clarisa, you are amusing."

"I mean it."

"Despite what anyone here tries to tell you, witches and mortals have far more in common than we care to admit. Men will start wars for land, and witches will betray covens for gold. There are good among both, of course, but none are without their faults."

Clarisa mulled his words in her head, and bit her lip, unsure of how to respond.

"Can you keep a secret?" he asked, jaw tense.

"Better than anyone I know," she breathed, watching the mist build up on the tendrils of Navir's hair. She couldn't remember the last time they were this close. It made her feel uneasy.

"That's why I trust you. Do you trust me?" He asked the last question with a serious glint in his eyes and grabbed her hand.

"Yes." She matched his serious tone. In truth, she knew that there was no other choice but to answer him this way. She wished she could pull her hand back, but curiosity was overwhelming her.

What was he about to tell her?

"Good."

"Navir, why did you come here?"

He brushed his hands through his damp hair, considering her carefully. "We need to trust each other, in order for us to finally rule this kingdom the way it should be."

"Navir, what are you—"

"And I'm sure you have heard the rumors, the storm is on its way, we can feel it charging through the air, it is awakening something upon these lands beyond our magic. You have proven yourself stronger than any witch.

You just need to harness it, let yourself become who you are meant to be. We cannot overpower the forces that will soon come upon us."

"What forces?"

"Mortals, as you may know and the Strix. A coven that was banished from the Blackthorn long ago for their . . . interesting ways of practicing witchcraft."

"What does the queen make of all this?"

Navir chewed the inside of his cheek, clenching his jaw. "She has not considered all of the options before her. I have been forced to forge alliances for the betterment of our kingdom. I do not wish for us to cower nor for our witches and magic folk to die at the hands of the mortals anymore."

"So, you mean she either doesn't know or doesn't approve."

"Both." He smirked.

"What you are talking about is treason, I do not wish to have any part in it, and neither should you."

"It isn't treason to discuss my birthright," he replied, his eyes flickering. "Your mother—"

"Let me worry about my mother."

"I don't want to see you destroying yourself in order to get a throne that is already promised to you."

"There are forces beyond your comprehension that will destroy us. My mother has done nothing to stop it but behead a few traitors. We will be weakened by the mortals; it is only a matter of time."

"Why are you telling me this?"

"Because you are the prophecy, and I am the one to make it come to fruition."

Clarisa could barely speak, unable to make sense of everything he was telling her. He leaned in close, tracing a flower-like pattern with his finger on her palm. "I have some things I need to take care of."

She held it up before her, watching as it glowed dark blue, then disappeared. He closed her palm and lifted her chin until their eyes met. His solemn, serious look beheld hers.

"Go back to the castle, I need you to stay alive. There are more people that want you dead than you realize."

THEO

TWENTY-TWO

Theo sat behind his desk, writing correspondence to his aunt in the Mistral Islands, a response to her apologies for missing his upcoming nuptials due to her ill health, when there was a knock at his door. He set the quill aside, and raised his head, "you may enter."

A guard opened his door, announcing, "Your Highness, Princess Adriana."

Theo straightened, his brow furrowing, his sister rarely visited him in his chambers, and never after dusk. "Let her in."

Adriana walked in wearing a dark-lavender bliaut gown, with her hair braided behind her. Her face was impassive as she entered and waited until the guard closed the door before speaking. "Good evening, Brother."

"Good evening, Adriana. Is something wrong?"

"No, no," she sat across from him, looking around his chambers.

"How long has it been since I last visited you?"

Theo followed her gaze around the room. "I–I am not sure. Perhaps since we were children?"

She nodded, looking toward her fidgeting hands in her lap. She seemed unable or unwilling to speak, so Theo continued. "It has been a while since we even spoke, now that I think of it. How are you, how is the court?"

She continued to focus her eyes on her hands. "It suits me, as all things do."

"Anything interesting?"

"No," she began, before sighing. "I am glad you are back home. The castle seemed rather dull without you in it."

"I would much rather be here."

"How was it?"

"How was what?"

"Larrea. War. Was it like what we've read in the histories?"

Theo shook his head slowly. The sounds of steel swords against wooden shields filled his ears, the cries of men as they fell off their wounded horses, how quickly they lost their lives amidst the chaos and confusion of weapons and bodies. His heart thudded against his chest; his hands felt clammy.

"No, unfortunately it was not."

"Do you want to talk about it?"

"I would much rather talk about anything else."

Adriana nodded, pursing her lips in concentration. "It appears your wedding is still set as scheduled. Father has sent men to add protections to the Winding Road to alleviate concerns by the other houses during their travel."

"I heard. I have sent Lady Helena my condolences on the passing of Lord Felix. Not that I believe House Mora is particularly keen on receiving reminders of his death. Apparently without any suitable heirs, his eldest bastard will be in line for the title."

"What is wrong with his bastard?"

"Nothing"—he smirked—"only that Lady Helena tried to have him killed a few times. I suspect we will see another death soon with all the bloodshed that family seems to bring upon themselves."

Adriana shuddered slightly, still fiddling with her fingers. "Do you believe it was the work of witches?"

Theo cocked his head. "Adriana, the witches are in the Blackthorn with a sea between us. They wouldn't dare come where they are not welcome and where their magic is weakened."

"I heard they have been causing quite a stir in Zafira."

"That is Zafira, not us. And even so, it is a small faction of peasants displeased with Lord Ybera. There is no evidence that they are witches as they claim to be."

"You do not seem to be concerned."

"I'm not, I have other pressing matters needing my attention as of late."

Adriana stood quickly. "Perhaps, I should go then."

"You can, but I'm confused. Why did you come here, was it just to talk about witches?"

She hesitated, biting her thumbnail nervously. Theo distinctly remembered occasions where their mother would admonish such behavior but decided to forgo the subject. He furrowed his brow.

"Did you know that Father wishes to continue fighting? That I am expected to wed to secure funding for this new war?" She stood tall, maintaining her composure, but her face could not conceal the bitterness lurking within.

Theo weighed his words carefully as he answered. "Yes."

"Why did you not tell me?"

"I'm sorry, I should have."

"I do not wish to marry."

"There are many suitable bachelors from wealthy families. I am sure that you will have a say in your future husband."

"The choice will be to the highest bidder and in case you have forgotten, that may be with any graying widower. He can't make me!"

"In case you have forgotten, I, too, am being forced to marry. And I did not have a choice in the matter."

"But you could still do as you please."

"What are you saying?"

"You are not obligated to the same binding customs that I am. You can take a wife, but you are not obliged to love her, obey her. You can seek comfort in the arms of someone else."

"Adriana, I do not plan to bring shame on our house with meaningless trysts and neither do I make up these customs."

"But you still benefit from them."

"I am a prince of Givensmir, I will do my duty as such and secure this alliance. You would do well to follow my lead."

Adriana narrowed her eyes at him, her face flushed in anger. A long silence passed before she spoke. "And what of Eve?"

"What of her?"

"Do you still believe you two can carry on as you do after this marriage is secured?"

"What are you—"

"Eve is betrothed to Lord Callum now." She raised a brow, challenging him.

Theo stepped back, a sinking feeling in his chest. He swallowed, measuring his voice. "Is this certain?"

"Callum told me earlier today."

Theo turned away from her, heat rising in his cheeks. He knew it, he knew the rumors were true. Rising jealousy threatened to take over his sanity, he took a few deep breaths to calm himself. Adriana came by his side.

"It is not my intention to hurt you. However, unlike you, I did not feel it right to keep this a secret before whispers reached you in court."

"Eve is my friend," he muttered.

"A friend you are in love with."

"She is your friend too."

"How well do we know Eve, truly know her?"

"We both know her better than anyone, or have you forgotten?"

Adriana groaned, and began to pace furiously before him, running her fingers through the end of her braids. Theo moved toward her, grabbing her by the shoulders and holding her gently still before him.

"Enough of this, Adriana, tell me why you are here."

She stared at him, a mixture of apprehension and concern in her eyes. Her lips trembled as she spoke. "Does Eve have magic?"

Theo released her, taken aback. He didn't respond, trying and failing to come up with an answer—any answer—to her ridiculous question.

"Does Eve have magic?" she repeated.

"No, of course not. And I would caution you to lower your voice, we don't want such rumors going abound. An accusation like that could mean her death, Adriana. Have you lost your senses?"

"There is something different about her recently. Something troubling, and I am not the only one to notice!"

"What are you talking about?"

Adriana let out a shaky breath. "I just need to know if you've noticed anything, seen anything, that might be unexplained about Eve. I wish I didn't have to ask, but I have no choice."

"Who is giving you no choice? You are not making any sense."

"I can't say."

Theo pounded his fist on the table. "Adriana, if you have no evidence, then leave me be. I am not going to entertain childish rumors about someone who has been very good to the both of us. She may carry the enchantress's blood but, thank the gods, she is nothing like her."

"How do you know? Have you ever thought to ask?"

"Enough!" Theo pointed at Adriana. "I have listened long enough. Eve has done nothing but speak your praises and here you are trying to dig her grave. This is not like you, Adriana. When I was shipped off to Larrea, I left behind a charitable, kind sister, not one focused on meddling in court gossip."

Adriana's tears fell down her cheeks like rapids in the eastern provinces, but she stood before him, silent. He took a deep breath, settling his tone before he continued. "Eve lost her mother and sister; tell me she has not lost you as a friend too."

To this, Adriana crumbled before him, her face etched in shame and regret. He began to move toward her once more, but she turned from him rushing out of his chambers. She tossed the door open, startling the guard, and ran from view. Even long after she had gone, Theo felt as though he

145

could still hear her sobs down the stairs and through the corridor, echoing a fear within her that he could not quite understand.

EVE
TWENTY-THREE

E ve watched as the royal enchantress walked past her toward the king's tower, the guards lining the corridor. Their faces revealed nothing as they eyed her mother passing by, stiff and tall in their gold-and-black armor, the sunlight reflecting brightly as if they were candles lighting her way.

"Mother!" Eve called out; it sounded muffled, like an echo in a cave. Her voice trailed on and on, repeating itself until it died away seconds later. Her mother paused, but did not turn around. Instead, she kept walking purposefully. Eve looked at the guards, her heart thundering in her chest, but no one appeared to hear her.

"Wait!" Eve rushed toward her mother, reaching her hand out to grasp her.

Yet, it fell through her mother's body, as if Eve were nothing but air. She retreated a few steps, her hands now shaking uncontrollably. Tears began to pool at the corners of her eyes.

What have I done?

She tried to steady herself as she raised her hands to her face. It felt normal; her skin was cool and smooth beneath her touch. She walked up to one of the guards, and tried touching his armor, but he was unaware of her presence and her hand fell through him.

How is this possible?

Her mother was near the end of the hall and Eve rushed toward her. More afraid of being alone with these strange men than with someone she did not fully trust. Her skin prickled at the thought, but a sudden hope bloomed within her. The enchantress held great power, perhaps she could bring Eve back where she belonged. She owed Eve that much at least.

Her mother held her chin high, her hands placed gently in front of her as she moved gracefully, her focus appeared solely on reaching the tower stairs now only a few feet in front of them. Eve noticed her mother took a deep, shaky breath as they approached a man standing there.

"His Majesty is ready to meet with you, Lady Lucia," he said, bowing as they approached. And Eve recognized him as Ser Cardo, former head of the royal guard. He died shortly after the king, Eve recalled, of an illness of sorts.

"I often wonder, Ser Cardo, how you can be so comfortable with all that armor weighing you down." Her mother smirked.

He ignored her, his eyes trailing toward the tower steps. "Right this way, please."

He reached out his hand, a grim look on his face, but her mother did not grasp it.

"Thank you, Ser Cardo, I can manage fine."

Before he could reply, her mother began to quickly ascend the steps. Eve followed close, hearing Ser Cardo huff behind her. Her mother seemed to be very much looking forward to the door at the top separating herself and this man. Once there, her mother tried to open the door, but Ser Cardo placed a hand on the looped, brass handle.

"We still have to follow customs, my lady."

Her mother stared hard at Cardo, but relented, lips tightening. Cardo opened the door.

"Your Majesty, Lady Lucia."

"No need to shout, Ser Cardo, I have eyes. I can see the damn woman in front of me," the king grumbled from his bed. He lay there in his nightshirt underneath silk sheets, part of him obscured by the embroidered curtains that hung from the top of the four-poster bed. Cardo grimaced but bowed and turned to leave, closing the door with care behind him.

Eve heard her mother breathe a sigh of relief and watched as she took a few steps closer to the king. Eve kept a short distance, trying to make sense of the situation unfolding in front of her.

This was King Byron III, father of King Eryck. He was much different now than what she remembered of him as a child and of all the paintings of his likeness. The portraits had not captured the loss of his vivacity in the end. He was aged, and there was a feebleness, a vulnerability, that unsettled her. His gray-speckled beard took over most of his ashen, pale face, his wrinkles like deep crevices in bark, and his features—which normally presented as strong and handsome—was now full of anguish and pain. She had never seen this version of him in anything but words on the pages of the histories she learned by tutors in the court. Yet, standing here in front of him, witnessing it true, made her nervous and disturbed.

"Your Majesty"—her mother bowed deeply—"I came as soon as I could."

The king waved a hand noncommittally. "Let us part with the formalities, shall we? I fear we are far past that now."

Her mother pulled a chair from a nearby table, placed it by his bedside and sat. "What plagues you, My King?"

"I was hoping you could tell me." He sighed, sitting up straighter. Her mother tried to help him, but he held up his hand to stop her. "The day I can no longer sit myself up, promise you'll suffocate me"—he nodded to the pillow next to him—"with that right there. It was always too firm for my neck."

She sat back down and smiled.

Something is wrong, Eve thought, *she is too calm.*

After a few moments of silence, her mother said carefully, "I do not have the answer for which you seek, Your Majesty."

"Do you not have the answer, or do you not want to tell me." He tapped his head.

Her mother widened her eyes very slightly, almost unnoticeable, before she relaxed and patted the king's hand. "The former, of course."

He nodded.

"Has anyone else mentioned what may have happened?"

King Byron coughed into a red-spotted handkerchief. "No. There aren't many men lining up to claim treason, shocking as that may be," he said sarcastically. "Death is not particularly reversible."

"You may not die."

"I am no fool, Lucia. I will die, and soon, I suppose."

"Shall I tell you when?"

Eve felt a knot in her throat; how casual her mother was with such a demented subject. Her mouth was dry, her heart sinking, but she could not tear her eyes away from what she was witnessing.

The king's cloudy green eyes met her mother's, a tinge of fear within them. They were almost asking her the question she knew was in his head, the question she could hear him practically screaming inside himself. "Do I want to know?"

"That is up to you, but I cannot stop what is to come."

The king blinked a few times and shook his head. "Best not know, then. Have to keep some modicum of suspense in my life, I suppose." He chuckled. "Ser Cardo with his hourly updates was driving me mad. I threatened him with his head should he come back to brief non-emergent matters. Now I am rather bored."

"I can imagine it is now too quiet in here," her mother mused, looking about the room. Her eyes landed on Eve, lingering for a moment, but then turned back to the king. Eve wondered if she knew she was there and shifted uncomfortably where she stood—wondering herself if that was something she wanted in this moment between her and the king.

"Yes, yes. If he wasn't too busy being my bitch the past five years, I would have taken more of a shine to him," the king grumbled. "I believe he is already plotting how to get in Eryck's good graces."

"Your son—" her mother began.

150

"My son . . . is everything I tried not to be. And in being a halfway decent king, I have failed in showing him how to be a good man."

Her mother began to protest, but the king hushed her as he continued. "This is not up for debate. In this room, right now as we are, you can speak freely to me. My son has become quite the brute, and by the time I paid enough attention to him to realize this, it was too late. I was never a good father, never much of a good husband to the late queen, I only lived to serve myself and the kingdom, in that order."

Eve knew his words rang true, knew that they summed up what everyone else believed, and what she had read in her studies. Hearing him say it, however, made her feel a bit of pity for the man.

"I have some things I want to tell you, that I should have long ago. They may make me a wicked man, but I hope that you will forgive me, one day, for them." He assessed her mother once more and she nodded slightly.

"When you were captured years ago, it was no accident that you landed in my throne room. For weeks, the court had been hearing of the young woman aboard a ship who could see the future, could read minds as if everyone were an open book, move things by simply thinking about it— it seemed unreal that someone of such abilities would be anywhere near Givensmir, much less expected to be docking in Catalina's Port."

"You have always kept good spies."

"That I have. You can thank Lord Wesley for that."

Eve pictured Lord Wesley, with his air of self-importance. She had no idea he was the reason her mother had been found. It unsettled her.

The king coughed once more in his handkerchief and took a deep breath, continuing. "Tales of such sorcery were reserved for describing those of the Blackthorn, the realm who kept their most gifted within arm's reach. How then, I had wondered, did a young woman with such incredible power, escape their lands? We were at war with Mytar, and losing, badly. Our kingdom was not going to survive this war the way we were going about it. We needed an advantage, and I was desperate to not see my kingdom fall."

He looked away, trying to temper another cough that threatened to reveal itself, but Eve felt that contrition was the more likely culprit. She knew how this ended, knew her mother was the one to kill him, despite what he had to say.

Why did this matter?

Her mother placed her hand on his. "Please, continue."

He blinked a few times, before wiping a few beads of sweat with another handkerchief. "I paid a thousand silver pieces to anyone who would bring you to me alive, and they did within days. You had come along so willingly; I told myself that I had saved you from a life of struggle and poverty. I know now that you had simply foresaw your kidnapping."

"I did," she said calmly, still clasping his hand. "I saw little need to have the company I kept be harmed trying to protect me."

"Perhaps that is the only solace to that matter. I hope you forgive me for tearing you away from it." He held his breath.

"I do, but I believe there is something more you wish to say?"

The king nodded slightly and raised his eyes to hers. "As you know, one of the men you sailed with came to our gates looking for you. I informed you that he was killed by one of the guards, as was reported to me by Ser Cardo. I did not want any potential distractions to your abilities, nothing that would entice you to escape."

"I remember."

"What I did not tell you, was that after our conversation, I learned from Lord Wesley that the man was actually imprisoned, questioned by my men to see if there were any more of your kind aboard his or any other ship. He refused to speak despite the torture, refused money in exchange for information, and escaped." He coughed a few times before continuing, "I kept the information to myself, to prevent you from going after him, but I see now that I was wrong in that matter. However, selfishly, I do not regret it."

Eve held her breath, his words settling inside of her, and goosebumps began to form along her skin. Her mother never mentioned anything about her past nor anything of this man to her. Even in her writings—which were recovered shortly after her death and repurposed in the histories as proof of her madness—there was no mention of a man who attempted to save her from the king. Who was he?

Her mother was still, her expression cold and unwavering as she listened to the king.

"In my final hours, I want to leave you with one last apology. Unburden myself, if you will, before I am to meet the gods. I forced you to witness the death of so many, to be a part of a war you never asked to be a part of. It is not easy, damn anyone who tries to convince you otherwise. Us mortals are cowards, fighting amongst each other for superiority, when in truth, we are among the weakest of creatures in this world."

He stared at her mother, assessing her reaction. Yet, a tender smile was the only thing she returned to him. Eve held herself, unsure of what her mother would say, a chill ran down her spine.

"You have my forgiveness. Thank you for telling me." She patted his hands and released him.

"I–I want to do something for you, for all the troubles you have endured on my behalf."

Her mother raised a brow, listening.

"As I said, my son does not seem to take to your kind so well, apart from you, of course. It is why I had him swiftly married off when I began to notice how his lingering affected your magic."

"And I thank you for it."

"Was I right to marry you to Lord Marcelo?"

"I do not believe your court would have kept me alive if you didn't."

"Good"—he placed both of her hands in his, all hint of humor gone—"you must find a way out of here before I die. Leave with your husband and daughters before the prince ascends, before he dismantles all protections I have held in place for you."

Her mother gave him a hard look in response.

Eve understood what he meant. Magic, for all its wonder, was not an invincibility; her mother—any witch—could be killed as any mortal could be. Her heart beat fast, her head swimming, her stomach in knots.

"If I had known that I would have ended this way, I would have ensured to orchestrate your escape myself sooner, but it happened so suddenly, and my messages are now being intercepted by Lord Wesley under Prince Eryck's order. My network, this court, is slowly learning that my illness is fatal, and I cannot protect you once they all confirm it."

Eve watched as the king's grip tightened on her mother. "Do you understand what I am saying?"

"I understand."

The king nodded slowly, assuredly. "May you live a long and happy life, my dear."

Eve felt a tear run down her cheek and squeezed her eyes shut trying to stop anymore from coming. For she knew that no words spoken, no wishes made to the gods, could prevent what happened next. Everything she had been told about this moment, the last interaction between her mother and the king had all been a lie. What else was a lie?

Eve blinked. She was sitting in her chambers, grimoire in hand, no longer in the past where her mother was.

"No!" she cried. "No, I need to know what happened!"

She tried touching the page, replicating what had brought her back fifteen years ago, but nothing happened.

Eve threw the book across the room, confused and frustrated by what she witnessed.

Is there a chance my mother didn't kill the king?
And if so, who did?
What else could be true?

She had to find out.

DAKON

TWENTY-FOUR

"**G**et up child!" Cerene shouted, lightly shoving Dakon with a broom out of his straw bed. He hopped to his feet dizzily as the woman continued to move him along. "I will not be here to wake you up every morning, child. Hurry along, we need assistance with the stables. The prince will be riding this morning. Come along!"

Dakon, dirty and soot-stained, threw on his tunic and shoes, much tighter now than they had been only weeks ago. He mumbled something incoherently under the continued orders she gave him.

"It may be your name day, and you may be seven, but that is no excuse for laziness," she chastised him.

As he made his way out of the servants' quarters, Dakon ran toward the stables, more to escape Cerene's shrill voice than actually wanting to assist with the horses. He hated tending to them, they reeked, and their manure was more than he could shovel, often taking twice as long to clean up compared to the other stable boys who were much older and faster than him.

The sun was beating down on him harsher than it usually did this early in the morning, and the sweat prickling on the edge of his skin began to itch. He wished he could tear off his clothes and run to the pond in the gardens, anything to cool himself. He remembered the last time he tried that, Cerene had scolded him in front of the other children. He decided to keep his tunic on.

"Been sleeping nicely, haven't we?" Bernal, one of the stable boys, jeered. He was a skinny, but short boy, no older than thirteen with a few missing teeth and long unkempt blond hair. There were four of them including Dakon, readying the horses for the prince's arrival. The other boys snickered as they continued brushing the horses and fastening the saddles. The marshal was nowhere to be seen, most likely ensuring the other preparations were in order for the arrival of the prince and his men.

Dakon ignored Bernal, already wishing he was still in his bed, pokey straw and all. *I hate the stables.*

"Hey, boy, look at me when I'm talking. That woman don't teach you manners?" Bernal continued, walking over to him.

"I don't have to listen to you." Dakon picked up a shovel.

"Is that what your mother said?"

"She's not my mother." Dakon opened one of the stalls, getting a shovel full of the manure, trying his best to ignore him.

"That's right, your mother was a whore." The boys howled with laughter alongside Bernal.

"She was not a whore," he grumbled, trying and failing to remember that he must ignore the boy's taunts.

"She sure was, my father said she was a crowd favorite," one of the boys chimed in, and the laughter continued.

Dakon shoveled some of the manure aside, trying and failing to conceal his tears for a woman he did not truly remember, but who was the cause of much of the teasing he received. He felt that he could hate her, this random woman, who abandoned him as just a babe, to the servant's quarters no less.

"Do you think she'll give us a chance?" Bernal jeered, making gross gestures with his body. Dakon only saw red now, red for the shitty task he was on, red for the fact that he was the smallest, and red toward all of them.

"My mother was not a whore!" Dakon threw the contents of his shovel at the boy. It landed square on Bernal's face, covering him in filth. The stables fell silent as the other boys watched Bernal and Dakon with shock. Dakon immediately regretted what he did, watching the dung fall from Bernal's face, now turning a reddish, then purplish color.

"You fucking bastard!" Bernal leapt at Dakon, and he moved out of the way in the nick of time. He stumbled into the dirt, turning as Bernal lifted himself off the ground. Without a second thought, Dakon ran.

He ran as fast as his legs would carry him, pushing toward the gardens just east of the stables. Behind him, he heard the stable boys giving chase, yelling and hollering like the wild men from Cerene's stories. *Cerene.* She would surely punish him for this, but he couldn't think about that now.

"Get back here, ya bastard!" he heard the distant yelling of Bernal.

Perhaps Dakon would best them, perhaps he would be able to escape them. His heart burst with hope, and he willed his tired legs to run through the thick vegetation of the unkempt part of the gardens putting the castle at a distance behind him. He ran as if his life depended on it.

Dakon pushed through the wild berry bushes and boxwood shrubs. Winded and breathless now, he hid behind them facing the path he came on. He tried his best to catch his breath silently, his lungs feeling as if they were about to burst from his body. His limbs were shaking uncontrollably as he heard the boys tear through the nearby bushes. Then they, too, went silent.

"I bet you he's hiding here," one of the boys whispered not-so-discreetly.

"He'll come out if he thinks we've left," said another.

"Good idea, Hamish, start walking out of the bushes, me and Tomas will stay put."

Dakon turned slowly, weighing his options; he was at the corner of the castle's curtain wall, no escape except the way he came. His heart thundered, limbs trembling for he knew they would surely be waiting for him, to do only the gods knew what. There were no guards present that he could see, and even so, as a child he knew they were not there to protect squabbling servants.

He heard Hamish loudly pushing his way through the bushes, making a show of leaving toward the main path. When he was gone, Dakon could hear the steady, but heavy breathing of the others. Dakon couldn't let them find him, not here, not where they could do as they pleased. He slowly began to crawl back toward the wall, trying to put some distance between them. The bushes barely made a sound as he tediously, frustratingly made his slow retreat.

Then, to his dismay, his knee snapped a twig in two, and the boys who had been silently looking the other direction, turned toward him.

"Get him!" Bernal yelled.

Dakon stood to run, but Bernal was quicker, grabbing him by the neck of his tunic, his hands reeking of dung and filth. Instinctually, Dakon kicked him between the legs, giving him a precious second to flee as Tomas helped Bernal up. Dakon scrambled through the bushes once more, so fast that he could barely make out what was in front of him, trying to stay off the main path which he could no longer see through the entanglements of thicker vegetation.

Then he fell.

Dakon tumbled downward, falling down the side of a hill. By not paying attention to what was in front of him, he had barreled through a weak point in the stone curtain wall. Rock crumbled at his feet, giving way to the momentum and pressure his body gave. Grass and mud fresh from the previous evening's rain covered his small body as he continued flying down and into a ravine. He hit his head hard on the pebbles of a thin river at the bottom, and the world went black.

Hours later, the dark of night settled upon the lands, bringing with it the usual group of nocturnal animals and insects. A soft, furry body climbed onto Dakon's chest and began licking at his face. He awoke with a start, disoriented and confused, the water from the thin riverbank had soaked his clothes clean through and it pained him to sit up. A dog-like creature leapt down, staring at him with fierce orange eyes surrounded by thick, black fur.

Dakon stood, fear gripping his heart as he recalled the events from earlier. He looked back up the hill where the castle loomed like a prison in his sight. No one would be out looking for a servant boy, the guards wouldn't waste their time on him, this he knew, but the stable boys would be. The thought of what they would do to him struck fear, his body trembling once more.

The creature began to slink away, backing up slowly before making its way to the edge of the forest across the ravine. He watched it turn to face him once more. Inviting him, perhaps, he wasn't sure, but he knew that he was too scared to go back. Too scared to face the boys that would be waiting for his return, Cerene would be useless to help when he was alone with them again.

"What are they going to do to me?" he wondered aloud.

The dog stared but cocked its head as if it had heard him.

"They are going to kill me, I think," Dakon responded to nothing. He looked back once more at the castle, barely visible now in the darkness that prevailed. He only knew of life in the castle, his entire short life amounted to serving others who would never really see him. Maybe falling through the broken stone wall was a blessing in disguise. He turned to the dog.

"What is it like outside? Is it safe?"

The dog did nothing but sit and stare.

"You are no good," Dakon grumbled, tears pricking at his eyes. He was scared, he hated to admit it, but it was true. He was terrified of what awaited him, but he also knew that he was more terrified of what he didn't know. And as he stared at the dog and the pitch-black forest behind it, he realized that he was unsure of how to survive without the little comfort the castle provided. Scraps of food were easier to obtain when he worked near the kitchens than he expected it would be in the forest, where things from Cerene's stories could kill him in an instant.

"I'm going back," he said in a shaky voice, tears streaming down his little cheeks. "Thank you for nothing." The dog stared at him as he began making the trek up the hill, slipping down every few seconds due to the thick mud. By the time he made it to the top, he realized that the hole through the stone wall was enough for a single person to fit through but was covered in thick brush and bushes so tightly wound that it was nearly impossible to notice. It was weakened and needed to be fixed, certainly, but he would worry about that later, feign innocence if it was brought up.

He stared once more down the hill toward the dog, whose orange eyes he could still somehow see in the distance, before it finally disappeared into the forest.

Dakon made his way through the gardens, keeping an eye out for the stable boys and hoping against hope that they had given up their pursuit. A naive hope, but one he wished the gods would grant him, nonetheless. He made his way to the southern end of the castle taking the long way toward the servant's quarters, when he saw them.

The enchantress and her daughters were taking an evening stroll through the gardens. It was too late to move once they laid eyes on him.

"Are you lost?" the enchantress called out, her voice a beautiful lilt compared to the rough demeanors he had grown accustomed to.

Dakon stood silent, soaking wet and muddy from head to toe, ashamed and embarrassed at being found in this state.

"Is he okay, Mother?" the youngest girl asked.

"He was running away from someone," the other said matter-of-factly.

"Three boys from the looks of it, Clarisa," the enchantress agreed, making her way toward him.

"I didn't mean to throw it, I swear it," Dakon began to plead, but the enchantress hushed him softly.

"Of course you didn't. That was not a nice thing the boy said."

"I didn't mean to break the wall! I promise I didn't."

"He broke a wall?" the youngest asked. "How is that possible?"

"Shhh, Eve, mind your manners," the enchantress scolded her daughter. Eve went silent, her face pouty.

"The wall is quite old, Eve," Clarisa responded. "It is no surprise that a part of it would give way after centuries of being left to nature."

"Eve, please ask one of the servants for a tunic, quickly."

Eve rolled her eyes but ran off.

The enchantress studied Dakon's face, her brow knitted, and eyes narrowed. He felt a subtle calm wash over him and recalled his journey out and back through the wall. He kept recalling the memory, almost involuntarily, a few times before he found himself focused back on the present.

"I-I'm sorry, m'lady," Dakon mumbled, eyes downcast.

"There is nothing to apologize for, Dakon," the enchantress said, calmly. "I will not say anything of the wall if you don't."

Dakon let out a deep, shaky breath but felt comforted by her words. He stood a little taller, righting his shoulders as he became aware of what would happen should a guard or servant find him speaking to the ladies of the court in his state.

"Promise?" he asked quickly, hoping that she meant it.

Dakon looked into her soft, brown eyes, feeling lost in them momentarily, before she nodded. "Yes, of course."

Eve returned with some clothes bundled in her hands and handed them to Dakon. He bowed to the ladies, a bit clumsily. "Thank you."

Before they could respond, he took off, hoping that no one saw their exchange. Accepting gifts from the court was frowned upon, but he knew his current tunic was nowhere near a potential repair. He made a note to avoid the southern part of the castle from now on. And as he entered the servant's quarters, he was surprised to notice that no one questioned his whereabouts, and even more shocked that the stable boys seemed to ignore his very existence. Almost as if the interaction never occurred. He dared not test it, slinking into his room.

That night, he dreamed of the beautiful enchantress and of black dogs in dark forests.

Dakon opened his eyes to the darkness and the sound of a heavy door shutting and locking in place.

"They're gone," a gruff voice said.

Dakon blinked a few times, trying to remember the last few moments. His dream, or memory rather, became hazy and pushed slowly to the back of his mind. He was now lying under a table obscured only by a tablecloth. The darkness loomed around him, and he could hear movement nearby.

It all came back to him: he was not seven, but a grown man lost in the slums and had been knocked unconscious.

"Thank you, Muli. You may leave us now," a deep voice responded. It sounded like the voice of the robed man who spoke amongst the crowd earlier.

Dakon tried to control his breathing as he listened for how many people there could be. Were there only two now, four, six? He felt for the daggers still sheathed on his belt.

He heard another door open and shut as he presumed Muli left the remaining members. His pulse quickened, hoping they would not think to look under the table.

"As we know, the daughter of the enchantress has reached her age of maturity. The time has come for us to act, to bring her to our side before she is lost amongst the mortals for good," the robed man said.

Dakon held his breath. *Eve*, they were talking about Eve.

"Reyher, she has been amongst the mortals her entire life. No doubt poisoned by the pernicious lies of the court, there is nothing to suggest she would join our cause," said a woman's voice.

"Not willfully, of course," Reyher agreed. "We only need her blood. A sacrifice to appease the gods."

"What of her sister?" another, a man.

Three, at least, Dakon thought, *two men and a woman.*

"The protections of the Blackthorn are far too powerful at this time. We would spend more time trying to break it and risk losing our cause. We are in a precarious position," Reyher replied, a hint of frustration in his tone.

"She never received her mother's magic. What good is she to us—to Isila—if we sacrifice her? The goddess may see it as an affront," the woman again.

"Talesa, her lack of magic is not our concern. She is one of two known half-witches born in over half a century. She may not have magic, but her blood does. Any child that could outlive death's kiss is surely chosen by the goddess."

"My spies have successfully infiltrated the castle. They will inform me when the time is right," the unnamed man responded.

"Good," Reyher sighed.

"What of the other problem?" Talesa asked.

The room grew tense and quiet; Dakon slowly slid out one of the daggers.

"What of it?"

"I have heard reports that few members of our faction have gone astray. Killing recklessly without your order. Surely that will bring some *complications* to our cause."

"The noble killers?"

"Yes, the very same."

Dakon felt a tugging at his shoe, he looked down to see the black dog, pawing at him from the other side of the tablecloth. His heart began to race, sweat now trickling down from his temples as he tried to quietly, carefully push the dog away.

"Were you not the one who convinced me to let them into our circle to begin with?"

"We cannot fight without others in our cause."

The dog continued pulling at Dakon's shoe with its teeth, making growling noises at him.

"Shh, move, *please*," Dakon begged, his voice barely audible over the arguing between the witches.

Then Dakon heard a loud knock, and his heart nearly gave out, the fear now clutching it in an icy grip. He looked down toward his shoe, the dog was gone once more.

It was silent, still. He could only hear his heart beat in his ears. Then, Reyher spoke, loud and deep.

"We have a visitor amongst us."

ANA

TWENTY-FIVE

Ana walked out of Clarisa's chambers, offering a ghost of a smile as she passed Brisa and Tabor standing outside. "I am glad you all made it back safely," she said. It was a statement, nothing more.

They nodded and went inside, closing the door gently behind them, leaving her alone in the hall. She moved through the winding corridor, taking note of the misty darkness that cast a dim night light from the windows. The air inside was frigid and gave her goosebumps as she moved like a ghost through the halls. As she walked, a cat appeared in her shadow, walking behind, then alongside her. She peered down, it now fully formed next to her, and scooped it carefully into her arms.

Ana pet its dark fur, soft and delicate in the candlelight that lined the halls and quickened her pace. The cat rubbed its head against her, a reminder to calm down and slow her movements. She didn't wish to draw any attention but felt as if the eyes of thousands were upon her. It was unsettling.

She continued until she found a door at the far end of the castle and pushed against the thick frame to let herself inside. Ana climbed the winding steps leading to the top of a solitary tower in the east wing overlooking the Dallise Sea. The cat jumped out of her arms and gracefully landed on all fours before proceeding into the center of the room.

It was a private chamber, fit for a royal, a certain royal. Ana took a few steps inside, gingerly taking in the expensive furnishings, the remarkable view of the sea from the sky-high balcony, and ran her fingertips along the sheets of the large bed as she passed it.

"How do you like it?" a masculine voice drawled from behind her.

Ana's breath hitched, and she turned quickly to face Prince Navir, who was now in nothing but a dark blue robe he was fastening lazily along his trim waist. For a brief moment, her eyes lingered on him, remembering clearly what she had to do. What she needed to do.

She batted her lashes coyly at him as he closed the distance.

"It is breathtaking, Your Highness," she said, masking her hesitancy.

He smiled as his eyes burned into hers. "Do you think anyone saw us?"

"No, Your Highness, I made sure to take the long way here."

"Good." He kissed her lips softly. Ana leaned in for more, knowing her part well, but he moved his head back assessing her. She lifted her lips and tilted her head. This seemed to please him, and he beckoned her toward the balcony.

There was a slight breeze, and the rain began to pick up, but he stood out there barefoot with nothing but his robe on. The rain dampened his dark hair, and he lifted his head up to the sky, letting it fall down his face. Ana stood confused, but followed him outside, not liking the feeling of getting wet, of the rain washing away the perfume she wore for this occasion.

"I thought cats were supposed to hate getting wet," she teased as she brushed her damp hair out of her face.

Navir smirked, turning toward her. "Good thing I'm not a cat right now."

"True," she sighed, this evening was turning out much differently than she expected. "What is it you're hoping to see out here?"

165

"Nothing, really."

They both stared out at the water a short distance away, the waves gently rocking along with the wind. The night was young, but no one meandered the grounds, focused more on getting their rest, than dealing with another night of torrential rain.

"I'm glad you asked me to come here. I've been wondering if I have been boring you lately."

"It's not every day that I need your assistance."

"How many people have been up here?" Ana pressed, trying not to be conspicuous. A dread rose within her hoping Clarisa never ventured along this part of the castle.

"In my chambers?"

"Yes."

Navir shook his head. "I don't know, between staff and members of the coven, it's hard to keep track."

"Have any women been here?"

"My mother is a woman."

Ana sighed deeply, not wanting the answer to the question equally as much as she wanted to know. "I mean, other women. There are . . . rumors."

Navir turned to her, lifting her chin slightly. "My dear, sweet Ana. You don't listen to silly rumors, do you? I thought you were far too sophisticated for that; I must have been mistaken."

"I didn't say I believed them, Your Highness. I only meant that I heard about your affairs and thought you should know."

Navir nodded, contemplatively.

"Does Clarisa know?"

Ana's heart sank. "Clarisa?"

"Yes, does she hear these rumors? Has she told you anything?"

"No, nothing." She breathed a sigh of relief. "Most of the coven still avoids her, and who can blame them?" Ana placed her hand in Navir's, trying to sound convincing. "She has the prize we all want."

"Clarisa is only a means to an end." Navir tightened his jaw, pulling his hand away.

"I know."

"She has what was supposed to be mine," Navir snarled. "It's something a simple witch like you couldn't understand."

Ana rolled her eyes before she could think to stop herself.

Navir squeezed her face between his hand, suddenly, forcefully. "Am I bothering you?"

Ana's breath caught before she replied, "N-no, Your Highness."

"Are you sure? Your rolling eyes suggest otherwise."

Ana was speechless, unable to think of how to stop this from escalating and began stumbling over apologies.

"I can't hear you over the groveling, and you know how much I hate groveling." He released her, shoving her face a little too forcefully aside.

"I–I am sorry to have offended you. I want nothing more than to make you happy in any way I can."

Navir glared at her. "You've seen what happens to people who disappoint me. I would hate it if you disappointed me." There was a deadly tone to his words, a venom that chilled Ana.

Malin.

"I know."

"I didn't expect my mother to be the jealous type." He smirked. "It appeared the mortal and him couldn't keep their hands off each other for days. A strand of her hair and drops of your potion had him lusting after her like a dog in heat."

Ana only nodded. Remembering her involvement leading to them getting caught at the wrong place, at the wrong time, by the right people.

"I'm talking to you, Ana," he growled.

"Yes. I'm sorry, My Prince."

"You serve me, remember?"

"I remember."

Ana hadn't let herself think about it too much, but as Navir glared at her, she wondered if perhaps she might know too much now. She needed to prove herself useful, prove that she was worth keeping alive.

"Do you? Because it seems like you are forgetting the whole reason you are back here. And if you can't do my bidding, then I may not have any use for you."

Ana nodded, tears pricking at her eyes, she knew that she was there to spy on Clarisa, that her entire duty was to maintain her trust, help her claim her power that she was too afraid to explore, but it was proving difficult. She had fallen in love with Clarisa months ago, much to her detriment. The only way to keep her alive now was to keep up pretenses with Navir.

She thought of how she could salvage this night, and blinked away her tears, thankful that the rain disguised them.

"I will one day rule in place of my mother. The covens need a true witch, one who has been born and raised in the craft to lead them against the mortals wishing to destroy us. Clarisa is the key to gaining my true power. If you are not on my side, then you are against me."

"I am always with you, My Prince."

He clenched his jaw, the rain falling down the ends of his tendrils. "She is the only half-witch in our possession. Her blood will bring us the grimoire."

"Yes"—Ana nodded, carefully considering her words—"the prophecy says you need blood of a half-witch."

"Are you mocking me?"

"No, Your Highness. But a word of caution. Her dying would rid you of *long-term* possibilities."

Navir froze, looking down at her with widened eyes before narrowing them warily. "Are you suggesting we keep her alive?"

"I am only suggesting that you do what you need to rule." She looked back at him with equal frankness, getting so close they were practically drawing the same breath. "Imagine what you could do with a half-witch dedicated to serving you. If her blood can resurrect gods, what else can it be used for?"

Navir's brows furrowed, ruminating over Ana's words. She needed to change the subject, and quickly.

"Let us not forget that I am powerful, too."

Ana pulled the string of the robe loose and placed her hands gently on Navir's chest as she kept her eyes locked on his. He watched as she began to slowly morph into something else, someone else, that she knew he so desperately desired. In seconds, Ana's black hair became several shades lighter, her brown eyes darkened ever slightly; she appeared as Clarisa in his arms. She touched him gently, and raised her hands behind his neck, brushing her fingers through his wet hair. She brought her face close to his, blinking away the raindrops on her lashes before locking her lips with his. He kissed her passionately, desperately, as if he had been waiting for this moment for lifetimes. The rain beat down on them as they were tangled in each other.

"You are lucky I'm in a good mood," Navir breathed between kisses.

"Let me take you to a better one," she whispered, biting his lip softly.

Ana could feel the magic within her, coursing through her veins, making her feel far more powerful than she had moments ago. She would keep Clarisa alive, no matter what it took.

Navir lifted Ana up, and she wrapped her legs tight around his waist. They continued kissing, falling deeper into their passionate embrace as he carried her inside.

EVÆ
TWENTY-SIX

I t was risky, she knew, carrying a book like this, even hidden in a satchel, but Eve was determined to scour the royal library for texts that could support what the grimoire showed her. It was late and she would be left unbothered at such an hour. Thoughts of Dakon entered her mind, to question him, but the idea of approaching him, confirming what she knew in heart to be true was too much. She had to do this on her own.

Eve walked into the darkened, large space, empty of its scribes and their apprentices in the odd time between twilight and dawn. She visited the library often, caring to sit amongst the texts and scrolls, learning about the history of Givensmir, the bloody battles and wars fought, the betrayals, the victories, the alliances. All things far more interesting to imagine in her head as she devoured the pages than anything her tutors lectured her about. To the annoyance of her handmaids, she was rather fond of reading, but never in her room, where books gifted to her throughout the years regarding the expectations of noble women and intricacies of needling sat untouched.

Girls of the court were expected to be well read and astute in order to bolster their marriage prospects and strengthen the alliances of their families. Yet, as she grew, she realized that women here were expected to be vessels of knowledge, not orators of them.

Eve felt as if eyes of the texts were watching her every move, expecting her to slip from her mortal veil. She calmed her nerves, breathing slowly, and cradling the bag tightly to her chest as she walked.

For days, she reflected on the night of the wedding announcement when everyone froze around her. She had almost convinced herself that it did not happen, that the shock of the evening caused her to hallucinate the freeze. Nothing like it had ever happened before, after all.

When it came to the matter of the ashes and the letter. She convinced herself that the handmaid had already lit the note on fire and hid the ashes in her pocket, attempting to use Adriana's fireplace to dispose of them. Unusual, but not impossible.

But the book, this grimoire, appearing in her room . . .

She was not so sure anymore.

Despite all the excuses she fabricated, there was something about those instances that pulled at her carefully orchestrated facade. It scared her.

The library was quiet in the late evening, and Eve did not hear a single soul as she moved around the shelves and tables. Candlelight was still aflame throughout the space, casting long, dark shadows throughout the room. They followed her.

Eve picked up one of the lone candles, and moved toward the dark, back portion of the library. She was not sure why she planned to go here, only that something, a force, perhaps, tugged her in that direction.

The scrolls and texts of this part were full of dust and cobwebs, untouched and most likely neglected for many years. She brushed it away and read the bindings of a few.

THE HISTORIES OF HOUSE EBRON—YEAR 200 THRU YEAR 750

KING BYRON III—LESSONS IN THE ART OF PATIENCE AND REVERENCE

TALES OF THE SHREWD GODS

ROCIO CARRANZA

ON THE GODDESS OF TRICKERY AND MAGIC—AN EXCERPT OF CONFESSIONS BY BLACKTHORN WITCHES

THE ERA OF ENCHANTMENT—A RECOUNTING OF THE ROYAL ENCHANTRESS'S TIME IN GIVENSMIR

She pulled the last one free from the shelf and turned it over in her hands. It was lighter than her grimoire, but the weight of it on her soul felt heavy.

Was this something she wanted to do?

Would she be better off tossing her book in the fire and returning this, going back to her blissful life at court?

She sat on the floor setting her candle down carefully beside her and read.

It is this scribe's expert opinion, upon researching the rumors, writings, and accounts of the royal court of Givensmir, as well as interrogations of imprisoned witches prior to their executions, that this text contains the most accurate depiction of the years 792-814, hereafter referred to as the Era of the Enchantress.

This work has been reviewed by the Gold Council to ensure our histories are reflected accurately and with care to the subject.

The following is a summation of the text in its entirety:

Centuries following the Era of Great Upheaval, witches and their craft were considered legends and folklore. The Blackthorn kingdom was regarded as home to cannibals, chaos-worshippers, and other sorts of feral beasts across the Dallise Sea. Magic was no longer in existence, and merchants who claimed to trade with the Blackthorn, though no solid evidence of such trade has been provided to this council, swore they were as mortal as any other. 'Witches are no more, the old king saw to that,' a common phrase amongst the Givensmir commonfolk.

In early 792, rumors abounded of a young girl who possessed extraordinary powers—gifts of telepathy, mind-reading, and clairvoyance—from the Blackthorn. It must be noted that this, too, was the very year Givensmir warred with Mytar. King Byron III ordered the witch be found and brought to him, against the pleading of his council. Witches, while predominantly folklore, still imparted fear and distrust amongst the people. 'It will anger the gods to indulge this folly, even if it were true,' Ser Leon James, Commander of the Armies, was rumored to have said.

Despite the opposition, the young witch, Lucia, was found disembarking a pirate ship from Catalina's Port, and came willingly. Rumors of her magic proved true, and every battle thereafter won by her ability to foresee the events and advise on changes to plans to ensure Givensmir's victory against Mytar. Thereafter, the king bestowed on Lucia the title of Givensmir's First Royal Enchantress, Blood of the Blackthorn, and Heart of Givensmir. King Byron quickly married her to a political ally in the court, Marcelo Rubianes, Lord of Rubianes Keep, to secure his province from a brewing civil war. The rise in taxes for lands east of the Mytar mountains sparked discontent amongst the citizens of Rubianes. Following the marriage, the king ordered taxes be lowered.

The royal enchantress was held in high regard amongst the court but was met with stark dislike among the people. They did not trust a witch from suspicious lands and an equally suspicious background. Not much is known from the royal enchantress that was not explicitly stated by her, and she held few spoken words of record outside of her advice to the king. During her twenty-two years as the royal enchantress, Lucia aided in the expansion of Givensmir to three more kingdoms—Mytar, Zafira, and Larrea—and aided in settling unrest amongst those who proclaimed civil war. King Byron III achieved what many could not, using the enchantress as his formidable weapon to maintain control.

The enchantress was not expected to birth children, as the histories of witch and mortal pairings were believed to be fatal to both mother and child. Yet, when it was announced that she had birthed a daughter, successfully, it was celebrated as a miracle amongst the court. 'The gods have brought favor among our lands!' the king is witnessed to have proclaimed to the Gold Council.

The daughter, Clarisa, inherited her mother's magic, and gathered significant devotion from those attending her. When a second daughter was born, it was met with equal anticipation, the king eagerly awaiting two half-witches with magic that could very well mean his and his heir's victory in all future conquests. His disappointment is well-documented upon discovering the second born, Eve, resembled her father—mortal—in all but his likeness.

Reports suggest the enchantress killed King Byron III through poison, seeking power and vengeance after years restrained at court. His son, the now-King Eryck heroically prevented her escape, slaying the witch in the process with the legendary dagger, "Mortal Defense."

Clarisa, aged twelve, disappeared shortly thereafter under mysterious circumstances. As of this writing, she has not been found and is presumed dead. Eve remains a ward of the court under Lord Marcelo's charge.

Eve closed the text, her chest rising and falling quickly as she attempted to control her breathing. All these events were not new to her but reading them again held new meaning she did not realize. She was not sure if she could trust it anymore.

She grabbed Blood of the Blackthorn again, opening it to the last page she left off at and tried to touch every bit of the page she could. Trying and failing to get it to replicate the magic of the previous night, trying to force the truth from it, the whole truth that was hidden from the Givensmir texts.

But nothing happened.

"Damn you, damn you," she seethed. In a fit of rage, she pushed on the book once more, setting it ablaze with her fingers.

Eve stood quickly, shocked, dropping the burning book in the process. Red and orange flames enveloped it, the sounds of the roaring flames took over, curling the pages into themselves, blackening them in the intense heat.

No!

She stepped on it, trying her best to extinguish the fire, to salvage any bit of the book that remained.

"Stop, stop, stop!" she pleaded, louder than she intended.

The flames grew and began to crawl along the floor like a demon searching for something to feed on. It engulfed the scrolls and books on the shelves, taking them into its fiery embrace. Eve quickly moved back, the heat singing the edges of her hair, and she closed her eyes, arms out defensively in front of her.

She would be discovered; this is how they would find out what she was. *"Burn with it,"* a voice said, *"or burn for them."*

"No!" she screamed. "Stop! Stop!"

Then, time held still once more, her heart pounding in her chest the only thing she could hear.

Eve lowered her arms, carefully opening her eyes to behold what became of the library. But nothing was amiss, the grimoire on the ground before her as if it never took to flame at all. She breathed shakily, as she reached out her hand to touch it.

Her heart nearly stopped when it disappeared and there was a knock on the entrance door of the library. "Lady Eve? Are you here?" It was one of the court guards.

She looked back where the book had been, confirming it was indeed gone. "Y-yes, I am!"

Eve stood quickly, standing just in time to see the guard approach. "My lady, Lord Marcelo has arrived and requests your presence in his chambers."

She stood shakily before the guard, trying her best to breathe calmly.

Her father, the man who turned her mother in all those years ago, was back in Givensmir.

DAKON
TWENTY-SEVEN

Dakon held the daggers fiercely in his clammy hands, waiting for them to surround him, waiting for the moment to strike. He dared to sneak a peek under the tablecloth, watching as the group rose from their chairs.

"I sense that he is here," the unnamed man said. He was tall and broad shouldered, with burn marks on his face and down his neck. He turned his face in Dakon's direction, and even took a step toward him. Dakon held his breath, trying to remain as quiet as possible.

"Then let us meet him, Ivan," Reyher said, grasping his arm.

Ivan narrowed his eyes, holding still for a moment, before he followed the other two out of the room, moving further into the building.

Dakon waited for them to return, waited for them to catch him as the unknown visitor listening in on their conversation. His heartbeat was erratic, thundering in his ears, unrelenting in his rising panic that he tried to quell.

They will find you if you stay. They will not let you leave alive.

He had to move fast, go out the way he came in, the large door to the front. He peered under the tablecloth once more, ensuring the three were truly gone before he slipped quietly from under the table. Dakon rushed to the large front doors, bolted by a thick brass lock. He pulled it, but it was stuck. He could hear the group beginning to return, their footsteps and whispers louder now.

He grabbed the lock with both hands now, struggling against it, using all his might.

"You there! What are you doing?!" he heard the angry shouts and running steps.

With everything he had in him, he thrusted the lock toward him once more, and it gave way.

A hand grasped his neck as he shoved the door open. Then, a blinding light and the screech of one of the Strix members as he wriggled free and began to bolt toward the bridge.

"He burned me! My hand! My hand!"

Dakon ran for his life.

Never daring to look back.

Somehow over the course of the night, he made his way back to the castle, sneaking his way to the servant's quarters as the light of day peeked through the trees. So panic stricken was he, that he did not stop running until he reached his room, sweaty and gasping for breath. Pazel turned just in time to catch him, red-faced and clearly hungover, but alive, nonetheless.

"For the love of—you scared us shitless, Dakon!"

He grabbed Dakon by the shoulders, inspecting and assessing him. "I thought you were dead! I'm truly sorry. Never again, I swear to you."

Dakon only nodded, he fought to keep his eyes open, the entirety of the night finally catching up to him as he spoke. "Pirates. Witches. Strix. Eve."

"A pirate?! Dakon you are a man amongst men, truly. Kilian will be relieved when he hears you made it. He felt terrible leaving you."

Pazel's words were garbled as he spoke, and Dakon's vision blurred, his head throbbing. He fell to the ground from pure exhaustion and the aftermath of rigid panic seizing any control his mind warred for. There was so much to say, not enough time, he needed to tell Eve. Tell her about the Strix and their plans.

"Dakon! He is burning! Someone help!" He could faintly hear Pazel's yells and footsteps as another voice cried out for a healer.

So much to say, but the only words that passed Dakon's lips were: "Tell, I need to . . ."

Then Dakon drifted off to a seemingly endless slumber of darkness and despair.

⚜

He awoke with a jolt, sweat dripping down from his temples as he tried to control his breathing. The room around him was cold, the dawn barely approaching but still a short time away, the other servants sleeping on their own piles of straw around him. It all came back to him in sudden, terrifying moments—an uprising, the Strix in the capital, their plan to kidnap Eve. *Eve.*

A pain resurfaced in his head, and he squinted his eyes shut trying to will it away. Dakon needed to do something, anything. He could not stay quiet while chaos threatened the realm, but how?

Cerene. She would know what to do, surely.

He stood, slid on his boots, and quietly tip-toed around the sleeping servants in their shared room. His skin was hot to the touch despite the feeling of the dank and dreary space. Perhaps, she would have a cure for a novice familiar tethered to a fire witch too.

EVE
TWENTY-EIGHT

E ve's father looked much older than she last remembered—dark circles under his eyes, deep-set wrinkles, and a tired smile.

"Good evening, my daughter."

He walked toward her on a cane taking considerable effort to move. She had heard of the injury he sustained in battle, losing a foot to infection, and breathed a sigh of relief that it was not his life that was taken instead, despite everything else that warred within her about him.

Eve moved to assist him, but he raised his hand toward her.

"I can still embrace my daughter on my own." He gave her a brief hug and kissed her temple before gesturing her to sit. He made a pained effort to sit across the desk from her, assessing her with his dark blue eyes.

"You have grown since I last saw you."

Eve nodded, unsure of how to reply.

"Thank you. How is Natalia and your son?"

"Your brother, you mean."

"Yes."

"Isidro is quite a handful, a mischievous little boy. But who isn't at four?"

Eve gave a faint smile. "Of course."

"I would like it if you spent some time with your stepmother and your brother. I think it would do you good."

Thoughts of Clarisa entered her head, the conversation her mother had with the king on his deathbed. She paid little mind to what her father was actually saying. She was far more focused on getting back to her chambers and finding out how the book worked, to go back and see what else it offered of her mother.

"Eve. Eve, are you listening to me?"

She lifted her head distractedly. "Yes, Father, apologies. I have not slept much."

Her father looked at her curiously, his eyes narrowed. "Does this have to do with Lord Callum?"

Eve stared into her father's eyes; she knew he approved of the match; Lord Callum admitted to receiving his blessing before asking her. She wondered if her response would have carried any weight at all. Marriage contracts were not particularly up for debate with women in the court . . .

"No, I—" She wasn't sure what to say, really. "I am quite fond of Lord Callum."

"Good, it is high time you be wed. In truth, I thought the king would have married you to one of his sons, but it was not to be."

"No, it was not." She wished the conversation to be over. To be back in the room, opening the book, touching its pages . . .

"So, if it is not Lord Callum that concerns you, what keeps my daughter up at night?"

Eve returned her father's disapproving gaze and decided to go for a different approach.

"I only wish Mother would have been here, to celebrate my betrothal."

Her father's eyes widened and narrowed quickly; he took in a deep breath.

"Your mother . . . well, she made her choices."

"Why?"

Her father pinched the bridge of his nose, squeezing his eyes tight before responding.

"I know," he began slowly, methodically, "that she wished for a power that did not belong to her."

When Eve did not reply, he continued, "It is by the grace of the gods that you are alive. And, might I remind you, by the mercy of the king, that you were not executed alongside her as her kin."

"Does the daughter of a traitor become the traitor herself?"

"No, however, her kind was not particularly welcome, and she did you a disservice with her actions. Actions that took years of mending and you as the king's ward to fix. Any lesser house would have not been given this second chance."

"And I am grateful, truly. I only wish—I only wonder if, maybe, perhaps, there was a reason for her actions."

"There is no good reason for treason, Eve." Her father shook his head. "It was my responsibility to the realm and your future that she be turned in. I could have lost you, too, had I not."

"Did you ever speak to her, before she did it?"

"I tried, but I fear she was too far gone by then, avoiding me at all costs, unless she was speaking about how we needed to escape."

"Escape?"

"Yes, she was fervently intent on trying to flee, certain that staying here would be dangerous. When King Byron, may he rest with the gods, fell ill unexpectedly, and I caught your mother trying to escape, it was then that I knew. I did not want to believe it, of course, and regrettably delayed my response because of it. For had I acted sooner, history would have been different." He paused, shaking his head as if the memory pained him. "Magic is a curse, never forget that."

"But Clarisa—"

"We do not know what would have become of Clarisa had she gained full control of her magic," he replied solemnly, "but as I have told you many times before, she is no longer with us. Do not torment this old man to revisit such a heartbreak."

Eve nodded, having heard all this before. Clarisa was smuggled out of the kingdom by someone her mother trusted, never to be seen again. Eve shuddered at the thought, tears threatening to surface.

"I love you, Eve, as I did your sister," her father said, the corners of his eyes glistening. "It has always been my greatest regret to not save her, I hope you know this."

Eve nodded, trying unsuccessfully to keep her tears at bay.

"I never wish for you to come to any harm. It is my vow as your father to always protect you, and I hope in that I have been successful."

"You have, Father."

He reached up, squinting his eyes to mask the pain his body had at the motion, and wiped a tear from her cheek. "Do not worry, my child, aside from appearance, you are nothing like your mother. You are good, you are kind, and if my accountant is correct, you have an inkling toward the finer things."

She let out a small, unexpected laugh between her tears, and he took it in kind, smiling.

"Now, tell me about Lord Callum."

DAKON

TWENTY-NINE

D akon approached Cerene's room and raised his knuckles to knock on the door.

"Come in, Dakon," he heard her say from within.

He opened the door slowly, peeking in at first. He had been here many times before, but for some reason, it felt intrusive for him to be here today.

Cerene's room was small, barely able to fit a small, straw bed, a stool, and a thin, flimsy wardrobe where her clothes and personal belongings were stored. She sat upon the bed, her hands folded in her lap as if she had been waiting.

Dakon stepped inside.

"I am sorry, it's early I know," he stammered.

"There is no apology to be made." She looked up at him. "I have been expecting you. Sit." She gestured to the stool.

He sat as she studied him.

"I am afraid my time is limited, and with so much to say, I do not know where to begin."

"I saw them," Dakon breathed, a shudder went involuntarily through his body. "The witches. They are building an army to take over the mortals."

She reached a hand out to him, then upon her fingers touching his skin, retracted them quickly.

"You need to control your magic." She handed him a cup, and he drank its contents. It felt cool and calming; he could feel the heat of his skin simmer down to normal.

"What was that?"

"Water"—she laughed—"with a bit of lavender. Lesson two, sometimes what is practical can be magical."

He laughed for a moment forgetting about his worries.

"They are called the Strix." Cerene held his hands gently. "They were banished from the Blackthorn centuries ago. Dabbled in dangerous magic, killing many witches in the process."

"They spoke of kidnapping Eve, something about her being the enchantress's daughter. What should I do?"

"You save her, that is your duty. You are bound to this witch, Dakon, that is not to be taken lightly. Her death could spell your ruin."

"Why did you not die with the enchantress?"

"I do not know, but some of my magic was lost."

"I don't understand."

"Every spell we do, every bit of magic we use, requires sacrifice. Some sacrifices are small, a minute lost, a piece of your soul. Others can be fatal. We thought sacrificing her power would be sufficient to bind Eve's magic, but she began to show signs of it returning. And when the last king was dying and the fates of her and her daughters seemed bleak, we did another, stronger, binding spell."

"And she sacrificed herself instead," Dakon breathed.

"Yes." Cerene nodded woefully.

"How can I keep her alive?"

"You must take her, far from here."

"I do not have money for passage."

184

Cerene stood and walked slowly to the wardrobe. She opened it, tinkering around with different items inside. She pulled out a small bag and placed it in Dakon's hands.

He opened it, revealing more gold and silver coins than he had ever beheld in his life.

"Cerene, how did you? I–I can't."

"You must and you will. There is something else in there too."

He fumbled through the coins and picked out a small book from it. No larger than his hand. He opened it revealing written instructions and depictions of creatures, plants, and even some humans. It was a book of spells. *This is real*, he reminded himself. It felt as if it was worth more in his hands than the coins.

"She has a book of her own. It will appear and disappear for her, until she can learn to properly summon it. Do not let it consume her."

"What if she doesn't want to come?"

"She will. And you will have to help her."

"Will I be able to?"

"That is only up to you."

Dakon nodded and stood. "Thank you, Cerene. I will never forget this." He gave her a fierce hug, being mindful of her frail state.

She held his face between her hands. "You have been much like a son to me. It has been my life's privilege to raise you."

Dakon kissed her on the forehead and began to walk from the room.

"One last thing," she said from behind him, and he turned to face her once more.

"Yes?"

She looked pensive and grave. "I will be killed in two days' time. Do not stop it. Do not change it. For my sacrifice is needed to protect you and Eve."

His heart dropped, "Cerene, no—"

"It is done, Dakon. Do not let my death be for nothing."

THEO

THIRTY

Theo stalked down the halls toward Eryce's chambers ready to accompany him to the sparring room, unnerved by his conversation with Adriana. His mind was plagued by thoughts of him and Eve, combing through them for any possibility of witchcraft on her part, but came up empty. Surely, Adriana was paranoid, unnerved by the news that she may be betrothed herself soon.

He moved quickly, noticing the rise of the sun through the open windows of the empty corridors—most guards were switching their posts, moving from night shift to day. His lack of sleep meant a grueling, but earlier rise than normal, hoping that his brother would distract him from the horrid thoughts that now seeped into him.

As he was about to turn the corner, he heard the creak of an opening door and stopped in his tracks. Lord Callum, disheveled in a white tunic, was slowly walking out of Eryce's chambers. Theo dashed quickly behind the corner, peeking out to make sense of what he was witnessing.

Eryce followed, pulling Callum back toward him gently. Theo watched as he touched Callum's face and kissed him. They whispered something to each other before Callum rushed out toward the opposite end of the corridor. Eryce quickly disappeared, closing the door behind him.

Theo stood, rigidly. He had no time to truly process his thoughts before a familiar voice spoke behind him.

"Good morning, Brother."

Theo turned startled, beholding Marc's smug face.

"It seems we now share the same secret."

Theo narrowed his eyes. "Who else knows?"

"Well, you, now." Marc smirked, before feigning shock. "Oh, did you mean who else? That is not my secret to tell, unfortunately."

Theo grabbed Marc by his collar, pushing him against the wall. "I will not play games with you, Marc!"

Marc snickered. "Games? We haven't played together since we were boys, Theo. Why start now?"

Theo felt his blood rise, and debated between punching him or letting him go. After a long moment, he lowered his head and took a deep breath, releasing Marc. "Tell me now."

Marc brushed himself off, tilting his head at Theo as he did so. "Men have *urges*, Theo, or did Father never talk to you about that?"

"I am not Eryce, I have no qualms with beating you right here." Theo's nostrils flared, and admittedly a small part of him wanted Marc to push him past the edge.

"Our brother is heir to this throne. Father is sick and old. What Eryce does with his time is of much importance to many people including our enemies. You would be a fool to think no one else suspects."

Theo's blood ran cold. "Is Callum one of our enemies?"

"Anyone who isn't us is a threat."

Theo bit his cheek, and paced before Marc, trying to make sense of the information. "Kings have had affairs for as long as time. This is nothing new."

"Validation? Is that what you choose? You are stupider than I thought."

"It's true, though."

"It is also true that Father has beheaded men for less. Do you think this information would stop him now? He has two other sons to choose from, *heirs and spares.*"

"You will say nothing!"

"I have not said anything, yet."

"All you have clamored for our entire lives is power, being a prince is not enough, you must doom your kin as well?"

"Eryce is not fit to sit on the throne."

"And you are?"

"We both know I have the courage to do what needs to be done."

"Only a coward would wish for war when he is safe behind his gates."

"Don't tempt me, Brother. I am more powerful than you know."

Theo and Marc held their deadly glares in a brooding tension.

"What has held you back, why are you biding your time with this secret?" Theo demanded.

"Perhaps, I do care for our family. We are bound by blood are we not?"

"You are not a benevolent man. Blood on your hands would mean more to you than those you share it with." Theo shoved Marc, his rage getting the better of him.

Then he felt the cool, sharp sensation of a blade on his neck. Marc smirked, holding the dagger out with a practiced hand, training it on Theo's flesh. Theo tensed, barely able to breathe without feeling the pinch of steel.

"Blood is blood. Inside our bodies, or out. In the end, it always comes out. You would do well to remember that, Brother. The walls have eyes, and they all belong to me. This *situation* is barely scratching the surface. And while you would sit and clean up Eryce's mess, I am busy making sure mine stays intact."

Loud footsteps echoed toward them. Theo met Marc's eyes, and watched as he slowly withdrew the dagger, placing it inside his belt.

"And that is how you surprise your enemies, Theo," Marc said in an uncharacteristically charming tone.

Theo stared at him bewildered and confused.

"I'm glad to see both my brothers finally getting along," Eryce quipped as he approached them, a genuine smile on his face.

Theo took two short breaths, and instinctively lifted his hands to his neck, feeling where the blade had just been. Marc placed an arm around Theo's shoulders hugging him close and returning Eryce's grin.

"As I told Theo. We are bound by blood."

ADRIANA
THIRTY-ONE

"Thank you, Princess. We are eternally grateful to the king." It was a common, and expected phrase, told to her frequently during her charity visits. A few times a year, she and the ladies at court would visit the common folk, bequeathing them coins, sustenance, and materials from the castle, all while ensuring her father was given the credit. The common folk believed it was due to his generosity and praised him for it, despite the fact that he never showed up to any of the events.

This portion of the charity required her to sit at a long table on a pavilion in the city square, greeting a few members of the crowd and providing them with a gift of their choosing from the table. They only had two items left, a bushel of vegetables and some fabrics.

She looked around, seeing familiar faces on her side of the pavilion. Her guards, those of her mother, a few ladies of the court, and Dakon. He was clad in a rather humiliating ensemble of loose-fitting, bright-colored clothing. She tried to avoid looking his way, her heart unable to bear how much it killed him to be seen by her this way. He had been avoiding her recently, and she wondered if he found out about her kiss with Timothy. She hoped not. Yet, he was present to entertain the crowd through song, and his voice was the only thing that lifted her spirits, slightly.

"Smile, my dear," her mother told her through a rigid smile of her own. "Wouldn't want to stir any trouble now, would we?"

Adriana internally rolled her eyes but smiled nonetheless to the man who selected the vegetables. "Many blessings to you and your family."

The man bowed generously, and followed the direction of the guard, walking down the steps and toward a couple of children.

The guards sent up an old woman next, who feebly climbed the steps with her cane. The sun beat down on the crowd, and the princess fanned herself, cursing whoever invented heavy dresses and thick fabrics. Sweat trickled down her brow and she used her handkerchief to wipe it away.

Finally, the woman made her way in front of the queen and bowed as well as she could, given her condition. "Good afternoon, My Queen, Your Highness. Many thanks to your blessings."

"We are pleased to hear it, please, the fabrics are yours"—her mother gestured to the piles of fabric left to carry—"though we can arrange for someone to take it to your home."

"Home? Oh, My Queen, you are mistaken."

"Where would you like us to send them, then?" Her mother looked impatient, and Adriana wished she could be back in her chambers, out of the sun, and away from this awkward conversation.

The old woman smiled tightly and shook her head. "I come not for your fabrics, but for your heads."

Adriana snapped her head toward the woman. Surely, she misheard her. "What?" her mother gasped.

"Your heads," the woman repeated.

Fear gripped Adriana's heart, and she barely had time to look up, before the crowd began descending on the man with the bushel of vegetables. Cries and screams rang out, and the queen no sooner rose, than the old woman began cackling as she transformed into a large, grotesque man.

Burn marks covered his body, large portions of his skin disfigured and vile.

"A witch!" someone from the crowd yelled. Her mother screamed and in seconds the queen's guard rushed the man, sending his body off the pavilion. The crowd started to climb the steps to Adriana and her mother.

"Run! Run, My Queen!" one of the guards screamed before becoming overwhelmed by the sheer mass of people before him. Most of the court ran in different directions in utter chaos.

Adriana and her mother ran to their carriage, where the guards rushed to meet them. Her mother entered first, and all Adriana could hear were the feral shrieks of the crowd close behind.

She reached out her hand to her mother, taking a step into it, before someone leapt at her dress skirts, pulling her to the ground.

"Help, Mother!" she shrieked, panic gripping her as she kicked the man in the face. One of her guards stabbed the man with his sword and began fighting with another, and another.

Her mother's guard, trying to fight off the growing crowd, closed the carriage door and rushed her mother off to safety before he, too, became overwhelmed.

"Adriana!" her mother screamed from the carriage.

Adriana stood quickly, running toward the carriage with her guard in tow, but a man jumped upon him. They were immersed in a brawl, and Adriana kept running, turning just in time to see the man crush her guard's skull with a large stone. She screamed, horrified, and the man looked up.

"There's one of them!" he pointed toward her, and a few members of the crowd began to run.

"Wait, wait!" she shrieked toward the carriage, but it was too late, it turned a corner and was out of sight.

Adriana's blood was pumping, running as fast as she could into one of the buildings. It seemed empty as she shoved herself inside.

Turning quickly, she set her eyes on a large table and shoved it with all her might in front of the door. Hoping and praying to the gods that it would hold the people back, at least until the guards came back for her.

But what if they don't? The thought clutched her, squeezing her with panic, and she started to shake and sob. She took a few steps back until she could hear the pounding of rocks against the building. They knew she was here, and they began to thrust themselves against the door. She rushed further inside, barreling through a back door.

She no sooner burst through then a hand was upon her. She screamed, fighting to free herself.

"Get off of me! Get off!"

"Shhh! Princess, it's Dakon!"

The princess stopped quickly, meeting his eyes. Then she heard the carnage raging inside. The sound of the door being smashed filled her ears. "Please, take me home!"

"Follow me." He pulled her hand, and they rushed into an alley.

She did not realize how unfamiliar she was with the capital until Dakon was pulling her through the street almost as if he were following someone or something. They moved quickly through alleys and street corners, past shops and hovels, pleasure houses, and taverns. The sounds of the raging crowd grew more and more distant, and still Adriana ran harder than ever.

They soon reached the back of the castle's curtain wall and Dakon moved a few of the stones, allowing her to scramble inside. Bushes and brush blocked her vision and impeded some of her movements, but he placed the stones back in their place and grabbed her hand once more, moving her through the castle gardens. She blindly followed, as if in a trance, as he hurriedly rushed her to an unfamiliar entrance along the side of the castle itself. They ventured left and right through passageways she had no idea existed, until finally, he opened a seal behind one of the pillars, leading them into the base of her tower.

It was empty, no doubt due to all the guards being summoned to control the crowd and find her.

"H-how did you?"

"I was able to slip past when they ran after your carriage. I saw you run into the home," Dakon said distractedly. "Did they hurt you?"

Adriana breathed deeply, before looking down at herself. Her dress was torn and tattered, her hands bloody, and her hair tangled and messy, but otherwise she was unscathed. "I don't think so."

In truth, exhaustion overwhelmed her, there was nothing more she wished to do than be in the safety of her room, sleeping under her covers like a child.

"I'm sorry this happened to you." He reached his hand out, letting her cheek rest on his palm.

"I-it was a witch, I saw it, Dakon, I swear." She trembled, remembering how the witch shifted in front of her very eyes.

"I believe you." He brought her in his arms, and she sank into his chest, feeling his heartbeat against her. They had never touched before, not like this, but part of her yearned to never have to leave his embrace.

He came back for her, and she owed him her life.

"I could speak to my father to grant you a rise in your station. Your courage more than deserves it. You could be—"

Dakon shushed her gently, kissing the top of her head as he held her. "I didn't save you for titles."

Adriana bit her lip as suddenly, thoughts of Timothy came to her mind. The night Marc caught them together. She dropped her hands and eyes quickly, taking a step back.

"Thank you. Truly, Dakon. I don't know how I can ever repay you."

"Are you going to be okay?"

She nodded, her lips quivering as their eyes met.

"It is you, not Timothy," she breathed, "isn't it?"

Dakon sighed and kissed her hands softly. "I wish it could be me, Princess."

Before she could respond, he ran down the hall and disappeared around the corner.

Moments later, as Timothy and the rest of her guards came rushing to her side, she could not find the words to describe her emotions for the servant who saved her life, a servant she was desperately in love with.

CLARISA

THIRTY-TWO

C larisa sat at the trunk of the blackthorn tree within the castle courtyard; it had grown so much, unlike the rest within the kingdom. From where she sat, it seemed to reach the heavens, its branches spindling out like broken fingers blocking most of the rainfall. It was stripped of its healing berries, awaiting a winter's hibernation where it would remain stagnated until the spring.

A few droplets made their way through the tree and were about to land on the space between her eyes, before she lifted a finger, freezing them in midair. She sat upright to study them, retrieving the crystal from her pocket and comparing them. The droplets were transparent and reflected its surroundings like small mirrors. She could see a bit of herself in it, trapped in the water. The crystal was back in its translucent state, as well, but the dark smoke within continued its unrelenting tap. She was not yet ready to let them free.

Clarisa opened her palm, and let the droplets fall.

She felt his presence before she heard him speak.

"Clarisa, Her Majesty, Saryn, wishes to speak to you," Tabor said, bow in hand and standing just out of the rain under the protection of the awning. Brisa stood next to him, calm and composed, her hair now a cropped silver hue. *My familiars*, she thought, *could be quite unfamiliar to me at times.*

Clarisa looked at what was left of the raindrops on her palm, no longer beautiful reflections, but something that slid through her fingers.

Clarisa walked into the queen's solar and bowed as she had done countless times before.

"You summoned me, Your Majesty?"

Saryn turned to face her, cup in hand. She was impeccably dressed in a navy gown, half of her hair braided up out of her face, the rest lay over her body in long, dark tendrils.

"Take a seat." She gestured toward the chair across the desk.

Clarisa sat, warily.

Saryn took a long drink from a cup, before staring her piercing blue eyes into Clarisa's. "Do you think I am a cruel queen?" She began to walk, behind and around Clarisa, as she spoke.

The question was odd, but Clarisa responded quickly, not wishing to offend by her hesitation. "No."

"Why do you believe we had to execute Malin and his"—she lifted her chin, as if contemplating the fitting words to conclude her question—"his mistress informant?"

"He betrayed the coven, Your Majesty, and the mortal threatened our safety."

Saryn nodded and continued walking around the room, poised and graceful. She placed her empty cup on the desk.

"Did the mortal look threatening to you?"

Clarisa cast her eyes down, remembering how afraid the woman was, begging for her life. She could feel Saryn's eyes on her as if they were burning holes in her head, then she could hear the queen pull at leaves of a plant, placing bits of them together inside the cup.

"We witches do not hate mortals. We ruled them once, long ago in the times of the original three. They worshipped us, praised us, and through us gave their lives in service of Isila." She scoffed as she tore the last of the plant into the cup. "Look at me, speaking as if I was there."

Clarisa raised her eyes, taking in what Saryn was saying. Not quite understanding their meaning. Saryn leisurely walked across the room and removed a few ashes from the hearth.

"As we know, after Isila fell, the gods saw to it that we witches were bound and limited by our power. Our strength in magic dwindled to small gifts and tokens passed down through generations. We are very much like mortals ourselves now, aren't we?"

"Yes, My Queen."

Saryn placed the ashes into the cup. Then, she twisted her wrist, around and around until the hilt of a small blade appeared in her grip. Clarisa tensed, unsure of how to act.

"We look the same, sound the same, and even *bleed* the same." To this, she cut her palm, letting drops of blood spill inside the cup.

Clarisa controlled her breathing, trying to keep herself unbothered by Saryn's words.

"It is a curse, truly then, that we should be at odds for so many centuries. Mortals unwilling to let us live as we choose, and us"—she walked to a small basin in the corner of her room, submerging her wounded hand— "unwilling to change to suit them." Clarisa watched nervously as Saryn wiped her hands with a small cloth, her cut now healed.

"I understand," Clarisa whispered, keeping her eyes distracted in her lap.

The two remained silent for a few moments, until Saryn spoke once more.

"You sit before me, two halves of a whole. A witch. A mortal." Saryn stood across from Clarisa, studying her. "As a little girl, I remember hearing stories of half-witches. 'Oh, how rare they are,' my mother would say. To have magic and mortality, it was unthinkable. To touch them, be in their presence, was to see a creation by the gods and for the gods. And I prayed to Isila every night, 'please, let me meet one, let me see what they can do. Just once.'"

Clarisa swallowed, feeling a lump in her throat. She shifted uncomfortably in her seat.

"I was about your age when I met my first. I was set to take over my father's throne, and in preparation he sent me on a journey to visit the other covens, to make our presence known to witches outside of the capital. It was exciting for me, I had never ventured far before, was not allowed. Meeting this man, however, was not quite what I had expected. The stories, the folklore, it all spoke of magic and witchcraft that would rival any potions, tinctures, spells, ever witnessed, uncontrolled and swayed by mortality. But he was nothing like the stories. He spoke like I did, felt like I did, everything about him was rather uninteresting."

"I'm sorry."

"None more than I. My father had us married, believing that this man was the one prophesied to find the book or that our child would be. 'A mortal heart, and wicked nature, my dear. None are more wicked than you,' he would laugh. I could still hear that laughter, even now, as I am speaking to you." She paused, as if measuring her next words carefully. "But like a good princess, I did what I was told. Married the half-witch and bore him a son. The only one that survived at least."

Clarisa bit her lip.

"Navir was supposed to be the prophesied prince. The one to find the grimoire and bring us our salvation, bring us back to a time when we did not have to cower like prey. But I learned in time that he was not like his father, not really. Mortality never suited him."

"I never knew, Your Majesty." Clarisa held her breath, unsure of how to react to such an admission.

"Not many do. The man did not last long after Navir was born, and I ruled fine without the constraints of that marriage pulling me from my duties." Saryn lifted a pitcher from the basin, filling the cup on the desk with it. "You are no longer a child under my care, but a woman now, Clarisa."

"Yes, Your Majesty."

"A woman who has grown into her power and has fascinated us all by your immense control and gentle soul. Surely, you are favored by our goddess."

"I only wish to live up to such a compliment."

Saryn smirked. "How admirable. Your mother would be proud, if she were here."

Clarisa nodded, furrowing her brow. She did not think of her mother often, did not remember a time where Saryn mentioned her in the last few years.

"Why do you think I had you kill Malin, when I could have had any guard do so?"

Clarisa swallowed, unsure. "Because I am here to serve you, My Queen."

"Hmm." The queen nodded, taking a sip from the cup. They sat in silence as Clarisa felt the queen's scrutinizing gaze upon her; she cast her eyes down to the rings on her fingers, random trinkets collected and gifted to her over the years.

"Witches do not wish to war with mortals. Do not wish to do anything but live as we do in harmony and peace. But to achieve that, sometimes we must do things we hate, hurt people who may not deserve it, for the greater good. Malin threatened that peace, and he needed to look upon your eyes, the one he swore to protect, and know he failed."

Clarisa knitted her brow, recalling Malin's final moments, his plea to her. *Find her, please.* Her skin prickled at the thought. She shook her head, finding the courage to speak. "What do you need from me?"

Saryn sipped her cup once more, studying Clarisa. She placed it down gently. "You will kill the lady of Mytar, the one set to marry the prince of Givensmir."

Clarisa's eyes widened. "Do you not wish I kill the king instead?"

"A broke king is of far more use to us than a dead one." Saryn pushed the cup toward Clarisa.

Clarisa stared at it, then back at Saryn, the queen who gave her a second chance at life. She took her in and kept her safe in the confines of the castle walls at a time when witches were being murdered almost daily throughout Serit.

This is not someone evil, Clarisa told herself, *this is someone trying to keep us alive.*

"You show great promise, Clarisa, and perhaps, one day soon, the book will come to you and Isila will lift us from the depths of our struggles so that we will not be the ones making such horrible decisions. But until then, we are bound by this eternal curse, to continue fighting against mankind until death takes us all."

She looked inside the cup, it bubbled beneath her gaze, and she could faintly hear screams from within as the bubbles popped.

"Please, don't kill me!"

This was not Saryn's blood, she thought, as goosebumps crawled over her skin. She looked up into Saryn's expectant gaze. "Drink, my dear."

Clarisa couldn't think of how to reply, her focus now on her drying mouth that now desperately craved relief.

EVE

THIRTY-THREE

Theo and Felicity's wedding proceeded normally, much to Eve's relief. In truth, she found it hard to focus on the event while simultaneously trying to grapple with everything that had occurred over the last few days. She knew she was a half-witch, that her mother had been a royal enchantress in the king's court before her death, but Eve had never shown signs of having magic. It was always Clarisa that was gifted, who was taken under her mother's wing to shadow her when she began to conjure water with her mind and hex objects at will.

What had brought about this change in her?

In the last few months, there had been a resurgence of witches in the kingdom—from rumors of them in Zafira, then the one burned at the stake just outside the city, and now, she shuddered as she recalled the events Adriana divulged to her, now, they were attacking nobles and royals in the streets and on roads.

As Elder Borgias droned on in his sermons, she wished for nothing but to be in her chambers with her grimoire in her hands. Her book, her truth, the light she could not see before. Perhaps, she had yet to uncover an answer to quell the chaos that was brewing around her.

"As the five will it, may this marriage be blessed in faith, trust, love, strength, and courage.

She considered her possibilities: could she truly give in to magic that might lurk beneath her skin or was there a way to return all to what it used to be. Magic, she had always been told, was sporadic, unpredictable, and now she knew it could even be dangerous. If that were the case, then surely it was her duty to learn how to control it, her responsibility to discover the truth the court did not want her to see.

"In the sight of the gods, and before the people of this temple, may you all bear witness to the union of Prince Theo Ebron and Princess Felicity Mytar."

She had done so well to avoid putting a target on her back, striving to bring pride to her house and become the darling of the court. As she mulled over her thoughts, Eve decided she wanted nothing more than to keep her magic a secret, to continue her facade as nothing but a mortal with an unfortunate, but dormant tie to witchcraft.

It can all be as it once was, she told herself, *I just need a little more time.*

"By the will of the gods, this union shall thrive for the good of the kingdom!"

"By the will of the gods!" the crowd chanted loudly, breaking Eve's concentration.

The bells began to chime beautifully in the temple, people stood to clap and cheer from their pews, and she followed suit. She lifted her eyes to Theo and his new bride, taking in the sight of them together. They kissed briefly and smiled at one another before presenting themselves to the guests. Together, they looked the part of royalty, befitting of their station, one could almost believe that they had known each other all their lives. Maybe even loved each other.

"That will be us soon," Callum whispered in her ear. Eve turned to him, startled, nearly forgetting that she was seated next to him.

"I hope we can be at least half as happy as they look," she replied.

He cast his eyes to the couple, as if considering his next words. "I will do my best, that I can promise."

Eve nodded, responding with only a tight smile. She dared herself to take in the sight of Theo and Felicity once more, hands joined together and raised for all the people of Givensmir to witness.

And for just the briefest of moments, she allowed her heart to crack, before thoughts of the grimoire began to plague her once more.

Eve was filled with the sound of music as she sat in the great hall. She mulled over the last few hours – watching the love of her life walk down the aisle and make sacred vows to another. How she was forced to watch them solidify it with a kiss, and how she was now at the celebration, sitting down, when everyone was up dancing about the room. The couples moved elegantly together, and Eve watched with longing eyes as Theo led Felicity to the center of it all. Felicity danced with such grace and agile movements; it was as if she were floating on air with Theo's deft hands leading the way.

Eve had a servant pour herself another glass of wine and downed it in one sitting. Callum excused himself to take care of business a short while ago. Pedro had gone to dance with one of the ladies at the table whose name she couldn't recall, and Adriana was dancing with a Mytar noble. She was alone and without an escort to leave the great hall, forced to feign politeness as a lady, of which she was failing miserably. Time seemed to somehow crawl, and Eve sighed heavily, taking in how upsetting this evening was turning out to be.

She groaned as she held out her glass again. Another servant stopped by to fill it up. Eve began to pull it back, intending to see how many gulps it would take to finish it, when someone picked it out of her hand.

"It almost seems as if you're avoiding a good dance."

Eve turned and stared into the hazel eyes of the man she loved, and her mouth went slack, her mind trying to push through the tipsy fog of the wine in her system.

"I–I am just tired. I might go back up to my chambers when my cousin returns."

They both looked toward Pedro who seemed to be thoroughly enjoying himself with yet another dance partner. Eve rolled her eyes, and internally swore to trip him up the stairs when they left this feast.

"Well, it seems to me that he is a bit preoccupied at the moment, as you should be." Theo sat in the empty seat next to her.

"I don't think anyone wants to ask the slightly drunk lady to dance," she scoffed, reaching out for her glass. Theo placed it out of her reach on the table.

"I think you have had enough for one night; wouldn't you agree?"

Eve held up her hands in mock defeat. "Whatever you say, Your Highness."

"Are you okay?" Theo stared hard into her eyes, his brow furrowing. If Eve had felt less emboldened by the alcohol, she would have certainly graced him with a bright smile and cheery disposition. However, right here, right now, she was neither of those things. She took a deep breath, calming her beating heart as she stared right back into those eyes, wondering when she may ever be this close to him again.

"No."

"No?"

"No."

"Why? Has someone offended you?" He looked concerned and took her hand in his. It was an electric feeling, a spark that jolted everything inside of Eve and made her quickly regain her senses. She pulled her hand out swiftly from his.

"I mean, I am not fine sitting down while everyone is out there dancing and having a good time. Please, fetch me a partner, Prince, someone dashing, find Lord Callum perhaps, wherever he is." She gestured to the sitting potential partners.

Theo seemed to avert his eyes and was neither amused nor did his concern wane. His jaw tightened and his eyes darkened.

"Are you sure?"

"Of course, I only want to enjoy tonight and celebrate you." She took a stilling breath, and smiled, putting all her effort in the task. "Truly, I wish you the greatest happiness. Princess Felicity seems like a wonderful person."

The ache in her chest throbbed as she practically choked out the last words, but Theo seemed to not notice, returning her smile. He truly was the most handsome man she had ever known, even if it was her heart that swelled the bias.

"This is why you are my greatest friend, Eve. You never cease to support me or amaze me if I am being honest."

"It is an honor to be your friend, Theo." She felt the tears prick at the corners of her eyes and turned away from him. "I am glad to see that you are happy."

"I am happy," said Theo. "It is a privilege to serve my kingdom, and I know this alliance is me doing my part."

Eve couldn't help herself, knowing that she may never get another moment like this. "Do you love her?"

He chuckled. "You are asking a man if he loves his wife?"

"Yes."

"You've asked me this before, remember?" he breathed, his eyes burning into Eve's. "I am sure I will grow to love her, though."

Eve nodded, feeling a bit disgusted with herself. "Of course." She nearly felt the admission on her lips, to rid herself of the shame at withholding her betrothal from him for so long.

It has been a couple of days, surely he must know by now.

"Enough of this depressing talk." Theo stood, saying, "The night is young, and I am appalled you have not danced yet."

"There aren't many eligible bachelors at the moment." Eve giggled.

"Well, then it is my duty to dance with you as your humble host."

Eve's breath hitched, butterflies fluttering in her stomach, and she felt her heart pounding in her chest.

"Will you honor me with this dance, Lady Eve?"

Eve nodded and prayed that her feet would not be clumsy beneath her, trying to recall all steps in her head as Theo led her onto the ballroom floor, filled with others dancing elegantly to the lively music. No one seemed to notice their discussion at the table, nor did they seem to care. Princess Felicity was twirling in the arms of Marc, oblivious to Theo's choice for a dance partner. Eve gave a sigh of relief as she placed one hand on Theo's shoulder, the other in his hand.

"Ready?" Theo smirked.

"Always."

Theo began to dance with her, moving elegantly as all his years of royal training had taught him, Eve kept up, an exquisite dancer in her own right, but kept her eyes downcast. The buttons of Theo's dark-gold coat glimmered from the chandelier above them as they danced, and she held her eyes firm on them, trying to keep herself from thinking too much about anything but the buttons and the dance. The music swelled at all the right moments and lulled them into a slower movement at others. Eve had danced many times with Theo, they would laugh and talk through their steps like the friends they were, but tonight, Eve's heart felt heavy knowing this may be her last time in his embrace.

"You are not usually this quiet," Theo whispered in her ear.

"I am not usually this tipsy," she remarked, and he laughed. The sound sent wonderful chills down her spine.

"Tell me a secret, Eve. Humor me."

"You know practically everything there is to know about me. No mystery here, I'm afraid."

"That can't be true, you are the most interesting person I know."

"Good, I planned it that way." She grinned.

"I meant it—that night," Theo's voice took a serious tone. "You will always have a piece of me."

"And you too, Theo."

"Always?"

"Always."

Memories of that summer night drifted in her mind. Their hands tangled in each other, their fervent kisses losing restraint as they lay atop the dewy grass, allowing themselves to be consumed by the raw emotions; not knowing if they would ever see each other again. She could still feel the sensation of their warm bodies pressed together in desperate need. How he whispered her name, like a cathartic release, as she pulled him deeper inside her. She had never felt pleasure like that before or since.

"Sometimes, I wish things turned out differently," Theo murmured, "not that I am ungrateful to be getting married, only that I wish it was with someone *different*." He spun her as he said this, her gown twirling with burgundy and soft pink hues. She smiled truly for the first time in a long time, feeling free and happy.

"Oh?"

"Someone who was a bit more like me, who I could confide in, trust with all my heart."

Eve held her breath as she twirled back into his arms and locked her eyes on him. His gaze was soft and there was a slight crinkle at the corners of his eyes as he returned her stare.

"What I am trying to say is that—what I really want you to know, Eve, is that—"

"Brother, mind if I cut in?"

The pair was interrupted by Prince Marc who placed a hand on Theo's shoulder.

Before either of them could respond, Marc continued, "Your *wife* claims to miss you."

The two of them faced Felicity, who was fast approaching them. Eve dropped her hands immediately, and Theo looked to Eve one last time, regret in his eyes.

"We'll talk later, I promise," he said to Eve, before turning to his brother, giving him a pointed look as he left to attend to the princess.

As the music continued, and the dancing around them, Marc placed his hand around Eve's waist, and she felt disgusted as she lightly placed her hand in his free one. They began to move steadily, and Eve had to begrudgingly admit that Marc was nearly as good of a dancer as Theo was. She kept her gaze fixed on the room around them, avoiding Marc's eyes and wanting the song to be over so she could grab Pedro and go back to her chambers. She noted that he was dancing with yet another lady, this time one from Mytar.

"It seems as if you are unhappy dancing with me, Lady Eve," Marc said slyly.

"Not at all, Your Highness," she replied curtly.

"You know, he is married. That means no more garden strolls, no more late-night conversations, no more *dancing* together."

Eve looked at Marc fiercely. "Yes, I am well aware."

"Are you? Because by the way you and the prince were talking, any reasonable person would have suspected otherwise."

Eve glared at him as they continued their dance, Marc spinning her quickly before bringing her back into his grip.

"I will keep that in mind."

"I am only looking out for your best interests. Surely you did not believe that my father would have allowed him to marry just *anyone*."

Eve remained silent, biting her lip and focusing on keeping herself calm. She did not want to let him under her skin, she wouldn't let him get to her. Even worse, she did not want a repeat of what happened at the welcoming ceremony.

"It must be a bit disappointing, though," he continued, "spending all your time on someone who you could never be with. Such a waste."

"We are only friends, Your Highness, nothing more."

"Of course, of course." Marc grinned, and it made Eve feel nauseous.

It wasn't that Marc was unattractive, but he often competed with Theo, and he was a known philanderer in the court. A snake in a human body and practically nothing like his brothers.

"What is it you want from me? You never asked to dance with me a day in your life unless forced to."

"I only wish to keep you in line, Eve. A half-breed throwing herself at a married prince would be unbecoming of this court, especially in front of the new additions to our family." He raised his chin to the lord and lady of Mytar who sat behind the royal table, talking with a few of the nobles. Eve recoiled slightly, the word *half-breed* snaking its way through her mind, an insult, but one she had not heard in a long time. At least, not in her presence.

"I've never known you to care so much about anything other than yourself, Your Highness," she gritted between her teeth. The music began to crescendo, and all the ladies were spun by their partners, Eve included, as she gave Marc another nasty glare. He only smirked in response.

"I would be very careful if I were you," he said as Eve was spun back into his embrace, his voice carrying a serious, venomous tone. "You never know who could be watching you."

Eve remained silent, taking in all that he was and wasn't saying.

What kind of threat is this?

"You know," Marc continued, lowering his voice, "there are other ways you can remain close to Theo, even after he is married. Ways that are deemed acceptable—even in the court—but it all depends on one thing."

Eve tensed as he whispered softly in her ear. "Tell me, can your skills in the gardens last summer carry over to his bedroom?"

She couldn't help herself, pulling away as the rage and disrespect flooded her system, overpowering her every will and control.

How did he know?!

Before she could think twice, at least twenty glasses at the nearby table smashed into pieces, startling the crowd as a few people shrieked. Eve stood still, trying to calm down before any more of her magic revealed itself. Marc pulled her back into his arms as everyone else began talking at once, moving closer to inspect the cause.

A booming voice echoed through the great hall. "It seems as if the festivities have caused our more drunken folk to behave rather inappropriately," the king declared as he rose from his seat, a crooked smile on his face.

The people laughed nervously before the servants began cleaning up the mess quickly and succinctly.

Marc released Eve, grinning as he kissed the top of her hand. "It'll be our little secret." Then, he winked before walking away into the crowd.

Eve thought about chasing after him, trying to make sure he wouldn't say anything, but knew it would only incentivize him more. She turned to Prince Theo, who was staring at her in confusion and concern. "Are you okay?" he mouthed.

She nodded, before quickly returning to her seat, where Pedro and Adriana were waiting for her.

"I think it's time to go," he said.

"I'll join you," said Adriana, reaching for Eve's shaking hands. "I should have feigned another sickness sooner."

"It's fine," Eve replied, feeling an anxious, fearful energy at how the night had progressed, at her sudden influx of strong magic, at Marc's threat, at Theo's sudden marriage, at everything. It fatigued her so greatly, she wanted nothing more than to be in her chambers, away from the rest of the crowd who was now talking amongst each other about the oddity of the situation.

"I just need some rest."

The two nodded and began to escort her quietly past the tables when more glasses began to break around them. The furniture began to shake and rattle as people began falling out of their chairs. The candlelight around them flickered before blowing out completely, leaving the great hall in near-total darkness. The crowd shrieked in fear, and Eve was cut by some of the glass.

"Eve, are you doing this?" Adriana demanded in a hushed tone, the screams of scared nobles and chaos surrounding them.

Eve looked incredulously at her, *why would she ask me that?*

"Of course not!"

Yet, she wasn't so sure. She did not feel any different, did not feel any sense of magic coursing through her as everything began to shift.

"What is happening?" Pedro asked.

Before she could reply a scream pierced the great hall, and all the candlelight blazed furiously again. Eve cowered on the floor next to Adriana and behind Pedro who stood as their shield.

"Gods," Pedro breathed, his eyes wide and mouth slack. Eve followed his eyes and beheld the shock of her life. Clarisa stood in the center of the room.

After fifteen years, she had come back.

And at her feet was Princess Felicity, dead.

210

CLARISA
THIRTY-FOUR

S lowly, methodically, Clarisa felt herself transported back into the castle that was once her home. She felt a sense of wistfulness and nervous energy as she tried to push past the ties that longed to be remembered. She never thought she would return, never imagined that if she did it would be to take a life.

Through the darkness that shrouded the great hall, the princess came into view. She looked back and forth in terror and confusion. People ran and screamed around her, some making their way to the entrance, while others were trampled by the sheer size of the crowd.

Clarisa continued toward the woman, calm and confident, and the people ran through her as if she were but a spirit in the air.

She had to protect the coven.

She had to remove the threats.

If this woman stood in the way of what needed to be done. Then so be it.

She willed the room to freeze, forcing everyone into a silent suspension of time.

The woman was frozen in place, lovely and captivating as she clung to a man's chest in fear. Her eyes were wide, glistening with panic. It was a shame, she thought, that someone so beautiful would have to die so cruelly.

"Make this quick."

"Time is running out."

Clarisa raised her hand out before her, channeling the magic of the witch's blood she drank earlier. Fire sparked from her fingertips, and with it drew a witch's mark, deep into the skull of the woman.

The woman shrieked and howled in pain and terror but couldn't move away. It was torturous to see, and Clarisa quickly ended her life as she did Malin's. Tears sprang into her eyes, as the woman slowly began her descent, clashing with the floor as a husk of her former self.

It was done.

"Come back."

"Come back."

The voices urged her from beyond.

Clarisa beheld the dead woman on the floor before her once more, holding what was left of her hand, it was naught but skin on bones. Ash riddled the floor around her, scalding and faintly glowing red in areas where the heat tried to refuse its destined fate.

"I'm sorry," she breathed.

Then she stood as time resumed. The candles flickered on, and she began to disappear into the haze as the crowd began to thrash and scream once more.

But before she could close her eyes and submit to the daze that gripped her, she saw Eve, standing as the chaos unfolded around her. Their eyes met, and within Eve's was one of shock, confusion, and rage. Clarisa could barely breathe as the great hall began to grow small and distant. She could not believe what she had seen. It was impossible, it had to be.

After fifteen years, Eve was still alive among mortals.

EVE

THIRTY-FIVE

"*It was a witch!*"
  "*A witch killed the princess!*"
  "*The princess is dead!*"
"*They have come back; they have come to kill us all!*"
The voices echoed throughout the great hall amongst the shrieks and mayhem that took over the crowd.

Eve stood stunned, rooted to the ground as Pedro shouted at her to move. Adriana was quickly removed by her royal guard, taken through a side door.

"Clarisa, that was Clarisa," Eve kept sputtering, shock still lingering over her. Pedro forced her to move, shoving her toward the main doors.

Lord Wesley confronted them as they began to rush out of the hall.

"Where do you think you're going, Lady Eve?" he drawled, grabbing her arm roughly. The crowd still ran amuck in chaos, most oblivious to their interaction. Yet, some now stopped to see what was unfolding. Eve heard the cries of the Mytar king as he held his daughter in his arms.

"I am seeing her to her chambers safely, Lord Wesley. Let my cousin go."

"The king has ordered that me and my guard to escort her there. We will be searching her room immediately."

"Retrieve the healer, damn you, the healer!"

"For what purpose?" Eve shouted, feeling his nails digging into her skin. She tried to pull her arm free. She could hear voices now as the crowd gradually began to focus on her.

"Did she do it?"

"Is she a witch?"

"Witch! Liar!"

Three more guards surrounded them, and Eve watched as Pedro laid a hand on his sword, unsheathing it. The room was now filled with more guards and a few of the royal healers rushed toward the body. Princess Felicity was surely dead, a bloody mark of three stars upon her forehead, singeing her skin. Eve forced herself to look away.

"No need to cause a scene. If she has nothing to hide, the king will have no reason to further suspect her."

"I have done nothing wrong." Eve stood between Pedro and Wesley. Her grimoire, they cannot take it from her, she would not let them touch it.

"If you do not come *willingly*, then I will be forced to have Ser Pedro executed on the spot for dereliction of duty."

A few members of the crowd gasped, and Eve turned to Pedro. His nostrils flared, and she could see him considering his very limited options as the guard encircled them.

"No! No, I will go," she shouted.

"Eve—" Pedro's eyes widened.

"Please, I do not want your blood on my hands."

He nodded, and after a brief deadly glare to Wesley, sheathed his sword. He took a step back as the guards rushed her, grabbing hold and bringing her through the crowd as they watched in horror. One of them quickly placed cuffs on her.

"What is this for?" Eve gasped.

"A precaution, my lady."

"They are arresting her!"

"There is no need for cuffs, I am perfectly capable of walking where I am told."

"They are *iron*. As I said, a precaution."

Eve felt her face flush, the fear of her situation settling in. The witch laughing and beaten at the stake. She couldn't bear it. Panic gripped her.

"I am not a witch. I possess only mortality and a love for the gods. You know this."

Wesley ignored her, pushing her to walk in front of him.

She could hear her damnation in the crowd as they trailed through the long halls toward the maiden's keep.

The walk to her chambers felt as if it were the longest of her life. Dread filled her insides as she realized the book would be found and only the gods would know what they planned to do to her.

They walked up the steps to her chamber door.

"Anything you wish to confess before we search?" Lord Wesley asked, narrowing his eyes at her.

Eve immediately thought of the grimoire, how it was hidden within her personal belongings, not easily found, but could be, nonetheless. She silently wished that her ability to freeze time would appear now, but it did not, much to her detriment.

"No."

He shook his head. "That was your last chance, witch. Wait here."

He positioned one of the guards to watch her and disappeared into her chambers. She could hear his gruff voice shouting, "Search her belongings, leave no stone unturned!"

Eve tried to still her breathing, to be calm before she damned herself, but thoughts of the book clouded her mind. She would be tried as a witch, guilty before she would even have a chance to speak her truth. That she was innocent. She was not a murderer. She was not a witch. Not how they believed.

Loud banging from the guards moving and throwing her furniture and belongings could be heard throughout the tower. Eve closed her eyes wishing it would stop, wishing that she would have gotten rid of the book when she had a chance, wishing she was anywhere but here.

Then she heard footsteps stumbling up toward her chamber.

Her father with his cane unsteadily moved up the steps, breathing heavily as he did so.

"Father!" she began to move toward him, but the guard held her in place.

"Don't move," the guard growled.

"Eve? Eve! What is the meaning of this?" He eyed her chains, mouth agape.

"I had nothing to do with it, Father, I swear," she yelled. "Please, speak to the king, have him release me!"

"I was told they only escorted you to your chambers, not that you were accused."

"I am not accused, Father—"

"Then why are you in chains? Why are they searching your room?"

"I do not know, please. I am innocent."

"Eve," he began slowly, still eyeing her chains, "what have you done?"

"I have done nothing! I possess no magic, no witchcraft, I am just like you, Father."

"They say no good comes from conspiring with the Blackthorn, but I did not listen . . ."

"Father!"

Lord Wesley came to the door then. "Ah, Lord Marcelo, how can I help you?"

"What is my daughter accused of?"

"The king has not named any specific charges but has merely asked that we search her chambers for any evidence of foul-play related to the princess's attack."

"On what grounds?"

"You will have to ask the king, my lord. I only do what I am told," he answered, but then lowered his voice to where only Eve and her father could hear, "but I am led to believe the king suspects witchcraft, and as the daughter of the enchantress . . ."

"I possess no witchcraft," she spat. "Father, please, believe me!"

Yet, her father looked distant, confused. "Not again," he murmured more to himself than to Eve.

"Let us hope not," Lord Wesley responded, then turned to Eve. "For now, we have found nothing, but this does not mean that you are released. You are to remain in house arrest until the king declares otherwise. Do not think about leaving your chambers, nor removing your bindings, or I may be forced to send you to the dungeons."

Eve's heart thundered against her chest.

The book was not found.

"I said, do you understand?" Wesley's voice came to her.

"Yes."

"Good." He smirked and took out a knife from his belt.

Eve stilled, eyes wide.

"Your hand, please, Lady Eve."

Before she could respond, he grabbed it and pricked her palm, drops of blood fell onto his blade.

She pulled her hand back quickly.

"Why did you—"

"Hope you sleep well, my lady," he smirked, and the guards escorted her into her chambers. As the door closed, she saw her father still stunned in the same position, staring at her as if she were now a stranger to him.

She closed her eyes and turned away as the door was locked, a guard surely on the other side.

When she opened them she beheld the horrid mess her room had become after their search. Drawers overturned, clothes strewn across the floor, a few papers and books tattered, ink spilled—her heart felt heavy and numb.

As her eyes moved toward her bed, however, she held her breath, eyes widening.

Laying as if untouched atop her tossed, torn sheets was the Blood of the Blackthorn.

THEO
THIRTY-SIX

Prince Theo paced back and forth outside his father's study, he could hear the king, the lord of Mytar, and their aides inside yelling over each other trying to determine their next steps.

"How does something like this happen?"

"Are you certain of what you saw?!"

"Someone must pay for this horrific act!"

The prince was a whirl of emotions—one second he was speaking to the princess and the next her face was shrouded in flames. A flame that started on her forehead and ripped its way through her. Ash was left scattered about her body like fingerprints. He shuddered at the memory; it was a fierce and cruel way to die.

"Brother, take a seat." Eryce gestured to a spot on the bench next to him. "It does you no good to hear them in this state."

Theo considered telling him to worry about himself, nearly bringing up Lord Callum in his frustration, but thought better of it and sat.

"I don't understand, how could this have happened? And why did they take Eve away? What does this mean for our alliance?"

"Quiet, Brother, calm yourself. They may hear you."

"I want them to hear me, they need to give me some answers. I have a dead wife and a friend who has been falsely imprisoned. I demand to know what is happening!"

Eryce tensed, assessing Theo before saying carefully, "Tell me again what happened."

Theo brushed his hands through his hair, frustrated. "My answer is still the same as I told them inside that room. Princess Felicity and I were speaking, it went dark, and I noticed a burn mark growing on her forehead. I pointed it out, and then she began to scream—I have never heard any woman in my life scream the way she did. In an instant her body shriveled. I tried to pick her up, but I didn't know what to do. I tried, brother, I swear, I tried—" Theo stumbled over his words, full of distress and anger. He began breathing rapidly, the terrible nightmare resurfacing.

Eryce stood to calm him. "There is nothing you could have done."

Theo grappled with his fear and anger, standing to pace again, fervently running his hands through his hair. Sweat prickled at his temples and his hands shook involuntarily.

Eryce grabbed him by the shoulder, sitting him down again. "I said sit, Theo."

Theo let out a shaky breath. It was terrifying to know that life could be taken so unexpectedly, would he be next? Who else was on death's toll?

"Look at me, Brother. Look!" Eryce said urgently.

Theo raised his eyes, beholding his brother's grave stare. "I want you to answer me honestly, swear to me you will and whatever your answer may be you have my word I'll keep it between us."

Theo furrowed his brows but nodded.

"Do you believe Eve had anything to do with this?"

"W-what? *Eve*? She was halfway across the room—"

"Has she confided in you that she can practice witchcraft?"

Theo kept his eyes locked on his brother's before scoffing into nervous laughter. "Eryce, our kingdom has rid itself of witches long ago—that *thing* with mother and Adriana, was an exaggeration. They were terrified."

Eryce narrowed his eyes. "And what of the attacks on the nobles, Zafira, the witch who was executed not so long ago?"

"Fear is the only thing causing our kingdom to come up with notions that witches have truly returned. We need to focus on who did this to Felicity, before going on wild chases for people who are hundreds of miles away." His lips began to quiver. He could not lose his sense of sanity, could not give in to this foolhardiness.

Eryce closed his eyes and let out a deep sigh. "No one but a witch could have killed her."

"In all our years in this castle, Eve has never once exhibited any trait of witchcraft or magic at all. She's perfectly mortal, I swear."

"How can you be sure?"

"She would have told me." But even as he said it, doubt began to creep in. *Would she?*

"You truly believe that she would have told the son of the king who ordered the extinction of her kind in this kingdom?"

"It is not her kind!" He wouldn't allow himself, couldn't allow himself to believe it. Yet, his voice cracked as he made his declaration.

Eryce paused, assessing him. "Theo," he whispered. "See reason, she is in love with you and you her."

Theo took a stifling breath; the words were now hanging in the air, and he knew he had to confront them.

"Even if what you are saying is true, Eve would never harm me or anyone in this kingdom. This was not her. I know it."

"In fifteen years, there is a lot we still do not know about her, about what she is capable of."

"I know that she is good, that she would never take part in killing someone, especially an innocent."

"I hope you are right." Eryce sighed, and Theo could nearly feel the tension emanating from him.

Theo stood and began to pace again, but his heart and mind were focused not on his dead wife, much to his shame, but on Eve, considering whether he really knew her like he thought he did. He tried to go over every encounter he could but came up empty. *It can't be.*

The study was still roaring with the voices of men that were not listening to anyone but themselves.

Over an hour later, the room began to empty of most of its occupants. The men walking out of the room were ashen and silent as they passed the princes on their way out. A few offered condolences to Theo, bowing with mournful regret at not having been able to help.

Theo only nodded, and thanked them for their support, unsure of how he should properly act in this situation. It was too uncomfortable and raw.

When the crowd dispersed, no doubt heading to complete their various tasks, the hall was completely silent again, but for only a short while. Minutes later, rapid footsteps were heard coming toward them from the dark corridor. Eryce and Theo both jumped up, readying themselves for what may come through the shadows. Daggers were drawn, and the hair on the back of Theo's neck stood; he nearly called out to see who was there before Marc and Lord Joseph II of Mytar, brother to the princess, stepped through.

"Goodness, Brother, haven't we had enough bloodshed this evening?" Marc narrowed his eyes and placed a fingertip on top of Theo's blade, pushing it down away from him.

"Our apologies, we are a bit on edge. We were not expecting anyone else," Eryce replied.

"The kings' men called upon us to attend a meeting, that is why we are here," Joseph said, eyeing the brothers suspiciously. "We are told to wait here until they call us into the room."

"Of course, please have a seat." Theo sheathed his blade and gestured to the bench along the wall.

Joseph shook his head, instead moving to the castle windows next to them. He silently took in the view of the grounds.

Marc took a seat. "Wake me up when they are ready, Theo." He smirked and laid the back of his head against the wall, slouching slightly with his eyes closed.

It took all of Theo's willpower to not hit him in the face. He walked toward Joseph instead to create some distance.

"My condolences, Joseph," he said softly. "I only wish that there was more I could have done."

"Call me Jos." He didn't look his way, but instead continued eyeing the view before him.

"Of course."

Another pause, then he sighed deeply before continuing, "My sister hated your lands, you know, said it was too flat for her liking. She much preferred the mountains of Mytar."

Theo only nodded.

"She would climb as high as she could go when we were children, and we would race to the top of one of the large cliffs to see who could behold the wondrous views first. You see, at the top you could see the ends of the world—I could reach my hand up and touch the sky if I wanted to."

"It sounds magnificent," Theo replied.

Jos continued looking out the window. "When she was six, she tripped while climbing up a rather slippery slope and fell a long way down. I raced to her, as fast as my legs could carry me, and when I reached her, she was lying there, still as death on the floor, and I can still feel how my heart stopped as I looked upon her sweet face, and the blood pooling from behind her beautiful hair. And I begged the gods to let her live, to let her come back to life—that I would protect her with everything I had in me. I must have recited every prayer I knew."

Jos turned to Theo, his eyes burning into his. "I begged the gods to let her live, only for them to burn her like a witch at her wedding."

The words struck Theo, and he had no time to reply before Ser Aznaro, head of the royal guard, opened the large study door.

"The kings are ready to speak to you, Your Highnesses, Lord Joseph." He bowed, then left quickly. Theo turned to Jos once more, each holding a serious look before following the others inside.

The twilight outside the study windows barely offered much light aside from the fireplace that dwindled with a faint flame. There were a few wooden chairs, a wardrobe, and shelves filled to the brim with books. A large desk was positioned next to the fireplace, and their fathers both stood behind it, whispering to each other in confidence before turning to behold them.

The men's expressions could not be more different. Theo looked upon his father, whose expression was dark, but held a confidence he could not understand. Lord Joseph was distraught, his face ashen and pale as he turned to receive them.

"My sons, this is a grave day indeed. We have lost a beautiful princess under extraordinary circumstances—"

"Out with it! Tell them what you know!" Lord Joseph demanded, the bags under his eyes were nearly purple, his grief etched on every inch of his face. Theo's heart dropped knowing the man would never see his daughter again.

"Yes, yes." The king coughed into a handkerchief before continuing, rather nonchalantly, "A witch's mark was discovered on the princess's forehead and the fire, as Prince Theo has told me, appeared to originate from that same spot. This heinous act combined with the Blackthorn's killing of our people is a call for war! We must act before we lose any more of our precious lives."

Theo could see right through what the king was doing, exploiting the princess's death as another reason to war with the witches. Yet, he was torn and begrudgingly had to admit his father had a point: there was a mark on Felicity, a mark that could not be explained, and the fire . . .

Could Eve really have something to do with this?

"I thought our kingdoms rid themselves of witches years ago?" Jos asked, a harshness to his tone. "Am I to believe we have left our homes bare of protections while we were out fighting your war?!"

"Mind your tongue before the king, Son!" Lord Joseph admonished. "I do not wish to lose any more of my children tonight."

Jos bit his tongue, nostrils flaring.

The tension in the room thickened, and Theo could feel all eyes on his father. King Eryck shook his head, walking toward Jos. "It is quite all right, Lord Joseph. Grief can make a man do foolish things. Foolish things that may have them meet the one they grieved for sooner than expected."

He was nearly eye to eye with Jos now. "Enlighten me with your wisdom, young lord. How does one get rid of an infestation?"

Theo watched, holding his breath as Jos blinked in response. "F-from within, Your Majesty."

The king nodded, pleased. He coughed again into his handkerchief and walked back to Lord Joseph's side. "You will find, gentlemen, that in our line of work, everything may appear enticing to those who do not know what lurks within."

"What do you mean, Father?" Eryce asked, evident confusion on his face that mirrored the rest of the room.

"It seems that while we have rid ourselves of most witches throughout the kingdom. Some have been able to successfully blend within our castle walls."

Theo's blood froze, *Eve?*

There was a knock on the door, and the king gestured for the guard to open it. The princes turned to see Ser Aznaro with Princess Adriana. Theo's heart sank, shocked and incredulous. Eryce turned to their father. "What is the meaning of this?"

The king ignored him and turned toward Adriana. "My dear, can you tell the room what you witnessed?"

The princess was shaking, nervously twisting a damp handkerchief in between her hands, she barely looked at Theo who stared at her with disbelief.

"Y-yes, Father."

"You are safe here, Adriana, you can speak freely," the king said, unusually sweet. It gave Theo a sickening taste in his mouth.

Adriana nodded hesitantly before proceeding, "I saw my handmaid turn a note to ash in her pocket. No candle, no fire, nothing to make it so. It happened before my eyes, but I refused to believe it was true, until— until—" She began sobbing relentlessly, and Eryce made his way to her.

"A note, turned to ash from nothing but her willpower, I see," the king mused. "And later we have a princess killed by fire . . ."

"Father," Eryce raised his voice as he consoled his weeping sister, "you have made your point, please let our sister go in peace."

"Of course, of course. Let us end this swiftly, Ser Aznaro?" He gestured toward the knight who opened the door, letting a few guards in with a feeble, old woman between them.

"What is going on?!" Theo demanded.

King Eryck ignored him and faced Princess Adriana. "Is this your handmaid?"

The princess's eyes were heavy, and she was speechless as her father demanded again, "Is this the handmaid you mentioned?!"

"Y-yes," she stammered, "Father, please—"

"What is your name, witch?!" The king turned to the servant.

"C-cerene, Your Majesty," the old woman croaked.

The king turned toward Lord Joseph. "Would you like to do the honors, friend?"

Lord Joseph's heavy eyes turned to one of rage and fury as he nodded, moving close to the weeping woman who was incoherently stammering.

"Why did you kill my daughter?!"

"I–I didn't kill anyone, My Lord!"

The king nodded to the guards who punched her in the stomach. She fell forward but was caught.

"No, please, don't hurt her!" Princess Adriana screamed.

"Ser Aznaro, please remove my daughter. Take her to her chambers. This is no place for a woman."

The knight nodded and swiftly removed Adriana whose howling and crying soon became distant as they moved down the hall.

Theo was shocked at what was unfolding before him.

Did she kill Felicity?

How could someone like her be responsible for such a crime?

After another blow to the woman, she began to screech as blood dripped from her mouth and nose. "Isila, save my soul!"

"We will solve nothing by beating an old woman! Stop this madness!" Eryce demanded.

"My daughter is the true victim! This woman let herself be controlled by witchcraft, a sign that she is not well among the gods, and for that she must die," Lord Joseph spat, the glare in his eyes like fire.

"I killed no one!" the old woman screamed.

"Liar!" Lord Joseph yelled and slapped her with the back of his hand.

Theo moved between Lord Joseph and the woman before he could strike her once more. "This is not the way!"

His father placed a hand on Lord Joseph's shoulder. "Friend, let us kill her properly so her magic cannot be used against us anymore."

Lord Joseph hesitated, breathing raggedly, his muscles tensing and trembling with rage. Finally, he nodded, and the king gestured to the guards to remove the woman.

When she was gone, the room fell silent once more, each person collectively trying to maintain calm in the chaotic scenario that had just unfolded before them.

Theo thought of Eve, and what would happen to her. Would she be released now that the woman was found?

The silence was broken by Marc.

"Witches?" Marc exclaimed. "In our castle no less. What other kinds of trickery is the Blackthorn up to?"

"Settle down," King Eryck said, turning once more to Lord Joseph. "We shall get our vengeance against this evil soon enough."

"Yes," he replied, "yes we shall."

"Summon Ser James," King Eryck said to one of the guards. "I demand he ready our ships and prepare our armies. I wish to maintain the element of surprise."

The guard nodded and headed swiftly out of the room. The princes stared at each other in shock.

"Father, we must be smart about this, we do not know what kind of forces they possess," Eryce pleaded. "You may be sending our fleet to certain death."

"My sister is dead, and you are worried about a few ships?" Jos retorted, stepping nearly toe-to-toe with Eryce. They glared at each other, only seconds away from a sure brawl before Theo pushed them apart.

Lord Joseph walked to Jos. "My son, you are the last of our line. You will stay here, there is another task I need for you to complete."

"What? No, Father, I must be in battle!"

"The princes of Givensmir honor us by avenging Felicity. You will marry Princess Adriana after a considerable time has passed to mourn your sister. We will continue this alliance for our family, we will not let her death happen in vain."

Theo ignored this, approaching his father. "We won't just be losing ships, we will be losing a sizable portion of our forces that are still coming back from war. Father, I implore you, we must plan—"

"Silence!" The king slammed his fist on the desk before going into a coughing fit. He wiped a bit of blood from his lip with the back of his hand. "You and your brothers will embark on this task, do not return until you bring me the head of their queen."

"You are sentencing your heirs to death!" Eryce growled.

"I have plenty of bastards!" the king snapped.

Theo looked upon his father in horror, the realization of what they were charged to embark on truly settling on him. This was meant to be a death mission. They were collectively silenced, even Marc whose eyes betrayed fear.

"So, it is done," the king murmured. "You can all leave. There is a lot of preparation to do, so little time."

"What will happen to the handmaid?" Theo asked, trepidatiously. He couldn't bring himself to inquire about Eve for fear of the worst.

His father held his gaze, a wicked smirk on his face, assessing Theo before he responded. "She will burn, like all witches do."

CLARISA

THIRTY-SEVEN

Clarisa waited on bated breath as the oracles slowly entered the circle. The three of them—Diani, Sybila, and Amia—shuffled one behind the other as if tethered by an invisible string. Diani was the eldest, frail and feeble, her tendrils white and thinning. Her face cracked and etched like bark as she moved slowly ahead of the others. Sybila stood tall and poised. Her long, chestnut hair braided down her slender back. Amia, the youngest, was but a child. She trailed behind the other oracles, calm and gentle, her smooth, tawny cheeks filled with freckles. Her hair cropped to her shoulders. Their hooded gowns, which were normally described as white in the grimoires they uncovered, were a dark gray.

"They are ready for you, Clarisa." Brisa gestured toward the center of the circle, moving her long, copper hair behind her shoulder. She offered Clarisa a weak smile.

"Focus," Tabor added, a hint of concern in his voice. "Reach out to us when you are ready to return."

She met their gazes and nodded. She knew what she had to do. Clarisa stepped into the circle, surrounded by her familiars and the oracles.

"You come seeking answers, child?" Diani asked as she lifted her chin toward the crystal in Clarisa's hands.

"She comes with questions," Sybila responded.

"Questions she is not prepared to have answers to," Amia finished.

The three of them murmured their agreement amongst each other.

Clarisa took a step forward. "I have come to request your wisdom."

"Speak, child. For you may not have many words left to you."

"Many words still upon her lips."

"Many words unspoken."

"I wish to know about my sister," Clarisa spoke up, louder than intended.

The oracles fell silent, their pale gray eyes upon her.

"My sister, who I believed to be dead, was very much alive. I saw as they chained her and took her away. I need to know what will happen to her, if she needs help."

"No," Diani spoke.

"No?"

"No," Sybila chimed in. "You do not wish to know if she needs help."

"You know the answer to that question," Amia said simply.

"But—"

"You wish to know if she is like you—like your *mother*."

"If she possesses great powers."

"Rare powers."

"That is not—"

"We are not asking."

"We know."

"You know."

Clarisa furrowed her brow, frustration surging through her body. Yet, the risks were too high to start a confrontation here, and there were still more questions left. She shook her head, ignoring their accusations.

"What will happen to her?"

"She may have a trial; she may die a red death."

"She may die cruelly."

"She may die."

"How much time do I have left? What can I do?"

"That is for you to decide."

"No one else."

"Only you."

She bit her lip, feeling herself lose control of the conversation. "I prayed to Isila as a child, she had every opportunity to speak truly to me about my family."

"The goddess does not reveal the answers to unspoken questions."

"She does not bend to the will of her creations."

"She does not—"

"I come to seek your foresight, not riddles." Clarisa began to seethe. She could feel her power rising, influencing her.

"Our foresight is a gift from Isila, child."

"As is your foresight."

"As is yours."

"I do not possess foresight—"

"Your dreams indicate otherwise."

"The dreams that wake you."

"The dreams that haunt you."

"Isila has watched me suffer for years in solitude, only for me to witness my innocent sister be imprisoned for my actions. If I am chosen by her, why must she trifle with me!"

To this the oracles did not speak but faced each other.

Clarisa noticed, losing the last bit of restraint she held on to.

"What is it that passes through you? Speak!"

The oracles faced her once more. A menacing look upon their faces.

"You are not who the prophecy speaks of."

"The prophecy names another."

"Another long forgotten."

"I am the forgotten one! I was left upon a ship for the Blackthorn. I alone bore the burdens of my family's demise. I possess the rare magic, the ancient witchcraft that flows through my veins. *I* am the Blood of the

Blackthorn!"

"You are not forgotten."

"Your heart, in chaos."

"Your soul, buried in the depths."

"No, it's me. It's always been me," Clarisa breathed, weakening before them.

"It can be."

"If you will it."

"If you *kill* for it."

Their words began to commingle, filling her head until their voices were like echoes in her mind. She clasped her hands on her ears and screamed as they began to reach out to her.

"Enough!" Clarisa shouted. "Enough!"

Then it was silent, eerie, and Clarisa raised her head slowly. The oracles were gone, and in their places were three stones upon the floor carrying a witch mark in blood.

"Clarisa?" Tabor rushed to her side as Brisa thanked the oracles and Isila for their wisdom.

"Yes," she replied, stepping out of the circle but unable to tear her eyes away from the bloodshed before her.

"We were able to place them back," Brisa said, winding the rope of the circle and placing it in her leather satchel. "Hopefully we need not to summon them again."

Tabor moved to collect the necklace and bloody stones, assessing them. "Why inform you that you are not of the prophecy, only to leave behind this?"

"It is a sign." She picked one up from Tabor's hand, inspecting it. It was a hag stone, a light tan in color with a sizable hole through it. There were few found throughout the Blackthorn, particularly in the southern shores. They were used to see through disguises of magic folk among other powers. She assessed the bloody witch mark branded on it. The same one she was forced to put on Felicity. "This stone is bound by the blood of mortality," Clarisa murmured.

No sooner had the words left her lips, then a startling thought occurred to her. Another who was bound in magic and mortality as she was. One who may indeed be wearing a mask among mortals.

Could Eve have magic, too?

Tabor handed a stone to Brisa. "Three stones for three of us."

"Perhaps they will help with your dreams, Clarisa?" Brisa asked.

But Clarisa did not hear her. Her mind now spiraling with revelations she never thought to admit, never considered. Her muscles tensed and a malcontented urge filled her. She had been so consumed by her internal struggles that she never once considered that maybe, just maybe, the prophecy was falsely bestowed upon her. That her entire life and purpose had been a lie.

Eve. Magic. Prophecy.

Without realizing it, her body numbed, and the stone fell from her hand and clattered on the floor. It became clear to her then that Eve was more than just alive, she was a potential threat to her destiny. Her purpose, her right to claim. The only reason she endured every struggle and overcame them with greatness. With her sister in the way of her fate, Clarisa was nothing, every hardship meant nothing.

The oracle's message was clear—Clarisa had a choice.

To save her sister and forfeit her destiny.

Or let Eve die and claim it for herself.

DAKON

THIRTY-EIGHT

The bells tolled relentlessly, raging against Dakon's skull as he peered from the top of one of the capital's buildings to the growing crowd below.

Booong! Booong! Booong!

He placed his hands on either side of his head, wishing it would stop or that he could destroy it with his bare hands. Dakon shut his eyes tight, trying and failing to stop time like he did in his fight with the pirate, but it was no use. Men were gathering kindling and setting up the stake just outside the city gates. He could see them work from a short distance as he leaned against the stone railing. Nothing, no force or power in this world could make him stand any closer.

Rumors flew through the servant's quarters about Cerene meddling in witchcraft and despite the love most of the servants had for her, many were enticed to provide confessions witnessing her acts of damnation.

"She confessed in the king's solar. It must be true."

No doubt torture had to have been involved. He shook his head, trying to force the thought from his mind. And now it was reported that Eve, too, had been arrested, many believing they worked together.

He pounded his fist on the railing, how had he let things get so wrong?

More reports surfaced that the castle would close its gates following the burning. With the Strix prowling the streets, he knew that time was precious and nearly gone. Even so, he could not tear himself away, not yet. There was something he had to see through first. He heard footsteps making their way toward him, their pattern so familiar he did not care to turn.

"Dakon," Pazel said cautiously, "I've been asked to summon you. The steward requests the full presence of the household staff."

Dakon turned and Pazel shifted uncomfortably under his stare. "Tell him to fuck himself."

"I figured as much." He took a few steps and put a hand on Dakon's shoulder. "I know how much she meant to you."

"Then why should I have to go?"

"Because innocent people are murdered every day in this place. You, me, Cerene, we are nothing but the dirt beneath this castle. Taking a stand right now and surely dying for it, is not what Cerene would have wanted for us."

Dakon looked in Pazel's eyes and saw only fear—truth and fear.

"I do not plan to die today, just like I do not plan to move from this spot until it's over."

Pazel sighed, and after a long pause leaned against the railing next to Dakon. "Then I suppose I will be here too."

"You do not have to be here. The risk is mine to bear."

Pazel looked toward the stake, and Dakon followed his gaze. Kindling and a sizable crowd surrounded it, hungry to take the frustrations and injustices of their lives out on someone. No matter their innocence. It was cruel and barbaric, to kill someone so good and wonderful just because they possessed something that was envied. Dakon was sure that if any mortal had the chance to possess magic freely, they would do so without hesitation.

"We are friends, Dakon. I go where you go."

Guilt and shame filled Dakon as he watched Cerene be transported through the jeering crowd. The city threw rotted food, spat at her and yelled obscenities as she walked the steps to the platform. It felt like none of it was real, a hazy dream, a nightmare, and it took all Dakon's willpower to stay put. To not try and save her, despite his promise. It gutted him; tears rolled down his face, and he was not ashamed to admit that this spectacle they were making of her was breaking his heart. It would have been easier to break his body than look upon her suffering.

But magic was not immortal. And fate could not be changed. *Spells required a sacrifice, and her spell must have been powerful to warrant this,* he thought.

The elder spoke, the crowd cheered, and the flames began to feast upon Cerene as if they had been starved for centuries. She screamed and wailed, and Pazel held Dakon, begging him not to look. But a powerful magic coursed through him, and before he allowed his grief to completely consume him, he wiped his eyes with the back of his hand. And willed the fire to roar strong. To kill her quickly, to give her a more merciful death than the slow torture they wanted her to suffer.

And it did. It roared larger than any fire he had ever witnessed in his life. The flames raced to the sky, feasting upon its air and devouring the stake, burning it to ash. The crowd and the elder jumped back and ran from the force of it, trying to extinguish it.

But her screams finally ceased, and as the tears rolled down his cheeks, he thanked her for everything she ever did for him. For protecting him from the fate she so cruelly had to endure. It was the best he could do for the woman who gave him a second chance at life.

EVÆ

THIRTY-NINE

Eve moved carefully, cautiously toward the book. It was untouched and showed no indication of being trifled with as her chambers had. Just as she lifted a hand to touch it, the book opened to where she had last left off. The colored ink began to fill the page, telling another story she had never heard before. Her heart thundered in her chest, her hands shaking as she awkwardly took the book in her chained hands. Fire sparked at the tips of her fingers as she let herself be consumed by its power.

For this would be her salvation.

Eve was no longer bound but walked through a hazy corridor she vaguely recognized leading to her father's former suite. It was dimly lit from the late afternoon sun and was empty except for a woman running to the steps leading to her father's study.

It was her mother.

Eve chased after her, feeling as if she were running through quicksand. She pulled herself up the stone steps until she caught up, barely able to slip through the door before her mother closed it behind her. She watched as her mother gasped for air, breathing heavily.

As if on instinct, Eve reached out to touch her; her fingertips barely brushed her mother's shoulder before her mother stilled. She turned toward Eve, her brow knit in confusion as she stared into Eve's eyes. It lasted no more than a second before her mother shook her head and rushed toward the desk.

She scribbled quickly, the ink from the quill blotting in some areas of the scroll, and Eve watched as she was forced to waste precious seconds cleaning it up to make it legible. Her mother's hands could barely contain their shaking, trembling uncontrollably. She blew on the words, reciting a spell of sorts to make them dry faster as she grabbed her husband's seal from his desk. Eve could hear footsteps beginning to climb the tower steps toward her.

"Hurry, Lucia, hurry," her mother scolded herself.

She rolled the scroll and sealed it quickly.

The steps were growing closer.

Eve backed to a wall, fearful of who it may be.

Her mother opened the cage, procuring a morning dove and fastening the scroll on its foot, reciting another spell over and over again.

A knock was on the door.

Eve clutched her chest, wishing she could disappear into the wall.

"Fly, and find him," her mother whispered to the dove as she released it out the window and into the darkening sky. It flew out and disappeared almost immediately, the spell taking its effect.

"Please make it over the castle gates," her mother whispered, before sitting at her father's desk pretending to read a book. "Come in," she said aloud.

"It is only me, dearest." Her father's voice. He opened the door, a look of concern flashed across his face. "I was told you came here. Were you looking for me?"

Eve watched her father, so much younger and full of life. He stood tall and broad shouldered, confident even without meaning to appear so.

Her mother breathed a sigh of relief. "Thank the gods, Marcelo, you scared me."

"Oh?" He furrowed his brow, and quickly closed the door behind him. "What is the matter, Lucia?"

Eve watched as her father held her mother's hands.

"The king will not make it past the week," she said softly.

Marcelo took a step back, mouth agape. "You have seen this?"

"Yes. Prince Eryck is making preparations for a swift ascension; he will be crowned officially the following day."

"How can this be? It was just a small illness."

"I cannot see the past, Marcelo, you know this."

Her father approached her mother, his shoulders slumped, his fingers pinching the bridge of his nose. The seagulls cawed, the people in the city below went about their usual business, as did those in the castle, but none of it appeared comforting to either of them.

"We must leave," her mother whispered.

Marcelo raised his chin, looking in her eyes. "They will suspect us of his killing if we do. Prince Eryck will surely seek us out with all his might."

"He will use that power to separate us all should we stay."

"Where would we go?"

"Across the sea—"

"The Blackthorn is not safe; you have told me yourself."

"It may be our only choice. For the past hour I have been going over the options, the choices that exist where death can be avoided for all of us. The mortal kingdoms may try to use you or the girls as bait for me to serve them, the Blackthorn is where I would be among others like me."

"But what of our daughters? There is no one like them there."

Eve understood what he meant. In stories, witches and mortals rarely had children together. The blood of a witch was too deadly for mortals, with many half-witches dying before they took their first breaths. In this century, Clarisa and Eve were the only known in existence.

"There is no proof that they are the children prophesied. For all we know, there could be other half-witches among us that have yet to reveal themselves."

"And you are willing to take that chance—to go back to a land you have not set foot on in over twenty years and expect for us all to be welcome? For Clarisa to be used for her power? For Eve to be at the mercy of those with it?"

"I cannot promise anything!" she yelled, and her father staggered, unsure of what to say. "My magic weakened the day I stepped foot on this godforsaken land, everything I am, everything about me you have come to know is barely half of what I could have been."

They held their stares, an argument begging to be released on both of their lips.

Her father sighed first. "Explain to me how we are supposed to escape. This place has been locked down like a fortress since the king went ill a few days ago. Even if we did, we could only sail for so long before the king's men caught up to us. There are no ships bound for the Blackthorn, nor has there been for decades from here, as you well know. And unless you are going to tell me you know a smuggler, I think we need to consider our options in staying."

Her mother paused, and bit her lip with uncertainty. Eve knew her mother's powers over the years had slowly been fading, her magic becoming less potent as time went on away from the blackthorns that gave witches their magic. *Her inability to foresee the king's demise*, Eve thought, *is an example of her waning power.*

"I do not know a smuggler, that is true."

"Ah, exactly wh—"

"But I know a pirate."

Before her father could recover the shocked look on his face, there was a fervent pounding on the door, and the shriek of a child.

"Eve? Clarisa?!"

They ran to the door, her father throwing it open quickly. Before them was a young boy, no older than seven years old, trying to free himself from the grip of one of her father's guards.

"What the hell are you doing?!" her father roared at the guard, who quickly released the child.

"Pardon me, Lord Marcelo." He stood, now only gripping the child's arm to prevent him from escaping. "The boy claims to have a message for you. He ran past me before I got the chance to escort him up here."

"Well, release him," he replied hurriedly, then faced the boy. "Who are you, what is your message?"

The guard let the boy go, and the boy gave him a wary look before turning to her father.

"I am Dakon, m'lord," he said, carefully. "The governess sent me to tell you that Eve has run away from her studies again. It was my job to tell you, not him!"

The boy stood proudly, as if filled with the confidence of knowing he completed a job well done. Her parents looked at each other and back at the young boy in a dirty tunic and rough hands for someone so young. *Dakon,* Eve thought, feeling goosebumps on her skin as she studied him.

"Er—thank you, Dakon. Please let the governess know we have received her message and have sent the guard to find her."

"Yes, m'lady." He bowed, too deeply, but then ran off down the tower stairs, nearly pushing the guard in the process.

"Little shit," the guard muttered under his breath, before turning back to her father. "Would you like me to retrieve your daughter, my lord?"

"Yes, please."

"She will be in the usual spot," her mother said. "The prince should be with her. I expect his father would want to see him."

"Certainly." he bowed and retreated down the stairs, mumbling his curses at Dakon who was now much too far to teach a lesson to.

The door closed, and Eve watched her father sigh heavily before turning back to her mother. "What is it that you are afraid of? What do you see that makes you feel that we must go immediately?"

Her mother narrowed her eyes at her father and pursed her lips. "Treason."

Eve blinked. She was back in her chambers, her hands shackled together and filled with ash. Confusion took over as questions filled her mind.

Who was the pirate?

Was it the man the former king spoke of?

What had she done that was treasonous?

Did she truly kill the king?

A knock at her door brought her mind back into focus, and she barely had time to hide the book under her sheets before Adriana was let into the room. She walked in, apprehensively.

"It seems you have made a mess of things," she said, eyeing Eve.

Eve took a deep breath. "This was not what I wanted."

"I know," she sighed. "I just need answers. We are friends—sisters, even—are we not?"

Eve moved toward Adriana, raising her hands to provide a hug before remembering her shackles. "You are my sister. My family—"

"Did you do it?"

"What?"

"Did you kill Felicity?"

"No, of course not. I was with you."

"It all happened so fast—"

"I have been shackled and thrown in my chambers like a prisoner. You know I would never do anything to hurt anyone, especially your brother."

Adriana took a deep breath and moved to Eve. "I believe you, truly, I do. It has just been rather confusing."

Eve cast her eyes down at the floor, unable to understand how things became so muddled.

"They have burned the woman who did it."

Eve looked back up quickly, thoughts of her sister in chains filled her with dread. "What?"

"It was my handmaid, the servant, Cerene."

241

Confusion hit Eve. "W-why do they think it was her?"

"Don't you remember? The ash in the pocket, my note, it was witchcraft, I'm sure of it. I was just too scared to say anything. But after Marc asked me about you—"

"Why would Marc ask about me?"

Adriana bit her lip, hesitating. "He believed you had magic. He asked for me to find out, and the only time we were alone when anything occurred was in the presence of the servant. I told him about it when he confronted me after Felicity's death."

Eve felt sick. This woman was killed as a witch for her mishap with the ashes. A terrible, fatal misunderstanding. But as she looked into Adriana's eyes, she could not force herself to speak, to say the truth. She pictured the witch from the execution, how horridly she had been treated by the people, how bruised and beaten she was. That would be her, too, and surely no one would save her.

Maybe this Cerene did have something to do with it.

Maybe the ash in her pocket was the woman's fault.

Eve considered this. Mulling over it with a desperate conviction. She did not know this woman, did not know what other evidence was used to convict her. It was not entirely impossible that another witch could have been hiding in the castle, was it?

Adriana continued speaking, but Eve was no longer listening. Her head filled with every tale, folklore, and story she could about witches. Everything that she had learned thus far about her mother and her time as an enchantress.

The grimoire, surely it would reveal the truth.

DAKON
FORTY

Dakon ran alongside Pazel and Beast through Catalina's Port, the wind whipping wildly at his hair as he dodged passersby and vendors in the streets. Pazel seemed to not notice his new pet, and Dakon decided to keep it that way as long as he could. He held the small bag from Cerene and his daggers strapped to his belt. This time, the way to the tavern was much clearer with Beast's guidance. They reached the tavern just before sunset, and he affectionately petted his gytrash, thanking him for his help. Beast licked Dakon's fingers before he walked into an alley and disappeared in the darkness.

The crowds of the street turned more feral with midnight's approach, and so Dakon grabbed Pazel and quickly ducked inside.

The barmaid blushed when she saw him. "What can I do for you, handsome?"

Dakon nodded, avoiding her gaze. "Where is the captain?"

"Which one?" She smiled teasingly.

"Captain Amarin. I need to speak with him."

She tilted her head toward the back of the bar. "He was busy with Madam Cristina, but he might be done and with his crew in the back."

"Thank you."

He moved to head in that direction, but she placed a hand on his. "You never told me your name."

Dakon looked into her pale-blue eyes, a curiosity and kindness within them. "It's Dakon."

"I'm Clara."

"Clara," he repeated, giving her a brief smile back. "Thank you again."

"Hi, Clara. Pazel." His friend lifted his hand to the barmaid. "You might have seen a man like me a few days ago puking on a pirate's shoe, it's my silly twin brother. I'm nothing like him."

Clara gave him an odd look and took her hand back quickly.

Dakon grabbed Pazel and pulled him to the back of the tavern.

"We are not here for a long time; I need you to focus."

"I know, she is in love with me; my sincerest apologies. I just can't keep them off me."

Dakon rolled his eyes as they approached the room.

It was a large suite, filled with tables and men drinking behind them. In the corner, laughing with some of the men was Captain Amarin.

"It might be better if you wait in the hall," Dakon urged.

"I was just thinking the same," Pazel replied, leaning against the wall.

Dakon nodded, took a deep breath, and entered. "Captain," he said breathlessly, "I wish to take you up on your offer."

Amarin looked him up and down. "And who are you?"

Dakon raised a brow. "I'm Dakon, the one who bested you in a duel days ago."

"Did you? I think I'd remember that." He laughed with some of the men at his table.

"I did—"

"The captain don't know you, boy," one of the men said, "get lost."

Dakon ignored the man, pressing Amarin. "You offered me to sail with you that night and I intend on taking it."

244

The man retrieved his sword. "I said get lost."

He pushed Dakon roughly, sending him to the ground. Dakon pulled his daggers out, jumping to his feet. Anger and frustration taking over. "I am not here to fight, but I will if I have to!"

They glared at each other until a roaring laughter was heard. Dakon shifted his gaze to the captain. "Oh, I remember you now, boy. That fire. Unlike any I've seen in a long time. Gio put down your weapon."

The man sheathed his sword once more, eyeing Dakon warily.

"Tell me, what changed your mind, boy?" the captain asked, gesturing to Dakon to sit across him.

"I want a fresh start, somewhere new. Far away from here."

"You look bloody miserable, I'd want a new start, too, if I had dog shit for a face."

Dakon ignored him as a few of the men cackled.

"Alonso, get him a drink."

Another man next to the captain handed him a clear liquid with a bitter smell.

"Drink up and think about it. We leave tomorrow before dawn," the captain continued, "if I see you on the ship, then, you're welcome to stay. If not, I wish you well and hope you don't end up dead."

"Dead?"

"Yes, boy. Haven't you heard," Alonso chimed in, "there's rumors of witches coming into Givensmir. Been growing a following here in the port."

Dakon felt as if the air were still and thick. He fought a rising panic as memories of the Strix in the locked building came back to him. Since then, he shuddered at even the mere thought of them. How close they were to grabbing him as he escaped.

In a city of thousands, it would have been impossible for them to find him. That was his only solace in the matter, the only thing that helped him go to sleep.

Could they still be looking for me?

"It's a bad omen, too many witches congregating like that," Gio mumbled.

"What do you think they want?" Dakon asked.

245

"Between you and me, I hear they're searching for the enchantress's daughter. The non-magic one," the captain said.

"Why?"

"To spill her blood, eat her, who knows. Point is, they plan on using her for something to further their cause. Poor girl probably has no idea."

Dakon took a long swig of his drink, nearly coughing the strong taste up. All of this he already knew, but to hear it again gave him chills.

"I bet they were behind the murder of that one princess. They probably meant to kill the half-breed and mistook the girl for her," Gio said.

"They don't look anything alike," Alonso scoffed.

"And you've seen either of them?"

"No—"

"Then shut up."

Dakon looked around the table, considering all that was said. Cerene said that his and Eve's fates were tied, for her to be harmed would damn him as well. He pivoted the conversation, focusing once more on his reason for coming.

"When are you sailing, captain?"

"Tomorrow before dawn, I said. Clean your ears, boy."

Dakon looked outside, the night was approaching. There wasn't much time. He downed the entirety of his drink, pounding his fist on the table as his face screwed up in response to the horrid, burning taste.

"I will be there. And I will bring two people for passage *and* your discretion."

Before the captain could respond, Dakon handed him a handful of the gold and silver coins. The captain smiled. "I like you Dakon. I think we will work well together." He placed the coins in his pocket. "A reminder, we don't wait for stragglers."

"We will be there," Dakon promised and left the room.

Pazel and Dakon nearly ran into a few tavern patrons on their way out. It was far more crowded than it had been the last time they were there. He passed Clara at the bar pouring cups, and she eyed him with amusement. Pazel waved, but she pretended not to see.

"Why do I get the feeling I won't see you again, Dakon?" she yelled as he neared the entrance.

"Because you won't!" he called back but left her with a genuine smile.

THEO
FORTY-ONE

Theo paced before Eve's door, debating the consequences of entering. A woman was killed for the murder of his wife, but all signs pointed to Eve's potential involvement, or at least, that was the opinion of the court. He was summoned to his father's study that morning, charged with a task that seemed nearly impossible to complete. The king's words hung thick in the air—*question her, or I will do it myself.*

It was his only opportunity to get the truth from Eve before they departed. After days of avoiding her, days of resisting the urge to visit and ensure her well-being, he was now forced to confront her. Answer for his unforgivable absence.

The thought unsettled him, and yet, selfishly rushing into battle unsettled him more. Far more than any other he was forced to participate in. The Blackthorn was an unknown territory, and it had been nearly eighty years since an invasion had been attempted, ending with the deaths of thousands of Givensmir's army.

Theo thought of Eve again.

Was she involved or was she truly innocent in all this?

If nothing else, he knew he deserved the truth.

He nodded to the guard, who let him in.

"Prince Theo, my lady," the guard announced before quickly retreating and closing the door behind him.

Eve was clearly startled and threw her sheets around as she leapt from her bed. Theo looked upon her in shock. Her long hair was tangled and messy, her eyes red and puffy, as if she hadn't slept since her arrest. Yet, her fingers, his eyes narrowed—her fingers looked as if they had been rifling through dirt or ash. *Ash.* His heartbeat quickened, hoping against hope that it was a mere coincidence. He moved his gaze to the fireplace, empty, clean, and seemingly unused.

"Theo, I've been waiting for you to come see me," Eve said, trying to brush her fingers through her hair and leaving bits of ash in them. "I am so very sorry for your loss."

"Thank you. I've been otherwise engaged, as you know," he said stiffly.

She moved toward him, arms cuffed but trying to raise them in an embrace, but he took a step back, placing his hand between them.

"I have come with a purpose, Eve. First, I wanted to make sure you are well—"

"This has been a deliberate misunderstanding."

"Is it?"

Her eyes widened. "You of all people should know I would never do anything to hurt you. Or anyone else."

Theo shook his head, unable to look at her, unable to see her in this state of distress. He squeezed his eyes tight before forcing himself to face her once more.

"My father," he began, sighing, "has sent me on a fool's errand to procure a confession from you."

"I did not kill the princess—"

"Not that kind of confession, Eve."

Her brow knitted. "Then what does he want?"

"I think you know already."

"I–I do not."

"Princess Felicity died by witchcraft, a witch's mark burned onto her forehead. The only evidence was *ash*"—he grabbed her hand and lifted it to her face—"care to explain?"

Eve looked at him in horror, stunned silent.

"I didn't want to believe it; I defended you against everyone who warned me. Please, tell me it isn't true—"

Suddenly, his hand felt hot as if touching steel in flame, and he released Eve quickly, swearing out loud. A bloody blister began to form on his palm. He held it in front of him, coming into full realization of who he was truly dealing with.

"Witchcraft," he breathed through gritted teeth. The pain of his hand was nothing compared to the pain in his chest, the devastation of knowing Eve had played him for a fool.

"Theo, no! I'm sorry! It's not what you think!" She rushed to him, trying to inspect his wound, but he brushed her off, wrapping it in a handkerchief from his pocket.

"Stop." He stood, moving out of her grasp.

She moved back. Standing helpless, tears began forming at the corners of her eyes. She was shaking, terrified.

"Please," she begged, "let me explain."

"How long?" he demanded.

"I—"

"How long?!"

Theo watched as Eve wiped tears from her eyes, holding herself as if she may fall apart at any moment. Her hands leaving ash marks and traces of his blood upon her dress sleeves.

"A few months, maybe less. I was terrified. I didn't know what was happening to me."

"How could you lie to me, *me* of all people?" His heart sank, the tension thickening.

"I couldn't tell you. I couldn't tell anyone. You know this. It would have been tantamount to a death sentence."

"I would have kept any secret of yours until my dying breath. I would have weathered the storms of our chaos to ruin than to face a lifetime of war and misery without you." Theo's heart was pounding, his anguish palpable, but he could not stop himself. "But you made a choice that I cannot save you from. Dammit, Eve, how could you not tell me?"

"Theo, I'm sorry," she whimpered, tears falling over her cheeks.

His shoulders slumped, and he brushed his hands through his hair in frustration. "Did you kill Felicity?"

"No, I swear," she said desperately, "that was not my doing."

"Do you know who did?"

To this, he watched as Eve opened and closed her mouth, biting her lip.

"Was it the servant? The one who was executed?"

Eve shook her head, shame prevalent on her face.

"Adriana was forced to give a witness statement—she was in shambles—and you knew. You knew the entire time it wasn't her!"

"I didn't know if she was a part of it, I only thought I saw someone else," she responded quickly.

"And who was that?"

Eve paused trepidatiously before finally uttering, "Clarisa."

"Clarisa?" Theo stood, bewildered.

"Yes—no. I don't know." She moved her hands over her face and through her hair in frustration. Theo couldn't tell what to make of this, of her words.

"You saw her, or you didn't. We are about to go to war with the Blackthorn, a princess is dead by their hand, and now you are telling me your sister—dead these fifteen years—may have been the assassin?"

Theo watched as Eve fell silent.

"Who are you, Eve? What happened to the girl I thought I knew."

"I am still me. I promise. I have not changed."

Theo raised his burned hand angrily. "*This* would seem to say otherwise. Eve, people are dead, and you have inherited the eternal curse. What do you expect me to do?"

"To love me in spite of it!" she shouted.

The words hung in the air between them, filling Theo with confusion and a sense of desperation. Eve stared nervously at him, breathing deeply, waiting for him to respond. After a few tense moments, he began to slowly close the distance.

She placed her hands in his again, this time cool to the touch, and held on fervently. "Please, help me escape this," she whispered. "Let us run away and be free *together*. The way we wished we could've that night."

Theo paused, staring into her eyes, reflected in them was the color of the rich earth they ran through as children, the amber tones of passion, of home, of comfort. He took in the beauty of the woman he knew to be his world, the one who visited his dreams, giving him hope of a peaceful future in the midst of battle. *It would be easier to move mountains than to let go*, he thought, but even so, he removed his hands from hers.

"I have loved you all my life. It was always you, Eve"—he confessed, breathing deeply and finding courage to speak the next words —"but I am tired of hiding in gardens and yearning for what could have been. And you deserve someone that could give you more than a summer night." His voice shook, and he took an unsettling breath trying to feign indifference. But the look in her eyes nearly broke him. He faced away from her, "I will tell my father nothing of what transpired here. And *if* I return, I will see to it that you are swiftly married to Lord Callum, to live in Teros—"

"No, I will not go," she said quickly, reaching out for his face, running her hand through his hair and holding him tight against her.

Tears ran down her cheeks, and Theo stilled, unable to find the resolve to move away nor in this moment did he want to. He searched her eyes for the truth of her words, and slowly lifted a hand to caress her cheek wiping away the tears. She focused on him, unwavering hope in her misty-eyed gaze. His soul crushed under the weight of his shame as he held her in his arms and forced the next words from his lips.

"I wish that love was enough."

Before Eve could answer, a knock was heard and the door opened to Lord Callum and the guard. "Lord Callum, Your Highness, my lady."

Theo and Eve took a step back from each other quickly.

"Should I come back at a later time?" Lord Callum asked, eyes wide in confusion.

"No," Theo said, turning back to face Eve once more, "we are finished here."

CLARISA
FORTY-TWO

The waves crashed against the shore, swallowing up men and sinking them into the depths of despair. Clarisa could see herself walking slowly through the carnage and chaos, providing her blood to the waters. The ships crashed into themselves, destruction just out of reach.

And the voice, clearer now, called out a name.

Eve! Eve!

This time, however, her dream went red.

Clarisa opened her eyes, a haziness taking over as she tried to breathe. Hands were around her throat, squeezing with all their might. Panic flew rampant and she tried to scream, tried to produce any sound for help, but all she could muster were winded, choking gasps.

A stranger, a man cloaked in black, sat over her, and she tried to push him away. They struggled and the man lost his grip. She used the opportunity to punch him in the throat. Her eyes watered, and she sucked in breath after breath as her body struggled to cooperate. She tried to scream, tried to make a sound, but her throat was bruised and swollen. The skin of her palm began glowing blue where Navir had left his mark, but she had no time to think about it.

The man leapt toward her and knocked her against a shelf, sending the items clattering loudly onto the ground. As they wrestled, Clarisa tried to summon her magic, but she was barely holding on to life, her vision blurring incoherently, her body desperate for air. The man pulled out a knife, lifting it before him, and Clarisa squeezed her eyes shut in terror.

Clarisa heard a *swoosh,* and the man screamed, dropping the knife, an arrow sticking out of his hand. Clarisa moved her gaze toward the source. Tabor was across the room, bow in hand, and Brisa rushed to Clarisa, knocking the knife away.

"Move back!" Brisa ordered, and Clarisa stumbled behind Tabor.

The man on the ground ripped the arrow from his hand. Blood began pooling at his feet.

"Who are you?" Tabor yelled, fitting another arrow quickly into his bow.

Clarisa could hear footsteps rushing toward them down the hall.

"They are coming," the man replied, a sly smile on his face as he backed into a corner.

Brisa pulled Clarisa to her feet. "Who is coming?!"

The man did not answer, but retrieved a vial from his pocket, drinking the contents quickly before facing Clarisa. His gray-eyed stare and monstrous smile chilled her to the bone.

"You will join me soon, *enchantress.*"

Members of the coven rushed into the room in time to see the man dropping to the floor.

Dead.

***

"He had the sigil of the Strix on his wrist," Clarisa said as she sat in front of her fireplace, staring into the flames, trying her best to make sense of its dance. Scrying into fire was far more difficult for her than water, but something about the flames called to her, and she tried to listen. Yet, as the flames licked the sides of the hearth, growing as it feasted upon the kindling, it said nothing.

"The queen has alerted the covens; they will inform us if there are any more among us"—Ana rested her hand on Clarisa's—"and the queen has doubled your guard. No one will enter without them knowing."

Clarisa shook her head. "They were banished centuries ago, why do they wish to come back now? What do they want with me?"

"I don't have the answers," Ana said, "but I want you to be safe."

"The ships, the ones from my dreams, they are coming for us"—Clarisa knitted her brow—"then I wake to someone strangling me."

Ana held her hand tight, allowing Clarisa to continue.

"I am not safe in sleep and not safe when I am awake. Even as I sit scrying before this damn fire, I am not safe!" She threw a bowl of water at it, reducing the flames to ash.

"You are safe with me," Ana replied.

"Am I?!"

She did not mean the words to come, and as soon as they left her lips, she regretted them. Ana looked as if she had been struck, a hint of confusion and shame in her eyes. Clarisa turned her gaze back to the ash, focusing on its gray and black hues atop bits of orange embers struggling against its inevitable demise. She could feel Ana's stare burning into her but refused to meet her gaze.

They remained silent a short while, before Ana finally stood. "You have no idea what I would do for you," her voice cracked, "what I have already done for you."

Even then, for some reason, Clarisa couldn't bring herself to take it back or face her. Without another word, Ana left the room, slamming the door behind her. Clarisa sat in front of the fireplace for a long while, staring into nothing and mulling over everything.

Something was coming—no, that something was here and wanted to kill her. No one could be trusted, not anymore. Navir's words echoed relentlessly through her head, *there are more people that want you dead than you realize.*

And with that thought, any intention she had to save Eve was gone.

DAKON
FORTY-THREE

"Dakon? What are you doing—I thought we were escaping?" Pazel called out as they ran in the direction of the castle. "I still am."

"I was hoping we'd be halfway to Bastard's Haven by now, not to the end of our lives."

"Shh," Dakon replied, agitated. "I just need to—I have something of great importance I need to do first."

"Wait, just wait." Pazel stopped, pulling Dakon into an alley. "If I am to come with you, you need to tell me what you are doing. I can't risk my life or my potential freedom without knowing what your plan is."

Dakon let out a breath. "I'm sorry. You're right."

"About time you noticed."

Dakon ignored him. "You may not believe me and trust me I barely do myself. But I have to rescue Eve, she is coming with us."

"Isn't she arrested for witchcraft?"

"Yes."

His eyes widened, and he shook his head. "Do you want to follow Cerene's fate?"

"No. But I made a promise."

"Are you in love with her?"

"No, you idiot. I"—he fumbled for the right words—"I made a promise to protect her. If she dies, I may die with her."

"Dakon, this is madness." Pazel gripped him by the shoulders. "You are willing to risk your life for a lady you've never met because you made a promise? Did this person have a death wish for you!"

"Not exactly."

"And how will you manage that? There are guards riddled throughout the castle. Unless you are going to tell me you have magic, too—" Pazel stopped, his eyes widening as Beast appeared next to Dakon.

Dakon bent to pet the gytrash. "Hello, friend." Beast licked his face and hands, happily.

"W-what is that monster?!"

"This *monster* is how we will get through the castle."

"Where did you find it?" Pazel was frozen on the spot as fear etched its way into his face.

Dakon couldn't help but laugh. "He found me. And he has a knack for direction."

"Is he going to slaughter all the guards and let us walk through unscathed?"

"No, but I am sure you heard the rumors."

"That touching wild beasts would mean certain death, yes I have."

"No, listen," Dakon urged, "the one of hidden passages throughout the castle. Beast will be able to lead us through them. He's already done it once."

Pazel paced in front of him. "So, you need to save this Eve. And then we can leave? This is ridiculous, even for you."

"I don't have a choice."

"Of course not. It is never easy with you handsome ones, is it?" Pazel sighed dramatically, "just give me moment."

"You don't have to come."

There was a silence that lingered and Dakon could see Pazel contemplating his options. He was just about to speak, when Pazel finally chuckled, shaking his head.

"And miss out on all the fun? This might be the most exciting and dangerous thing I ever do."

Dakon smiled.

"Besides, you need someone to watch your back—with the fighting and all."

"You are a shit fighter."

"It was an off day."

Dakon rolled his eyes. "If you come with me, you need to protect yourself and do as I say. Do you understand?"

"Yes, yes, I swear it on my mother's life."

"You have no mother."

"Okay, my father's."

"You have a father?"

"No, but I need something to swear on, so you'll trust me."

Dakon took a deep breath, pinching the bridge of his nose; at least if he died, it would be with a modicum of humor at the end.

"Last chance," Dakon whispered as they climbed the hill next to the curtain wall. Beast ran through the wall, and Dakon could see him through the hole in the stone waiting impatiently on the other side.

"I'm with you." Pazel replied, swallowing nervously.

Dakon nodded and they both squirmed through the opening in the curtain wall, closing it carefully behind them with the stones. He fought to maintain control of his nerves, coming back here when the guards were closing the gates and increasing their security may prove tricky. They followed Beast through the gardens, trying to blend in as they normally would. A few guards strolling by noticed, but otherwise paid them no mind.

Beast led them to a small cellar door in a remote part of the castle grounds.

"I didn't realize this was even here," Pazel whispered as Dakon pulled it open, revealing a dark space beneath. He prayed that Beast was taking him the right way.

"Neither did I."

They climbed into it and lit a torch before they closed the hatch. The torch was barely helpful in the darkness that shrouded them, but at least he could see Beast just ahead. They walked through the tunnels and climbed various steps with dead rats and spiders until bits of light began to trickle in at various spots along the wall.

"What is this?" Pazel wondered aloud.

"Spying holes," Dakon mused, "from when this castle actually had decent spies."

"Where do they look into?"

"The various rooms and corridors of the castle, I suppose."

"Have you spied on people here?"

"No."

"Why not?" Pazel asked as he began to peek into a few.

"I see no reason to—aren't you supposed to remain quiet?" Dakon pulled him from one of the holes.

"Oh, yes, I am the epitome of silence."

Dakon glared at him as they moved through the secret passage. He knew the hall leading to Eve's chambers was relatively quiet and the stairwell was coming up. Only a few more steps.

"Hey, Dakon," Pazel whispered, "look at this."

He gestured for Dakon to peek through the hole, and his heart sank.

Dozens upon dozens of guards were lining the hall in front of Eve's chambers.

"This is going to be harder than we thought," Pazel breathed.

"I've faced better odds, that's for sure," Dakon mumbled. "Let's hope they're still stacked in my favor."

EVE
FORTY-FOUR

S he could barely hear Callum's words—his vitriol at her circumstances, his declarations to have her freed immediately, his scheduled audience with the king—all of what he spoke barely broke past her shock. She was grateful, but the weight of everything felt all-consuming and torturous. A pang of guilt clawed its way through her as Callum kneeled, grasping her hands between his. He stared into her, his eyes soft and gentle now.

I do not deserve this man.

"I am here for you, Eve," he kissed her forehead, "I will be back as soon as I can, I promise."

She could barely move, barely speak, as he walked away with a determined stride. Then she was alone once more.

How could it be, that such a short time ago she was a noblewoman with her life and prospects ahead of her, and now she was reduced to a criminal in shackles? She twisted her wrists, trying and failing to get comfortable with the iron chains so tight.

Theo was gone, Callum was gone, a woman killed for her sister's crime, and now, she was alone to think about what may happen to her. *It was vile*, she thought, *how Felicity looked in her father's arms*. She was barely a body, as if she had been sucked dry of everything save for her skin like a thin blanket over her bones. Eve shuddered.

She felt for the book beneath her pillow, its leather binding oddly comforting, and drifted into a fitful sleep allowing herself to give in to her body's fatigue.

There was a knock, soft at first, and then a light tapping.

"Eve," she heard a whisper through the wall. "Eve, it's me, Dakon."

I am being driven mad, she thought, *the book has rid me of my sanity*. Yet, when she reached under her pillow, she did not feel it. She lifted the pillowcase, and saw it was gone.

She did not have time to think about it as the tapping grew, capturing her attention once more.

"Eve. Come here, there's a friend with me, don't panic."

Eve sat up from her bed, then, startled and confused. She turned in the direction of the sound from within the wall. It sounded like two people bickering with each other. She carefully climbed out of her bed, and walked toward it, fumbling a bit with her shackles as she removed a painting that hung on her wall.

There was a small hole behind it from whence the voices came, barely noticeable in the wall if she did not hear them beckon her. She approached it, peeking inside. It was dark and dank, save for a torch light that a thin, scrawny man was holding. Dakon stood next to him with a large, monstrous dog.

"Have you come to save me, Dakon?" she whispered, nervously.

"Yes, that is what familiars are for."

"Familiar? I thought you said apprentice?" the man said, confused.

Eve was not sure what to make of him. "Who is that?"

"I am Pazel, my lady." The man bowed awkwardly. "I am here to be your *apprentice*."

Dakon elbowed Pazel in the ribs. "I'm sorry for him. I am a novice myself, but the binding spell has ended. Your magic is coming back, and I need to help you escape before it's too late."

Binding spell? Familiars? Apprentices?

"I don't understand," she whispered urgently, taking a second to peek at her door, praying that no one would burst through. "They may be back any minute, I don't know what is going to happen to me."

"The king will summon you to his tower this evening."

"How do you know?"

"We've been listening to his conversations through the walls," Pazel chimed in, "thanks to Beast."

Dakon pet the monstrous dog. "He will lead us through these hidden halls to where you and the king are. I will be far better able to help you escape there."

"Why not here, now?"

"This wall does not open like the ones near the king's. And"—he paused nervously—"have you seen outside your chambers, past the stairwell lately?"

"No," Eve breathed. "I haven't left since they brought me here."

"It's an army out there," Pazel blurted. "Me and Dakon wouldn't be able to cut through and save you. Not even with Beast."

Eve bit her lip, she did not realize how much of a threat the court expected her to be.

"My magic grows as yours grows," Dakon said gently. "I do not possess enough, nor can I control it well enough to get you through that kind of force."

"We share magic?"

"We are tethered, as I said. I am only as safe as you are alive, if that helps you feel better somehow."

Eve considered this, but recognized she did not have many options, "I trust you, Dakon."

"This is new to me. And I will explain when we have escaped and are safe. But there are people who want are calling for your execution, and others who want to use your magic."

Eve let out a shaky breath, she did not realize how dire her situation had become, foolishly believing that Theo's or Callum's request to free her would have been enough to resume as normal. She was such a fool. Tears threatened at the corners of her eyes.

Dakon moved closer. "I was told you had a book, keep it safe. But if it disappears, let it."

Eve furrowed her brow. "You know far more about me than I do you."

"Trust me," he replied, "I wish I did."

Eve nodded, then remembered he couldn't see her. "Where will you take me?"

"I have a plan that should be worked out by the time we come back."

"You are going to leave me?" she gasped, louder than intended.

"I will be back," he promised. "There is someone I need to speak with first."

THEO
FORTY-FIVE

The ships were anchored along the port, rocking gently in the night—the sails barely moving in the uneasy stillness and lack of wind. An elder of the clergy prayed loudly from the scriptures for their safe return. Hundreds of men were silent, listening to the prayers they hoped would lead them to victory, as did Theo. To come home successful after another needless campaign, to capture lands that were not theirs by right, but by force, disturbed him.

Theo looked around at the faces of the crowd, some familiar, some not, most likely farmers and men of the countryside they rarely visited. A haunting night fog clung around them, choking their spirits as the elder now raised his hands, and cried out, "May the gods have mercy on us, and may they accept the dead into their kingdom of immortality!"

Theo noticed the elder's robes moved like a ghost around him, his pale face and balding head adding to the vision. It scared him, reminded him of the ungodly force they were planning to invade. It had been centuries since the last successful ship ported in the Blackthorn, and decades since they were last invaded unsuccessfully. The histories came to him, gripping his heart like an icy fist. The last invasion barely came back with enough men to man a small boat. *It is a curse*, he thought, *the inability for the witches to leave for long, and the inability to be conquered.*

He began to truly wonder, then, if this would be the last time he would walk on these grounds, if it would be the last time he would look upon the castle, his home, and see his mother, his sister, his father. Moreso, if the conversation he had with Eve would be their last.

The elder finished his sermon flinging holy oil at the crowd for their final blessing repeating the same phrase over and over again.

"By the will of the gods!"

It became real to many as Theo again looked upon their faces, those young and old. This would not be like any other battle. This was a war against nightmares.

"I saw a raven in my dreams, brother," Eryce said as they boarded the ship. "It unsettles me."

Theo turned to him. "What is to come unsettles me."

"Do you think we will come back?"

"I don't know."

The men began to board the ships, too few to sustain a war, but enough to begin a skirmish. This was foolish, Theo thought again for the hundredth time, the faces of the men around him confirmed it. They all knew these ships may very well not return.

Theo and Eryce moved in silence toward the mainmast, allowing the crew to board around them.

"If by some miracle we return from this, there is something I must tell you. Something I wanted to tell you long ago."

Theo looked upon the slight fear in his brother's face, the stoicism he tried to muster to hide it. He briefly thought of Lord Callum leaving his brother's room and wondered then if it was the right time to speak of it.

"Whatever it may be, I will always have your back, Brother. As I know you have mine."

Eryce let out a deep breath and took Theo in for a brief hug. "This is why you are my favorite brother."

"I am honored. However, between me and Marc it's not much of a choice."

Eryce knit his brow. "Speaking of, where is Marc?"

"He has already boarded our ship. Apparently, he is now an expert sailor."

Eryce let out a low laugh. "Let us hope, for our sake, he is."

Theo looked around the ship and those surrounding them waiting for the command to set sail. In the darkness, there was no one save for Eryce and Pedro that he recognized aboard their ship. Each man focused on their task silently, not much like how it normally had been when they would set sail in the past with conversations abounding.

"It appears we have new men."

"Father tasked Ser James with summoning whoever remained in the city. Our army experienced some logistical challenges returning from Larrea, many men have still yet to set foot back in the capital."

Theo shook his head. "Then we are among bakers, blacksmiths, and butchers instead of swordsmen."

"I am sure the baker will be the strongest of them. Have you seen them wave their pins around at thieves?"

Theo took the bait, an involuntary smile creeping on his lips. "I wager the butcher is half a swordsman already, only he needs to aim at the living."

Eryce chuckled for a moment, then looked out toward the water. "I wonder how they will sing of our ill-fated attempt."

"It may start off with a mad king sending all his heirs to die for pride."

"Or greed, but there are already too many songs of greed."

"Maybe it will be about two brothers who adventured to death's door together."

Eryce turned to Theo, placing a hand on his shoulder. "I like the sound of that."

Theo returned the gesture. "Let us go to war, then."

"To war."

The sounds of anchors being hauled filled Theo's ears, and then, as the ships moved further out in the water, silence. The Dallise Sea was known for its treachery, rich in lore about monsters lurking in its depths—it was why their trade routes favored south of the Mistral Islands. The maps Theo studied estimated a three-day journey to the Silver Port of the Blackthorn. Now, as they steered their ship northwest, Theo felt a sinking feeling at the pit of his stomach, the taste of the salty air too thick, the lack of nature blessing their journey—not even a seagull to bid them farewell. This was a fool's venture. To disturb the unknown was to invite chaos. And they would soon find out how death greeted its guests.

DAKON
FORTY-SIX

"I see the princess."

Dakon stilled. "Are you certain?"

"She is sitting on a chair reading a letter. I see her right there."

Dakon ripped Pazel away and peeked in. Adriana was sitting at a chair, reading from parchment that looked familiar . . .

"Should I call for her?" Dakon asked, suddenly nervous and doubtful.

"You have to say goodbye, this is the best chance you have."

"What good would it do?"

"You did not bring me all this way and leave your witch in her chambers—well she was there anyway—to not see the woman you love." Pazel leaned against the wall. "I am tired of your restraint—"

No sooner had he leaned, than the wall began to protrude into the princess's room. A small opening from which he could enter.

The princess began to scream, and Dakon ran out, holding his hands up to silence her.

"Adriana, it's me, it's Dakon."

He heard footsteps racing toward her chambers and she hid him quickly under the bed.

"Princess!" a tall, blond guard called out. "Is everything okay? I heard screams."

"I–I—" she began. "I saw a spider, but it's quite all right now. Thank you, Timothy. I'd like some privacy, please."

Timothy furrowed his brow and took a quick look at the room. Dakon held his breath, hoping he wouldn't enter and look left where he would surely be able to notice the protruded wall. But instead, he nodded and retreated, closing the door behind him.

"Dakon, what are you doing here?" Adriana whispered, pulling him out from under her bed.

Dakon breathed deeply, his heart thundering in his chest, as he tried to pat down his dirty tunic, "I–I came to say farewell, Princess."

"Farewell?"

Dakon looked into her hazel eyes, full of wonder and care. For years how he longed to stare into her beautiful eyes, to have the privilege to gaze upon her face this close. He moved closer, closer than he would have ever dared before. Adriana's brow knit in confusion, but she stood her ground. He knew he only had precious moments left before he had to go back to Eve. The adrenaline spiked a courage in him he had never felt before.

"Yes, Your Highness. I must go."

"Go? Why?"

"I don't have time to explain."

Adriana bit her lip, confusion and sadness overtaking her features. "I–I will miss you, Dakon."

He nodded, lifting her hand to his lips. "It was a privilege to be your confidant. A privilege that I will dream about for the rest of my life." He began to turn away, unable to bear the disappointment on her face any longer.

Adriana reached for his hand suddenly, grasping it quickly, but firmly in hers.

"Dakon, wait."

The sound of his name sent a fluttering in his chest, and he turned to face her once more.

"It's you, isn't it. Please, at least tell me the truth before you go."

Now or never, you fool. He took a deep breath, shame filling him.

"Yes, I–I am sorry for ly—"

Before he could finish responding, she placed her hands around his neck and kissed him sweetly. Her lips soft as they embraced each other, deepening the kiss, her hands in his hair, and his on the small of her back pulling her closer. He would have traded every bit of himself he could, to whatever gods really existed out there, to be with Adriana like this for the rest of his life.

He felt a tug at his shoulder, and knew it was Pazel. There was no more time.

He pulled away slowly, watching as a small blush formed on her cheeks.

"I only wanted to kiss you," she breathed, her eyes fluttering open, "I hope you don't mind."

"Of course he didn't, Your Highness." Pazel bowed clumsily and pulled Dakon towards the open wall. "I'd say this was his best-case scenario."

"I didn't mind," Dakon said, brushing Pazel off. "I will cherish it forever."

"I won't say a word, Princess. Ask him, I am the epitome of silence."

Dakon shoved Pazel, gesturing him to leave.

"Goodbye, Dakon," Adriana said, a bittersweet smile on her face. "Don't forget me."

Dakon walked backward as Pazel ushered him behind the wall, taking a final look at the woman of his dreams, to keep the memory of her smiling at him locked in his soul.

EVE
FORTY-SEVEN

Eve had never truly thought of death before this day.
Never imagined how it would feel to draw her last breath, to say her last words, to leave with so much unfinished. Yet, as she walked down the darkened corridor, clad in more iron chains held by the king's guards, she thought about it.

How would it feel to die?

Would death grant her an audience, or would it be perpetual darkness?

Would the gods she had been forced to pray to all her life come to her, let her into their immortal kingdoms, embrace her as a daughter of theirs?

Would it hurt, when the king killed her?

How would he do it?

Thoughts of the witch pulled behind the horse through the streets clouded her mind, sending shivers throughout her body. She would never make it, never be able to muster the strength or courage to face death in such a barbaric manner. She would sooner die of fright.

Eve felt an ache in her chest, the familiar fear creeping up her spine, as the guard knocked on the king's solar door. Her book, she hoped, was gone for good, perhaps appearing for another unassuming witch in the world. A small voice echoed through her head: *they would not need a book to justify killing you.*

"Come in," she heard the king say.

Her flesh crawled, and she kept her eyes downcast as they pushed her inside. They dropped the chains at her side, and she felt tied to the spot. It was difficult to even stand straight with the weight pulling her down.

"Leave us," the king drawled.

"But, Your Highness," one of the guards protested, "for your safety would you not wish one of us here with you?"

There was a tense silence interrupted by the king coughing.

"Your Highness?"

"Damn you," he said after his coughing fit. "Get out or I shall have your friend there slit your throat!"

She listened as the guards retreated quickly, shutting the door behind them.

Eve stared down at her feet, unsure of what else to do. She tried to recall all the excuses she came up with over the past few weeks, reasons she should be spared, ways to explain her magic away as folly or gossip. Yet, in the moment it was all lost on her. The truth echoed louder than she expected in her skull. The book would not let her forget who she was. Even if it damned her.

"Apologies for the way you have been treated, Lady Eve. I asked that they restrain you to your chambers, not that they harm you in any way."

Eve raised her head, facing the king. He stood confidently before her, his eyes betraying his words. She sincerely doubted it, but she was in no position to question it. Not when she was unable to summon her magic at will.

"I understand, Your Majesty."

"Do you? Understand, that is."

"You believe me to be responsible for the princess's death." She kept her eyes fixed on him, trying to gain a sense of the direction he intended.

Any way for her to manipulate the conversation in her favor as she had done so many times before.

"I don't actually," he replied as his lip curled. "Not directly that is."

"I had nothing to do with her death, Your Majesty," she began.

He raised his hand to silence her. "There have been reports of a peculiar nature lately. Notes turning to ash in pockets, glasses breaking without a cause, a princess tragically dies, and you," he raised a brow, "lingering in your chambers for hours and hours reading a book of magic."

Eve's eyes widened, her mouth slack as fear gripped her.

"Do not try to deny it, my dear. My sources are well-placed."

"I–it is not what you think."

"Oh, but I think it is. You lied to me, Eve. I do not take kindly to those who lie to me."

She shook her head, the only thing she could do. She was a child; she did not know then that she possessed any magic.

He continued. "Perhaps that is your greatest trick of all—playing us all for fools as the mortal child of the enchantress. A stupid, mortal girl."

Eve began to shake, feeling helpless and trapped. The chains felt heavy on her wrists, and it took everything in her to remain standing. She was caught; no amount of words would change the outcome.

"What do you want?" she breathed, sweat pricked at the surface of her skin from the effort to remain as she was while her strength waned.

The king retrieved a key from his pocket and unlocked a box on his desk. "I want you to use your magic . . . for me."

Eve looked at him, shocked and dumbfounded.

No.

"I do not know how to control it," she said.

"Then *learn*, quickly."

"It is not that simple."

"Make it that simple," he growled, "or I will give you a witch's death, and it will be slow, I promise you."

She breathed raggedly, her options before her impossible.

"Which would be a shame, as I would hate to destroy this." He opened the box, pulling out the grimoire.

Rage seized her suddenly as her eyes lingered on it. She needed it, to save it, to cut his throat and take it from him with her bare hands if she had to. She tried to move forward, but the chains were too heavy. She growled out loud, noises coming out of her from voices that were not her own.

"Oh, so this does have some importance to you?" The king smirked.

"Leave. It. Alone," she seethed.

"No," he said, "I don't think I will. I can't have you using it against me or killing anyone else for that matter. Not after all the trouble I went through summoning it."

"I will kill you!" the voice within her screamed. Something was trying to escape her, to control her, but it was not powerful enough, yet. She tugged and thrashed against the chains, but to no avail.

"There is a great deal of magic in your blood," he smirked, "thanks to your mother, I learned that I would only need a drop from a powerful witch to summon what I wish."

Eve recalled Lord Wesley pricking her with his knife, and she was stunned silent.

The king laughed, placing the book back in the box.

"Let us discuss how things will go from now on." He pulled a chair a safe distance in front of her, and sat, arms crossed before him.

"I will never give you my magic."

"You are not listening"—he sighed—"I said I wanted to use it, not have it."

"Never."

"What a shame, I hope you realize the book is not the only thing I have over your head."

Eve narrowed her eyes at the king, before hearing a familiar voice call out, "Eve! Eve!"

She turned quickly toward the door, but the chains held her back, "Callum?"

There were footsteps on the other side of the door, a loud sound, and then silence. Eve held her breath as it opened slowly, revealing a battered Callum at the feet of a few guards. His nose was bloodied, his eye blackened.

Her flesh crawled as the king said behind her, "Now are you willing to talk?"

DAKON
FORTY-EIGHT

Dakon felt bittersweet as he rushed through the tunnels with Pazel and Beast. Beast trotted ahead of them, understanding his way through the tunnels better than Dakon ever hoped. He felt they were close; they had to be.

"How does it feel to kiss a princess? Did her lips feel like gold?"

"No," Dakon whispered, "focus."

"Then they tasted like it, I'm sure."

Dakon ignored him as they picked up their pace.

They reached Eve's chambers, the various spy holes allowing him to see inside. It was empty.

"Where could she have gone?"

"Maybe they released her?"

Beast tugged at Dakon's tunic, pulling him back to the hallway where the guards were previously lined up. He peeked through the hole; they were all gone. Beast whined against the edge of the wall, clawing at it.

Dakon ran a hand in Beast's fur trying to calm him. He felt the wall for a familiar incision, and upon finding it pushed slightly. It gave way allowing for a brief space to enter the corridor.

"What are you doing?"

"I just need to see something."

They both rushed up the steps into Eve's chambers, and Dakon felt the sheets for the book Cerene had told him about. Making sure it was not left behind. It wasn't there.

"Fuck," he cursed, "we need to go now."

The door opened suddenly as a guard entered the room.

"Well, well. If it isn't the king's fool. Aren't you supposed to be kissing ass and telling jokes?"

Dakon nodded. "We were just leaving."

Beast began to growl, positioning himself between the two. Dakon wished he could be real, but Timothy showed no signs of noticing the gytrash.

"And what do you think you're doing?"

"Looking for Lady Eve." The best he could come up with on the spot. *Foolish, foolish idiot.*

"You just missed her. I escorted her to the king's tower." He smirked, tilting his head.

"We will be leaving," Pazel said shakily, pulling Dakon's arm.

Timothy held up a hand. "No, I don't think either of you will be going anywhere." He pulled out his sword. "Shame, I expected the king would have let me kill you in front of an audience, especially once he hears of how you laid your filthy mouth on the princess."

"How do you—"

"I heard through the door as you savagely kissed her, stripping her of her dignity. Only question is how you hid when I burst through the door."

"Watch yourself," Dakon spat, pulling out his daggers.

"It's you who's been sending her those love letters, isn't it?" He chuckled behind the monstrosity of his sword. "I would thank you seeing as though I've been taking the credit. But I don't know what's worse, a fool loving a princess or a stable boy knowing how to write."

The tension thickened as they stood their ground, weapons drawn.

"Pazel, get out while you still can."

Pazel nodded, slipping out of the room. Beast turned, whining. "Leave," Dakon breathed, softly, "Help Pazel find his way."

The dog whimpered but disappeared.

"Coward," Timothy laughed.

"No more than you, fighting a man without a sword."

"Some kills come easy I suppose."

He leapt toward Dakon, sending the full force of his blade into the stone floor as Dakon moved out of the way just in time.

"Fight me, fool!" Timothy slashed his sword through the air.

Dakon held his defense, keeping his daggers before him. They were dinner knives against the massive sword in Timothy's hands. He tried to focus on an escape, but his path from the room was blocked.

Timothy ran toward him again, nicking Dakon's shoulder. Blood oozed out onto his tunic and the floor.

Dakon twisted and cut Timothy's face with his left dagger, stepping back quickly out of range.

Timothy reached out and touched the cut, his nostrils flaring and his eyes narrowed. "You missed."

They battled, metal clanging against metal, Dakon trying to dodge the fatal blows and Timothy using his sword to try and overpower him.

Dakon blocked another blow by Timothy, pushing him back in the process. The guard fell back, sword falling from his grip. Dakon leapt onto Timothy and quickly plunged the dagger into his side, more a flesh wound than anything.

Timothy howled in pain, and Dakon removed the dagger, his eyes wide with shock. He had never tried to truly kill a man before, never came close in all his time sparring with the princes or even his fight with Amarin.

Timothy punched Dakon hard in the face, sending him onto the floor where they grappled for control of his daggers. Dakon thrashed against his weight, shoving him aside. He barely had a moment to breathe before Timothy grasped the long sword and bore his weight down on Dakon.

He swung the sword, and Dakon barely caught it between the cross of his blades. He struggled against Timothy's strength, he was no match for him, not like this.

"Any last words for your princess? I'll make sure they die in this room." Timothy spat, blood trickling down his face and onto Dakon.

Dakon felt his muscles fatiguing, his hands began to give way as the sword pushed deeper toward his throat, drawing beads of blood. He closed his eyes, trying to fight his fate that was sure to come.

Then, he heard a loud thump and felt an instant relief from the struggle. He opened his eyes. Pazel was now standing over a limp Timothy, a broken chair on the floor in front of him. Dakon shoved the guard off him, the weight making his shoulder scream in pain.

"Who's a coward now?"

Dakon breathed a sigh of relief as Pazel helped him up. "Certainly not you, my friend."

He caught his breath, and lifted his hand to his neck, the blood not as bad as he imagined it would be. He wiped it with the back of his hand.

Beast appeared, licking Dakon's face. He grabbed him in a quick hug and stood quickly. *Eve.*

He could almost feel her pain within him. It burned, something was burning inside of him. They had to move, now.

He handed Timothy's sword to Pazel. "Use this only when you need to. If something happens to me, you must escape. Go to Catalina's Port, and board Captain Amarin's ship. Let him know it was me who sent you in my place. Understood?"

Pazel nodded, admiring the sword in his hands. "My first sword and fight. They were right, you are a bad influence on me."

EVE

FORTY-NINE

"Do him no harm, and I will answer your questions." Eve felt a sickening in her stomach as she said the words. Her eyes narrowed, wishing she could burn him on the spot, wishing she could freeze time, or use any of the powers she might have gained from her mother. But she was helpless, unable to summon them now when she needed them most.

"That's what I thought," the king replied with a sneer before addressing the guards. "Be sure to hold him in full view of Lady Eve. Should she slip, so will your daggers on his throat."

"Don't," Callum groaned, "Eve."

Her heart ached, and tears pricked at her eyes as she beheld him, beaten and restrained before her. She turned back to the king, jaw tightening.

"You know exactly what I wish to know." He moved toward her.

"Stay away from her!" Callum yelled, trying and failing to leap out of the guards' grasp. Before Eve could respond, a guard punched him in the stomach, dropping him on the floor.

"Please, stop!" she yelled.

"Mind your tongue, Lord Callum, or she may end up in your shoes."

Callum writhed on the floor in pain, grunting and spitting out blood.

"Now, as I was saying," the king turned his attention to Eve, "how long have you had the curse."

"Th-the curse?"

"This will be quicker if you do not feign innocence, child. Answer me true."

Eve held still, her voice caught in her throat. To answer would be to damn her. To answer would be to damn anyone who held association with her.

"Break his arm," the king said aloud.

"No—!"

A horrid snap filled the air and Callum's cries echoed the solar.

"I don't know! Months ago—please, please let him go!"

"Ah," the king said calmly, "so we have an understanding now. You answer my questions, and he lives. You don't and there may not be any of him left by the time I'm through with you."

Eve nodded as he pulled a dagger from his royal robes, holding it out for her to see. It held a black hilt encrusted with blood diamonds atop an iron blade.

"This dagger was used to kill your mother."

Eve turned her head to the side.

The king eyed her as he continued, "It was once believed that witches' blood ran black as their souls." He lifted the dagger up slightly, as if holding it out to catch the moonlight, admiring it. "I was sorely disappointed to see that she bled red, the same as all mortals. For all her power, she died fairly easily. For all her power, she could not take my crown nor supersede the will of the gods."

"I know the story."

"Then you know how it ends for those with magic here. Those who practice witchcraft and worship those vile gods."

Eve remained silent, wishing that her iron chains would turn to dust at her feet, that she could truly summon her familiar and fly out through the window like in the stories.

"I tried to give your mother a chance, but she was only concerned with bloodshed and power. For years after, I had to clean up the mess, the filth, of your kind in this kingdom so that only you remained."

Eve snapped her head at him, eyes wide. "What do you mean?"

The king lifted the corners of his lips in a vile smile "We will do things differently this time, *enchantress.*"

"I am not an enchantress."

"Oh, but you are. Your mother passed her gifts onto you in death. And I have been waiting for the moment it manifested. I will have the power my father was too weak to control. You will not have the high standing or influence that she had. You will remain a prisoner here at my beck and call until you are of no use to me. You will tell me what I need to know to take more land and power, until I am the sole ruler of every kingdom I can get my hands on."

Eve stood horrified, trying in vain to move herself back, but he grabbed her arm quickly. The touch of his skin on hers, volatile and rough.

Then the truth revealed itself in his eyes.

KING ERYCK
FIFTY

Prince Eryck valued two things above all: power and loyalty. The one did not exist without the other. It was something his father, the soon-to-be late King Byron III had told him time and time again. The gruffness and growl his father's voice would have as he said them, the emphasis he put on nearly every syllable still raised goosebumps on his skin. Eryck could not recall a time when his father said anything of affection, but *power* and *loyalty* were the words that echoed inside his head when the candles were burned to the wick and the sheets were pulled nearly to his chin.

Even as a grown man, a seasoned warrior who had seen combat countless times, even as he watched his father on his deathbed, shouting those words like a madman before he finally gave in to his illness—a cruel sickness that he had been fighting bitterly for over a week—he could still feel his words upon him like a viper wrapping around and squeezing his throat as he had done so many times before.

"Power! Loyalty!"

His death couldn't come fast enough, and Eryck nearly had a mind to stab him in the neck to quiet the senile old man, but the doctors and witnesses present for the imminent death kept him grimacing in a dark corner of the room instead. When his father finally quieted, two healers approached the bed with caution, nodding to each other as they began to inspect the king and feel for any other signs of life.

Eryck watched with annoyance and contempt as their movements were more theatrical than deft. As if they were proving their worth to him in sight of all the men present. Eventually, the healers whispered to each other and turned to face the room, their faces grave, but stern.

The grand healer, a middle-aged man with a balding head and a weathered, tired face. He looked upon Prince Eryck, his eyes a mixture of sincerity and concern before announcing, "gentlemen, King Byron III is with the gods now. May he rest in peace among the five in their eternal paradise. By the will of the gods!"

"By the will of the gods!" the room chanted. Eryck remained tight-lipped in the corner, uninterested in the formalities.

"Now, long live King Eryck! Long may he reign!" the healer roared, kneeling before him.

The group of nearly twenty men and both healers pounded their chests with their fists and kneeled alongside him:

Long Live King Eryck!
Long Live King Eryck!
Long Live King Eryck!

The now-King Eryck left, refusing to linger in the room of a man who disgusted him beyond comprehension, whose dead face was twisted into a snarl and whose bulging eyes looked as if they were going to leap out of their sockets as he lay in his filth. Not one of the men in the room dared to follow him, giving their new king his space.

Power and Loyalty.

King Eryck recited this to himself, guards in tow as they always were, striding confidently through the corridor toward the throne hall. The guards opened the heavy, wooden, double doors without him asking, and he stood a moment to take in the room before fully entering. The throne hall was dark, with only a few torches lit near the entrance, the midnight sky filtering in from the arched windows on either side of the throne, barely providing any semblance of additional light. Eryck took a few steps inside, this room appeared far smaller than he had recalled from earlier that day, and it disappointed him. Perhaps it was his father's presence that made the room seem infinite, something he would now have to make a reality.

He walked further toward the center of the room and faced the throne itself. The massive chair consisted of gold finishings, befitted with cushions of the same color embroidered with black thread, the impressive colors of the kingdom. Large gold-and-black curtains were strewn behind it, connected to an intricately detailed archway of gold. King Eryck rested his eyes back on the throne. A fearsome outline of a black merlion, claws raised, its snout baring its fearsome teeth, was sewn into the front cushion, reminding all those who looked upon it that only someone with *power* and *loyalty* could deign to rest their back on it.

Would he dare?

Even before the official coronation?

He would.

King Eryck ascended the few steps with ease, taking note of the queen's throne. It mirrored the design and detail of the king's but was smaller in size, far less intimidating. He scoffed, thinking how his wife, Alondra, would look sitting next to him, so meek and polite. It was laughable really, how someone of his status could even deign to waste his space with such a pathetic woman.

The only thing he could concede in her favor were the sons and daughter that she bore him. Otherwise, he would have tried to kill her long ago. He pushed the chair lightly, found that it was rather heavy, and pushed it harder until it toppled over. Eryck laughed as the thud echoed across the empty throne room, a guard peeked inside, but he waved him away and was alone again.

If his marriage hadn't been arranged before he could talk, he would have rejected the notion of even meeting anyone as dull as Princess Alondra. However, his new position could warrant an accident or two if she tried to step out of line.

He smirked at the possibilities of that idea and reached his hand to his father's chair—his chair now. It was smooth and cool underneath his fingertips, and he walked around once to get a better view of the throne his father would have beaten him senseless for touching or nearing. It was sturdy, made of strong Teros darkwood, and much, much heavier than the queen's chair—*good.* King Eryck sat, feeling in good spirits.

"Ser Phillip," he called from his throne.

One of the guards, a tall, dark-haired man entered the room and bowed. "Yes, Your Majesty?"

"Bring me the enchantress."

Soon, the guard returned with a woman at his side. She was dressed in a long cerulean cloak over a teal, silk dress that pooled the floor behind her, the hood of the cloak covered her head and most of her face. He gestured for Ser Phillip to leave them, and he did, closing the large doors behind him. The enchantress walked slowly toward his throne, her heels making clicking sounds along the white tile of the throne hall. For a few moments, her heels were the only sounds in the entire world, it was music to his ears.

As she reached the bottom of the throne steps, she curtsied deeply. "Your Majesty."

Eryck enjoyed this, and watched as she stood back up, taking in the woman before him. "Lucia. How are you this fine evening?"

"My evening was fine until I was removed from my chambers in the middle of the night," Lucia spat, her face still lowered.

Eryck chuckled in response; he appreciated her poisonous temper; her fire and passion were some of the reasons he was infatuated with her, beyond all sense and reason. Lady Lucia was the royal enchantress, and the sole woman and witch of the Gold Council. Over the decade, she proved a worthy asset to his father as her visions were tantamount to the success of the kingdom's battles and their recent win against the Zafira territories over a year ago, much to the delight of King Eryck and the crushing heartbreak of his wife who was raised in its capital.

While Lucia remained at the court she was under the protection and watchful eyes of his father. A father who was dead now.

"My, my, you are feisty when you're tired. Why don't you remove your hood so that *your king* may look upon your face."

Lucia hesitated at first, but then slowly raised the hood and settled it on her shoulders. Looking back at him was one of the most striking women Eryck ever laid his eyes on with smooth, bronze skin, bright, brown eyes, and thick, dark, curly hair that fell just below her breasts. She was enchanting, indeed.

"What do you want?" Her words were venom.

"I only wished to share this moment with you."

"Go share it with your wife."

He ignored her and changed the subject, annoyed, but not wanting to rid himself of his good mood. "Tell me a vision, Lucia. *Enchant* me."

"I do not wish to enchant you."

"Why not? Especially since there is nothing standing in the way of us now."

"There never was an 'us.' "

King Eryck lifted himself off the throne and walked toward her. "I have seen you eyeing me, I know that you feel as I do. As I always have for you."

Lucia seemed to change her approach and righted herself, squaring her shoulders at him. "I did not mean to deceive you, Your Majesty."

"You are forgiven, now, let us start anew." He continued his approach, closing the gap between them.

"Yes, that would be wise." She moved backward toward the entrance of the throne hall, keeping her eyes fixed on him warily.

Eryck picked up his stride and grabbed her waist, pulling her close to him. "You wouldn't want to punish your poor husband or daughters, would you?"

She looked at him, wide-eyed, and tried to pull him off her, but his grip held firm.

"Lucia, you no longer have to fight it, you and I can rule this kingdom. You and I can rule all the kingdoms. No one can stop us."

He leaned in to kiss her, holding the back of her head with his other hand. Eryck was finally going to get what he had been desiring after all these years. His lips touched hers and he felt as if he were the magic one, as if he truly understood what invincibility was. All the time spent waiting for her was worth every bit of torture and tediousness.

Then, before he could do anything further, he felt a stinging pain on his lip—she bit him.

He pulled his face away and pushed her forcefully, she had drawn blood. *How dare she do this to her king*, he seethed internally and wiped his lip with the back of his hand. She began to run to the doors.

"You are going to regret that." He raced after her, grabbing her by the hair and forcing her to the ground before she could reach it.

She pulled out a dagger from her cloak, swinging wildly. She cut him deeply below his eye and stabbed him in the flesh of his side before he managed to grab her wrist and squeeze, forcing her to drop it. He got atop her and pinned her to the cold floor.

"Your Majesty"—tears began streaming down her cheeks—"please, spare me."

He slapped her with the back of his hand, anger seething into every bit of his body.

"You dare to lay a finger on your king?!"

"Let me go!" she cried.

"We will rule every kingdom on this earth until there is nothing left. You will do this for me. You *will* make this happen."

She struggled against him, using whatever force she had to try and push him off her.

"No!" she screamed.

He could not understand why she was acting this way. He had to make her see, make her understand. She spat in his face as she pushed her hands against his chest, trying to throw him off. Fury swept over him then.

"You will love me," he snarled, and placed a hand on her throat. "You. Are. Mine!"

His anger blinded him, sending him into a turmoil that he had never felt before. A rage that consumed him, that sent him to the point of no return. Lucia clawed at his hand, gasping for air, trying in vain to push him off her, anything to free herself, but he was far stronger. He could hear the crack of her bones under his grip.

He did not mean to kill her, only to subdue her, to make her see reason, to make her understand just how much he loved her, to listen to him, to love him back.

It was only when the guards opened the doors to the throne hall seconds later, accompanied by a few lords from his father's chamber, did they witness him sobbing over the dead enchantress.

"What happened, Your Majesty," one of the lords gasped.

The king looked down upon Lucia, her face now pale and lifeless; she was still the most beautiful woman he had ever seen. He closed her eyes with his fingertips, his heart sinking, and body sagging as he began to rise from over her. The pain of the flesh wound sent him back onto his knees in agony. His vision was becoming hazy, and his consciousness was waning. He tried to concentrate on something, anything, to keep him awake.

His eyes landed on the dagger next to him. It was black with blood diamonds encrusted in the hilt designed in the typical fashion of the Blackthorn realm where Lucia was raised. At least, that's what he believed. It was covered with his royal blood, dark red and dripping onto the tiled floor. It terrified him as his mortality reflected back to him with each drop, and his paranoia rose.

She could have killed him.

Fear filled his eyes as he began to formulate the reasons for such a treasonous act. As he stared down at this dagger, he realized that this woman—this witch—beneath him was far more dangerous than he ever thought possible. A snake in his court.

He gripped the dagger, eyeing it carefully. His reflection was muddled in the bloody blade.

There was no doubt in his mind that she came armed because she intended to kill him tonight, even after all he was willing to give her. After

290

he professed his love to her, she was ready to rid him of this world, of his birthright, of his kingdom. She tricked him with her witchcraft to fall in love with her in the first place, to be unable to resist her. The possibilities of her evil works were unlimited.

Eryck raised the dagger, high above his head, and before the men in the room could stop him, he plunged it into her heart. Angry tears felt hot and stung his eyes as they trailed down his face. He yelled out in pain and rage until he began to cough.

He coughed horrendously until blood began to drip from his mouth, the taste of it, iron and bitter against his tongue. He could hear the healers making their way down the corridor rushing to him. There were various loud voices that echoed outside of the throne hall. The guards and lords were getting closer now in panic.

Eryck took a last look at Lucia who, with her eyes now closed, looked as if she were merely sleeping; his father was a fool to trust a witch, no matter how beautiful, and he would make sure to rectify that mistake.

"The enchantress tried to kill me," he breathed, "bring me her daughters." Then he fell to his side, and the men who approached him gasped before roaring into intense shouts of confusion and chaos.

And as King Eryck succumbed to the black haze of unconsciousness, he uttered something that shocked the room into complete silence.

"Power. Loyalty."

<hr />

The memory flooded the king, paralyzing him as he looked upon Eve's deadly gaze—she looked so much like her mother. As if his vision carried it in fragments, he felt the dagger slip from his hand and into hers.

He blinked once, and there in front of him was the enchantress.

EVE
FIFTY-ONE

The king's memory filled Eve with horror and rage. The truth of her mother, the lies she was forced to face every day since the destruction of her family—the emotions, the raw carnage she wanted to inflict, her wrath, would be nothing like this world had ever seen. In an instant, the room and people froze around her. She could hear the crackle of the flames engulfing the room before she saw it.

"*Summon me.*"

A voice spoke to her, familiar and cold, but she let it flow within her, guiding her next movements. The iron chains turned red on her wrists, the heat melting them into molten bits of metal that clanged as they fell to the floor. Her eyes locked onto the king's as he watched her frozen in terror.

"*Let me in, Blood of the Blackthorn.*"

Eve closed her eyes and felt the power and magic flowing within her. She was no longer the lady of Rubianes Keep; she was something far more deadly. She grabbed the knife from his clammy hand and stabbed him in the heart, pushing until he collapsed on the floor.

Eve was no longer herself, but she felt a sickening relish in who she was becoming. She knelt next to the king, her now-red-colored eyes alight with the fire taking over the room around them, ensnaring life in its deadly grip.

"Goodbye, Eryck," the voice flowed through her as she whispered in the king's ear. She plunged the dagger deeper as the king grunted in frozen pain. Blood pooled around the hilt of the dagger and onto her fingertips, it flowed from his mouth like a river. It was as if someone else had taken over Eve, something had amplified her wrath into a harbinger of death.

She faced the box, ready to grasp the book once more.

"It is safe now," the voice whispered within her.

Eve could feel herself nod and turned away, walking calmly out of the chambers and through the flames unscathed. The guards were frozen, their knives still positioned tightly against Callum's body.

"Together we will be the fire that rules the world."

Eve lifted her hand, guided by a cool confidence she had never before experienced, and in an instant the guards fell to the floor, dead.

Stop it, she thought, *I don't want to kill anyone else.*

"We are the fire."

Leave! Leave! She tried to scream through the force that fought within her.

Her hand began to raise shakily before her, pointed toward Callum.

No!

With every force of her strength, every bit of her that was left in her body, she struggled against what was to come.

NO!

She no sooner thought this than Eve slumped to the ground, her muscles ached, and her energy felt depleted as if the magic consumed all her strength. Yet, the flames persisted in the king's chambers and the dead remained as they were. She stood and stumbled toward Callum, who began to writhe in pain once more.

"Callum, Callum, get up!"

"Eve," he whispered, lifting a hand toward her, slowly taking in the room and bodies. "Eve, what happened? How did they die?!"

She could see the panic rising within him, coming to the realization. The flames now moved past the king's chambers beginning to engulf the curtains in the hall they were in.

Then came the shouts from a distance. *More guards*, she thought, and her heart quickened, as she searched around the tower for a place to go. *Where were Dakon and Pazel?!*

"We need to leave, *now*," she replied, pulling him to his knees.

"You—you're a witch," he sputtered.

"I will tell you everything you want to know, but we have to leave, please!"

He stared at her for a moment that felt like an eternity, before finally, he nodded. "I trust you."

Eve watched as Callum tried to lift himself on his broken arm, stumbling back to the ground. He tried once more, grabbing one of the swords from one of the dead guards as he stood.

The curtains fell, flames shooting up high and strong. With dread, Eve realized it was blocking the only other path away from the tower. They stepped back from the immense heat and both looked down the stairs as their only means of escape. Stairs from whence the frantic shouts and orders yelled could be heard. Callum breathed heavily, then faced Eve, a solemn look on his face.

"Eve . . . you must run when I give the signal."

"No—"

"If there are two, maybe three, I can give you a chance to escape."

"No, I won't let you!"

Callum grabbed her hand. "Please."

Eve gripped him tight. "I will not abandon you, Callum!"

The guards were at the base of the tower steps, but there was nowhere to run. Time seemed to still around them as they held each other, staring fiercely into each other's eyes. *He deserves the truth, it is now or never.*

"I love Theo," Eve whispered, shakily, "but I love you, too."

Callum smiled gently, sadly. "And I love Eryce. But I made you a promise to love you and I meant it. Every word. In this moment, there is

294

no one I would rather see the end of my life with."

Eve trembled against him, terrified as the heat of the flames began to lick at her skin. It cracked and roared through most of the tower, smoke filling the room.

"I love you, Eve."

Callum kissed her then. Passionate and desperate, knowing they would not make it out of this alive. She pulled him close, and deep inside wished it was Theo, and for a moment, she convinced herself it was. Just as she knew he wished for Eryce.

And the fire began to creep toward them, surrounding them as if they were flies caught in its web.

THEO

FIFTY-TWO

I t wasn't only his father's intention to battle against such a powerful, unfamiliar force that concerned Theo. Yet, he could not place where his building dread was coming from as the days passed, only that it existed and now he could no longer ignore it. The more it sat with him over those two days, the more he came up with potential reasons he was so troubled, besides the expected death before him.

He thought it odd that his father would even agree to send all three of his sons, all his heirs, on a mission that could have been completed by a more skilled reconnaissance team if surely the Blackthorn was so dangerous. He even considered it bizarre how unusually quiet Marc seemed from the other end of the ship, remaining aloof rather than boisterous. Theo wondered if it had to do with the fact that Marc had not set foot outside of Givensmir his entire life or if the weight of his father's desire to have him join the army as his brothers did secretly frighten him.

A thick, white fog permeated the sea around them, barely giving them enough visibility to see a few feet ahead of them. Stories of the monsters that lurked within these waters plagued him, pirates and krakens, horrid beasts of the witches' creation. However, they encountered none of that; it was the smoothest sail he had ever experienced. Not so much as inclement waves or weather.

The only thing Theo felt was the prickling on the back of his neck, the feeling that they were being watched, but couldn't tell from which direction. The only semblance of life in these waters was the occasional sound of waves lapping against the ship and the light breeze against the sails.

This was no simple undertaking, the risk of attacking land by sea with nothing but brute force was tantamount to a death sentence for the first few waves of men, if not all of them. Surely the Blackthorn would be positioned with archers, and typical defense forces along the castle walls.

Theo couldn't shrug the cold grip of something inside of him, his breathing deepened, and his pulse quickened; there was something very, very wrong.

He walked to Eryce, who was fastening daggers to his hips by the steer.

"Brother, I have an eerie feeling about this place," Theo murmured, trying not to alarm the men around them.

"I've been having the same feeling," he replied, turning to Theo.

"This is a fool's errand; a death sentence."

"We have always been fools to the gods."

"I fear our gods have no presence here," Theo replied, looking around at the other men who were conducting their preparations solemnly in silence for the bloodbath that surely lay close ahead. "I recommend having Marc stay behind with the rallying party. We don't want to risk all of us at once with his indiscretion."

"It would bring shame on him to not fight."

Theo only nodded but felt a dryness to his throat. They held their silence for a few moments.

Eryce put a hand on Theo's shoulder. "I have not been honest with you, Brother."

Theo eyed him, nodding slightly. "I know."

Eryce appeared speechless, opening and closing his mouth.

"You and Lord Callum. Your lack of an heir thus far . . ."

Eryce looked at the wooden boards beneath him, taking a deep breath. "He is my soulmate, Theo."

"Eryce—"

"Tell him for me, if I don't make it out."

Theo grabbed his brother by the shoulders. "You will have to tell him yourself. We will survive this."

Eryce brought him in for a hug, and Theo held his brother close. Because in truth, he knew if this battle didn't kill Eryce, their father surely would.

Eryce moved to the main deck, assisting in battle plans with the commander. Theo remained by the steer, trying to make sense of the sinking feeling he continued to have.

The ship was slick as a drizzle began making the fog that much more eerie. Theo cursed at his father under his breath and wondered why anyone allowed the old, and obviously deranged, man the continued power to make any decisions.

Pedro moved next to him. "Your Highness," he whispered, "I wanted to tell you it has been an absolute honor and privilege to be your close friend. May the gods have mercy on our lives."

"You have been the greatest of friends, Pedro."

"I am perhaps your only friend." Pedro smirked.

Theo chuckled, "I would say the same for me, except you are often found in the arms of so many women. I fear there may not be any room for friends in your life."

"They are dalliances, Your Highness. You are the confidant I will battle beside for the rest of my days"—Pedro stilled, suddenly, looking out toward the sea—"even if they are numbered."

Theo leaned against the railing, not realizing his white-knuckled grip on it. "The feeling is mutual."

Pedro leaned next to him, his brows furrowed. "My cousin, Eve—"

Theo's jaw tightened. "I told my father she was innocent. That she had nothing to do with Felicity's death."

Pedro nodded, mulling over this. "She cannot control who her mother is. But I can promise you, by all the five gods, that she would never hurt anyone. She does not have a wicked heart."

"I know."

"Will they release her?"

"My father said there is no reason to keep her confined. The threat has been dealt with."

"That is what Lord Wesley told me. It settles my nerves to hear it confirmed."

"Lord Wesley?"

"Yes, he came to visit me before I arrived at the shipyard."

"Why?"

"He inquired about—"

Then a scream ripped through the fog.

And hell broke loose.

Theo turned toward it and watched as their ships fell into anarchy.

"Mutiny!" someone shouted.

Theo's eyes darted around, adjusting toward the rest of the gray that now surrounded them. A large force climbed the sides of their ship, using ropes to leap between vessels. They moved stealthily and quickly, practically racing up the sides as if it posed no hardship to them at all.

No.

"Pedro, find Eryce, go now!"

The mutineers on his side pulled themselves up over the ship, and Theo withdrew his sword quickly, slicing one through the midsection, before they could make it over. Pedro swung his sword and killed one as he made his way down the stairs but struggled to pull his sword from the body, as another man jumped on top of him. They struggled as the man retrieved a dagger and attempted to pierce Pedro's chest, only held back by Pedro's grip on the man's wrist. Theo rushed to him, just as the man's eyes began to emit a bright, white light. It momentarily surprised Pedro who began to let up on his grip. Theo plunged his sword into the man's back just in time.

Pedro pushed the man off him and stood, his eyes wide and bewildered. "Wh-what was that?!"

"Witchcraft," Theo breathed. "These are witches!"

Pedro's eyes were wide as beheld the sheer size of the forces overtaking the ship. Men seemed to come in from every ship Givensmir sent to the Blackthorn, overwhelming them.

Theo's eyes landed on Eryce who was embroiled in his own sword fight near the mainmast.

"Go, aid Eryce!" Theo ordered. "I will find Marc!"

Pedro ran, fighting his way through the crowd, but became overwhelmed as he tried to fight two witches.

Theo ran to the left flank, where he could barely see Marc, injured on his back, as Eryce fought a man next to him. He was closing in, but still about fifty feet away. He ran as fast as his legs would take him, pumping his arms to propel him; his right one feeling the strain of its previous injury. He willed himself to ignore it, despite its growing intensity. With the weight of his sword and the daggers concealed on his person, his lungs were on fire, and he whipped through the air trying in vain to reach Marc and Eryce before it was too late. Through the bit of moonlight that poked through the fog and clouds overhead, Theo could now better see what was happening before him.

His soldiers were all in battle, some falling as the witches began using their various mystic skills against them. Eryce was in a heated sword fight with one, each expertly taking aim and defending themselves. Marc was clutching his side with one arm as the other held a death grip on his sword. His fingers were stained red.

Eryce deflected a blow by the witch toward his neck, but in doing so slipped on the wet floors beneath him. He scrambled to turn with his weapon raised, but the witch, having a heartbeat to hone his power, blinded Eryce with a white light and plunged the sword into his torso.

"No!" Theo yelled, and he swung his sword just in time to cut off the witch's head before he had a chance to blind him next. The head rolled toward Marc who screamed and kicked it elsewhere.

Theo knelt by Eryce, trying in vain to plug up the wound with his hands, anything to keep the spread of blood from getting worse, but it was in vain. The wound was too deep, and Eryce stared at Theo as he desperately tried to aid his brother.

"Theo." He coughed, blood spurted from his mouth. "Theo."

Theo held his brother's gloved hand, holding on tight as his tears came. "No, don't you dare! You're going to be fine; we will take you to the healer, we will fix this."

"Shhh," he whispered, coughing again. He looked paler, even in the darkness. "Listen."

Theo fell silent, trembling as he gripped his brother's hand.

"Don't . . . don't," his brother tried to say, but death was coming too quickly. "Don't . . ."

Then, it was silent. There was no gasping for air, no breathing, nothing. He did not have time to think about his brother's words before Marc spoke, standing now as if he were perfectly unharmed. "Now it's only you and me."

Theo barely registered what he said, shocked and devastated—Eryce had died in his arms.

But Marc inched closer, and Theo looked up in time to see him pull a dagger from his belt, repeating what he said. "Only you . . . and me."

Before Theo could grab his sword, a sharp pain exploded in his ribs, a pain that nearly blinded him, and he yelled out in agony. He turned, as Marc withdrew the blade of his dagger. "Marc? What are you doing?!"

Theo looked at his younger brother with shock. This was not his brother, but a sinister, evil man who now waved his dagger in front of Theo's face. The chaos around them seemed distant as the pain radiated quickly. Theo knew that he would not be able to maintain consciousness long.

"It's prince and heir to you. Did my act fool you—the scared baby brother?"

"Why?" Theo blinked tears of pain, holding his side as he tried to breathe, to stay awake, he had to fight somehow.

Marc pushed him to the ground. "Because it's mine and you were in my way."

Then Marc swiped the air, taking aim at Theo's neck. Theo barely twisted away in time and kicked Marc's feet from under him. The action jolted a new wave of torment throughout his ribs and body. Theo screamed from the pain, and it was all he could do to continue moving. Marc, who had dropped the dagger from his fall, scrambled to try and grab it, but Theo grabbed Marc's foot and pulled back with as much strength as he could muster. Marc, a glint of fear in his eyes, turned and kicked Theo in the face.

Theo backed away quickly from Marc, who now pulled Eryce's sword to him and stood, breathing raggedly from the skirmish.

"You don't want to do this, Marc," Theo pleaded, knowing that he did not have much time before he met the same fate as Eryce. "This is not you. Prove to the world that you are good like I know you are."

"Damn the world," Marc spat. "One day, I will rule it all."

Marc raised the sword, and Theo knew that with all the fight he had left in him, his body was unable to comply. The wound had gone through his ribs and punctured his stomach, bleeding out profusely; he was beginning to go into the haze of unconsciousness. His arms and legs were shaking from the blood loss, unable to work on just adrenaline anymore.

Theo closed his eyes, accepting this realization, and prayed to the gods that they make it a swift death. He could hear the swooshing of the sword, slicing the air with its deadly intentions; it would be the end of him. His mind briefly flashed images of his brother, his sister and mother, and then of Eve. His heart ached and he wished he could see her once more.

He opened his eyes in time to see Pedro, bloodied and disheveled, shoving Marc out of the way. The sword landed inches from Theo's head and stuck in the wooden railing. With not a moment to spare, Pedro leapt toward Theo, taking them both overboard and into the frigid, dark sea.

CLARISA

FIFTY-THREE

It was her dream turned into reality. The ships crested the edge of the space where the night sky and sea met, breeding chaos beneath a storm as they sailed toward the Blackthorn.

Clarisa was in a trance, being led by some intuition that did not belong to her. Her bare feet padded along the wet sand; the thick fog clung to the air around her. Rain pelted the weary witches who tried in vain to stop the mortals. But all Clarisa could think of was the water. She belonged to the sea; it was hers and hers alone.

Tabor and Brisa followed close behind. Witches formed enchantment lines along the beach, praying to Isila to cast away their enemies, summoning their combined powers to do their bidding.

Clarisa pushed through the center of the formation, pausing just before the water. It swayed back and forth, trying in vain to touch her.

Giselle pushed past them. "What is the meaning of this?!"

"Your only chance of survival."

"Together we will survive, not alone. Do not ruin us with your pride."

Clarisa ignored her.

The high priestess narrowed her eyes, her lips thinning. "You dare defy my authority?"

"Those ships will not wait for your authority. I know what I must do."

Giselle scoffed. "I will not stand aside to a *half-breed*."

Clarisa's chest rose and fell in quick succession, her hands trembling in anger. "One more word, and I can kill you instead."

She laughed. "You have no power over me. I am a line between us and our goddess."

Clarisa felt a force over her that she was no longer in control of, anger, and deep resentment. "Lines can be broken."

The high priestess's face twisted in agony, her body seizing as she fell to the ground, her arms spasming chaotically. The witches stopped their incantations, rushing to their fallen priestess.

"*Stop her!*"

"*The priestess!*"

"*Someone get the healer!*"

Clarisa closed her eyes as the delicious feeling of retribution and vengeance took over her. She raised her head and arms, letting the power flow through her. The high priestess began screaming viciously, horribly in pain.

Tabor rushed to Clarisa. "No! Stop, Clarisa, this isn't you! Come back, come back to us!"

"*She is dying!*"

The moment seemed to drag on for a lifetime, but when Clarisa opened her eyes, only seconds had passed. The high priestess stopped convulsing, breathing deeply and gulping in air.

"As I said"—Clarisa narrowed her eyes—"I know what I must do."

The high priestess's eyes widened in terror, the witches around them frozen in fear.

Clarisa moved past them confidently, her bold brown eyes changing into an enchanting blue gray, the magic within transforming her. She could hear Tabor and Brisa scuffle with witches who tried to stop her claiming she would disrupt the spell.

She paused before the water, retrieving a dagger from her hip and breathing deeply.

"Do not fail me," she whispered under her breath as she lifted it toward her hand.

Before she could think twice, she quickly sliced her palm, the pain intense and throbbing. She walked into the sea, letting the blood spill and become one with its dark waters. As soon as they met, the ships began to break apart in the near distance and lightning struck the sea, the heat setting them on fire. It was intense, and quick.

Her dream was no nightmare, but a premonition, made real before her eyes.

She raised her hands toward the night sky, letting the blood flow down from her wound and trickle down her arm. Clarisa could picture the armies perishing in the sea, sinking further in as the foliage of the destruction weighed them down. The energy flowed through her, the sickening madness of power taking over. Nothing else seemed to matter, not the mortals drowning in the sea, not the witches cowering behind her, and not the sister she had doomed. She was death itself.

<hr>

Dead bodies of the men began to wash ashore as the night sky transformed into hues of light gray blurred by the rain. It was only when she heard a voice, that she woke from whatever had taken hold of her. A voice that sounded familiar calling out the name she had forgotten about in her dreams.

"*Eve!*"

"What is wrong?" Tabor asked.

"*Eve!*"

She snapped her eyes open, lowering her arms as she turned to face the sound. It was distant, but clear. Clarisa ran toward it, rushing as fast as she could through the sand.

"Wait, Clarisa! Where are you going?" Brisa cried out behind her.

She could hear them rush toward her but continued her sprint.

Clarisa crested a sand dune and stopped. Before her was a face she hadn't seen in nearly fifteen years.

Theo.

He was disheveled and wet, having come in from the sea. His arm was twisted awkwardly behind him as blood began making a pool beneath his body and into the sand. He kept whispering her sister's name between garbled chokes of water.

"Theo!"

She ran and knelt next to him, "Theo, stay with me!" She placed her hands on his wound, focusing on trying to heal him with any magic Isila would give her, any enchantment she could remember from Ana. After a few moments, Theo's eyes began to flutter as her face twisted from the pain.

"Eve?"

"No, no it's me. It's Clarisa."

Tabor reached Clarisa then, retrieving his arrows, he quickly nocked one into place.

"Clarisa, step away from him. He may hurt you!"

"Stop! I know him! He is from Givensmir."

"That makes him your enemy. Let me kill him."

"No, please!"

Just then a voice echoed from a nearby distance. Running toward them was a man in equal disarray, with dark tendrils and eyes.

Pedro?

Clarisa was stunned silent, unable to process.

"If you hurt him, you will have to go through me!"

"Who are you?!" Brisa asked. Tabor flexed the bow in Pedro's direction.

Pedro looked between Theo and Clarisa, unarmed and eyes wide, wounds prevalent on his flesh and blood soaking his tunic. He raised his hands defensively, recognition spreading over his features as he beheld Clarisa.

"Y-you're alive," he breathed.

Clarisa couldn't respond, couldn't think of anything to say otherwise. She heard the high priestess and members of the coven rushing toward them. She stared down at Theo who had passed out in her arms, his wound barely closed. She swore, frustrated and out of time.

"What is the meaning of this?" Giselle demanded.

Pedro continued staring into Clarisa, and she could hear him beg just under his breath. "Please."

"The high priestess asked you a question!" one of the witches growled.

"I–I am Theo, the prince of Givensmir. This man, *Pedro*, is my sworn knight, he is heir to one of the richest provinces in the kingdom."

"Clarisa, is this true?" Tabor asked, concern taking over.

Clarisa looked between Pedro and Theo, unsure of how to respond, but Pedro's eyes bore into hers, pleading and desperate.

"Enemies!" she heard her coven shout. "Kill them quickly!"

"No! No!" Clarisa cried. "He speaks true."

Coven members eyed the scene before them. Clarisa knew it was strange—her holding the head of a mortal as she pleaded for their lives. She stood her ground.

"He is the prince, and his knight is in my arms. We need to spare them; we can use them as leverage."

"Take them to the healers and then the dungeons," Navir ordered, appearing suddenly as he walked toward them.

Clarisa watched as Theo and Pedro were swiftly removed. And she only hoped that she made the right decision. Her heart pounded and she trembled under the weight of what just happened. Her cousin, and her old friend, both now taken by the coven.

As the crowd dispersed, Navir walked to Clarisa, gesturing Tabor and Brisa to move aside. "Give your witch a moment." He waved them away, but they only shifted slightly, unwilling to leave her truly alone.

He brought Clarisa into a hug, wrapping his arms around her as she began to shake uncontrollably. The voices, the power, the deaths, her blood.

Navir turned her around, making her take in the beach before her. Rain hit her forcefully, sending drops down her face and through her hair.

"Look at what a few seconds of your true power has caused." He raised his hand, and tilted Clarisa's chin toward the water.

The bodies continued washing ashore, replacing the normal morning tides. Filling the sands in blankets of red and faded gold. Clarisa's heart raced, her breath caught in her throat, and her eyes watered at the hundreds of men that now painted the scene before her.

"I am not angry, my dear, Clarisa," he whispered. "I am in awe."

She could barely speak as the bodies kept coming, littering the ocean as far as she could see. Never had she seen the beautiful blue water turn red under the rising morning sun.

EVE

FIFTY-FOUR

E ve closed her eyes as she and Callum embraced, waiting for the guards to finally make it up the stairs. They could hear their swords being unsheathed and one of them making commands to the other.

She wondered if it would hurt, or if she would die quickly. Eve prayed that the sword could end this now, for she could not bear to prolong her fate anymore.

Then, she heard the sound of stone groaning against stone. Her eyes flicked up, blinking through the smoke and fire. A wall moved from the left.

"Eve!"

Two men rushed out of it. *Dakon! Pazel!*

"We must go, now!"

Before she could respond, they grabbed her and Callum and forced them into the wall, closing it tightly behind them. She and Callum coughed viciously; she had not realized how weak her lungs had become and how much it hurt now to breathe. For a small, fleeting moment, thoughts of finding the book filled her head, *where did it go?*

"Who are you?" Callum choked out between gasps.

"Dakon. I'm here to save you." He looked to Eve, who was now staring back at the wall they came through. *How did it know the book was safe? Maybe, I have enough time . . .*

Dakon grasped her hands tightly. "Eve, we have no time, the castle is closing its gates and doubling the guard. You will get it back, I promise."

She turned to him. "Is that possible?"

Beast began to tug at her dress. Eve tugged it back, impassively, waiting for Dakon's response. "I know that it will come back to you. It only wants you."

Eve could only nod in response as Dakon grabbed her arm.

"Follow Beast, if you can see him, he knows where to take us."

"I see," she managed, and rushed behind the animal.

Eve could hear Pazel as he helped Callum down the steps in the dark.

The group rushed through the tunnels. Smoke began to follow them as the fire consumed all in its wake. She could see holes through the walls allowing bits of light to filter through their path.

"Quick this way!"

Most residents of the castle seemed to be waking, screaming at the fire coming from the king's tower. Eve's heart thundered in her chest. They stumbled into what she believed to be the servant's quarters where people were running amuck with unfettered chaos. Beast rushed through them like a ghost, as the rest of the group had to dodge bodies rushing to and fro, ignoring yells for them to return.

They barged through the servant's entrance and ran outside to the gardens, where Beast waited impatiently for them at the edge. She barely noticed as they passed the pond she and Theo had spent their childhood in. No time to think about that now. Just make it out alive.

"Halt!"

Eve turned just in time to see a group of knights pointing and starting toward them from a short distance away.

"Do you have a plan to get us out of here?" Callum asked as they rushed through the thicket and thorns.

"Trust me," Dakon called out, "keep going!"

They sprinted deeper into the brush, and it became more entangled as they forced their bodies inside. It clung to her dress, skin, and hair as if begging for her to stay, clawing its way and drawing blood. Eve's lungs were on fire, she had never run this hard in her life, the air was struggling to make its way through her body.

They went this way!

The witch was with them!

Eve's lungs felt as if they would burst, her limbs screamed for rest, and sweat and damp hair covered her face as she followed.

Finally, they came to the end, and Eve's heart dropped.

"A fucking wall?" Callum growled. "It's too tall to scale!"

Eve watched as Dakon struggled with the stones. Something about this felt oddly familiar. As if she had been here before. She touched the stone wall, and the feeling of running with Clarisa as a child came back.

This was how we escaped.

"Help me push and we can go through it!"

Pazel and Callum, with his good arm, shoved their weight against the wall. Beast paced back and forth anxiously, whimpering and whining until, thankfully, the stones gave way.

"Hurry!"

They squeezed through, just as they heard guards swiping through the brush with their swords, calling out for them. In their hurry, they tumbled down the steep hill. Pain radiated throughout her body as she endured more cuts of brush and the beating of rocks against her skin as she made her way to the bottom.

There was a small ravine, barely trickling water through from what she could tell. She pushed her body up, her arms shaking as they struggled to lift her torso. The rest of the group was getting to their feet.

"Is everyone alive?" Dakon asked.

"Yes," she groaned.

"I think so." Callum coughed bits of blood on his tunic.

"I'm not certain anymore." Pazel spat out a tooth.

"Down there! They escaped through the wall!"

Instinctively, they all ran to the edge of the forest, hiding within the shrubs. Dakon faced them, a grave look on his face. "We are headed to a ship in Catalina's Port. Come if you want to live or stay and wait for them to find you."

He pointed up at the break in the wall. Eve looked up and saw at least one guard successfully make it through with his armor intact.

<hr/>

They ran in the night toward the port, stopping only to catch their breath in the city. Guards roamed the streets, and already news of her and Callum's escape had reached the city watch. She could hear them bark orders to one another as she hid with her group in alleys and abandoned buildings.

Time was no longer on her side, but the sea was only a short distance away. Eve crossed the bridge between the capital and Catalina's Port and could see the waves as they rocked gently under the approaching dawn. And a bit further out, a ship.

They could all make it. They had to make it.

Beast continued running through the slums, leading them through broken streets and darkened alleys. Finally, they reached a cove. Eve inspected the massive rocks jutting out from the sand and water leading up to where they approached. They would have to climb down to reach the bottom. She peaked over. Thankfully, it was not that far should she slip.

Slip.

She squeezed her eyes shut and the memory came. Clarisa slipping down and her father grabbing Eve before she could follow. It was becoming clearer now, and her body shook at the memory.

"We're almost there—" Dakon no sooner said this, then hooves could be heard behind them. Two knights were rushing toward them, more following not too far behind.

"Halt! Halt!"

They were gaining speed, but Eve could see the ship in the distance. A small boat wading just off the shore to row them to it. They were so close. They just had to go down. She had to do this. There was no other choice.

"Make it to the boat! Make it to the boat!" Dakon was yelling.

Beast had disappeared, and Dakon and Callum helped Eve into position until she got her footing. Then Dakon slid alongside her, climbing down to her right. Pazel did the same on her left. She was nearly at the bottom, when she finally looked up.

Callum stared back, a sober look in his eyes. "I meant what I said," he called out, "in the tower."

He began to stand.

"Callum! What are you doing?!"

"Take her, Pazel!"

"No!"

Eve tried to fight against Pazel, but Dakon came and grabbed her. Practically carrying her through the sand and into the boat. Dakon threw her inside as Pazel jumped in and grabbed the oars.

"Callum!"

She could see from a distance, three more knights on horses now surrounded him. As if time itself had slowed, she watched in horror as he retrieved his sword and took the first swing with his unbroken arm.

Then, they surrounded him.

Eve screamed, thrashing against Dakon and watching as the sheer force of the guards obscured Callum from view. Even when they pulled her up onto the ship, she could only see golden armor glinting red in the dawn.

"We need to go far from here. Somewhere no one from Givensmir will be able to find her!"

Voices shouted around her, but Eve could barely process what they meant. She sat silently next to Pazel in the captain's quarters while Dakon and the captain argued before them.

"I need to know what you're doing, before I go around fulfilling promises that may end up with me dead!"

"I paid you to take us somewhere safe, not to ask questions!"

"That was before you brought me a fucking witch!"

"Say that one more time and I'll cut your other ear off!"

"Stop!" she seethed. The voice of the magic within her began to wake itself. This time, she did not smother it.

What remained of her despair melted away to rage and wrath. It was not a curse to be a witch, of that she was certain. For power corrupted even the fairest of beings. It was truly the only thing that reigned over mortal and magic minds alike even if it meant both of their demises.

Power like the king's, power like *Clarisa.*

By killing the princess, her sister set off a course that was immovable and deadly. The only reason Eve was here, the only reason she had to endure the pain and suffering of her imprisonment, the brewing war, of losing Callum, and possibly Theo, was because of her. She damned her kin by resorting to chaos and destruction. All her power and never once did Clarisa think about how her actions would affect Eve. Never once did Clarisa even seek her out in fifteen years.

Very well, then.

The men quieted, watching as she rose from her seat. Eve, feeling the power within her, coursing through her veins, walked to the captain. He stood speechless before her as she glared at him with her red-colored eyes, relishing at the tinge of fear in his.

She lifted a hand before him, and he flinched. Eve smirked and flipped it over to reveal her palm. Within it a small flame appeared, glowing bright against her skin.

"My name is Eve, daughter of the enchantress, and Blood of the Blackthorn. And I am the witch of whom you speak."

The cabin was silent, save for the crackle of the flame in her grasp. The captain stilled in shock and awe as Dakon and Pazel knelt beside her. The sun filtered through the cabin window, and the water glistened beneath it. She would reach the end of where the sky and sea met; she would venture out to nowhere. To find her sister and end this centuries-long war between the mortals and witches. Because, for the first time in her life, she beheld a magic that she would no longer hide.

For fire is not meant to cower in the dark, but to burn bright in spite of it.

MARC
FIFTY-FIVE

Marc tossed his helmet into the sand as he stalked up the beach toward the castle, the armor glinting against the sun and weighing him down. It had been three long days of a journey back in the only ship that made it out of the chaos. What was left of his father's army after the witches' attack followed close behind him.

All were members of the Strix, who would prove to be worthy allies against the Blackthorn when the time came. He rubbed the sweat from his forehead, thinking about how much effort and planning went into orchestrating so many deaths. Marc never planned to truly embark on the Blackthorn, it was a foolish, disastrous plan made by a mad king. He made sure his father's loyal men perished in the Dallise Sea.

Knights of the king's guard and notable council members met him, faces ashen as the realization of their brutal defeat dawned on them.

Lord Wesley, Elder Borgias, and Ser Aznaro came to meet him.

"My Prince, are your brothers close behind?" Aznaro asked.

Marc met his eyes with a steely gaze. "No. One is dead, and the other was plunged into the sea."

Aznaro's eyes widened, speechless.

"So, he is dead as well," Elder Borgias breathed somberly.

"I must go see my father; it should come from me."

He took a step forward, but Lord Wesley placed a hand on his shoulder. "My Prince, the king is dead."

"Dead?"

"Reports believe that Lady Eve was responsible."

"Where is she?"

"She—she has escaped, Your Highness," Ser Aznaro said.

"You are telling me some half-breed witch was able to escape a heavily guarded castle after murdering the king?"

"Y-yes, but—"

Marc gave him an incredulous look before calming his features, pulling Aznaro close. "You are in charge of his personal guard, are you not?"

Aznaro only nodded.

"And what were your vows? I can't seem to remember."

Aznaro's eyes widened. "That I should die for my king, protect him with my life and those of the innocent."

"Well," Marc said with a sneer, "it doesn't seem like you held up to those, now did you?"

Before Aznaro could respond, Marc pulled out a dagger and shoved it into the guard's neck. "So, I won't be needing you."

He tossed the body to the side, leaving the dagger in place as he looked upon the rest of the knights and council before him, staring in wide-eyed shock.

"It seems I am the next in line, gentlemen. Elder, I assume you brought what you needed."

The elder fumbled for a moment, stepping over Aznaro's body with a sickening look of dread on his face. "Yes, Your Highness."

Borgias gestured to the crowd of knights, nobles, and the remnants of the army to circle around them. His eyes not meeting Marc's as he retrieved a crown from within his robes. Its golden hues shone brightly in the sun, the black jewels encrusted along the stems circled the front of the sigil of his house.

Marc took a knee before Elder Borgias, as silence came over the crowd of men. The only sounds were the waves washing ashore and the seagulls in the distance.

"Until such time preparations can be made, in times of war we must make do with the circumstances we are given," the elder announced to the crowd. "As such, in the presence of our brave soldiers and beneath the skies of our five, I say these sacred vows."

He began to recite the words:

"May The Creator give you faith in times of darkness,
May The Sage guide you to reign just,
May The Lover guide you to reign true,
May The Warrior give you strength against the wicked,
And above all, may Death protect your soul.
This crown forged through centuries of your blood,
Is now entrusted to you.
May you reign as one chosen by the gods."

Elder Borgias carefully set the crown on his head. "Marc Ebron of the Mistral Islands, King of Givensmir and the Four Seas, Defender of Mortality and the Faith of the Five! Long may he reign!"

Marc stood as the crowd began to chant:

"Long reign King Marc!"
"Long reign King Marc!"

In this moment alone, he held all of which his father could only dream of: power and loyalty.

"Your Majesty"—Lord Wesley bowed before him with a wicked smile on his face—"there is something you need to see."

<hr>

Marc entered the dank and cold dungeon, rats skittered across the floors away from the group and their torches. He followed Wesley toward the end and waited as the dungeon master unlocked the door. He opened it with a long creak, and two guards rushed inside subduing the prisoner.

Marc walked inside as a guard brought him a small table and a satchel. Marc did not look at the prisoner as he calmly placed the bag on the table, opening it slowly for him to see. Inside were various knives, scalpels, and other such tools. When they were meticulously laid out before him, he finally raised his head and faced the prisoner with a cool, sinister look.

"Well, well, Lord Callum, I hear you like to conspire with witches these days."

"Damn you, Marc!"

A guard punched Callum in the stomach, and he began to bend until the other guard held him up. "This is the king you are speaking to!" the guard spat.

Marc held up his hand. "There is no need for that, thank you."

He watched as Callum kept his eyes downcast, coughing blood onto the floor. Marc lifted Callum's chin with a rough hand and relished at the terror in his eyes.

"Where has our little witch run off to?"

Callum spat in his face. A guard quickly kneed Callum in the side, and he groaned on the floor, weak and feeble. Marc pulled out a handkerchief, wiping his face and smirking.

He lifted a sharp scalpel from the table, making a show of inspecting it against the faint light peeking out through the barred windows.

Marc smiled as he moved toward Callum, lifting the scalpel to and fro in front of him. The guards brought Callum back onto his feet, holding him tight in their grip. He shoved the handkerchief in Callum's mouth until he was sure he was barely breathing.

Marc brought his lips close to Callum's ear. "Your loving prince is dead. I saw it myself. The blade went clean through his body." He smiled viciously. "He might have even called out your name, I can't seem to remember."

Callum groaned and cried through the gag, his face red and eyes heavy behind the bruises.

Marc stood, then, looking down on this pathetic man. He raised the scalpel once more.

"Let us begin, then, shall we?"

AUTHOR'S NOTE

The inspiration for this book came one dreary, rainy, December day as my family and I were on vacation. We were driving through the quiet, country roads hours east of Seattle, and I began to daydream—as I so often do—while staring at the evergreen trees that filled the scene around us. They were massive clusters of Douglas Firs that appeared as shadows in my eyes and whose peaks nearly reached the heavens and overtook every inch of space in the forests.

Four consecutive thoughts hit me then:

How easy would it be to get lost in there?

What if someone was trying to escape through those trees?

What if it were children – sisters, even – trying to run through them?

How far could they get?

Thus, as they say, the rest is history, and after completing a few short stories and de-prioritizing my unfinished works, I focused solely on *Blood of the Blackthorn*.

The questions had manifested itself into an idea of two magical sisters torn apart as they tried to escape through the forest. Then divided further by lies, manipulation, and the societies that raised them. Societies, I might add, that are antagonistic towards each other due to centuries of bloodshed and fear instilled within them. Of course, all carefully orchestrated by the leadership of their respective kingdoms. No good deed goes unpunished.

It is no secret that women and marginalized communities through time have been harmed by hateful rhetoric due to fearmongering. The kingdom of Givensmir is an example of this. Witchcraft, in this story, is not easily controlled or manipulated by mortals, and therefore seen as a threat. Continuous propaganda through folklore and word-of-mouth all contribute to this message, amongst the mortals in this story, that witches are the enemy. To convey this, months of research went into learning about witchcraft throughout history and in our modern day. Including the different communities that have either embraced or disparaged it over time. For example, hundreds of years ago simply possessing an object made from a blackthorn tree could be seen as practicing witchcraft and had fatal consequences. To be even associated with witches, no matter one's innocence, could have been enough to damn a person . . .

The inspiration for this book is more than popular culture; the complexities of practicing within a coven, as a formalized tradition or religion, or as an individual can look different. No one witch and their craft are the same in the real world, just as they are not all the same in this fantasy world.

This, I hope, has been prevalent with Eve and Clarisa's approach to accepting their power in their own time, in their own way. Or even with Dakon and Pazel, who may find witchcraft is something found later in life whether through blood or an appreciation of it.

As a final disclaimer, this book is purely fiction, based in a fantasy world where magic and witchcraft can look far different from our everyday life. It is my sincere wish that if you find yourself staring off into the forest, perhaps in a daydream state, that this book comes to mind and you smile just a bit remembering how it made you feel (good and a bit magical, I hope).

To conclude it must be noted, dear reader, that I could spend a lifetime researching and never come close to knowing everything there is to know on the subject, no matter how fascinating.

That is the beauty of reading, I suppose, each time we pick up a book it always teaches us something new. So keep reading.

With Love,
Rocio

ACKNOWLEDGMENTS

This work has been a long time in the making, and as such, I have collected quite the support system along the way.

Allen, my personal history buff and partner, for humoring and educating me as you read through each chapter and provided your expertise. Our long-winded discussions regarding the complexities of empires and power struggles throughout time were not in vain. Though, of course, any liberties taken in this book are of my own accord. Thank you can never be enough for your time, energy, and support as I burnt the midnight oil making my dream a reality.

To my siblings—Dallas, Adriana, Pedro, and David—I am wholeheartedly grateful as you listened to me talk relentlessly about the book I planned to publish one day. You have been my greatest confidants, providing me with wisdom and guidance as I navigated this new chapter of my life.

My editor, Heather, who has incredible patience and kindness. You truly reinvigorated my passion for this work when imposter syndrome kept creeping in. I am eternally grateful for your non-stop, hilarious reactions to nearly every scene. It made me smile, tear up a little, and laugh a lot. Your tact, humor, and professionalism are what I wish every author to have in an editor.

To the witch communities, both online and in person, who were open and welcome with my endless questions and curiosities. I am forever grateful for your insight and wisdom as I ventured into new territory.

Finally, to the book community. Your unwavering support felt like a giant hug when doubt would creep in. For embracing me before I had anything to show for it, this book is, quite literally, thanks to you.

About The Author

ROCIO CARRANZA is the author of this and several other works, including *Lana Lang* published with Sad Girl Diaries literary magazine and *Miss Reliable* published with Griffel Magazine. She has an MBA in Strategic Management and lives with the ever-jovial Allen and their two sons in Austin, TX. *Blood of the Blackthorn* is her debut novel.

Visit the author online:
www.rociocarranza.com

Instagram & Threads:
@rociocarranzawrites

Bluesky:
@rociocarranza